The Cities

THE CITY OF RAVENS

Richard Baker

W0019056

THE CITY OF RAVENS

©2000 Wizards of the Coast, Inc.

All characters in this book are fictitious. Any resemblance to actual persons, living or dead, is purely coincidental.

This book is protected under the copyright laws of the United States of America. Any reproduction or unauthorized use of the material or artwork contained herein is prohibited without the express written permission of Wizards of the Coast, Inc.

Distributed in the United States by St. Martin's Press. Distributed in Canada by Fenn Ltd.

Distributed to the hobby, toy, and comic trade in the United States and Canada by regional distributors.

Distributed worldwide by Wizards of the Coast, Inc., and regional distributors.

FORGOTTEN REALMS, RPGA, and the Wizards of the Coast logo are registered trademarks owned by Wizards of the Coast, Inc.

All Wizards of the Coast characters, character names, and the distinctive likenesses thereof are trademarks owned by Wizards of the Coast, Inc.

The sale of this book without its cover has not been authorized by the publisher. If you purchased this book without a cover, you should be aware that neither the author nor the publisher has received payment for this "stripped book."

Made in the U.S.A.

Cover art by William O'Connor
First Printing: December 2000
Library of Congress Catalog Card Number: 00-102620

9 8 7 6 5 4 3 2 1

UK ISBN: 0-7869-2017-3
US ISBN: 0-7869-1401-7
620-T21401

U.S., CANADA,
ASIA, PACIFIC, & LATIN AMERICA
Wizards of the Coast, Inc.
P.O. Box 707
Renton, WA 98057-0707
+1-800-324-6496

EUROPEAN HEADQUARTERS
Wizards of the Coast, Belgium
P.B. 2031
2600 Berchem
Belgium
+32-70-23-32-77

Visit our web site at **www.wizards.com/forgottenrealms**

Dedication

For Alex and Hannah
I hope you never use up all your wonder.

CHAPTER ONE

Jack Ravenwild scrambled over the parapeted roof of House Kuldath and grinned in delight. The night air was heavy and wet with the first storm of spring. Water ran from his face over his stubbled skull, shaved just over the ears and closely cropped in a distinct widow's peak.

Jack was a small man, with a wiry build and a round, friendly face that was perpetually split by a jester's mocking smile. Dark eyes glittered gleefully over an impish nose, a wide mouth, and a thin trace of beard along his jawline.

"Hurry, hurry!" he called softly over his shoulder. "The rain stands to ruin my best suit."

All around him, the moss-grown shingles and leaning spires of the city's rooftops stretched out into darkness. Jack studied them with deliberate disinterest. Behind him, a single hairy arm groped for a handhold on the rain-slick rooftop. A moment later, Anders Aricssen hauled his head and shoulders to the parapet, grunting with effort.

"If you find yourself concerned about the condition of your clothes," he gasped, "you might consider helping me up, instead of capering up there like some kind of rubbish-heap weather vane."

"Rubbish-heap weather vane, indeed," Jack

said sniffing. He considered himself dashingly dressed for the moment. The night's work demanded clothes that fit like a shadow over a grave, so the small man wore snug leather breeches, a loose shirt of dark gray cotton, and a leather doublet stiffened and padded, all in black. A rapier was slung high on his left hip in a thin wooden scabbard wrapped in black velvet, and a matching poignard rode on his right hip. Pausing a moment to brush the water from his dark cloak, he stepped over to the edge of the roof and offered his hand to Anders. "Come on, then."

Anders clasped his arm and dragged himself onto the flat roof, slipping and scrambling awkwardly. He straightened slowly, unfolding a frame more than a foot taller than his companion's. While Jack was dressed in dark leather and a voluminous cloak that billowed in the wind, Anders simply wore weathered buckskins that left his golden-haired chest bare to the elements.

"Are you certain you didn't use sorcery to magic yourself up that wall? That was not as easy a climb as you'd led me to believe, friend Jack."

"Why resort to magic when natural aptitude suffices?" Jack replied. He took two light bounds across the slick shingles and balanced a moment with his feet athwart a brick chimney, watching streamers of smoke wind about his legs. "Black as old pitch tonight, friend Anders," he laughed. "Why, I couldn't have picked a better evening for my enterprise!"

"*Our* enterprise," grunted Anders by way of correction. "That would be *our* enterprise, Jack. It concerns me when you make mistakes like that." While Jack occupied himself by hopping casually from one parapet to the other, ignoring the forty-foot fall below, the tall Northman unwrapped a heavy broadsword not too much shorter than Jack himself and slung the blade over his shoulder. He stood eye-to-eye with Jack, despite the fact that the

Ravenaar man now balanced on a crenellation a good cubit higher than the rooftop upon which Anders stood. "Speaking of which, you still have not told me what prize we seek tonight."

Jack led Anders across the rooftop to a small stone slab in one corner. "Below us, as you well know, is the warehouse of House Kuldath. The five brothers Kuldath hail from some distant land far to the east. Their principal trade lies in carpets of exquisite workmanship, rumored to be hand-woven by sixteen enslaved princesses forced to labor at the brothers' command in order to prevent House Kuldath from collecting on a debt owed by their destitute father."

Anders frowned. "Carpets. That's bad. They're quite heavy, and in this rain, they'll get heavier still. That will be a lot of work."

"No, no, forget the carpets. We're here—"

"Ah, so it's the princesses, then. They're even heavier than carpets, but unlikely to become heavier with a soaking. Manageable, I suppose."

Jack sighed. "Forget the whole carpet story. The important thing is, the five brothers Kuldath are quite wealthy, and in celebration of an extremely successful season, they recently purchased a set of five perfect rubies from the jeweler Shorlock Revahl, each one to give to his wife. We shall relieve them of the responsibility of caring for these small baubles."

"Rubies," Anders said, nodding. "That's much better. So how do we do this?"

"Below there," Jack said, pointing to the stone slab, "lies the hitherto inviolate inner sanctum of the brothers Kuldath. With some careful scrying, I have determined that the first floor of this building is the Kuldath Emporium; the second, their main warehouse; the third, their living quarters; and the fourth, the private offices and secret vaults of the house." Jack donned a pair of soft leather gloves and pulled his hood over his face. "The room below is reserved for the storage of their very finest carpets. Two rooms away is a locked strongbox wherein the rubies lie. You shall remain in the carpet room and stand guard, while I steal the strongbox."

"I don't see why you need me along, if that's the case," Anders replied. "One of your ability should be able to handle that quite easily."

"There may be a complication," Jack admitted, "involving a guardian demon who watches over the wealth of the house."

Anders turned to stare down at him. "Am I going to have to fight this demon?"

"It's extremely unlikely. I anticipate that we will reach our goal and retreat before any encounter with the guardian becomes remotely possible. I merely asked you to come along to handle that one chance in a hundred— nay, a thousand—whereby the demon may become aware of our presence." Jack knelt by the trapdoor and spoke the words of an opening spell, gently passing his hand over the latch. With a small rasping sound, a bolt on the other side slid out of the way. Before the blond-bearded Northman could reconsider, Jack opened the door and dropped inside.

He landed on a soft stack of carpets, surrounded by deep gloom. He'd always had a knack for feeling his way around in the dark. Without stumbling, he glided forward to the storeroom's door and cracked it, peeking out into the hallway. A checkered wooden floor and ornate chestnut paneling gleamed in lamplight outside the storeroom. Watching for any sign of movement, he heard Anders drop into the room somewhat more awkwardly than he had.

"Stay here, good Anders," he said quietly, "and be ready to come swiftly to my aid if I call for you."

"May I ask a simple question first?"

"Of course."

"How do you intend to divide five gems, Jack? Four or six present no problem, of course, but five are difficult to split between two partners."

Jack closed the door to the narrowest of cracks and turned back to Anders. "Well, each of us shall have two rubies to start. That is only fair."

"That makes four," Anders observed. "Do you mean to tell me that you will leave the brothers Kuldath the fifth gem, in order to ensure a fair and evenhanded split of the take?"

"Of course not. I shall have it," Jack replied.

Anders scowled. "Your certainty unsettles me, friend Jack. How did you arrive at this decision?"

"It is a simple matter. I conceived tonight's adventure, and I reconnoitered our means of ingress. Therefore, I shall take the greater part of the treasure." Jack set his hands on his hips, putting on an expression of lordly indulgence. "Your assistance is important, of course, so I cheerfully assign to you two-fifths of tonight's take. You will note that I deal with you honestly and without deceit before the work commences. Others in our profession might conveniently allow the question of the fifth gem to go unanswered until the prize was in hand. That, in my experience, leads to rash actions and hurtful words."

"I am not reassured," the Northman replied.

"Why, you should be, friend Anders. I am in all things and in all ways the very soul of honesty. Not only do I pride myself on my true and forthright nature, but I believe that I can claim to have never knowingly allowed a falsehood to pass my lips. The slightest deceit is quite beyond my capabilities, and every day I fervently pray to be struck down in the most horrible and grisly fashion imaginable should I fail to live up to my own exacting standards of decent and moral conduct."

"And what is that?"

"Decent and moral conduct? Why, I define—"

"No, no, not that. The most horrible and grisly demise imaginable. What would that be?"

Jack raised his hand as if to answer, thought for a moment, and then lowered it. "I'm not entirely sure." Momentarily nonplussed, he tapped his finger on his chin and then gave up with a shrug. "I'll think on it. Are you satisfied with the arrangements?"

Anders grimaced. "I accept, under one condition: If I end up fighting the demon, I get the fifth gem."

"I assure you, that condition is completely unnecessary," Jack said.

"If that is really the case, then you should be able to agree to it without hesitation. Now, do you agree to my condition?"

Jack winced and offered a weak smile. Anders was much smarter than he looked. "I do, although perhaps we should define 'fighting.' "

"Easily done. If I find myself in a situation where it's trying to kill me, or I'm trying to kill it. Now, if you please, resume your burglary."

The small thief opened the door and slipped out into the hall. He furiously considered some kind of strategy by which he might have avoided conceding the last gem to the Northman but fell short. He glided past several doors emblazoned with the symbol of the House Kuldath, an anvil crowned by five gemstones, and wondered idly if in the near future the brothers would amend their house symbol to a plain anvil. Jack had carefully studied the interior of the building through various divinations and seeing spells over the last week, committing the entire plan of the building to his memory. He knew, for example, that the door immediately to his left led to the personal quarters of Aldeemo, eldest of the brothers, and that the door across the hall led to a linen closet backed by a secret stairway that led down to the emporium on the first floor. Talent in both sorcery and thievery made possible thefts that mundane rogues or honest sorcerers would never have attempted.

He reached the end of the hall, where a door sheathed in green copper sheets warded the upper vault. Here Jack knelt and fished out a couple of small picks from a pouch at his side, expertly picking the lock with a moment's work. He glanced over his shoulder; at the other end of the hallway, Anders peered out of the carpet storeroom, watching intently. Jack winked at him and opened the copper door, quietly sliding inside.

The room was a small, crowded place fitted with five counting desks all in a row, awash in bagged coinage and precarious stacks of iron strongboxes. Had Jack a mind to take it, the coinage itself would have been an epic success . . . but he was after something more impressive than hundreds of pounds of coins. He worked his way to the back of the room, where a small iron box rested in an alcove in the wall. Cautiously, he inspected the niche and the box, using his poignard gently to raise the front edge of the box.

The weight of the box held down a small spring-loaded trigger, just visible under the center of the container. "Perfectly predictable," Jack muttered. Taking the box out of the niche would trigger some kind of alarm or trap. He could probably disarm it, but did he need too? Suddenly the answer struck him. He laughed softly. "Of course!" Carefully, he fished another set of picks from his pouch and set to work, quickly opening the small box right where it sat. If he didn't move the lockbox, he wouldn't trigger the trap, and that meant that all he had to do was remove the rubies from the box without removing the box from the niche. With one final click, the box opened.

Five perfect rubies glimmered darkly inside.

Jack grinned. He pushed the lid back out of the way, exposing the five rubies to view. Then, as a precaution in case removing the weight of the rubies might be sufficient to trigger the spring-loaded catch beneath the box, he fished out a small wooden dowel from his burglary kit and wedged it in place to hold the box firmly down on the bottom of the niche. That done, he produced a small silk cloth from another pocket and folded the five rubies inside. "And that is that." He grinned.

Something snuffled and grunted outside.

Jack froze. He held his breath, listening intently. Then he mumbled an invisibility spell, fading from sight as the familiar words and energies worked the magic in the accustomed way. Even as he vanished, the counting-room door slowly swung open, creaking on its hinges.

A hulking, bearlike shape stood in the door. Leathery bat-wings flapped and shuffled as it advanced into the room. Demonic red eyes glowed in the center of an ursine face crowned by curling ram's horns.

"Come out, come out, little thief," the demon hissed. Its voice was thick oil poured over a hot stove. "I can smell your magic, I can hear your heartbeat, I can taste your spoor in the air. You cannot hide from me."

Jack decided to try anyway. He held himself perfectly still, breathing slowly and silently.

The demon advanced into the room, snuffling and spreading out its limbs to grope for him. "I see you have borrowed my masters' rubies, little thief," the creature hissed. "Put them back now, and I will allow you to live."

Moving very slowly, Jack crouched low and began to feel his way forward. The only way to escape was to dive under the creature's grasp and bolt before it could turn to follow. He tightened his grasp on the gems, held in his left hand. Then, before he could lose his nerve, he jumped to one side and scrambled under the monster's outstretched paws.

"*Anders!*" he called.

The demon roared and slammed its monstrous talons against the wall, trying to catch hold of Jack or pin him in place, but Jack dropped to all fours and scrambled past the guardian. Coins glittered and crashed in the darkness. The monstrous creature whirled with impossible speed and sprang after him, talons grasping blindly for him, its stinking breath hot on his neck. Jack gained his feet in the hallway outside and fled for his life.

At the far end of the hall, Anders broke his cover and charged forward, unsheathing his broadsword with a shrill ring of steel. The demon roared and spat a gout of flame at the swordsman, driving him to the ground. For one long, flawless moment, Jack saw nothing between him and his route of escape but the dark crevice of the storeroom door. He put his head down and ran for all he was worth.

Then a door opened right in front of him, and Aldeemo Kuldath stepped right into his path. Pale and wizened, the easterner blinked his eyes sleepily while drawing back the string of a small hand crossbow. Jack, still invisible, crashed into him at a dead run. Both thief and merchant sprawled to the floor. Aldeemo's crossbow fired with a sharp snap, embedding its tiny quarrel in the middle of his own left foot. Jack's rubies flew from his hand and scattered across the polished wood floor of the hallway, skittering and dancing like droplets of wine.

"My foot!" howled the merchant.

"My rubies!" wailed Jack. His invisibility faded, spoiled by the collision.

Roaring in rage, the demon leaped over both to meet Anders's charge, as the Northman shrieked a battle cry and sprang forward with his blade flashing. The guardian's claws and teeth snapped and gouged huge furrows in the paneling. Anders dodged and slashed, parrying the attack and hacking away at the monster with furious strokes.

"That's three!" the swordsman cried. "Do you hear me, Jack? That makes three!"

While the swordsman and the demon traded desperate blows, Jack shook his head, clearing the cobwebs, and scrambled after the rubies. The first one he reached for was kicked aside by a careless step of the guardian demon; the second, Aldeemo reached first. He groped for another ruby and seized one . . . just as another door opened and Ospim Kuldath stepped into the fray, armed with a long cudgel.

"Thievery! Burglary! Chaos!" the second Kuldath shrieked. "Summon the Watch!" Then he stooped and picked up the fourth ruby.

"Discretion is advised," Jack muttered, then decided to leave while he could. "Anders! Get out!" He jumped to his feet and darted past Ospim, ducking under a swing of the club, and threw himself into the secret storeroom in the middle of the hall—there was no way to get past the demon and Anders, engaged in their furious duel.

"Stop! Come back here!" Aldeemo cried. He tried to scramble after Jack, sprawling to the ground again when he tripped over the quarrel stuck in his foot. The lean, bearded merchant screamed a string of curses in some uncouth eastern tongue and clutched his injured extremity.

Anders snarled a curse of his own and started giving ground, retreating back to the carpet room. At the right moment, he jumped back and slammed the door in the demon's face, barring it with one swift movement. The creature lowered its massive head and butted the door hard enough to split one of the planks. Hoping that Anders had sense enough to make his escape while the demon battered down the door, Jack retreated into the linen closet and groped for the catch to the secret door. An anxious moment later, he found it and bolted down the secret stairway.

One ruby still clutched in his hand, he burst out of the secret door into the Kuldath business floor and threw himself out of the first window he encountered in a spray of broken glass. Without breaking stride, he rolled to his feet and pelted for home. Instinctively he avoided the bobbing torches and angry voices of the local watchmen converging on the scene, slipping into a dark alleyway and resuming his mask of invisibility.

It could have gone worse, Jack told himself.

An hour later, Jack sat in the crowded warmth of the Cracked Tankard and quaffed a clay mug of ale. The Kuldath ruby rested in the innermost pocket of his doublet, a mere handspan from his heart, and he reveled in the cool impression it made against the ribs of his left side. As always, he'd claimed his seat on the back wall, midway between the stairs leading up to the Tankard's private rooms, a doorway leading to the kitchens and then the alleyway beyond, and a small window fronting on De Villars Ride. He'd learned through necessity that he could fit through that window in a pinch, and he now counted it among the seven possible exits from the room.

The Cracked Tankard was not the roughest taproom in Raven's Bluff, nor the oldest, nor the one most frequented by thieves and swindlers, nor the one with the cheapest ale or the sauciest barmaids. It was instead a pleasant combination of all these things. Situated on the western end of the Anvil, the heart of the city, the Tankard not only made an excellent meeting place, but it also collected rumors and news in much the same way that the lowest portion of an awning collected rainwater. All manner of things in Raven's Bluff ran downhill to this one spot.

By Jack's guess, midnight was two hours gone, and still Anders had not showed up at their arranged rendezvous. He chose not to worry too much. The blond-bearded swordsman was one of the best brawlers he knew, and he was as comfortable racing across the city rooftops as the rocky cliffs of his distant homeland. It would take more than an angry demon and the brothers Kuldath to prevent his escape. Jack had partnered with Anders before in similarly daring escapades; if he knew the Northman, Anders would be along sooner or later.

Observing that his ale was almost gone, Jack held his mug in the air and called, "Briesa! There must be a hole in this cup, for it is empty again!"

Across the taproom, a pretty dark-haired barmaid waved him off. "I'll get to you as soon as I can, love," she replied over the din.

"I have been waiting to hear you speak those words for weeks now, Briesa," Jack replied.

She rolled her eyes and turned away, six tankards brimming in her hands as she danced off to a table of rowdy Sembians. The girl was very pretty, a few inches shorter than he was, and quite fetching in the busty barmaid's blouse and dress. Jack grinned to himself and drained off the last of his mug, designs upon Briesa's virtue forming in his mind.

When he looked up from the empty tankard, he found himself gazing into the eyes of an exquisitely beautiful woman dressed all in dark leather. Hair as dark as midnight spilled down her shoulders. Eyes that smoldered with sultry promise and ebon fire studied him with calm, collected confidence. A long, slender sword was sheathed at her hip.

"Good evening," she said in a clear voice marked by a faint burring accent. "Are you called Jack Ravenwild?"

"I might be," Jack admitted, setting down his cup with some care. "If you owe Jack Ravenwild a substantial sum of money, then I am certainly he. If, on the other hand, you intend to run him through for some imagined slight long forgotten on his part, then no, I don't believe I'm the one you're looking for." He paused, studying the woman, and then added, "If, perchance, you have heard of his prowess in the arts of love, and yearn to find out if half of what you might have heard is true, then I am most certainly Jack Ravenwild."

She smiled coldly, a smile that didn't touch her eyes, and settled into the chair opposite him. "I'll take that as a long-winded yes, although I don't owe you money, I don't mean to kill you, and I don't have any particular interest in your romantic prowess. I'm here to talk business."

"Business?" Jack sighed dramatically. "Well, business it is, then. To whom am I speaking?"

"You can call me Elana," the dark-haired woman said. She shifted slightly in her seat, clearing her sword arm and moving to make sure that the table would not interfere with a sudden draw. Long, lithe muscles flexed along her forearm. Jack realized that her face and figure showed not a trace of softness—she didn't wear the sword for show. She was a panther, a tigress, absolutely confident in her own abilities.

"What can I do for you, Elana?" Jack asked. He offered a subtle smirk, unable to resist the temptation to jest a little with her. He hated serious people.

"I hear," said Elana, "that you excel in finding things. I would like you to find something for me."

"You have heard correctly. There will be, of course, a

pittance of a finder's fee. I would charge you nothing for my services, but if word got out that I'd worked for free, why, then I should never be solvent again. What are you looking for, dear Elana?"

Elana started to speak, and then held her tongue as Briesa approached and replaced Jack's mug of ale. The barmaid glanced at Jack and hid a smile, as if to say that Jack had no need of troubling her anymore with his suggestions, now that he had female companionship. Jack winced. It might take weeks to convince Briesa that he was discussing business and business alone with the lovely Elana.

"Anything for your companion, Jack?" the barmaid asked.

Elana glanced up at her. "I'll take whatever he's drinking."

"Right away, miss," Briesa said. She whirled off into the crowd, a serving tray balanced on her shoulder. She didn't notice the long, thoughtful look Elana gave her as she moved away.

"You were about to say?" Jack prompted.

The swordswoman returned her attention to him. "I'm looking for a book. A very old, rare book that I have good reason to believe is somewhere in this city. I'm willing to pay you five hundred pieces of gold for your help, plus a bonus if you actually recover it for me."

"What kind of bonus did you have in mind?"

Elana smiled in a predatory fashion. "I don't have too much more money at my disposal, but I'm sure you can think of other ways for me to reward you for a job well done."

Jack set down his tankard and sat straight up. She was toying with him, he was certain of it. On the other hand . . . "What can you tell me about the book? Anything you can volunteer at this point will help me to find it for you."

The swordswoman leaned forward, lowering her voice. "It is called the Sarkonagael," she said quietly. "Eight years ago, it was brought to Raven's Bluff by an adventuring mage named Gerard. I do not know exactly where Gerard got it or how long he had it before he came here. But I've asked after Gerard already, and it seems that he disappeared on some failed enterprise about six years ago. All I really know at this point is that the Sarkonagael was in this city then, and it was brought here by Gerard."

"What happened to Gerard's belongings when he didn't come back for them?"

"Apparently, the landlord who owned the house Gerard and his company were renting chose to sell off all the band's trophies when they didn't come back for them."

"So the Sarkonagael was sold about six years ago from the estate of an adventuring band. That may be useful," Jack said. There were a limited number of book dealers in Raven's Bluff, and any such sale would have been attended by some of them. The odds were very good that the Sarkonagael might be sitting in someone's bookshop. He smiled at the prospect of an easy five hundred gold crowns . . . and the attendant bonus. In fact, he might do well to make the job seem much harder than it really was. He could fabricate any kind of tale about daring burglaries or skullduggery. "One last question: Why do you want it?"

Elana waited a moment while the barmaid returned with her ale. She took a small sip, watching Jack over the top of the mug. She deliberately set down the mug and licked her lips. "I collect old books," she said. "That is reason enough."

Jack laughed. Somehow he doubted that Elana collected many books, but she was entitled to maintain her fictions. "It will do for me, my lady," he replied. "Now, for matters of pay—"

Elana forestalled him by reaching into her leather coat and producing a small pouch. She dropped it on the table in front of him with a reassuring jingle of coinage.

"You'll find twenty five-crown pieces in the purse," she said. "Call it an advance. I now consider you to be in my employ. You'll receive the balance when you produce the book or convince me that it cannot be found in Raven's Bluff. If that is the case, I expect you to spend at least a month searching diligently for it—and I'll know whether you really look for it or not."

"My lady, I normally require half the promised fee in advance—"

"Of course, dear Jack. And since you are so generously foregoing that requirement, I am prepared to offer the bonus of which we spoke. Generosity engenders generosity, true?"

Jack smiled. He found himself wondering whether Elana had another gold crown to her name or not, but for the moment he didn't care. If the job was as easy as he suspected, a hundred crowns was sufficient reward . . . especially with the bonus included. "All who know me speak well of my generous nature, my lady. Of course I shall accept the arrangement you propose. Now, how shall I get in touch with you to report any progress I make?"

"I shall contact you when it becomes necessary," Elana said.

"But it may be a day, or two days, or a week, or a month," Jack said. "I hardly know how long it will take me to find your book until I complete the task! And, to be perfectly honest, I can be very difficult to find sometimes."

"I found you once. I can find you again when I need to." Elana took another deep draught from her ale and stood up. She drew the back of her hand across her mouth and donned a pair of gloves, tugging them over her fair hands. "I am afraid I have other business to attend to. I will find you when I need to speak to you, dear Jack. In the meantime . . . please exercise some discretion. I do not want it widely known that I seek the Sarkonagael."

"I understand perfectly," Jack said. Belatedly, he rose also. "I am the very soul of discretion. You need not have any fears on that account."

"Good," said Elana. She drew up her hood and stalked away, graceful and purposeful all at the same time. Jack watched her go, bemused. He sensed that he was out of his depth in dealing with her, but at the same time, the Kuldath expedition had not gone as well as he would have liked, and he could always use the money. Still, something about her unsettled him. Working for competent and dangerous people was one thing, but Elana clearly regarded him as nothing but a temporary associate of no real account. She'd simply played with him the whole time, a cat toying with a mouse.

"I am *not* a mouse," Jack laughed. He sat back down again and sipped at his ale, watching the crowd swirl and shout. He waited another hour and then went back to his room in Burnt Gables. A ruby, a purse of gold, a beautiful lady, and a mysterious mission, he mused. Perhaps this was not a bad night after all.

The next morning, Jack visited the disreputable sage Ontrodes, who kept his house in a particularly poor part of Shadystreets. Whistling a merry tune and dressed splendidly in soft dove gray and midnight blue, Jack pranced through the streets of the city, greeting all who passed by with mirthful grins and generous bows. The steady drizzle affected his spirits not in the least, and the mire of Shadystreet's muddy lanes and deceptively deep puddles did not slow his steps at all. He had a mystery to solve and a lady whose favors he sought. What more could he ask of a morning?

The home of Ontrodes had once been a small sage's

tower, a cottage with a round stone turret nobly looking out over the Fire River across a green marsh filled with waterfowl. That had been close to a hundred years past. In the thirty-odd (or was it forty-odd?) years that the place had been in the care of Ontrodes, ramshackle wharves and rotten old warehouses had fenced in the riverbank, squalid hovels had encroached upon the sage's fields, and the tower proper had almost fallen over, leaving nothing but a tottering edifice perched precariously on the edge of utter ruin.

Jack rather liked the place; he thought it unassuming. He stepped up to the cottage door and thumped it soundly, careful not to knock *too* vigorously lest he precipitate the final demise of Ontrodes's home. "Ontrodes! My friend! Awaken, and provide me the benefit of your advice!"

A long silence followed, then a clatter and a horrible sort of honking sound that might have been the old man clearing his throat. "Advice?" coughed the old man from inside. "I advise you to go soak your head in a piss-pot! I know your insolent voice, Jack Ravenwild, and you'll gain more wisdom in that fashion than you'll ever gain from me! Now, go away, and don't even think of returning until at least an hour past noon!"

"Have you been in your cups again, then, Ontrodes?"

"It is no concern of yours, Jack! Leave me be!" A rattle and a thump sounded from inside. The sage coughed loudly and mumbled more curses under his breath.

"Why, I am deeply concerned by the slightest illness in any of my friends," Jack replied. "My solicitous and compassionate nature demands no less. If you suffer from too much indulgence, perhaps I can find some way to improve your spirits."

"That is the very problem!" Ontrodes suddenly appeared at the door, yanking it open with a grunt of effort. He stood there blinking, a short, paunchy man dressed in a wine-stained robe. White tousled hair crowned his red face, and a haze of untrimmed whiskers clung to his round jowls. "I sell my learning for the benefit of all, yet vagrants like you come and pick through my knowledge like curs sniffing through a heap of offal, refusing even the courtesy of a proper payment. Thus am I compelled to buy cheap, miserable Ravenaar wine instead of some more noble brew from Procampur or perhaps even fair Chessenta. And I awaken with ten angry goblins holding a war dance inside my head! Now, unless you have good gold in your pockets and some cure for my screaming skull-ache, leave at once!"

Jack bowed deeply and offered his most earnest smile. He dropped a small purse with a handful of Elana's gold pieces in Ontrodes's hand, and then he drew from his blue doublet a small silver flask. "Gold for your wisdom, and a fine elven brandy for your skull. The sublime bouquet is guaranteed to waft your perception to noble heights and charge your peerless mind with grand designs and astonishing visions." He laughed aloud. "If nothing else, I have improved your *spirits*, haven't I?"

The old sage slapped one meaty hand to his face and stood there for a moment as if to keep his brains from fleeing his head outright. Then he looked Jack in the eye. "I can see that you have no mercy in your heart. You might as well come in, then."

"Excellent!" Jack replied. He could feel a successful conclusion to his mission no farther away than a cheap brandy-flask and a terse, to-the-point discussion.

CHAPTER TWO

So, my dear friend, whose wisdom knows no bounds," Jack began, "have you perchance ever heard of a book called the Sarkonagael?"

He lounged in a vast, overstuffed easy chair in the first (and only safe) floor of Ontrodes's tower. The tools of Ontrodes's trade—books both old and new, well-known and obscure, mundane and magical—stood in great stacks throughout the cramped chamber or threatened to spill out from crowded bookshelves. The stuffing of the chair reeked of mildew, and a pile of tiny mouse droppings was located atop one arm in the exact spot that Jack wanted to rest his hand. He deliberately noted the location of the offending material and kept his hand in his lap.

Ontrodes squinted in thought and allowed himself a swig of the brandy. "Well, my dear boy, whose idle flattery knows no shame, I do not believe I have ever heard that name before." The sage laughed harshly, which led to a small fit of coughing. "You may have wasted your ten gold crowns and your cheap brandy this morning."

Jack frowned. As far as sages went, Ontrodes was not very reliable. There was a reason he was widely known as the disreputable sage Ontrodes, but he worked for next to nothing, and for exactly nothing some of the time, since his constant dissipations required a steady stream of small amounts of cash. Adventurers, rogues, and other ne'er-do-wells with a shortage of funds could usually obtain some useful scrap of information from the sage, when a well-researched answer from a real sage might cost far more than they could afford. He waved his hand at all of the books stacked head-high in the room.

"Surely you must have some hint of it somewhere in all this?"

"My particular area of expertise lies in wines, brandies, cognacs, sherries, and other exotic elixirs," Ontrodes rumbled. "No living mortal knows so much about such concoctions as I. Anything else I happen to pick up is merely incidental to my study of wines and liquors. I can say without hesitation that the Sarkonagael is not a vintage known to me, nor is it a book in which vintages are discussed, since I should then own it."

"That is not extremely helpful. How about a mage named Gerard, who would have made a name for himself as an adventurer about eight or ten years ago?"

"Can't say I've heard of him." Ontrodes said after a moment's thought, "A book called the Sarkonagael owned by a mage named Gerard, eh?"

"Something like that," Jack said with a wave of his hand. He had to remind himself to watch where he set it down. "Are you sure you don't have *something* about it in one of these books somewhere? I admire your intellect, but I cannot believe you have committed the entire content of your library to memory."

"More than you might think," Ontrodes said. He took another swallow from the silver flask. "For Sembian swill, this is not so bad. It's a shame you couldn't get your hands on some real elven brandy. That, my friend, is the very nectar of the gods."

"I'll see what I can do next time," Jack said. He pushed himself to his feet and discovered that he'd parked his right hand directly amid the mouse droppings. He winced and brushed it off on the other arm of the chair. "I thank you for your time, dear Ontrodes. If your wisdom fails me on this occasion, it is surely due to my inability to ask the right questions, as opposed to a degeneration of your mental faculties brought on by age and excessive drink."

"A moment, Jack," Ontrodes said wearily. "What did you call it again?"

"The Sarkonagael?"

Ontrodes scowled and cast one bleary eye over the formidable piles of books littering the chamber. "I'll take a look, but only if you swear to bring me real elven brandy if I find something."

"I so swear, instantly and without reservation," Jack said. "Thank you, my friend!"

"Save your thanks. The real brandy costs more than a hundred gold crowns for a flask this size." Ontrodes sighed and dismissed him. "Now, leave me alone. I have work—"

There was a knock at the door. "Hello? Ontrodes?" called a woman's voice from outside.

The sage mumbled imprecations under his breath. "It appears that everyone desires my wisdom at an unreasonably early hour today," he said. He shuffled to the door and opened it. "I am Ontrodes," he said. "Who are you?"

On the doorstep, a tall woman dressed in red silk and leather waited. A curved dagger was thrust into her belt and a slender wand was sheathed in a special holster on the other side. Her eyes, green and wide, smoldered under a short-cropped shock of brilliant red hair. A fine blue tattoo of an arcane sigil marked her left cheekbone. She crossed her arms imperiously in front of her and glared at him.

"I am the Red Wizard Zandria," she said. Her voice was sharp and commanding. "I understand that you know everything there is to know about wines, brandies, and other liqueurs. Is that true?"

Ontrodes blinked in surprise. "Why, yes. Yes, it is true."

"Good. Then perhaps I can retain your expertise in this matter." Without waiting for an invitation, she marched into the sage's cottage, studied the armchair doubtfully, and then settled herself on the corner of the desk. She was strikingly handsome, with a pert figure and a challenging strength of character in her fine-featured face. She glanced at Jack and asked, "Your business with the sage is done?"

It was more of a command than a question. Jack smiled and bowed deeply, reaching for her hand, but Zandria didn't offer it. He quickly recovered and straightened. "In fact, I had just concluded my business with Ontrodes. I am delighted to meet you, my lady Zandria. I am called Jack Ravenwild, and I possess no little expertise—"

"A pleasure to have met you, Jack," Zandria interrupted. "Perhaps we'll see each other again soon. Please, do not allow me to delay you any longer."

The rogue spread his hands and forced a smile onto his face. He'd suffered through enough condescending dismissals to know one when he saw one. That didn't trouble him at all; he would have loved to plumb the limits of Zandria's courtesy by deliberately ignoring her not-so-subtle hints. Not only did he delight in baiting beautiful women, but Zandria was clearly a mage of some skill and confidence—a Red Wizard of Thay, no less!—and she had urgent business with the most inept sage of the city. Jack smelled clandestine deeds and secret doings, and the mystery grew moment by moment into a consuming obsession he was helpless to resist.

Only one thing to do, then. Jack bowed deeply and

swept his hat from his head in a courtly bow. "As it so happens, I have great toils and wondrous works to attend. Farewell." He turned to the sage. "Ontrodes, I'll be back tomorrow to see how your search progresses."

The old sage was still gaping at Zandria. Apparently he was so used to dealing with rogues and empty-headed swordsmen down on their luck that he'd never expected to have a competent, confident professional seeking his advice again.

"My search?" he managed to ask.

Jack sighed. "The S-thing, once owned by the man named G," he hissed as he passed by.

"Oh, right, of course, I'll get right to it," Ontrodes said absently. Without looking, he waved a hand at the rogue. "I'll see you later then, Jack."

Mustering what dignity he could, Jack made his way outside and stood in the drizzle at the sage's doorstep, looking up and down the street. He nodded at a passing pair of porters carrying heavy casks on their shoulders, and then dashed quickly around the back of the sage's house. Splashing through ankle-deep mud, he circled the tower and found a shuttered window facing the alleyway. He scrambled about three feet up the tower's side, just high enough to lay his ear against the damp wood of the shutter.

"—the crypts," Zandria was saying, speaking rapidly in her clipped, clear voice. "The Lady Mayor has taken an unusual interest in the relics of Sarbreen of late, and I have long suspected that the guilder's tomb conceals an entrance into an extensive hidden vault. But I cannot actually find the place! All I have is this unfathomable riddle of an inscription."

"It's quite odd," Ontrodes agreed. "'Mark carefully the summer staircase and climb it clockwise thrice.' That makes no sense at all, does it?"

"Not really. I'd hoped you would understand it."

"Understanding may yet come to me, my lady. Cedrizarun is well-known to me. I have often wished that I had lived six or seven centuries ago, so that I might have sampled some of his works, all handmade and lovingly aged by the old dwarf himself." The sage cleared his throat; the floorboard creaked as he moved inside. "See here, this part of it: 'At the center of all the thirty-seventh.' That clearly refers to Cedrizarun's incomparable Maidenfire Gold of '37, claimed by some to be the very finest dwarven brandy ever distilled north of the sea."

"You mean this?" Zandria asked. "I thought that might be what it meant."

Jack could hear Ontrodes's gasp even through the shutter. "Oh, my lady," the sage said with awe in his voice, "I will gladly give you five hundred gold crowns for that bottle of brandy."

The mage laughed aloud. Her brusque, commanding manner vanished in her laughter; it seemed to bring out a carefree girl Jack never would have suspected. Then the glimpse was gone. "I fear not, sage. First of all, I paid far more than that for this bottle. Second, I will not uncork it or allow it to be uncorked until I am certain that I know the meaning of this riddle. I have a feeling that the Maidenfire Gold wouldn't fare well in your care."

"On the contrary, my lady, it should fare very well indeed! Who else could appreciate it more than I? Who else could revel in its exquisite bouquet, delight in every depth of its perfect flavor, comprehend with each loving sip the work of a master craftsman at the apex of his art? Oh, it would be a disservice to the world—and to dead Cedrizarun himself—if I allowed any but the most discerning and educated of connoisseurs to sample that liquor!"

Jack knew in that very instant that, regardless of the

consequences to follow, he would have to get his hands on the brandy and drink it with complete and total disregard for its marvelous reputation. The notion struck him as so humorous that he snickered out loud, turning his face into his shoulder to stifle the sound—a moment too late.

Zandria threw open the shutter with a gesture of her hand, dislodging Jack from his perch on the tower wall. He flailed for balance for one long, comical moment before falling flat on his back in the muddy alleyway behind Ontrodes's home. Staring up at the gray sky and the gentle raindrops, Jack grimaced in disgust.

"My new clothes are ruined," he observed.

"Count yourself lucky if that's all I ruin," Zandria snarled. Jack raised his head from the muck and looked back up at the window. The red-haired mage glared at him, the wand in her hand. "I don't much care for eavesdroppers, thieves, swindlers, or whatever you are under all that false charm and pretentious manner."

Spread-eagled in the mud, Jack adopted the most earnest expression he could find. "I would only insult you if I made any attempt to deny that I was listening to your conversation, my lady. I did eavesdrop, and you have my most humble and sincere apologies." He smiled in what he hoped was an apologetic manner, and then added, "I only listened in because I so desperately wanted to help you. I allowed my instinct to aid others in need to momentarily overthrow my common sense."

The mage blinked in astonishment. "You expect me to *believe* that?" she said.

"I never lie," Jack said. He slowly picked himself up off the ground, doing his best to brush the mud from his clothes. It was of little use. "Why don't you show me the inscription you were speaking of? And that bottle of brandy? Maybe I can piece together your riddle for you. I have a real knack for that sort of thing."

"I believe I'll solve it without your help!" Zandria rapped her wand sharply on the windowsill. "Now get out of here before I turn you into a toad or a newt or something worse!"

Ontrodes peered over her shoulder at him. "I believe she means it, Jack," he said. "Shame on you, listening at my window! My learning is my livelihood. When you make use of it without paying, why, you are stealing from me!"

"I shall begin to investigate this matter on your behalf this very instant," Jack assured Zandria. "How else can I demonstrate my good intentions? I'll let you know the moment I make any progress."

"Get out of my sight this instant!" the mage shrieked.

Jack gestured and mumbled the magical words. He faded into transparency as the spell of invisibility settled over him. "As you wish, my lady," he called out. Then he squelched off through the mud, phantom footprints appearing one after another as he strode off boldly. He hummed merrily until he was out of sight. "Two riddles, two ladies, and two mysterious prizes! What next, I wonder?"

Absolutely confident of immediate success, Jack spent the rest of the day visiting every bookseller he knew of, obliquely inquiring after the Sarkonagael. He was careful to come around to his point slowly and without excessive enthusiasm, but as it turned out, Jack's precautions were wasted. He didn't find a single glimmer of recognition among any of the six booksellers he spoke to. Grudgingly he conceded the possibility that the mysterious Elana might have already investigated the obvious possibilities. That was unfortunate, since it meant that Jack might have to work and work hard to unearth the book. He considered quitting outright, but then he found himself thinking about her raven-black hair and her perfect face. The prize just might justify real exertion.

At sundown, Jack turned his steps toward the Cracked Tankard. It was too early for the familiar crowd, but he was hungry and thirsty, and he hoped against hope that he might encounter his lovely employer again. He took his accustomed spot and handed Briesa one of Elana's five-crown pieces for a huge trencher of beef and boiled potatoes, plus a sturdy mug of the Tankard's best ale.

"Keep it," he told the barmaid. "We'll call it a line of credit."

"Don't you owe us some money already, Jack?" Briesa said with an impish smile.

"No more than a silver penny or two. That should more than address the balance of my debt, in addition to any small charges I incur over the next month or so," he replied.

Briesa took the five-crown piece and set off on her rounds. When she returned a little later, she informed him that the proprietor had told her in no uncertain terms that five crowns covered Jack's tab from nights past and his meal tonight. No line of credit was forthcoming, however.

Jack was just mulling over the possibility of changing taverns to some more trusting establishment when a huge figure in a dark cloak appeared at his table and hauled out the opposite chair without invitation. He looked up, a protest forming already, but he was silenced at once by a massive hand clamping down on his wrist. With a furtive look to the left and the right, the figure lifted the cowl of the cloak just enough for Jack to catch a glimpse of blue eyes and a somewhat singed blond beard.

"Anders!" he said in surprise.

"Shhhh!" hissed the big Northman. "I've been followed all day. Don't give me away!"

"Of course, of course," Jack replied. "Tell me, how did you fare when the brothers Kuldath drove us from our rightful take?"

"It was a harrowing escape, my friend," Anders said. "The storeroom door held against the demon just long enough for me to climb back up to the rooftops. I fled at once, darting from housetop to housetop, but the demon pursued me! Did you notice that it had wings?"

"Now that you mention it, yes, I do recall wings. The high road was perhaps not the best choice of escape routes, given a pursuer who could fly."

"I was forced to find refuge in the waters of the harbor, where I remained until sunrise, when the creature gave up and returned to its masters' home. That was a long, cold night."

"I waited for you here," Jack said. "For what it's worth, the ale was decidedly inferior last night, and they let the fire burn down to a small, sad pile of embers that didn't warm the room in the least. You were really better off in the harbor."

Anders let the remark pass without comment. His eyes had fixed on Jack's sizable plate of steaming beef and potatoes. "When I climbed back to the wharves this morning, I was spotted by Kuldath agents. They reported me to the city watch, and I spent the whole day eluding their search. As it so happens, I never found an opportunity to replenish myself after shivering in the cold, foul waters of the inner harbor all night long. You wouldn't mind if—?"

"Please, be my guest," Jack said generously.

It was easy to agree, since Anders was already attacking his dinner with the ferocity of a ravenous bear. He winced as the barbarian devoured the entirety of Jack's one-crown dinner, and washed it down with great gulps of Jack's fine ale.

"So," Anders managed between gulps, "do you have my ruby on your person?"

"Your ruby?" Jack managed. "Friend Anders, did I not tell you that I failed to carry off any of the rubies? My ill-timed collision with Aldeemo scattered the rubies all over the floor, and I was forced to flee ere I recovered any of them."

"Odd," Anders said. "I am certain that I saw you pocket one ruby before you left the scene. Shall I help you check your pockets to make sure you haven't forgotten anything?"

"Oh, *that* ruby! Well, yes, of course I managed to get away with the ruby you saw me pick up."

"Excellent! You may deliver it to me at your convenience."

"Well, I had thought that I would wait a couple of weeks and then fence the thing, so that we could then split the loot. Sixty-forty, as we agreed."

"I look at it like this," Anders said. "You promised that, if I happened to fight the demon, I should get three gems, and you should get two. To put it another way, I should get one more of the rubies than you. Since we have in our possession only one ruby, then it seems clear to me that I should keep it. Thus, I would have one more gem than you."

"What you propose is completely intolerable!" Jack protested. "I would see no reward at all for weeks of exhaustive planning, endless nights of scrying and spying, and of course the sheer physical peril of the adventure itself! I cannot be left empty-handed!"

"You are correct, friend Jack," Anders said thoughtfully. "We must sell the gem and split the proceeds. I will take sixty percent in lieu of my three gems, and you may have forty percent in place of your two."

Jack fidgeted in his seat. The five Kuldath rubies together would have fetched thousands of crowns. Now he stood to gain less than a tenth of that!

"I shall sell the gem at once, then," he said wearily, "and I will deliver your due share by the end of the tenday."

"Perhaps I'd better attend to it," said Anders. "I wouldn't want you to be troubled with remembering exactly how much you sold the ruby for. It might damage our friendship if you accidentally reported that you'd sold the gem for, say, six hundred crowns when you'd really sold it for seven or eight hundred."

"I would never—"

"I'm sure. Give me the gem, and I'll make sure you don't." Anders held out his hand.

Jack thought things over for a moment, fuming over the fact that Anders didn't trust him. The fact that he'd entertained the exact scheme suggested by the Northman was entirely beside the point. On the other hand, he could generally count on Anders to do exactly what he said he was going to do. The Northman was about as honest a cut-throat as you could find. In any event, Jack had several other prospects for success, and he never knew when he might need a big, strong swordsman close at hand.

"Very well, then," he said with a sigh. He reached into his vest pocket and pulled out the small, hard bundle wrapped in black cloth. "In all seriousness, I think you would be well-advised to wait a few days before you try to sell it."

Anders grinned. "I'm surprised, Jack. I thought I was going to have to beat you severely in order to make you see things my way." He scooped up the silk-wrapped ruby with one big, callused fist, then stood and tugged his cowl in place over his face. "Don't worry about the gem. I'll ride up to Tantras first thing tomorrow to dispose of it."

Tantras! What that really meant was that Anders was riding out of town with the entire sum of their take from the previous night, and it would take days before Jack knew if he was coming back or not. Trust of that sort was generally foreign to Jack. He managed to paste a feeble smile on his face and nodded.

"That sounds like a good idea," he said weakly. "I'll expect your return in four or five days then."

"Might be a little longer, depending on the spring mud," the Northman said over his shoulder as he left.

Jack watched him go, frustrated by the completely unacceptable way things had turned out. He was so pre-occupied that he didn't notice the two men sitting in the opposite corner rise to their feet and casually meander toward him until they stood shoulder-to-shoulder, towering over him.

"Would you be Jack Ravenwild?" said the first. He was a short, stout fellow with a round, sallow face and a small, pointed goatee. His voice purred like a well-fed cat.

"Don't bother lying," said the second. "We already know you are." This one was tall and lean, with long hands and a longer face. His yellow eyes stared out of deep, dark sockets like small, feral creatures hiding under rocks.

The rogue shook himself out of his self-pity and looked up. "Why in the world would you ask me who I am then?"

"Perhaps you could tell us where your large friend is going," the first man said.

"We know that he told you," the tall man added.

"Who are you, and why do you care?" Jack asked.

"I am called Morgath," the fat man said. "My companion is Saerk."

"Who we are doesn't matter," Saerk said. "Who we work for does."

"We are employed by an organization that provides a type of *insurance* to various mercantile companies of the city," Morgath said. "Last night, one of our clients suffered a small loss. We are investigating his claim, so to speak."

"They were robbed," Saerk said. "By a large, blond-haired Northman and a small rat of a burglar who knew some magic."

"That is all very interesting," Jack said, "but I don't see what it has to do with me."

"We have reason to believe that you may have a more intimate knowledge of this case—" Morgath said.

"We know you were responsible," Saerk interrupted.

"—and we expect you to see to the return the stolen property—"

"Or we'll kill you if you don't," Saerk finished.

Jack looked from the one man to the other. "If I were the man you were looking for," he said, "I would carefully consider your warning. However, I have no idea what you're talking about, I don't have any property of yours or your employer's, and until just a few moments ago, I'd never seen that barbaric fellow in my life. If you'll excuse me?" He stood and started to push past the two.

Morgath and Saerk caught him by the arms and pushed him back down into his seat. "We're not unreasonable men," Morgath began with a pained expression. "In fact, we feel that your talents do you credit. Not very many rogues could have pulled off the stunt you pulled off last night in House Kuldath. We'd rather work with you in a mutually profitable arrangement—"

"—instead of cutting you up like live bait and dumping

you in the harbor for the sharks," Saerk finished. "You've got three choices, Jack Ravenwild. Sign up, ship out, or sleep with the fishes." With that, the two thieves sauntered away, smug smiles on their faces.

Jack watched them leave. He picked up the tankard Anders had emptied and swirled it, hoping to find some significant amount of ale left, but the Northman had drained it dry. Then, as the two reached the front door, he muttered a small spell and conjured up an unseen hand. As swift as an arrow Jack directed the invisible presence to the bar and seized a full pitcher of beer. Then he dumped the entire contents on the head of a big, burly longshoreman by the door, dropping the pitcher to the ground right at Morgath's feet.

Roaring in rage, the longshoreman leaped to his feet. "Why, you—"

Morgath stood staring in amazement at the pitcher. When he looked up, it was just in time to observe the impact of the dockworker's fist on the end of his nose. He howled and fell. Saerk drew a dagger, as did all three of the longshoreman's companions, and in less time than it takes to tell, both thieves were involved in a vicious, violent bar brawl complete with knives, chairs, low blows, and cudgel-armed bouncers wading in to break it up.

Jack laughed aloud and slipped out the back door.

The next morning, Jack woke early, bathed himself in bracing cold water, shaved, and then dressed in his very finest clothes—dark blue hose, a shirt of impeccable Mulhorandi cotton, and a stuffed doublet of green and yellow brocade. He donned a short cape that matched the hose and selected a soft, burgundy cap with a long feather in it. Then he pulled on rakish boots of brushed leather and buckled on his rapier and poignard. Jack attired himself with great care every time he visited Lady Illyth Fleetwood.

The day was clear and bright, by far the best day of the spring so far, but Jack hired a coach despite the fine walking weather. He had the coachman drive him six miles beyond the city walls to Woodenhall Manor, the home of the Fleetwood family. The ride took the better part of an hour, which Jack used to admire the scenery outside the city. As far as he could remember, he'd left the city no more than ten times during his entire life, and he'd never been farther away than Woodenhall. He was a Ravenaar, born and bred.

The coach turned into the lane leading to the Fleetwood Manor, rumbling to a stop in front of an impressive veranda before a palatial estate. Liveried guardsmen stood watch over beautiful grounds and hedged gardens, attending a great wooden manor house that was big enough for dozens of family members and three or four times their number of retainers, guards, servants, and guests.

Jack told the coachman to wait for him, then strode up the steps to the nearest servant and said, "Please inform Lady Illyth that the Landsgrave Jaer Kell Wildhame humbly requests an audience this morning."

The servant bowed. "At once, sir. Would you care to wait in the study?"

Jack made a show of acquiescing. "That will do quite well, thank you."

He allowed the servant to show him to a comfortably appointed drawing room and busied himself with examining the decor while he waited patiently. He noted several small items he might pocket and sell later but restrained his larcenous impulses. The Lord Jaer Kell Wildhame was no petty thief!

"Jack! What a surprise!"

Almost dancing in delight, Lady Illyth Fleetwood swept into the room and embraced Jack. Despite the fact that she was well past her schooling and into the years when a noblewoman was expected to be safely married and already raising a child or two of her own, Illyth had never lost the look of girlish enthusiasm and wide-eyed eagerness one might expect of a lady ten years younger. Where other ladies primped for hours over the exact set of their hair and fretted for days over which dress best suited them, Illyth absently kept her long, black hair in a shoulder-length cascade of soft midnight and favored simple, comfortable dresses more suited to a merchant's wife than a nobleman's daughter. Her fingers were habitually marked with faint ink stains instead of painted nails. Illyth was an accomplished scholar and prided herself on her personal library, assembled book by book as her interests carried her from one topic to the next.

Other than Ontrodes, she was the next best thing to a true sage he could consult with, and she would gladly work for nothing at all—if Jack managed to pique her interest in the topic at hand.

"Hello, Illyth," he said. He bowed deeply. "You are lovelier than ever! I find myself wondering how it is that I've allowed two months to pass since I saw you last."

"Because you're a fickle and flighty scoundrel," Illyth said with a smile.

As far as she knew, Jack was the wandering son of a minor nobleman from the Vilhon Reach, seeking his fortune abroad since his older brother had inherited his father's lands and exiled him into penury to keep him from marrying the woman he loved. Illyth thrived on stories just like that, and Jack had been carefully embroidering the tale of Jaer Kell Wildhame for Illyth's benefit for the better part of a year now.

"Lovely, wise, and cruel, all at the same time," Jack said. "How do your studies proceed, Illyth?"

"Well enough. I've spent a lot of time over the last couple of months studying the natural environs of Woodenhall—sketching the lay of the land, tracking just how many creatures of what sorts inhabit the manor, keeping records of the weather, things like that. It's all quite fascinating—but I can see that it would just bore you. How about you, Jack? Is the theater open yet?"

"Oh, I need to find another sponsor or two, and a play worth producing," Jack replied. He'd met Illyth a couple of years ago, when he was occasionally employed by various theaters in the city. Many of the noble patrons of the arts enjoyed inviting actors, playwrights, and artists of note into their social circle for a time. The rich and powerful engaged in a subtle competition to attract the most interesting personages into their retinue, in the same way that they might bid against each other to own the most striking paintings or to stock the most outrageous menageries. Ingratiating himself among the well-to-do of the city was one of Jack's favorite pastimes.

"In fact," he said, "I was hoping you could help me on the matter of the play."

"Help you? But how?" Illyth asked.

"I know that last year you became interested in the topic of heroes, adventurers, and freebooters who'd made their homes in Raven's Bluff," Jack began. "I've got an idea for a smashing production based on the deeds of one of these adventurous sorts, but I'd like to verify the details of the story and make sure that I get it all right. Historical accuracy is very important to me."

"I'm glad to hear it!" Illyth exclaimed. "I can't tell you how much it annoys me when a playwright doesn't even bother to do a bit of research. Who did you have in mind?"

"A mage named Gerard. As I understand it, he passed

through the city and mysteriously vanished about six to ten years ago. Have you ever heard of him?"

She frowned prettily. "Hmmm . . . no, I don't believe so, but I've got hundreds of names recorded in my papers. If not there, then I might dig up some information at the Wizard's Guild, or at the Ministry of Art. What did Gerard supposedly do?"

Jack realized that he'd better tread carefully. He had to give Illyth a good reason for why he wanted to know about Gerard, one that would match his cover story. "I'm not really sure. My play is actually about a rival of his, and I wanted to cast Gerard as a villain. Supposedly, he owned a book called the Sarkonagael," he said. "Can you look into it for me?"

Illyth thought about it for a moment, and then nodded her head. "I'd be happy to, Jack, on one condition."

"Oh?"

"I need a partner in the new Game of Masks. It's going to start in just three days, and they say that the prize is a real Dragon's Tear! You're clever, and you've worked as a player before. I think you could be very good at it, if you just gave it a try!"

"The Game of Masks?" Jack tried not to wince. The Game was a noble diversion, an ongoing series of play-acting events wherein the participants took on various roles and tried to solve puzzles, stumble through a plot, or play at great deeds. He supposed it was fun . . . but it would take a lot of time, probably one evening in every three or four for the next couple of months. More than that, if he played seriously, and Illyth would demand no less than a serious effort on his part. It would also cost a lot of money to stay in the game, more money than he could put his hands on.

Unless Anders came through with his share of the Kuldath ruby.

Or he and Illyth actually won the Game prize. A Dragon's Tear would compensate him quite nicely for his time and trouble. And how hard could it be, really? Most of their competition would consist of foppish noblemen and bored ladies groping their way through a stale plot of some kind. Jack, on the other hand, was a professional. He lied, cheated, stole, and played at being someone he was not as a way of life. He'd cut through their silly Game like a shark in a barrel of codfish.

He looked up at Illyth, a little breathless, a little too fond of her books, but a charming and pretty girl who thought he was romantic, tragic, and entertaining all at the same time. If playing at the Game made her happy, why not?

"All right," Jack said. "When do we start?"

CHAPTER THREE

As it turned out, the Game was not scheduled to begin until the following night. Jack promised to pick up Illyth at sunset (yet another expensive carriage ride! he lamented), then returned to the city and dined at the Cracked Tankard. Following that, he called on Ontrodes to see if the sage had made any progress in the Sarkonagael riddle, but the old sot hadn't even started to look into it yet— he was too busy working on Zandria's dwarven runes. When Jack complained, Ontrodes pointed out that she paid him in real coin, while Jack simply promised a flask of brandy and would undoubtedly deliver the cheapest and most miserable brew he could pour into a nice-looking flask. So Jack returned to his rooms in Burnt Gables and went to bed.

The next morning brought a cool, steady wind off the Inner Sea and a gentle rain that promised to last all day. Jack foraged through his larder for something to eat, discovering a wheel of cheese and a small barrel half full of last fall's apples, now sweet and wrinkled. While he ate, he considered his next move. He decided to press forward with his investigations on Elana's behalf. This time, he would go straight to the source.

When he finished his breakfast, Jack turned

his attention to his closets. His rooms comprised half of the loft of a warehouse stocking sail canvas, barrels of pitch, great reels of rope, and dozens of other items useful to the Ravenaar shipyards and provisioners. It was an odd arrangement; Jack paid nothing for the space, and in return he was obligated to guard the warehouse from others of his profession. Since no self-respecting thief would try to carry off loot such as planks or ballast stones, he didn't have to work too hard to protect the place. Jack had furnished a fairly comfortable and well-appointed apartment in the building's upper story, and if the place was stiflingly hot in the summertime and intolerably drafty in winter, it was free.

The warehouse offered one other virtue Jack enjoyed—it provided ample storage for anything he stole and wanted to keep. He had almost a dozen closets stuffed full of various knickknacks and odds and ends he'd pilfered. Jack systematically searched through his closets for attire suitable for a visit to the Wizards' Guild, and found a heavy rune-embroidered robe of dark blue brocade over fine cotton. He pulled the robe on over a pair of baggy red breeches and pointed Calimshite slippers, adding a simple red fez to complete the outfit.

"I need a dangerous-looking staff," he muttered, critically examining his appearance in the mirror.

He settled for an iron rod about two feet in length, capped by a serpent's head of copper. He formed a simple spell and placed an invisible rune on the serpent rod, so that it would seem to be magically enchanted if examined by anyone who could detect such things. Then, with one more adjustment to his fez, he trotted down the rickety stairs out into the streets.

"I am a formidable wizard," he said aloud. "I have urgent business at the High House of the guild. Delay me at your peril!" No one was close enough to note his words. Adopting an expression of stern determination, he stomped off toward the Uptown district.

The High House of Magic was a large building of black stone, designed to resemble a castle in strength and majesty despite its surroundings. It was simply a well-made hall with false turrets and a decorative parapet, but the structure loomed over its neighboring buildings, a stodgy old gaffer knee-deep in disrespectful children. Without hesitation, Jack bounded up the short flight of steps leading to the front door, taking them two at a time. Then he hammered his iron rod against the door in the most imperious fashion he could imagine.

"Open up at once!" he cried. "The Dread Delgath demands admittance this very instant!"

The door opened slowly, with a monotonous creaking of wood. A wizened old porter stood there, squinting up at him (quite a feat, considering Jack's own modest stature). "Eh? What do you want here?"

"The Dread Delgath has come to grace your impoverished fellowship with a mage of the highest caliber and most impressive credentials," Jack said.

"And who would that be?" said the old man.

Jack glared at the doorman. "Why, me, of course! Whom else could I possibly be referring to?"

"Ah, I see," said the doorman. "Well, why don't you come in, and I'll summon Master Meritheus to discuss your potential for membership."

" 'Potential for membership', indeed! Why, the Dread Delgath should—"

"Right this way, sir," the old man said.

He turned and scurried inside so quickly that Jack had to dart after him in a most undignified manner in order to make sure he was inside rather than out when the door creaked closed again. Jack found himself standing in a dark-paneled foyer, dim and dusty, the air thick with dust and the faint, mysterious scents of exotic incense and alchemical experiments. The old man was nowhere in sight.

Jack waited a long moment, and then, just as he was about to strike off on his own, he was surprised by the sudden appearance of a tall, heavyset wizard in voluminous robes. The wizard was a young man with a round, sallow face and a drooping black mustache; he resembled nothing so much as an overfed house cat with a lazy inclination to toy with its prey.

"I am Meritheus. So, you're interested in Guild membership?" he said in a bored voice.

"The Dread Delgath is indeed interested," Jack said. "In fact, the Dread Delgath is so pleased by your magnificent guild house and your friendly porter that he shall refrain from charging you for the privilege of his company. Access to your library shall be sufficient for his compensation today."

Meritheus merely raised an eyebrow. "Our thanks. Now might I see some small demonstration of your powers? We would like to ascertain whether or not you are really a wizard before we consider your application."

"Under normal circumstances the Dread Delgath might incinerate you for your insolence, demonstrating his powers quite thoroughly!" boomed Jack. "However, the Dread Delgath is from time to time moved to small and compassionate acts, and thus he refrains from destroying you utterly. Attend, sir!" He reached out and seized the magic in the way he always had, shaping a spell of chaotic energy that swirled around him in a green spiral.

In the blink of an eye, Jack stood behind the wizard. He reached out and tapped the fellow on the shoulder; when the Guild wizard turned, he disappeared again, now standing back in his original spot. He tapped the wizard on the other shoulder, and then magicked himself to the top of a nearby bookshelf, where he perched like a brightly colored bird.

"Witness how the Dread Delgath masters time and space! I can be here—" he vanished, taking up a position on the other side of the hall— "or there!" — now standing on his head at the opposite end of the hall. He vanished again, appearing right before the young wizard. "Or anywhere, for that matter!"

The young wizard frowned. "I have seen spells such as that before, but I did not see how you cast it. Are you using some kind of magical device to accomplish your teleportations?"

"Faugh! The Dread Delgath needs no crutch to employ his magic!" Jack thundered. He dropped the iron rod to the floor and repeated his instantaneous vanishings again. "My magic is simply too advanced for one of your minuscule accomplishments to comprehend!"

Meritheus pulled a small notebook or ledger from the sleeve of his robe and readied a pen. "I'll take your word for that," he said dryly. He looked Jack up and down, and then started to write. "Name: Delgath—"

"The Dread Delgath!"

"The Dread Delgath, then. Specialty: None—"

"Master of time and space!"

"Very well, then. Specialty: Master of time and space." Meritheus narrowed his eyes and scratched angrily at his book. "Rank at entry . . . your spell of demonstration would seem to indicate full membership over neophyte or associate status, but I do not have the authority to vest you in a more advanced circle."

"The Dread Delgath shall, of course, demand immediate attention to that matter," Jack replied. "However, for the nonce, he recognizes that you are merely a powerless functionary incapable of making any bolder decision without the express consent of your superiors. Fill in your book as you see fit."

"Very good, then. Your application for membership will be considered in three days' time, when the Guild council meets. If you are accepted, you will be required to pay a small entrance fee—"

"Insignificant," Jack said with a wave of his hand.

"—of five thousand gold crowns," Meritheus finished. "After which, of course, your monthly dues will be twenty-five gold crowns. Unless, of course, you convince the council to accept your immediate promotion into the inner circles, which would be somewhat more expensive than that."

"Five thousand gold crowns?" Jack asked in a small voice.

"The Dread Delgath, master of time and space, surely does not balk at such a trivial sum?" Meritheus asked with an expressionless face.

"No, of course not!" Jack roared. He waved his arms in disgust and paced in a small circle. "But, for the sake of argument: if, perchance, for reasons unknown and unfathomable to mere mortals, the Dread Delgath elected not to advance such a pittance at this time, what other options might be open to him?"

"In that case, the Dread Delgath might be interested in our 'affiliate' membership. The cost is only fifty gold crowns."

"Describe at once the privileges and responsibilities of such an arrangement," Jack said.

"Affiliate members are entitled to attend any social events the Guild sponsors, such as our twice-a-tenday Fifthnight gatherings and our monthly Revels Arcane. You will receive a comprehensive briefing on the laws and obligations of practitioners of the magical arts within the city of Raven's Bluff, and you will receive limited access to the Guild library."

"Limited in what way?"

Meritheus consulted his book. "You may use the common areas of the library between the hours of sunrise and noon, on the third and eighth days of each tenday."

Jack thought quickly. Today was the twenty-third day of Ches, and the third day of the week. "Including, I take it, the remainder of this morning?"

"Were you to deposit the affiliate membership fee now, then yes, I suppose for the rest of the morning." Meritheus rolled his eyes.

"Then the Dread Delgath so agrees!" Jack cried. He immediately counted out ten five-crown pieces from the now-spent advance Elana had provided him with and pushed the gold coins into Meritheus's hand. "Take me to the library, at once!"

The mage simply pointed. "The second door on the left. And please, remember to be quiet."

Jack marched off at once to the indicated door. He hadn't planned to spend the rest of the money that quickly, but a membership with the Wizards' Guild might be useful. He'd never considered it before; he wasn't a real wizard, and it was very expensive. He could pass for a mage at need, perhaps commanded more arcane powers than many who claimed full membership. And, if it was a mere fifty crowns standing between him and the clue he needed to locate the Sarkonagael, then he stood to come out ahead.

He threw open the library door with complete confidence and stepped inside. It was a surprisingly small, cluttered space, a series of four or five small vaulted chambers illuminated by high, narrow windows spaced evenly along the wall. Heavy bookshelves stood an arm's length apart in a dozen serried rows, jutting out into the room like the piers along the Fire River. Several mages glanced up in annoyance at Jack's entry; he took no notice of their presence and strode over to the librarian's desk, where an angry-looking woman of indeterminate years worked furiously to catalog several stacks of books. She ignored him as long as possible, until Jack cleared his throat so forcefully he immediately started a coughing fit.

"Yes?" she snapped when he finished.

"The Dread Delgath requires your assistance," Jack intoned.

"Who's that?"

"I am the Dread Delgath!" Jack declared.

"Does the Dread Delgath refer to himself in the third person because of some disorder of the mind, or is it simply a puerile attempt to invest a measure of imaginary confidence in an otherwise inadequate personality?" the librarian asked. She waited a moment, watching Jack choke in rage, and then shrugged. "Never mind, I suppose it doesn't matter. What is the Dread Delgath looking for?"

"Records of old memberships," said Jack. "From about six to ten years ago."

"The last bookshelf on the right holds Guild records. You'll find membership rolls and the minutes of Guild council meetings on the second and third shelves. Try not to damage any of them, if you please."

"Damage them! The Dread Delgath—"

"—Would be much more welcome here as the Silent Delgath," the librarian said, cutting him off. She frowned and returned to her work, shaking her head.

Jack sniffed and abandoned the field. He went to the shelf the librarian had indicated and began to pull volumes at random, looking over the material to determine what was available. It was not very well organized at all; few people seemed to have any real interest in Guild business that was several years out of date, not when the other shelves held insights into the working of magic, the treasures and hoards of wizards long dead, and all manner of dark and dire secrets of power and wealth. "To work, then," he said with a smile.

Jack had expected to find some immediate clue regarding the fate of Gerard and the disposition of his tomes and grimoires, but he soon discovered that serious research was not a matter of pulling one lucky record from the shelf on the first try. He spent the better part of an hour rummaging through the records and made no progress at all until he struck upon the strategy of examining the records of Guild dues paid and unpaid. Leafing backward a year at a time, he found Gerard's missed Guild dues listed among the dozens of other wizards who'd failed to keep up with their monthly membership fees. Then it was simply a matter of checking through consecutive records to determine when Gerard's account had gone into arrears and when it was closed altogether.

In a few minutes he had his information: Gerard had made his last Guild payment in the month of Eleasias, Year of the Sword. For twelve months the Guild had recorded his failure to pay, closing out his membership in Eleint of the Year of the Staff. On a hunch, Jack examined the minutes of that month's Guild Council meeting . . . and there he found that the Council had ordered the wizard Durezil Nightcloak to attend to Gerard's tower and dispose of the missing wizard's affairs in order to recover the missing dues.

"How very generous of them," Jack said with a smile.

Suffused with the delightful taste of success, he replaced the old record and helped himself to the most recent, searching for a record of Durezil's listed address or Guild status. He flipped quickly through the pages, whistling merrily.

Until he found the entry reading: *Durezil Nightcloak, Initiate of the First Circle. Deceased as of the Fourth day of Alturiak, Year of the Unstrung Harp. Reported mauled to death by hungry trolls and subsequently devoured. Membership account closed by order of Meritheus, Assistant Secretary for Rolls of Membership, on the Ninth day of Mirtul, Year of the Unstrung Harp.*

"Dead? How inconsiderate of him!" Jack muttered. "How spiteful to live five full years from the day he dealt with Gerard's effects, only to die a year before I had need of his services! What kind of a man would do such a thing?"

None of the other wizards on hand deigned to answer, although Jack received a few black looks. He replaced the book on the shelf and stood there a moment, thinking hard about his next move. He might have to look into where Durezil had gone off to before getting killed, perhaps he'd kept the Sarkonagael when he handled Gerard's final arrangements. He tugged on his finger-thin edging of beard, studying the shelves in front of him with a blank look.

"Oh, no! Not you!"

Jack blinked and looked up. There, not a yard away, stood Zandria, her arms full of heavy scrolls. The beautiful mage scowled, fury descending over her features in a mere moment.

"This is the private library of the High House of Magic," she hissed. "How dare you creep in here to paw through these tomes! The unmitigated gall of it!"

"My dear lady Zandria," Jack said, raising one hand to forestall her tirade, "I have just this morning become a member of this esteemed Guild. I am a scholar and a practitioner of the Art, just as you are. We are peers and professionals; your outburst is unseemly."

"You are no peer of mine!" Zandria said angrily. "You are here with some larcenous scheme in mind, I am certain of it! When I get to the bottom of it, I promise you, you'll wish you had never crossed my path!"

Jack smiled and plucked the topmost scroll from Zandria's arms. "What have you got here? Maybe I can be of some assistance." He studied it with some interest.

"Get your hands off that!" Zandria snapped. She dropped her armful of books and scrolls on the nearest table and wheeled on Jack, snatching the scroll out of his hands. "Your juvenile stunts don't amuse me in the least. I will see to your removal at once!" She replaced the scroll on top of the pile and marched off to the librarian. She began to harangue the woman in an angry whisper, frequently pointing at Jack.

Jack watched in idle interest for a few moments. Zandria apparently managed to convince the librarian that his presence deserved some further investigation, and with a scowl in his direction, the woman rose from her desk and led Zandria out into the hall. He gloated privately, imagining Zandria's delicious frustration when she discovered that he had every right to be in the Guild library—and then his eyes fell on the stack of research Zandria had left on the table. "Ah, I might be able to help you after all." He laughed to himself.

With a confident air he sat down at the desk and efficiently rifled through the titles and texts the adventuring mage had left behind. "What have we here?" *Dwarf Runes and Marks. A Survey of Crypts and Sarcophagi. Ciphers and Codes. A Study of Tombs. Winemaking and Vintners. Eralme's Encyclopedia of Eastern Vintages.* A few dozen letters. A handful of mercantile books recording hundreds of transactions. "Quite a little mystery," Jack observed, "apparently involving a dead dwarf or wine maker—that Cedrizarun fellow she questioned Ontrodes about, I suspect."

Jack leaned back and set his slippered feet on the table, doffing his fez and staring into it absently as he considered the riddle. He knew Zandria's kind; the city of Raven's Bluff was full of them, bold and certain adventurers searching for monsters to slay, wrongs to be put right, and treasures to be found. A Red Wizard of Thay, utterly confident in her abilities, desperately interested in seemingly random topics linked only by the name of Cedrizarun, a deceased dwarven master distiller. Either Zandria was a liquor aficionado of epic proportions, or she was on the trail of some wonderful and richly rewarding adventure.

What Jack didn't know about the pursuit of wealth wasn't worth knowing. "She'll need my assistance, no doubt of it," he concluded. He returned his attention to Zandria's stack of books and uncapped one of the scroll tubes, emptying its contents onto the table. It was a piece of new parchment smeared with a carefully rendered charcoal rubbing, sandwiched between pieces of waxed paper. He rolled it out on the table and studied it.

The rubbing showed a detailed carving or relief from some unknown source. A smiling sun-face looked down on a vineyard, bordered by an elaborate scrollwork of curling leaves. In the center was stamped a dwarven mark that Jack didn't recognize. And, in a banner across the bottom, a string of impenetrable dwarven runes was carved. Fortunately, someone had taken the time to record a translation in a different hand beneath the dwarven writing:

> *"Other hands must take up my work*
> *Other eyes my works behold*
> *At the center of all the thirty-seventh*
> *Girdled by the leaves of autumn*
> *Mark carefully the summer staircase*
>   *and climb it clockwise thrice*
> *Order emerges from chaos; the answer made clear."*

"What an obtuse riddle," Jack muttered. He found a piece of blank parchment and set it over the top of the charcoal rubbing; then he worked an old spell he knew. Under the soft chaotic energies of Jack's sorcery, the blank parchment began to darken and smudge, taking on every detail of the rubbing exactly as it appeared in Zandria's parchment. Whistling under his breath, Jack folded the new copy and stuffed it into his robe. Then he picked up the scroll tube and started to replace the mage's rubbing.

"Put that down at once!"

Zandria stood in the doorway, Meritheus and the librarian at her side. She raised her hands to work some spell of great destructive potential, but the two Guild wizards restrained her in a panic.

"Please, my lady, the books!" the librarian cried.

"You must respect the sanctity of our fellowship!" Meritheus added. "Guild members do not engage in spell-slinging within these walls."

"Bugger the Guild!" Zandria shrieked. "He's been rooting through my books! If you don't want me to incinerate him in your precious library, you'd better get him out of here this very minute!"

Meritheus looked at Jack. "Master Delgath, it is now well past noon. If you please, affiliate members must confine their visits to the library to the morning hours."

"The Dread Delgath does not care for your petty rules and bylaws," Jack replied, "but in the interests of fostering good relations with his lesser fellows, he shall now absent himself from the premises." He paused and then added, "He also wishes for you to look into the rude behavior of one Zandria, who has offered the Dread Delgath nothing but contempt and suspicion despite his earnest efforts to assist her."

"The Dread Delgath would be well advised not to press his luck," Meritheus observed dryly.

He stepped aside and indicated the door with a jerk of his thumb. Jack gathered his robes about him with the greatest dignity he could muster, and then strode out of the room without even a glance at Zandria, who glared at him with undisguised loathing.

Jack tried not to notice how quickly the doorman hustled him out into the street, and he paid no attention to the rather authoritative *boom!* of the door slamming shut behind him. He patted his breast pocket and set off for home.

After a sparse lunch of black bread and sharp cheese at the Cracked Tankard, Jack headed back to his apartment to change his clothes. He threaded his way through the midafternoon hustle and bustle of the Anvil without even noticing, his mind working on the various riddles before him. Many of the streets were so choked with wagon traffic and long lines of porters carrying heavy burdens that other pedestrians were forced to detour blocks out of their way to get around the crowds.

While he walked, he considered his next step. Illyth Fleetwood expected his presence at the Game of Masks later in the evening, but he had most of the afternoon free. He could inquire after the belongings of the mage Durezil using some of the same sources he'd checked out when he was looking for Gerard, or he could buy a flagon of strong drink for Ontrodes and see if the old sage would let slip some information about what exactly Zandria was looking for and whether or not Jack might beat her to her prize. He grinned fiercely and leaped up on an empty hitching rail, then to the ramshackle overhang that ran from building to building along Morlgar Ride, balancing easily as he ran over the mud and the crowds of the street. It didn't matter, not a bit. The world was full of possibility, and any course he chose was guaranteed to produce extremely satisfactory results.

"I am amazing!" he cried aloud, and it didn't trouble him at all that no one in the crowd seemed to agree with him.

He reached his apartments and changed his clothes, dressing in his customary attire of gray and black. The Dread Delgath was not needed again this day, and Lord Jaer Kell Wildhame didn't have to come out for a few hours yet. In the meantime, Jack had business as Jack. He buckled his sword belt around his waist and hung his rapier and poignard at his side. Then he trotted down the stair and out into the street.

The fact that he was thinking about three or four different things probably contributed to his failure to note the cloaked figures watching his door. Without a word of warning, Jack was seized from behind and dragged off the street and into a nearby alley mouth. He was punched once in the stomach, hard; when he doubled over, somebody pulled his cape over his head and ran him into the nearest wall so hard that Jack saw nothing but stars for a good five or ten heartbeats.

One hand clamped across his middle and the other pressed to his skull, Jack looked up and got his first good look at his assailants. One was a big, brawny fellow, clean shaven and good looking, with black hair and clear gray eyes that showed not a hint of friendship. Despite the angry, purposeful look on his face, he seemed to exude authority. Jack had seen his type before—some kind of lawman or agent of the city's lords, charged with a list of duties and responsibilities as long as his arm and deadly serious about discharging each and every one. He was evidently the one that had manhandled Jack.

The other assailant was a woman with pronounced elf features and a shoulder-length sea of brilliant copper hair. She might have been a half-elf—her height and build were too statuesque for a full-blooded elf. Her dark eyes were not any warmer than her companion's.

"In a hurry, Jack?" she asked.

"Not at all," Jack rasped, trying not to show how much his stomach hurt. "If you could perhaps persuade your companion to pummel some other passerby, I should be delighted to spend the rest of the day in your company. But I am afraid you have me at a disadvantage, my lady. To whom am I speaking?" He started to push himself up, but the big man stepped forward and kicked his arm out from under him; he sat down again hard.

The woman smiled coolly. "We'll ask the questions," the woman said. "So, where are you going, Jack?" She wore a jerkin of metal-studded leather over green wool breeches and a shirt of fine mail. A slender long sword was sheathed at her side. "Be honest now."

"I thought I might take a stroll in the fish market. I miss the wonderful aroma when I'm away from the place for too long."

The big man shook his head and reached down to grab a handful of Jack's hair. He thumped Jack's head against the wall once, hard enough to start the stars in Jack's eyes again.

"Think of a better answer than that," he growled, "and don't waste our time."

"You wouldn't be on your way to meet Myrkyssa Jelan, would you?" the woman asked.

"Myrkyssa Jelan?" Jack blinked to clear his eyes and shook his head to make sure he was hearing correctly. "The *warlord* Myrkyssa Jelan? Enemy of the city, leader of Jelan's horde, ten feet tall and magic-proof Myrkyssa Jelan?" He tried to keep his face straight, but despite himself, a snicker crept into his voice, and then a snort, and finally a full gusty guffaw. "*Myrkyssa Jelan!* Oh, my lady, you are making a fool of me! Myrkyssa Jelan, indeed!"

Two years ago, the Warlord Jelan had ravaged all the Vast with a great horde of mercenaries, goblins, ogres, and giants, finally bringing all her forces to bear on Raven's Bluff. The army, led by Lord Charles Blacktree, had sallied forth to meet her in the field. Skirmishing and forays had followed for months, culminating in a week-long battle in which Jelan's onslaught finally failed on the sixth day of continuous fighting.

"No, I am afraid that I do not have the pleasure of Myrkyssa Jelan's acquaintance," Jack managed to gasp, "but I was hurrying to meet the sceptanar of Cimbar and the king of Cormyr, who even now plot a dastardly double-pronged attack on our fair city. Consider yourselves warned!" With that he lapsed into raucous laughter again.

Muttering under his breath, the big man stepped forward and seized Jack by the collar. "This is no joking matter. We have reason to believe that the Warlord's agents are at large in the city. She means to lay the city to waste. I mean to stop her. Don't laugh at me!"

"Honestly, I don't know what you're talking about," Jack said.

The dark-haired man hauled Jack to his feet and drew back one hand to strike Jack across the face, but the rogue twisted out of the warrior's grasp and backpedaled an arm's length. He set his hand on the poignard's hilt.

"Your attentions are unwelcome, sir," he said with a light laugh. "I thank you for the jest, but I must excuse myself." He paused and then added, "The Simbul expects me shortly, and I cannot keep such a lovely and important lady waiting, if you understand me."

The man halted. He deliberately pushed his cloak clear of his right shoulder, revealing a longer and heavier shirt of mail than the woman and a heavy broadsword at his belt.

"I think the question is, do *you* understand me?" the man said. "Don't trifle with us, street rat."

"You say you don't know anything about Myrkyssa Jelan. Interesting. I can produce a dozen witnesses who saw you meet with a woman named Elana at the Cracked Tankard a couple of nights ago," the woman said. "What did you talk about?"

"Even if that is correct, which I don't admit for a moment," Jack said, "there is no law against sharing an ale with an acquaintance in a tavern."

"Perhaps you should concern yourself with the question of who Elana is really working for, Jack Ravenwild. Spies need dupes, after all."

"I am nobody's dupe!"

"Don't be so sure of that." The man set his hand on his sword hilt. Jack followed the motion with his eyes, spotting a tattoo on the back of the fellow's sword hand—a hawk in flight, stooping with its talons extended. "Now, answer my friend's question."

Knights of the Hawk. Jack shook his head, still trying to clear the cobwebs. He'd managed to attract some very prestigious attention indeed. "I might. But first, tell me why the Knights of the Hawk are interested in Elana. And who you are, for that matter."

The man scowled. "You can call me Marcus. This is Ashwillow. Remember the names."

"Have no fear on that account," Jack said. He rubbed his head. "I won't forget you."

"We want to have some words with Elana," Ashwillow said. "We have reason to believe that she's involved in some undesirable activities, the kind of activities people get imprisoned for. Or possibly hanged." She stared hard at Jack by way of extending the threat.

"Have you seen her?" Marcus asked.

"Not since I spoke to her the other night," Jack answered.

"What exactly did you talk about?" Ashwillow asked.

"She had lecherous designs upon my person, but I informed her that my personal standards of conduct could not possibly accommodate her lustful wishes," Jack said. He dusted off his cape and rearranged his clothes. Then he deliberately pushed his way past the two city knights. "Our conversation included nothing that could possibly be of interest to two such brave and noble defenders of the city."

"We'll be keeping an eye on you," Marcus called after him as Jack walked out of the alley. "If you're withholding information, you'll be called to account for it later."

Jack bit down on his reply and left without another word. He'd be keeping an eye on them, too.

CHAPTER FOUR

The coach clattered to a halt on the wet cobblestones, rocking gently back and forth as its motion stopped. Liveried footmen hurried forward to open the door, dressed splendidly in white waistcoats and green caps. Jack ignored the offered hand and jumped down, thrusting his chin into the air and tugging at his finest coat to smooth the fit. He motioned the footman aside and turned to help Illyth descend. The noblewoman smiled and took his hand, climbing out of the coach with care.

"Oh, Jack," she breathed. "Isn't it *wonderful?*"

Jack glanced around. The coach stood in the driveway of a noble's palace, one of a dozen or more coaches and carriages lined up along the way. Paper-covered lanterns glowed softly over the manor grounds, and bright light streamed from every window. Music played elegantly in the distance, the strains floating through the air like an imagined kiss. The laughter of lords and ladies rose from all sides, a pleasant buzz that was inviting and intriguing. The evening was cool and damp, the air heavy and still after the rains of the last few days, but the lawn was green and dark, and the house lights gleamed on the wet stone walkway.

"It is fortunate that we have arrived upon the scene," Jack replied. "Your presence is the only delight this gathering lacks, my lady."

Illyth laughed aloud and blushed. "Oh, Jack! Flattery will get you nowhere." She pulled at his hand and tugged him forward. "Come on; let's go inside! I can't wait to get started."

The rogue indulged her with a patient smile and followed. Behind him, the coachman cleared his throat, but Jack never turned around, and he was pretty sure that Illyth hadn't noticed. He'd led the fellow to believe that a substantial gratuity might take the place of the coachman's standard rates, and since Jack was nearly destitute, he wasn't about to give away anything he didn't have to. The coachman wouldn't leave, but he might not be so quick to take Jack as his fare next time.

He trotted up the wide marble steps of the palace a step behind Illyth and swept into a grand foyer without deigning to notice the chamberlains who stood by the door. In the grand ballroom beyond, a hundred or more guests conversed and danced in a swirling mass of wealth and privilege, dressed in some of the most outrageous and exotic costumes Jack had ever seen. He studied the glittering assembly for a moment in wry amusement, feeling very much like a wolf among some very wealthy and carefree sheep. Then the crowd parted to permit the passage of a tight knot of unmasked lords and ladies, exiting even as Jack and Illyth stood in the doorway.

"It's the Lady Mayor!" Illyth gasped, so awestruck that Jack almost laughed.

"So I see," he replied, with a patronizing smile.

He quietly drew Illyth aside to make room for the lady's party, and bowed graciously as she approached. Lady Mayor Amber Lynn Thoden was a strikingly handsome woman, he noticed, surprisingly young and feminine for such a lofty position. She acknowledged the greetings of Game-players with a dazzling yet insincere smile and accepted their attention with unconscious confidence, a goddess receiving her just due. A burgundy gown showed her striking figure quite nicely while remaining in the bounds of good taste, and a silver circlet, the emblem of her office, encircled her dark tresses. Several high lords trailed in her wake, high city officials and dashing army commanders attending their lady.

"Lady Mayor," Jack murmured. "Your loveliness defies comparison this evening."

Lady Thoden raised an eyebrow and turned to study him more closely, her smile shining on Jack but somehow never reaching her eyes. A cool strength and confidence in her gaze struck Jack as disdainful, cold, almost calculating. At the same time she glowed like the sun among the crowd. She offered her hand, and Jack bowed low to kiss it with a sweeping gesture.

"Do I know you, sir?" she asked in a light voice.

"Lord Jaer Kell Wildhame of Chondath. My lady, a visitor in your fair city," Jack replied. He'd seen the Lady Mayor at a distance on two or three previous occasions, but he hadn't realized the beauty and strength she carried in person. Like Elana, but armed with weapons far sharper and more subtle than mere swords. "I shall on this instant declare Raven's Bluff my home until the day I die, for how could I ever leave the enchanted place that wrought a beauty such as yours?"

He started to say more, but the Lady Mayor withdrew her hand and nodded graciously. "I suppose I must abide here as well, for how could I deny you the opportunity to weave words such as those? I hope you enjoy your stay, Lord Wildhame. I bid you goodnight." Then she was gone, sweeping past Jack while the Lord Chancellor and Lord Swylythe briefly introduced themselves and followed behind. Jack scarcely noticed, his eyes still on the Lady Mayor as she left.

"'Your loveliness defies comparison?'" Illyth snorted and caught Jack's arm. "It might be nice if you could spare a compliment or two for me, Jack!"

"I have long since given up hope of discovering a compliment that could do you credit, fair Illyth," Jack replied. He caught her hand and kissed it as well. "If I were to call the sun a candle flame, I should shame both myself and the object of my praise. When I find the words to suit you, I shall never cease to give them voice!"

Illyth laughed and blushed. "That's better, I suppose. Come on—we must get our masks for the Game!" She led him into the robing room, where a handful of attendants in blue and silver awaited. "Lady Illyth Fleetwood and Lord Jaer Kell Wildhame," she told them.

"Lady Illyth," the chief attendant said with a bow. He was a large man, with broad shoulders and a bearlike beard tempered by the twinkle of humor in his eyes. "Lord Jaer. We're so very glad you could attend. I am the Master Crafter Randall Morran, and I will serve as the chief storyteller, moderator, judge, master of ceremonies, and facilitator of entertainment for this challenge of the Game of Masks." He turned his attention to a large wardrobe nearby and searched it thoughtfully before handing two simple masks to them. "Please, try them on. If they are uncomfortable, we shall adjust them."

Rolling his eyes, Jack doffed his splendid feathered cap and handed it to the footman. He pulled on the mask and turned to look at Illyth. A ghostly white crane with striking black plumage seemed to stand in her place, although he could vaguely glimpse the suggestion of a beautiful woman in an elegant gown through the illusion.

"Quite effective," he admitted. "How do I seem to you, Illyth?"

The crane laughed softly. "I find myself addressing a rather sly-looking fox in a gentleman's coat," she said. "It's curiously appropriate. And I?"

"A stately crane, very wise and beautiful," Jack said, "also appropriate. So, what now? How is the game to be played?"

"Listen now to the tale of the Seven Faceless Lords," intoned the Master Crafter. "A long time ago in a distant land, seven wise monarchs named Alcantar, Buriz, Carad, Dubhil, Erizum, Fatim, and Geciras ruled well and faithfully seven rich and prosperous kingdoms: Unen, Dues, Trile, Quarra, Pentar, Hexan, and Septun. In their wisdom, the seven monarchs placed the defense of their land in the hands of a great and powerful enchantment. The spell was bound to the monarchs' lives, so that as long as one did live, the land would be unassailable.

"Then, to ensure that no foe undid the enchantment by striking down the monarchs, each of the seven kings went secretly to dwell in the lands held by another monarch, living humbly among the people. When they must perforce appear in public, the monarchs hid their faces and names behind hoods: Red, Orange, Yellow, Green, Blue, Purple, and Black. Thus no one knew where each king dwelt or even what each king looked like, and the land was ruled well for many years.

"Alas, an enemy arose whom even the wise monarchs did not anticipate. One by one the descendants of the original Seven Lords turned to evil. Their peculiar arrangement made it impossible for the champions of the people to unseat the fallen lords, since even if one were exposed and defeated, any of the other six might loose the great enchantment upon the land to exact a terrible vengeance. And now, the only way in which the land may be freed of the rule of the Seven Faceless Lords is if each monarch's identity and the kingdom in which he dwells is learned by a true and faithful hero, so that all may be exposed and defeated in the very same stroke.

"So, my Lady Crane and my Lord Fox, you have begun the quest secretly to determine the identity of each of the Seven Faceless Lords. Over the next seven weeks, each lord will host a revel celebrating the seventh century of their houses' joint rule. Tonight you are guests at the Red Lord's Revel. May your search be fruitful, for all the land demands justice!"

Jack nodded. Seven lords, seven names, seven kingdoms. All one had to do was to hit upon the correct alignment out of the, just a moment, three hundred and forty-three possible combinations. Simple persistence should win the day.

"That doesn't seem too hard," he said aloud.

"Oh, and you should know," Randall Morran added, "that you are entitled to make only one guess. Should you guess wrong, the Faceless Lords will destroy you at once, thus removing your characters from the game."

"Is that all?" Illyth asked.

"No, my lady," said a second attendant. "Each pair of participants begins with a clue as to the identity of one of the Faceless Lords. By carefully conversing with the other guests and exchanging clues, you should eventually identify each lord's name and dwelling place."

"And our clue is?" Jack asked.

Master Crafter Randall Morran consulted a large leather-bound tome. Then he opened a small locked chest sitting on the credenza and rifled through its contents, producing a small ivory token stamped with gold filigree and printed with small lettering. "Here it is, my lord."

Jack took the token and glanced at it. *Dubhil is not the Orange Lord,* it read.

"If you are wise, you'll ask to see the another player's clue token when you exchange information," the second attendant said. "Some unsportsmanlike players might deliberately mislead you otherwise."

"Perish the thought," Jack muttered.

There was one strategy out the window. He passed the token to Illyth, thinking hard. It would be very difficult to get information out of another player without providing information of presumably equal value; that meant that any clever and thorough player would make progress at about the same speed as any other clever and thorough player. Of course, the tokens might be faked or stolen. Or, for that matter, that big leather book where the Game judges apparently kept a roster of players and clues might be borrowed for a time and then carefully replaced.

An unsportsmanlike player had a few options open to him, at least. Jack nodded to himself. It might not be so bad, after all.

"One more question," Illyth asked. "What happens if a participant guesses wrong and removes himself—and therefore his clue as well—from the Game?"

"Good question," Jack said.

Illyth was somewhat gullible and given to romantic nonsense, but there was nothing wrong with her reasoning. When she put her mind to it, there were few puzzles she couldn't figure out. If he could possibly accept the notion of losing fairly, he might have even considered tackling the riddle without deceit, relying on nothing more than her logical powers and his own guile.

"Oh, we've already thought of that," the Master Crafter said. "There are a handful of vital clues that we are watching out for. If a player with one of those clues faults out of the Game, we will reintroduce his clue by secretly reassigning it to a randomly determined player who is still in the Game. Never fear, my lady Crane; we'll make sure that a solution is possible for any who still choose to play." He guided them over to the elegant doors leading into the ballroom and bowed. "The Red Lord's Revel awaits, my lady!"

"Thank you," Illyth murmured. She took Jack's arm, and together they descended the small flight of steps leading down and into the grand room. Figures merry and fierce thronged the floor, bears and leopards, dragons and serpents, falcons and sparrows and gulls. Some danced, while others conversed gaily, and still more sampled the various hors d'oeuvres spread out along the shining side table. Striding through the center of the throng, the Red Lord moved with grace, confidence, and an air of subtle cruelty, a tall man (or woman?) in a scarlet robe and a seamless, eyeless hood of the same color.

"Lord Fox, Lady Crane," said a grinning satyr at Jack's elbow. "I see that you have just arrived. Perhaps you might consent to an exchange of information in order to begin the evening's riddle."

Illyth shrugged. "It seems as good a place as any to start." She started to hand her token over, but Jack deftly caught her hand.

"A moment," he said with a smile. He winked at her and turned to the satyr. "Your strategy, sir, is simple. You wait here near the place where newcomers enter, and offer them a fair trade—your clue for theirs. Thus you gain dozens of clues at the expense of one."

The satyr-masked man laughed. "I see you have no small instinct for gamesmanship. Well? How about it?"

"We would be parting with the entirety of our knowledge in exchange for a twentieth, perhaps a thirtieth, of yours," Illyth said, catching Jack's eye. "That doesn't seem quite so fair."

"I can hardly be held responsible for your late start," said the satyr. "Do you want my clue, or not?"

"We'll show you our token if you show yours, and tell us three other things you have learned," said Jack.

"My clue, plus one more," the satyr said.

"Make it two, and you'll have a deal," said Illyth.

The man grimaced—a difficult expression through the horned mask—and agreed with a nod. "Very well, then." They exchanged tokens; the satyr's read *The Black Lord is the brother of Geciras*. "Here are two clues more that I have learned: Alcantar does not dwell in Septun, and the Blue Lord does not dwell in Dues." He offered a shallow bow and moved on into the party.

"This is going to be very difficult to keep straight," Illyth said quietly to Jack. "I should have brought a journal and a pen."

"A sound idea. We'll do so next time, although I suspect that everyone else will have the same idea. In the meantime, I suggest this division of labor: You commit the confirmed clues to memory, while I'll memorize the unreliable ones."

"Confirmed and unreliable?"

"Clue tokens we have seen, and clue tokens we have heard about secondhand. I don't doubt that our satyr friend made up the two clues he told us, but on occasion, someone may deal with us in good faith. And if we have unreliable clues that don't contradict each other, there's a chance they might be the truth."

"Do you think that he was really lying to us?"

Jack simply laughed. "I would have, had I been him. Come on—let's see what clues we can learn and what deceits we can spread." Arm in arm, they moved on into the Game of Masks.

By the time midnight drew near, Jack had learned three important things.

First of all, he'd learned that many of the players were

not interested in rushing willy-nilly toward the collection of every clue at hand. In fact, there weren't more than a dozen or so serious competitors who were trying to hound out clues as quickly as possible. For the majority of the Game players, the entertainment of the evening lay not in solving the puzzle but in *playing the Game itself.* It boggled Jack. Many players made small talk or thought up stories to tell about other players or the Red Lord, weaving a complex plot around the rather trite story that the Game coordinators had invented to justify the riddle. Players refused to trade clues, offered to trade clues if Illyth and he would do something to forward their own little plots and efforts, or just casually dismissed Lord Fox and Lady Crane outright, telling them to come back later.

Secondly, Jack learned that it was possible to deftly pickpocket clue-tokens from passersby, especially on the crowded dance floor. He managed to pull off the feat three times during the course of the night. Of course, he couldn't figure out how to let Illyth know that these clues were reliable, but he figured that he'd solve that problem later.

Finally, Jack learned that it was extremely inadvisable to be caught at filching tokens. Near the end of the evening, Jack found himself standing near a man concealed beneath a panther mask as black as coal. The fellow was engaged in a conversation with a pretty serving girl next to the buffet sideboard. Jack sidled up behind him, filled a plate with food, and casually bumped the man as if by accident. The panther jumped and whirled on him, at which point Jack "accidentally" spilled his plate.

"Oh, please excuse me," Jack said. "How clumsy of me."

"No apology needed," the panther said, examining his clothes to see if any food had been spilled on him. He swayed a little, apparently a little in his cups. "No harm done—here, what's this?" Quicker than Jack would have believed, the drunken man reached out to seize his wrist with the abrupt celerity that strong wine sometimes imparts. Lord Panther twisted Jack's wrist, staring at his own clue token. "Huh? In a hurry to see my clue, eh?"

Jack winced. He shouldn't have pressed his luck—a good pickpocket worked with an accessory or two to help pass off loot quickly, just so this sort of thing didn't happen. "Ah, I'll agree that this looks bad," he said. "I assure you, sir, that this is completely accidental, a freakish coincidence. I would never deliberately stoop to such a crass tactic." He began to gain confidence in his bluster. "In fact, your accusation is unjust and undeserved. The Red Lord's vintages have fuddled your wits."

"How dare you deny your guilt when my token is in your hands!" Lord Panther growled. He seemed to be sobering quickly.

At that moment, Illyth disentangled herself from a nearby conversation and made her way over. "Hello, Jack. What's the trouble?"

"Ah, my Lady Crane. I sincerely hope that you adhere to higher standards than your companion here, or do you intend to seduce me in order to gain access to my token?"

Illyth stiffened. "I intend nothing of the sort. In fact, I don't much care for your words, sir."

"And I don't much care for finding this guttersnipe's hands in my pockets," Lord Panther said. "You should be more careful in choosing your associates, my lady."

"The lady has nothing to do with this," Jack said. "Listen, I am a reasonable man. Although I am under no compunction to do so, I'll show you my token by way of negotiating a mutually acceptable solution to our disagreement."

Lord Panther pried his token out of Jack's hand. Then he shoved the rogue hard with his free hand. Jack kept his feet but knocked over a side table in doing so. A chorus of breaking dishes drew the attention of everyone nearby.

"I have no wish to settle anything, you cutpurse," Panther said. "Acknowledge your guilt and apologize this instant, or leave this Game at once."

"Hold!" The crowd parted as the Red Lord appeared, tall and stately. "What quarrel disturbs my revel?"

"It seems you have invited a thief to your party, my lord," Panther said, nodding at Jack. "I caught this cretin pawing through my pockets."

"Lord Panther misunderstands," Jack replied. "It was a simple accident."

"I misunderstand nothing," Panther snapped. "Come on, you. You're leaving right now."

"Wait," the Red Lord said. "This is my revel, and I shall decide matters of justice. You claim that Lord Fox is a thief. Lord Fox denies the charge. There can be only one resolution."

"What's that?" Jack asked, more than a little concerned.

"Trial by combat," the Red Lord said. "We shall let truth and piety decide the quarrel. No unrighteous man can stand before the truth. Bring me a pair of dueling swords!"

Jack was fairly certain that that statement was not necessarily true, but he was *quite* certain that he didn't want to fight a duel this very instant. Was this part of the Game, a mock fight to assuage Lord Panther's damaged honor? Or did the Game players and organizers expect to see blood on the marble floor before the night was through?

"I would be delighted to oblige, Red Lord," he said carefully, "but I have recently endured a long and debilitating sickness—not contagious, no need to worry!—and I'm not really up for a sword fight at the moment."

"If you will not stand against your accuser, Lord Fox, we must rule that his claims are founded in truth and judge accordingly," the Red Lord said. "How can it be otherwise?"

"Perhaps I could designate a proxy?" Jack asked.

"In the kingdoms of the Faceless Lords, no such practice exists," the Red Lord intoned. "Why, you might choose a proxy based on nothing more than sheer physical skill for the purpose of gaining an unfair advantage!"

"That would never occur to me," Jack said, pure sincerity in his voice. "It was the farthest thought from my mind." He licked his lips and rubbed his hands nervously at his hips. "What of a battle of wits, then? Or a contest of balancing plates upon our heads? If Lord Panther is challenging me, don't I as the challenged have the privilege of choosing the weapons?"

"All true gentlemen know well how to argue with their blades," the Red Lord said, "and, if you have the strength of your convictions to shield you, no harm can possibly come to you. Now will you meet Lord Panther's challenge or not?"

Jack let the silence stretch so long that the gathering crowd began to grow restless. He might have ignored them despite the approbation in their eyes, but his gaze fell on Illyth. Even through the mask, he could see the mortification in her downcast face and slumping shoulders.

He couldn't disappoint her on the first night of the Game. "I accept the challenge," he declared in a ringing voice. "Lord Panther has allowed your fine drink to addle his wits, my lord. I would rather not fight a man in such a state and did earnestly make every effort to avoid this passage of arms. I only hope that I can avoid injuring him in some lasting way!"

"Not only do I call you a thief, but a braggart and a buffoon!" Panther said. "By Tyr's sainted ears, don't you ever shut up?"

A servant trotted up to the Red Lord, bearing a large wooden case. He opened it and bowed, presenting two fine, matched blades to the Faceless Lord. The cloaked figure studied the swords for a moment, then nodded in satisfaction.

"Clear a circle fifteen paces across, in the center of the floor!" he commanded. The crowd surged back in response to his voice. Conversation fell to an excited buzz as the players whispered and speculated.

Jack found himself standing on one side, a gleaming sword in his hand, watching Lord Panther stalk back and forth, working his muscles to loosen up. The other man seemed bigger, stronger, and not anywhere near as drunk as he should have been.

"Jack, please be careful," Illyth begged.

"I cannot abide his insults," Jack said calmly. "Justice must be attended to."

The Red Lord moved to the center of the circle and raised his hands. "Gentlemen, shall three touches serve honor tonight?"

"Fine," grunted Lord Panther.

"Of course," Jack replied.

"Excellent. Whoever leaves the circle, loses his weapon, or asks for quarter shall lose on the instant. When I lower my hand, you may commence." The Red Lord backed away, his arm high. Then he dropped it like an executioner's axe.

"Have at you!" Panther bellowed. He leaped forward, lashing out in a head-high cut that might have decapitated Jack outright if the smaller man hadn't ducked under the swing. Jack riposted with a sturdy thrust straight ahead, but Lord Panther twisted his lean hips and allowed Jack's point to glide past without making contact. Panther countered with a backhanded slash under Jack's blade, and now Jack had to leap as far as he could straight up into the air, drawing his feet up under his body and grunting with effort. "Ho! Stand still!"

"Careful!" Jack said. "You might hurt someone."

He dashed aside, and spent the next ten or twenty heartbeats darting round and round inside the circle, trying to stay ahead of Lord Panther's powerful swings. The man was no casual student of swordplay—he was well acquainted with what he was doing, and he didn't seem to care if a "touch" took off one of Jack's limbs by mistake. When Jack tried to stand his ground, the man launched a reckless flurry of slashes and thrusts that instantly threw the rogue into complete defense, ducking and parrying to keep Panther's blade at some safer distance. He decided he'd picked the wrong man to pickpocket.

"Stand and fight!" the lord roared.

Two quick passes of the blades, and then Lord Panther hammered through Jack's guard and slammed the blade into the thief's upper thigh, a blow that spun Jack to the ground and made the dueling sword flash a brilliant white light. The bystanders gasped and roared in delight.

"One touch for Lord Panther!" the Red Lord cried.

Stunned, Jack gingerly felt for his wound, expecting to see his blood pouring out of a gash half a hand deep, but he felt nothing, other than a deep, shocking sting. He rolled over and looked at his leg. There wasn't a mark on him. The swords, he realized. They're enchanted! They don't cut!

"Do you yield?" his opponent snarled.

"Hardly," Jack said. He pushed himself to his feet. His left leg would stiffen up later, but for now it held his weight well enough. He could take a sting or two. "A child's blow, feebly struck. I permitted it so that you would not lose your spirit."

"Excellent," the Panther said. "I shall endeavor to strike you harder then!"

"Continue!" the Red Lord commanded.

Lord Panther charged up fast, his blade flashing, but this time Jack dived forward and rolled up underneath his opponent's guard. He felt Panther's sword miss the crown of his head by inches, whickering past his ear, and then he stabbed the point of his own blade into Panther's groin. The blade flashed white and jolted in Jack's hand, imparting its painful message.

"Ha!" he cried.

The audience groaned in dismay. Lord Panther made a strangled sound and dropped to his hands and knees beside Jack.

"Basely struck," he gasped.

"One touch for Lord Fox," the Red Lord said. Some in the audience hissed in disapproval. "That was an ignoble blow, sir."

"My apologies, lord," Jack said, scrambling to his feet. He hopped away on his good leg, grinning devilishly. "I thought my opponent was shorter. Would you care to yield?"

Lord Panther climbed to his feet and stood a moment with his hands on his knees. "I'm not ready to yield yet," he said slowly. With great care, he straightened up and swung his blade slowly left to right, right to left, as if reminding himself of its weight.

"Gentlemen, continue," the Red Lord said.

This time, both combatants circled cautiously. Thrust and parry, thrust and parry, the blades clanged against each other with shrill rings. Jack held his own for a time, although he recognized that Panther was a better swordsman than he—and then Lord Panther launched a feint that caught Jack squarely on his weakened left leg, and as Jack's knee buckled, Panther reversed his attack and whipped the blade of his sword fast and hard against the back of the rogue's head.

White lights exploded in Jack's eyes. He tumbled to the marble floor like a puppet with its strings cut. His right ear was filled with a roaring sound that wouldn't go away, and the sword went skittering from his hand across the stone. He lay on his back, staring at the bright lights popping in front of his eyes for what seemed to be just a moment. Then he drifted down into deep, soft, darkness.

The next thing Jack knew, he found himself staring up at a lovely, pastoral scene of green fields and dancing nymphs, his skull aching as if it had been split in two. He was in a small, dark-paneled room, resting on a large, soft divan. The ceiling was painted elaborately and finished with a lovely gold filigree, framing the picture above him. There was no sign of the Red Lord or Lord Panther or any of the other guests.

"I seem to have misplaced the party," he announced to no one in particular.

"The Game's over for tonight," said Illyth from somewhere behind him. She sat down beside him and leaned over to study his eyes. "You've been unconscious for almost an hour. Do you think you can walk?"

"Aid me, dear Illyth, and I'll find out," Jack said. He accepted her arm and gingerly sat upright. His legs were rubbery but serviceable. Very carefully, he reached up to feel his head, and discovered a long knot the size of a hen's egg just above and behind his right ear. "Ooooh," he moaned.

"A hard blow. I'm surprised you woke up at all." Disapproval tightened Illyth's voice, and there was no gentleness in the viselike grip she maintained on his upper arm. "You could have gotten yourself killed, Jack. You're no swordsman!"

"It may seem that my talents lie elsewhere," Jack admitted. "My style is unorthodox, though, and it would be difficult for the untrained observer accurately to measure my skill. Lord Panther simply struck me a lucky blow."

"But you refused to back down, even when you could see that your opponent was better than you."

Jack's wits must have been addled from the knock on his head. Without thinking about it, he told the truth. "I couldn't disappoint you," he said. "I know you've had your heart set on the Game."

"Perhaps you should have considered that before you tried picking pockets," Illyth scolded him. "Honestly, Jack, I'm dumbfounded. You should know better than that!" She walked him toward the door, steadying him with one arm. Jack valiantly ignored the nausea and dizziness and allowed her to lead him through the abandoned banquet hall to the foyer and the driveway outside. Jack's coach was long gone, but it seemed that the master of the house had hired a couple of carriages for the convenience of his guests, and Illyth had a footman hail one. "I can't believe you resorted to stealing clues!" she hissed as they waited for the coach.

"It wasn't quite like that," Jack said. They clambered into the carriage and settled themselves. Then the coach clattered off into the night. They rode together in silence for a few minutes. Each jolt of the wheels sent fiery spikes through Jack's skull; he groaned softly with each rut or misplaced cobblestone. Between bumps he looked over at Illyth, but the noblewoman was glowering out the window at the city streets. Jack winced—he couldn't allow her to become so upset that she'd drop him altogether. If nothing else, he needed her for the Game. He decided to engage her scholarly leanings and change the subject at the same time. "I found something about Gerard today," he offered.

He guessed right; she couldn't resist an opening like that. "Really?" she asked, looking over at him.

"I visited the library of the Wizard's Guild and studied old membership rolls," he said. "You would have been proud of me, my dear, hours with my nose in a musty old book, trying to ferret out a clue!"

"Perhaps you might be salvageable after all," she said. "Go on."

"I discovered that the Guild assigned one Durezil to catalog and close up Gerard's rooms when Gerard did not return from his last adventure."

"Durezil? The fellow who was eaten by trolls?"

Jack nodded in appreciation. "Why, yes, in fact, the very wizard. I'm surprised that you would remember such a thing."

"Oh, the great majority of the adventurers I studied died in very mysterious circumstances. Durezil stands out because his companions not only returned to Raven's Bluff, but they actually recorded the circumstances of his end."

"What of the Sarkonagael or any mysterious books in Durezil's possession?"

Illyth frowned, thinking. "I seem to recall that Durezil's companions sold off most of his belongings and split the proceeds," she said. "I'd have to consult my notes to be certain, but I seem to recall that a wizard calling himself Iphegor the Black might have bought many of Durezil's old books."

Jack grinned. "I know where Iphegor the Black lives," he said. "My thanks, Illyth! I am in your debt."

"I thought you wanted to know about Gerard for some kind of play production, Jack. Is it this book that you're really interested in?"

"Oh, from what I've heard of Gerard, it was important to *him*," Jack said quickly, "and I'm thinking of increasing the role of Gerard in my play. Or maybe I'll cast the book as the villain and say that it uses its owners to do terrible things. Now what do we know about the Game riddle? Let us pass the rest of the ride by assembling our clues and analyzing them."

The coach rumbled on through the city streets.

The next day passed by Jack in a skull-splitting haze. He tried several times to climb out of his bed but failed on each attempt and finally resolved simply to spend the entire day in bed. He also found himself wishing Lord Panther significant and hopefully long-lasting dysfunctions from the one solid blow Jack had managed during their duel. By early evening he rallied enough to drag himself out for a hot skewer of grilled beef and onions at Nimber's Skewer Shop, little more than a windowed kitchen on a busy corner of the Skymbles. Eating something served to steady him greatly, and Jack thought about his next moves as he sat under a wooden overhang near the skewer-shop and watched people plod through the mud and the rain. Elana, Zandria, Illyth . . . he certainly did not lack things to do!

Jack spent the rest of the evening and most of the day after making inquiries in various quarters regarding Iphegor the Black. He also wandered past the mage's tower and studied it carefully, thinking about what he would have to do to break in. He considered briefly the notion of knocking on the door and simply asking Iphegor how much he wanted for the book—there might be a tidy profit to be made by acting as a broker in this instance. But three factors dissuaded him from that course of action: first, Elana seemed to be cautious with her purse and probably couldn't afford to buy the book outright; second, Iphegor's ill temper was legendary; and finally, Jack didn't want to put the wizard on his guard by asking openly about the book. If the wizard refused to sell it, of course he would take steps to make sure that the prospective buyer wouldn't resort to thievery.

By the end of the day, Jack had a good idea of what he would have to do to get his hands on the Sarkonagael.

He deliberately ignored his trepidation about the enterprise, assuming an attitude of supreme confidence. If he believed it possible, then it was surely possible, and nothing could prevent the success of any enterprise he cared to undertake. He headed toward the Cracked Tankard to celebrate his resolve and contemplate his coming reward.

Briesa was not there (he recalled that the fifth day of the week was her night off), so Jack simply stood at the bar and ordered a hunk of roast beef and a plate of boiled potatoes to go with his dark ale. He was just about to dig in when a cloaked and hooded figure moved up beside him and clamped a strong hand on his arm.

"Hello, Jack. Why don't we find a quiet table where we can talk?"

"Elana!" Jack exclaimed around a mouthful of potatoes. "What a pleasant surprise!"

He seized his plate and his mug and hurried after the swordswoman, who was already threading her way toward a quiet alcove in the back of the room. It wasn't Jack's usual spot, but it was perhaps even harder to spy on if not quite as close to the room's exits.

As he sat down, Elana drew the privacy curtain shut and lowered the cowl of her hood. Her strong beauty was undiminished—the dark eyes and raven hair, the soft lips, the lean grace. Jack decided that he'd have that book even if he had to fight his way through a horde of guardian demons to get his hands on it. Elana simply watched him for a moment and then smiled sardonically, as if she could guess at what he was thinking and was simply amused by it.

"Well, Jack Ravenwild, have you found me my book yet?"

"Possibly," he said. "I have a very good lead, dear Elana, although I confess I am exceedingly curious to discover why you want it."

"It's good to want things that you can't have," she replied. "It keeps your ambition sharp. I see no need to take you into my confidence, Jack, not any deeper than you already are."

"Be that as it may, I still don't know exactly what the Sarkonagael is—"

"But you know *where* it is?" she asked, interrupting him.

"I'll know for certain tomorrow," Jack said. "If all goes well, I'll have the book in hand by tomorrow evening."

"What do you mean, if all goes well?"

"The book is the property of a person who is likely to object to its removal from his collection."

"Who? Who has it?" Elana leaned forward, her eyes burning with intense interest.

"Why, I can't tell you that," Jack said with a laugh. "I told you on the occasion of our first meeting—I work for half in advance, half upon completion of the work. As of this very moment, you have paid me one hundred gold crowns out of a promised five hundred, plus a very generous bonus arrangement should I recover the book for you. But if I let you know exactly where the book is, why, you might forget the balance of our contract—and the attendant bonus—in your enthusiasm to claim your property, and then where would I be?"

"I don't go back on my word once I give it," Elana said in a hard voice.

"I never said that you would, dear Elana. I merely observe that some of my employers have had difficulty in recalling the exact terms of a bargain once I delivered what they wanted."

Elana studied him for a long moment. "You don't want me to beat you to the book. Very well, I can appreciate that, but I'm going to insist that you tell me something of its whereabouts, so that if something happens to you I won't have spent my money in vain."

"Understandable," Jack conceded. "In that case, I would ask for an additional one hundred and fifty crowns up front to make up the balance of my advance."

The swordswoman's eyes flashed in anger. "Are you attempting to change the terms of our agreement?"

"I never agreed to disclose all information as I discovered it," Jack replied. "You are requesting me to do so now, so I am merely attempting to set a fair value on it. After all, the last thing you said to me on the subject was that you'd pay me the balance when I bring you the book or when I present evidence that convinces you that it cannot be found in Raven's Bluff. I can't show you any evidence of that sort, so I'd better produce the book."

"You agreed, at least tacitly, to a reduced advance in exchange for the bonus on delivery," Elana pointed out.

"True," Jack agreed. He offered a fierce grin. "A partial or complete payment of the bonus would certainly count toward my advance, but I didn't want to bring it up unless you did."

"I see," Elana said. Her anger faded, replaced by some emotion that Jack had a harder time identifying—calculation, perhaps? Suddenly, she rose in her seat and leaned across the table, reaching behind his head with one hand and kissing him hard. His whole body jolted as if he'd been shocked.

Jack recoiled in surprise, but Elana refused to release him, and after a moment he returned her kiss with a building fervor. She teased his tongue with hers, her breath soft and hot on his face. He cupped her face with one hand and boldly extended the other to caress one perfect breast protected by the leather and steel that she wore, and then she pulled away, returning to her seat while Jack strained forward to maintain the moment's contact.

Elana smirked at him and then reached into a deep

pocket, pulling out a small purse that jingled when it landed on the table. "The balance of your advance, and a hint of your bonus if you succeed," she said sweetly. "Now, what's your lead?"

"Iphegor the Black," Jack said blankly. He slumped back into his seat, looking up at the ceiling to regain his composure. "A wizard named Iphegor the Black. I believe that he acquired the book from another wizard named Durezil, who may have acquired it from Gerard's belongings when they were sold off after his disappearance."

"Is it reliable?" she asked.

"It's guesswork, but it makes sense," he admitted. "I rarely have the advantage of incontrovertible evidence and confirmed sightings. My gift lies in my intuition for weaving suggestions and suppositions into facts."

"In other words, you're a good guesser," Elana said. She shook her head and started to stand. "Well, I will allow you to play your hunch, Jack. That's what I hired you for, after all. If you're right, bring the book to me three nights from now."

"Here?"

Elana snorted. "Do you have any idea of how many people watch this place? No, I'll leave word for you. Make sure you wrap up the book or cover it somehow."

"My lady," Jack said in a pained voice, "I am not unfamiliar with exchanges such as these."

"I suppose so," Elana said. "Good luck tomorrow. I'll be keeping an eye on your progress." With that, she slipped out of the privacy curtain and disappeared into the crowded tavern floor.

Absently, Jack counted the coins in the purse and picked at his dinner. To tell the truth, he would have told her anything for the kiss alone.

CHAPTER FIVE

You have some dishonest purpose in mind," said Tharzon, splashing through the knee-deep water of the sewer tunnel. "I can tell, Jack Ravenwild. In all the time I have known you, you have never approached me without some perfidious scheme at hand."

"Dishonest is a relative term," Jack replied. He struggled to keep up with his dwarven companion. The heavy spring rains now roared through the old mason-work sewers in a loud torrent, threatening to carry him away if he stepped too far to the center of the channel. "I have no doubt that the man I intend to rob came by his treasure in an underhanded fashion."

Tharzon, on the other hand, seemed to have no concern for the rushing waters. Like all of his kind, the dwarf was as solid as an old anvil, with the strength of a hale human constrained in a thick frame four feet in height. He was a professional acquaintance of Jack's, a master tunneler and lockpick who made his living by burrowing in on his prizes with careful deliberation. "So stealing from a thief is an honest act then?" The dwarf barked laughter, a sound like wet gravel sliding down a hill. "Two wrongs make a right!"

"Today I'll choose to believe so," Jack replied.

He frowned in distaste at his surroundings. He'd replaced the fine clothes and noble trappings of the previous few days with what he thought of as his working clothes—black leather over gray cotton, all veiled in a fine dark cloak of light wool. But his flesh crawled as he contemplated what might or might not be scurrying past him in the rainwater. Jack was more fastidious than he cared to let on, and he would never wear these clothes again without imagining a faint whiff of the sewers in the fabric, no matter how many times he cleaned them. "Are we almost there?"

"Almost," Tharzon replied. "So, what's this dwarf-work mystery you wanted to ask me about?"

"Have you ever heard of Cedrizarun?"

"The master distiller of ancient Sarbreen?"

"The very one. I take that as a yes."

"Of course!" Tharzon said. "I've spent a human lifetime exploring old Sarbreen and studying the lore of my fathers. Cedrizarun's name is still revered among my folk."

"Can you think of a reason why a Red Wizard—leader of an adventuring company—might become intensely interested in Cedrizarun's resting place? Specifically, a riddle or an inscription on or around the tomb?"

"Certainly. Your mage seeks the Guilder's Vault."

Jack looked up so quickly that he knocked his head on the tunnel roof. "The Guilder's Vault? Hold a moment, friend Tharzon, and tell me of the Guilder's Vault."

Tharzon looked back over his broad shoulder. His eyes smoldered beneath his heavy brow, and gold bands glinted in his ringleted beard. He paused in the next intersection, a high chamber where water streamed down from the glow of daylight above, and set his lantern on a ledge high on the wall.

"What do you know of old Sarbreen, Jack?" the dwarf asked, hunkering down on a dry ledge.

"A great dwarven city, built about seven hundred years

ago but destroyed soon after. Raven's Bluff sits on top of Sarbreen's ruins. Many of these sewers are old dwarf-work . . . as are cellars, vaults, and catacombs underneath much of the city."

Tharzon shrugged. "About as much as a human might be expected to know, I guess. Well, let me tell you a little more. These passageways were indeed built by master masons of the City of the Hammer, but carving stone and delving chambers is not all that there is to a city. Dozens of masters skilled in the other arts—armorers, weapon-smiths, jewelers and miners and woodcarvers and glass-blowers and all the others—ruled thousands of skillful craftsmen. That was the wonder and the strength of Sar-breen, my friend. Skill and industry, ceaseless labor in a great thriving city that shone for a brief moment as the richest of all dwarven holds.

"Everyone knows the work of the old stonecutters, but the master masons were only a part of Sarbreen's Ruling Ring. Other masters whose works do not survive today were held in high honor, too—swordsmiths whose blades are scattered from here to Waterdeep, merchants whose wealth now lies in dragon hoards or lost at the bottom of the sea, and others. They were sometimes known as Guilders, since they led guilds of craftsmen.

"Cedrizarun was the master distiller, the maker of dwarven spirits whose fire would consume any lesser mortal who dared imbibe them." Tharzon offered a sere smile. "My folk delight in work well done, but we also delight in strong drink, and it's said that none crafted a better spirit than Cedrizarun. He was an old and honored dwarf when Sarbreen was first built, and he wielded great influence as a Guilder.

"He died before the fall of the city and was entombed in the old manner, with his riches about him. Few of the other Guilders or the master masons received such honors. Sarbreen was sacked a short time later, and most of Cedrizarun's peers died in battle, their hoards carried off by the cursed orcs and vile drow who worked Sarbreen's doom. But Cedrizarun's tomb has not yet been found." Tharzon fixed his eyes on Jack. "What do you know of this mage?"

"She's found Cedrizarun's crypt. In fact, she's recorded some kind of inscription or riddle in or around the tomb." Jack thought for a moment, and then reached into a waterproof pouch at his hip and pulled out the parchment copy of the rubbing. "She's been trying to figure out what this means," he said, handing it to Tharzon. "I suspect that she knows that something of great value is hidden nearby. She is desperate to solve the riddle."

"And you think that I can solve it for you?" the dwarf asked. "Instead of asking me to solve the riddle so that she can loot the Guilder's Vault, I would prefer that you ask the mage where Cedrizarun's tomb lies. We can solve the riddle and respectfully remove the Guilder's wealth ourselves. My people laid it to rest; it is only fitting that I, as their heir and descendant, should bring it back into the sunlight again."

"I doubt that the mage of whom I speak would find such a plan agreeable," Jack said.

"Then she should not be advised of its details."

"Indeed. We can safely assume that my acquaintance will not willingly divulge the location of the crypt to me. That implies that I can only come by the knowledge we require by some means she would resist. I must trick it out of her, steal it from her, coerce her into telling me, or simply watch her closely and see if she leads me to the spot I seek."

"Throw a sack over her head and tie her up," the dwarf suggested. "You can hold her feet over hot coals until she's more cooperative."

"Subtlety is not your strong suit," Jack remarked. "Your plan is simple and direct, but I'd rather obtain the knowledge without giving her reason to suspect that I've learned her secret. Then she would have no cause to be angry with me, since she won't know what I've done."

"With my plan, you could just slit her throat and drop her in the harbor when you finished," Tharzon said. "She might be angry with you, but she couldn't do anything about it."

"I am not a murderer, friend Tharzon. There's no art in it."

"So you say. Well, don't rule it out as an alternative if more subtle tactics fail, eh? Pragmatism can be very practical." The dwarf stood and shook off his heavy cloak, looking at the rubbing from Cedrizarun's tomb. "Can I keep this?"

"If you like. I have other copies now."

"Fifty-fifty, if I break the riddle and you find the tomb's location?"

"I find that eminently agreeable," Jack said.

What he left unsaid was the obvious: If he cracked the riddle *and* found the tomb himself, Tharzon didn't need to be included as a partner. If the dwarf had any brains in his head—and Tharzon did—he must have noted that Jack didn't mention the identity of the mage who'd found Cedrizarun's tomb. Jack therefore guaranteed that Tharzon wouldn't have an opportunity to cut out Jack in just the same manner. One couldn't make a living at thievery, skullduggery, smuggling, and swindling without a certain willingness to discard obsolete arrangements at need or at least plan for the possibility that would-be partners might do so at *their* need.

"Good," Tharzon grunted. "Now to the other business of the day. This wall here stands between you and the wizard's cellars." He rapped on one decrepit masonry wall, off to one side of the sewer chamber. "My guess is a foot of hard stone, four or five feet of fill, and then another foot of stone in the cellar. This is old dwarf-work, built to last."

"We're here already?" Jack studied the obstacle. It would take a solid day of digging, and the noise would be considerable—especially breaking through the cellar walls on the other side. And who knew what sorts of magical traps or horrifying monsters might be locked up in a wizard's cellar?

"I have to admit that I'm surprised. Digging in the sewers isn't your normal method, so to speak."

"Iphegor's tower unfortunately offers no windows, and the rooftop is steeply pitched and sheathed in copper. Making use of the front door—the only entrance visible from the street—seemed to be somewhat rash." Jack offered the dwarf a predatory smile. "However, I should think that, were I a powerful and suspicious necromancer, I might want more than one exit from my tower. Let us search the area and see if we can't spot a secret door in this vicinity."

"I've already earned my forty crowns by leading you to this spot," Tharzon said. "If you want my assistance in breaking in, you'll have to cut me in on the take."

Jack rolled his eyes, but he reached into the folds of his cloak and retrieved a small purse. "Your fee, good Tharzon. I will point out that I'm offering to cut you in on the Guilder's Vault, which is a far more valuable prize than the musty old book I seek today. And I'll also point out that if you simply help me find Iphegor's bolt-hole but choose not to dare the perils of the tower's interior, you aren't really helping me break in—you're still guiding me to Iphegor's tower, which is what you agreed to do for these forty crowns."

The dwarf scowled. "A fine distinction, if one exists at all." But he started to examine the masonry wall closely, rapping his thick knuckles against the bricks and running his massive hands over every stone in reach. Jack joined him, working slowly along the passageway for a fair distance both up and down the tunnel. After a moment, Tharzon harrumphed. "A hollow space here, Jack, but I think that your wizard has used some magic to conceal the door, since I cannot find it."

Jack hurried over and worked the spell that rendered magical emanations and auras visible to him. As he expected, a five-foot-tall section of wall about two feet in width glowed with the unmistakable stigma of an enchantment. "Good work, Tharzon."

"Is it covered by some kind of illusion?"

"I'll see," said Jack. He frowned and worked the spell that undid other magics, muttering the words and making the gestures he'd learned to shape the spell. He concentrated on the door's ensorcelment and sharpened his will into a white-hot blade, seeking to sunder Iphegor's concealing spell, but Jack's spell of negation failed, unable to pierce Iphegor's handiwork. "That is not fortuitous," he murmured.

"You can't undo the spell?"

"No, Iphegor appears to be too strong for me, but I have other ways of opening recalcitrant doors, including some that don't try my strength directly against the wizard's."

Jack licked his lips and tried again. This time he simply worked a spell of opening that was designed to bypass Iphegor's defenses, not overwhelm them. Green chaos swirled and danced around his hand, soft wizardlight twisting into strange shapes and formless energy.

The wall shimmered and warped as the secret door swung open, spoiling the illusion. A dark passageway led inwards from the sewer. Jack grinned.

"Not so hard after all," he said. "I shall return in a few

minutes, friend Tharzon. Tharzon?" He turned to look for the dwarf.

Tharzon hurried down the sewer away from Jack. "This is where we part ways for now," he called over his shoulder. "If things go poorly inside, it would be advisable for me to be well away from here. I don't need to wait on the appearance of an angry archmage looking for accomplices!"

"Your confidence in my abilities bolsters my courage and steadies my hand," Jack grumbled. "What if I need your help?"

"I'm sure you'll do just fine," Tharzon said. "Farewell!"

Jack sighed and turned back the doorway. He worked spells of dark-seeing and invisibility, then another that would miscue any divinations cast upon him . . . say, by an angry wizard trying to locate an intruder and call down some horrible doom upon him.

With one hand on his sword hilt, he ducked his head and stepped into the darkness.

The secret passage wound halfway around the cellar, with two right-hand turns before it ended at a strong-looking door covered in dire runes. Working carefully, Jack studied them and disarmed the spells of locking and warning and killing, erasing crucial runes from each without setting off the spells in question. Negating them magically was out of the question; Iphegor was simply more powerful than he was, but even magical traps could be defeated with careful work. It took Jack almost half an hour to get through the secret passageway, but he finally opened the inner door.

He found himself in a small storeroom of alchemical supplies. Shelves full of perfect glassware custom-blown for particular sizes, shapes, or qualities lined the walls.

Jack ignored the glass (although it would certainly be quite valuable to the right buyer) and moved to the opposite door, cracking it open and peering outside.

He looked into a long, low vault lined with doors much like the one he was peeking out of. Wizard-lights burned in greenish globes suspended from sconces on the walls. Weirdly enough, a thick haze or fog hung in the air. It surged and welled to the impulse of air movements too subtle for Jack to sense. At one end of the vault a stone staircase with wide steps and ornate carvings led up into the tower proper. Still invisible, Jack slipped out into the main chamber and ventured glances into each of the rooms that opened out into the vault. Most were workrooms or storerooms, jammed with interesting oddities and arcane reagents. I'll check each in detail if I don't find a library upstairs, he told himself.

The last door on the right-hand side was ajar. A voice within mumbled and whispered, sibilant echoes rasping over the cold stone floor.

Jack glided silently to the doorway and gently pushed the door open another handspan, peering inside. A tall man in black robes chased with gold trim stood with his back to the door, intoning a spell from a great, musty spellbook. He held a small vial filled with dark liquid high in one hand, while tracing the words to speak with the index finger of the other. The trappings and accouterments of wizardry surrounded Iphegor, beakers and alembics and retorts bubbling and frothing, strange golden hoops drifting through the air. Malformed things slithered and hopped across the floor, incomplete familiars animated through some vile sorcery to serve at their master's beck and call.

Jack peered at the musty tome from which the wizard incanted. Could that be it? Or was it simply one of Iphegor's own workbooks or references? He decided that he'd leave the wizard to his work for now and search the rest of the tower while Iphegor was occupied. He'd find a way to search the workroom later if he had no luck elsewhere.

Moving softly through the mist, he crept up the stairs. The steps had the look of dwarf-work, just a couple of inches too shallow for Jack's comfort and elaborately carved with images of warriors and dragons. The staircase debouched onto a wide, airy hall marked at one end by a strong double door and a gleam of sunlight beside the jamb. "The main entrance," Jack observed.

He quartered the ground floor and found a small kitchen staffed by two strange, pale serving women toiling monotonously with Iphegor's pots and pans in utter silence. A small roast was sizzling over the fire, red and cool, just spitted. Good, Jack thought. That won't be done for two or three hours, so Iphegor isn't planning on dinner anytime soon. The rest of the floor held a dining hall, a sitting room with sparce furnishings, and a large pantry whose contents seemed unremarkable. Jack continued up the stairs to the next floor.

Here he found what seemed to pass for Iphegor's personal chambers. A large trophy room filled with all manner of dead things and a curio room dominated by a ticking orrery of bronze and iron made up one side of the second floor; the wizard's private rooms made up the other side. Jack searched both leisurely, pocketing a few items that caught his interest—a silver urn filled with incense, a funereal mask of gold inlaid with lapis lazuli, and a small statuette of a whitish metal carved disturbingly in the shape of a monstrous being with tentacles and wings. The wizard's personal chambers seemed comfortable enough if tastelessly furnished with gilt couches and decadent arrases.

The stairs climbed one final time to a conjuring chamber or astrolabe ringed by a series of deep alcoves. Each antechamber contained several bookshelves, and these were filled to overflowing by a vast collection of books, tomes, scrolls, and tablets, gathered together in an untidy clutter.

"Ah-ha," said Jack. "This is more like it. Now, where did he put it?"

"Here now," squeaked a high, rasping voice. "Who are you?"

Jack paused in midstep, looking around in near panic. No one else seemed to be present. "Never mind," he said, and advanced farther into the room.

"Does Iphegor know you're here?" Again the piping high voice.

"Of course," Jack replied, now seriously alarmed. He carefully scrutinized every corner of the room, searching for the other presence. "I am a mere disembodied voice conjured by his hand. I have no objective existence beyond his passing whim."

"Ha!" said the voice. "I think you are a thief hiding behind a spell of invisibility. Oh, won't you be sorry when Iphegor learns you are here!"

Jack swung his head from left to right, following the voice with his ear. It seemed to be coming from the high corner of a bookshelf . . . there! A small dark mouse perched between two heavy tomes, was studying him with beady eyes!

"You would be the wizard's familiar, then?" Jack said.

"I am," announced the mouse. "As such, I am very well acquainted with Iphegor's arcane repertoire, and I can assure you that disembodied voices are not to be found among the dozens of spells, enchantments, curses, and blights at his command, so therefore you are a thief!"

"It is, of course, widely known that a wizard's familiar can communicate mentally with its master," said Jack. "I cannot understand why you have deigned to address me instead of summoning Iphegor upon the instant to strike me dead with his terrible powers."

"Oh, I will in just a moment," the mouse said, "but first, I think I would like to see you plead for your life. If I am satisfied with your abject surrender, I may allow you to swear allegiance to me and then permit you to escape unharmed, so that you may serve me another day."

"I fail to see how that furthers your master's purposes." Jack silently glided forward, marking the exact position of the mouse.

"Iphegor represents a temporary arrangement at best," the mouse said, thrusting its whiskered chin into the air. "I have far greater designs than perpetual servitude to such as he. And so I am carefully building a network of daring, skillful, and suicidally loyal agents to aid me as I prepare my ultimate seizure of power. You may perform your obeisance now."

"Before I begin to grovel," Jack said, "I would like to ask a question. Could it be possible that Iphegor is at this moment so engaged in the spell he is crafting that your mental summons to him goes unanswered? In which case you would desperately gamble on the most arrogant bluff you can imagine in order to delay me until you can gain his attention?"

"That is two questions," the mouse declared, "and no, it is not remotely possible. Rule out any hope of escape, my lackey, and grovel before me in abject terror."

Jack reached into the bookshelf with the speed of a striking serpent and seized the mouse in his invisible hand. The mouse squeaked once in fright as Jack's spell faded, ruined by his sudden motion. The rogue held the whiskered rodent before his face and offered a wicked smile.

"I am not a particularly strong man," he said cheerfully, "but I am quite certain that I could crush every bone in your body by tightening my grasp. Do you agree?"

The mouse gulped. "I wish you wouldn't."

"If I recall correctly, a wizard's familiar not only shares a mental bond with its summoner, but it also shares a link of life energy or vitality. No familiar survives its master's death, I have heard, and a powerful wizard might be rendered virtually helpless by the sudden demise of his familiar, true?"

"Actually, no," the mouse squeaked. "It doesn't work like that at all."

"Oh. Well, then, I guess I have no further use for you. Good-bye, mouse." Jack began to tighten his grip.

"Wait!" the mouse cried. "Please! You were right! I was lying! Please don't kill me!"

Jack grinned. "Very well, I shall not, unless I am startled by the appearance of Iphegor himself, in which case I will kill you in an instant. I advise you to think twice before attempting to summon the wizard here through your mental link." He leered at the tiny creature until it scrunched its eyes closed in fright, and then laughed. "Now, I have business to attend. Perchance do you know where Iphegor keeps the Sarkonagael?"

"Please don't make me tell you that," the mouse whispered, a very small sound indeed.

"The longer we delay, the more likely it is that Iphegor and I meet, and I might be forced to squeeze you until your little bones snap and your little orifices trickle bright red blood and your little eyes pop out of your little head."

"Behind you. The second shelf!" the mouse wailed. "Please don't say things like that! I have a delicate constitution."

Jack searched the alcove the mouse indicated and found, on the second shelf, a large tome bound in black leather with massive silver clasps. With his free hand he fished it out of the bookshelf and examined the cover. It was an ominous-looking thing, with a silver skull embossed in the center and dire runes inscribed at each hasp. The title was stamped out in silver chasing: *The Sarkonagael, or Secrets of the Shadewrights*. He stuffed it into the pouch at his side and turned to go.

"You're going to let me go now?" the mouse asked hopefully.

"Soon," Jack said. "For now I deem it advisable to travel in your company."

He glanced around the summoning chamber one last time and then retreated down the winding staircase. Green wizard-lights threw strange, twisting shadows against the walls and gave everything a pale, unhealthy luminescence. The rogue quickly passed through the wizard's chambers and followed the staircase down to the ground floor.

No one was around. Jack trotted softly over to the tower's only door and paused a moment to whisper a spell that changed his shape, taking on another face and another appearance. He didn't want someone outside the tower to mark the departure of someone answering to his description. After a moment's thought, he molded his shape into a tall, strong swordsman in leather armor, with black hair, clear gray eyes, and the tattoo of a falcon showing on the back of his hand. Marcus would serve as well as any.

"Any traps or wardings on the door?" he asked the mouse.

"No, not from this side," the mouse answered dejectedly.

"Excellent. You and I shall take a short walk down the street, and when I am well clear of the tower, I will set you free—provided Iphegor does not interfere."

"I haven't told him a thing," the mouse said.

Jack let himself out and strode out into the street, blinking in the daylight. It was gray and overcast, but after the dim shadows of the wizard's tower, it seemed as bright as noon on a summer day. He set his clenched fist near the hilt of his sword, hoping that no one would notice the tiny gray head sticking out between his thumb and forefinger, and slipped into the crowd, walking away from the tower without a backward glance.

He was three blocks away when Iphegor finally caught up to him. There was a flash of light and a puff of sulfurous smoke directly in front of him. The wizard stood before him, livid with rage, nostrils flaring and eyes bright as burning coals.

"Hold right there," the wizard said in a hiss. "Your doom is upon you, defiler of my home!"

Jack thrust the mouse into his face and squeezed a little. "Careful, Iphegor. I have your familiar!"

The mouse squeaked. "Not . . . so . . . tight!"

Iphegor the Black, dread bane of mighty swordsmen, nightmare of rival sorcerers, doom of hulking monsters and plunderer of ancient lore, blanched in horror. He gaped openmouthed for a full five heartbeats before collecting his wits.

"Harm one hair of that mouse," he said in a deadly quiet voice, "and I shall order your bones to tear themselves free of your flesh and spend the rest of eternity marching endlessly across the face of the world. Now who are you?"

"They call me Marcus," Jack said with a shrug.

"Very well, then, Marcus. You will now put down my familiar, making no sudden moves. If you follow my directions explicitly, I may allow you to live. Any questions?"

Jack nodded sagely, absorbing the threat. He lowered his hand as if to set the mouse upon the ground.

"One question," he said. "Ever see a mouse fly?" Then he hurled the tiny creature as high into the air as he could throw it.

Iphegor looked up, agape in indignation. Jack chose that exact moment to punch the tall wizard in the knob of his throat as hard as he could and then turned to run.

Iphegor goggled in agony, choking for breath as he collapsed like a poleaxed ox. The wizard's eyes stared vacantly up at the airborne rodent, now at the very apogee of its arc. Jack dashed for the nearest corner, sprinting for his life. He didn't think he'd killed Iphegor, and that meant that sooner or later the necromancer would get around to being extraordinarily angry about the whole affair.

"Catch me, Master!" squeaked the mouse in terror as it fell, tiny limbs flailing vainly in the air.

The wizard gurgled and lurched awkwardly, throwing out one hand in a herculean effort. Incredibly, Iphegor managed to catch his tumbling familiar in the palm of his hand before collapsing on his back in the muddy street, spread-eagled. His face was a distinct shade of blue, but he finally managed to draw a great rattling gasp. Passersby glanced at each other, then carefully stepped around the prostrate mage and continued on their way.

"I . . . I think I'm all right," the mouse piped. "Oh, thank you, Master! Thank—" And that was all, for at that moment the wheel of a passing cart rolled right over mouse and wizard's hand both, crushing each beyond hope of repair. Bones crunched and blood ran; Iphegor, eyes bulging, let out one hideous strangled cry, sat bolt upright for a moment, and then fell back into the mud like a black banner pulled down in battle.

Jack checked his pouch to make sure the loot was still there and then trotted off down the street. He had to hurry if he was going to make it to the Fleetwood estate in time to escort Illyth to the Orange Lord's ball.

☉

Two hours later, Jack and Illyth stood on a terrace overlooking the sea, listening to the gentle strains of music drifting out from inside the white palace behind them. It was sunset. For a few minutes at the end of the day the red sun seemed to hang below the heavy overcast sky and above the slate sea, painting both sky and city with fiery scarlet and brilliant gold. The Game attendants must have marked the masks of the previous session, since Illyth was once again Lady Crane and Jack stood resplendently dressed as Lord Fox.

"We must have twenty clues here, not counting the hearsay, and I still don't feel as if I'm any closer to solving this puzzle," Illyth complained. She scratched notes into a small journal, thoughtfully studying the pieces she and Jack had accumulated so far. "If only some of the clues told you something in the affirmative, instead of the negative!"

"That would be far too easy," Jack pointed out, "and the organizers would quickly exhaust their store of clues. If you provide a clue that so-and-so is the Red Lord, why, you eliminate six of seven possibilities, but if you instead hint that so-and-so is *not* the Red Lord, you have only eliminated one of seven possibilities. It's annoyingly clever."

Illyth sniffed. "And what of this one? *The Black Lord is the brother of Geciras.* What are we supposed to make of that?"

Jack smiled. "First of all, it's another way of saying that Geciras is not the Black Lord. You should mark it as such. Secondly, it might be a clue-and-a-half, so to speak. When we find a clue that says *Geciras has but one brother, and he is king in Septun,* then we'd know that the Black Lord rules Septun."

"We need a lot of clues," the noblewoman muttered. Jack started to reply, but she poked him in the chest with her forefinger. "Oh, no. No more stealing tokens, Jack. I'll win fairly or not at all."

Jack grimaced. "Very well, although I think it likely that others may not feel constrained by your sense of fair play."

"Then I suppose we shall have to try harder."

Illyth finished writing and slipped the notebook into a small purse at her side. Jack had noticed many players similarly equipped tonight. Illyth might not want him to steal anymore tokens, but borrowing someone's journal might be very useful. Or, for that matter, filling a journal with *false* clues and then leaving it someplace where an unscrupulous player would rifle through it might also be useful. Illyth interrupted his scheming by grasping his hand and dragging him suddenly toward the ballroom inside.

"Come on, Jack! Let's have a dance. I want you right where I can see you."

They joined a sea of gracious, swirling figures gliding across the marble floor, arm in arm as they paced through the measured steps of a stately quadrille. Jack didn't know the steps, but he watched the noblemen around him and picked it up fast. He'd always had a knack for dances, even if his tastes ran more to reels and kicks. And it made Illyth happy; she laughed in delight at each turn and pirouette. Jack shrugged to himself. There were worse things that making Illyth happy, even if she had too much money to court honestly and too much sense to seduce dishonestly. But for a short time he could imagine that he belonged among a shining company like this with a beautiful noble lass like Illyth on his arm.

"So did you find what you were looking for?" she asked him suddenly as they promenaded across the floor.

"I beg your pardon?"

"About Iphegor, Durezil, and Gerard. The play you're working on."

"Oh! Of course." Jack thought of the Sarkonagael, currently hidden in a very secure spot with several spells of concealment on it. He wasn't supposed to meet Elana for two nights yet, but the book ought to be safe enough. "I am very close to finishing the script," he laughed, "and I expect a very handsome fee when I deliver it to the person who commissioned my work, a very handsome fee, indeed."

Illyth offered a wry smile. "And I thought you worked only for the love of the art. All right, Jack. The curiosity is driving me insane. What are you *really* up to? There's no play, is there?"

"If I told you that I am at this very instant furiously plotting the last scene, would you believe me?"

"Probably not," Illyth admitted.

"Then I had better not tell you that," Jack replied. The dance ended, to a spontaneous patter of applause from the dancers. Jack and Illyth clapped politely as the musicians bowed and set down their instruments. "The terrace again? It's warm in here."

"In a moment," Illyth said. "I must visit the powder room first."

"I'll be outside," Jack said.

He strolled back out to the terrace and looked out over the city. The palace was located in the Foreign District, a fine ambassador's house that was virtually a fortress within the city's walls. Orange flickers of light danced along the streets below as lamplighters made their rounds in the shadowed streets. He leaned on the balustrade, listening to the sounds of the city settling in for the evening—the distant clatter of dishes, a carriage passing along the cobbled streets nearby, a dog barking a short way off. Absently he paced the length of the terrace, down to a small private garden where smooth stone benches rested in a bower of green ivy.

Voices murmured ahead of him. "Indiscretion engenders opportunity," Jack said softly to himself. And Illyth had said that she wished for more clues, hadn't she? Eavesdropping was certainly less questionable than pickpocketing. Jack stealthily glided closer, straining his ears to listen.

"—that be enough?"

"Few will be armed. We can determine which of them are carrying weapons early in the evening, and perhaps drug their wine before we move. It shouldn't prove difficult to place our own men among the serving staff." Jack heard a man's voice, low and confident.

"What of the Watch? We'll need at least half an hour to be thorough, and we won't be able to afford any interruptions." A woman, her voice as sharp as a shard of glass.

"We'll create a distraction, a tavern brawl on the other side of town, or perhaps a riot. Yes, a riot. That would be an effective diversion."

"I hope you understand the risks I am taking," the woman said. "We will get only one chance. If we fail, all our heads will roll."

"Such is the price of failure, my lady. We must—"

"Jack! Where are you?" Illyth called from the terrace nearby. Jack quickly retreated toward her, holding up his hand to warn her, but she didn't notice. "Oh, there you are. Where have you been hiding?"

Someone moved behind him. Jack whirled; from the shelter of the high green hedges a man and a woman appeared, their features covered by the illusory masks of the Game. The man wore the orange and black stripes of a tiger, while the woman wore an elegant emerald shimmer that was reminiscent of a mantis. They regarded him coldly for a long moment, and then walked away, retreating back into the crowded ballroom as he watched them go. Illyth moved up beside him, and set her hand on his arm.

"What is it?" she asked.

"Those two," Jack said. "They were plotting something, my dear. I overheard them talking about how they would divert the Watch when they were ready to strike."

"Strike? Against whom? For what?"

Jack frowned. It was almost certainly none of his business, but what were they up to? He hated it when he discovered plots that were not his own. An assassination, perhaps? A coup? A simple robbery or theft?

He shook his head. "I do not know, Illyth, but they marked Lord Fox and Lady Crane as they left. We should be careful about protecting our identities from this point forward. They might not want us to find out what they were talking about."

"Ah!" said Illyth. "A new plot within the Game!"

"I do not think so," said Jack.

CHAPTER SIX

By the end of the Orange Lord's ball, Jack knew three things. He knew that Erizum was the Blue Lord. He knew that the Green Lord ruled Dues. And he knew that Lady Mantis and Lord Tiger meant him no good at all. In fact, they desperately wanted to find out who he was and what he knew.

Jack and Illyth had determined Erizum's identity through sheer good fortune. In the process of exchanging clues honestly with other players (the only method that Illyth condoned, unfortunately), they'd simply amassed five clues to the effect that neither Fatim, Alcantar, Dubhil, Geciras, nor Carad was the Blue Lord. That left Buriz and Erizum, and then they'd found a clue that read simply *Buriz is either the Red Lord or the Green Lord.* Clearly, some of the clues were simply better than others and offered the potential for a faster solution than simple elimination of possibilities. Jack decided that the Buriz clue must have been one of the key pieces that Randall Morran had mentioned when explaining the rules of the Game at the beginning of the Red Lord's revel, three nights ago.

The Green Lord's kingdom was somewhat more problematical. Jack knew it to be true, but he couldn't tell Illyth that he'd puzzled it out, because he'd done so by using his spell of copying to duplicate the stolen journals of two other players before slipping the books back into their owners' possession. Small thefts such as these had to be carefully timed, since early in the evening the owners were still sober and vigilant of their notebooks, while later in the evening the trickle of departing guests left the party much less crowded and made it harder to remove someone's book inconspicuously. And, of course, Jack couldn't rule out the possibility that someone might have made a false journal in the hope that it would be stolen and examined.

He solved that problem quite elegantly by convincing Illyth that they should split up for a while to obtain clues on their own. "After all," he pointed out, "We will double the rate at which we acquire information."

"But most of those clues will be unconfirmed," Illyth said. "We have only one token to show, so you would only be able to trade rumors."

"On the contrary, *you* will only be able to trade rumors. I will take our token for now."

"Just a moment! Why do you get the token?"

"Two reasons, my dear Lady Crane," Jack crooned. "First, you are by your very nature trusting and thus deserving of trust. You will fare better without the token than I would, because lying to a rogue such as Lord Fox is easy, but what true man could look into your eyes and utter a falsehood?"

"I can think of one," Illyth muttered.

"Second, if I have the token to trade, you will know that I am acquiring true and accurate information, and you will therefore have no cause to question my methods or the results I obtain at the end of the night."

The noblewoman studied him suspiciously. "To tell the truth, Jack, I find myself wondering what new scheme you can implement with the token under the guise of fair play. Besides, I don't think the rumors are all that important. Another player could say anything they liked to me about a token they claim to have seen, and how could I possibly know that they were telling the truth?"

"That is the beauty of it," Jack said. "When we compare our notes at the end of the night, we will simply *assume* that any unconfirmed clue we have acquired is actually false. Sifting through the rumors is the real challenge of this Game. If we wait until we have seen every clue token, we will certainly lose to someone who has seen fewer tokens but is willing to hazard all on a guess. Therefore, the key must lie in making the best use of our unconfirmed clues."

Illyth frowned, a gesture that her crane mask displayed as a subtle lowering of her bill and an introspective cast to her eye. "We should add to our notes a remark about which players have provided us with which clues," she said. "That way, we could more easily confirm rumors, or at least catch some of the more unscrupulous players in a lie. Very well, you can have the token, and I'll see what rumors I can trade. But try not to start any duels tonight!"

So Jack found an opportunity to circulate the most incredible and outrageous lies he could imagine, while presumably "acquiring" the information he'd gleaned from the rival journals. When he returned to Illyth at the end of the night, he conveyed a dozen of the clues he'd stolen from the journals as "confirmed" by examination of another player's token. Combining these with their own notes led to the discovery that the Green Lord ruled Dues, again by process of elimination. "See?" he told Illyth. "We are making substantial progress. I am absolutely confident that we will be able to solve the riddle in one more good session."

"I think two is more likely," Illyth replied. The hour

had grown late. The party was breaking up, with masked nobles and players gracefully making their exits in pairs and small groups. "The Yellow Lord's tournament is in three days' time. Will you be there?"

"I cannot contemplate the thought of failing you," Jack said. "Of course I will be there." They drifted toward the robing room to turn in their masks and depart, waiting patiently as the players before them unmasked in secret and exited the other side of the room. "Should we meet beforehand in order to examine our clues together and build a solution?"

"An excellent idea," Illyth said. "Why don't you come to Fleetwood Manor an hour or so early, and we'll compare notes."

Jack grinned. The carriage rides to Illyth's estate were costing him an arm and a leg, but he couldn't possibly let her know that. "Consider it done—" he started to say, when he looked past Illyth's shoulder and noticed Lady Mantis watching the two of them like a hawk preparing to swoop down on a pair of field mice. Her green gown and glittering mask concealed malice so intense that Jack could almost feel it where he stood.

"Jack? What is it?" Illyth watched him for a moment, then glanced over her shoulder. "It's that lady you met earlier tonight, isn't it?"

"Yes," he said, "although I wouldn't really say that I have the pleasure of her acquaintance." He looked around for her companion, Lord Tiger, and failed to spot him. Ahead of Jack and Illyth, two Game attendants opened the door to the robing room and ushered in another pair of players, closing the doors behind them. The line advanced a couple of steps. "I don't see her escort anywhere, do you?"

Illyth looked around the ballroom. "He wore a tiger mask, right? I don't see him."

Jack tugged at his chin, thinking. "Tell me, Illyth, if you were discussing the details of some nefarious plot and discovered that a masked player had overheard your conversation, what would you do?"

"Why, I would try to identify him, so that I could confront him later and determine whether or not he heard anything important."

"And how would you do that? Might you resort to unpleasant tactics to ascertain what had been discovered?"

Illyth glanced over at Lady Mantis. "Jack, this is just a game. This is the way the Game of Masks works—plots within plots within plots. The Riddle of the Seven Faceless Lords is simply the plot device against which the *real* Game is played, a game of acting out parts and making alliances, a game of innuendo and intrigue that the players themselves create as they go along. That's the Game of Masks."

"It's also a regular gathering of the wealthiest and most powerful people of Raven's Bluff," Jack said. "If I were not the very soul of honesty, I might be tempted to use the Game as a convenient tool in furthering my own ambitions and designs outside the Game events. Perhaps by embarrassing or eliminating rivals."

"You have a sinister and suspicious mind, Jack."

"Every day I regret that I am not more generous and trusting, dear Illyth, but I suppose I must make the best of the talents I have been given." The line advanced again; Jack and Illyth were next in line to remove their masks in secret and leave the party. "Humor me for a moment: where is Lord Tiger?"

"Who knows?" Illyth said crossly. "The washroom? Drunk under a table? Perhaps trysting with a secret lover in a private room of the house?"

"Good answers all," Jack said. "I think he's outside,

watching the entrance to the foyer. Lady Mantis will note when we go inside to remove our masks, and then she'll send someone—that servant there, by her side—to tell Lord Tiger that we are inside. When we leave, Tiger will identify us. Lady Mantis and Lord Tiger desperately want to know who Lord Fox and Lady Crane really are, and they mean to find out in just a few more moments."

"He might not know who we are, even if he does mark our appearance," Illyth said.

"True, but he could have us followed, or he might be able to ask anyone standing outside awaiting a carriage who we are. I might be difficult to identify, but I suspect you will be more easily recognized."

Illyth hugged her arms and suppressed a shiver. "Damn it, Jack. Now you have me thinking the same nasty and suspicious thoughts you're thinking. Should we delay removing our masks?"

"They'll simply wait as long as they need to. The longer they wait, the more players leave, and the easier it is to be certain of our identities."

"We can probably identify them in turn," Illyth pointed out.

"To what end?" Jack asked. "All we know is that they talked of something that sounded very suspicious. Who would move against a Game player based on that information?"

"So what should we do?"

"Fox them, of course. We'll leave without allowing ourselves to be observed." Jack drew Illyth out of the line for the robing room and led her across the ballroom to one of the antechambers. Lady Mantis watched them go and made a show of casually strolling in their direction, keeping an eye on them without following too closely. Jack and Illyth slipped behind a curtained alcove; then Jack turned to Illyth. "I know a little magic," he said. "I'll work a spell of invisibility on us both, and we'll walk right by Mantis and Tiger."

Illyth stared at him. "*You* are a mage?"

"Merely one of my many talents, dear Illyth. I consider myself a renaissance man, well versed in a variety of skills and exploits. Now, I will cast the spell first on you. Take hold of my sleeve so that we don't lose each other when I make myself invisible too." Jack mumbled the words of the spell and worked the gestures and passes necessary to form the emerald energy into the shape he needed; Illyth, looking both surprised and delighted, faded from view. He waited until he felt her hand on his arm and then worked the spell for himself.

"You're invisible," whispered Illyth's voice in his ear.

"As are you, my dear. Now, stay close to me and try to move quietly."

"What of our masks?"

"We'll take them with us tonight. I don't think the Game attendants will mind too much, provided we bring them back for the Yellow Lord's Tournament." Jack set his hand on hers, and they strolled back into the ballroom arm in arm. Lady Mantis and her servant stood there, waiting and watching. Few Game players were left, a handful of handfuls scattered about the floor, laughing and gossiping as the attendants began to clean the room.

Jack altered their course so that they passed right in front of Lady Mantis. Illyth gasped in alarm and tugged at his arm, but he grasped her hand firmly and carried her along.

"Good evening, Lady Mantis," he said aloud. "I do hope you have enjoyed the party. Perhaps we'll see you outside. Good night!"

Mantis nearly jumped out of her shoes. "Who's there?" she snapped. Jack simply laughed and walked off, leading Illyth away.

"Are you insane?" Illyth hissed in his ear. "Now they'll know how we eluded them!"

"True," Jack admitted, "but Mantis and Tiger will spend days wondering whether or not invisible spies are listening in on their conversations and reporting their every action to the proper authorities. It should cause them no little worry."

"It should make them all the more interested in discovering who we really are!" Illyth groaned. "You never settle for half measures, do you?"

"Bold statements and daring actions are the hallmarks of confidence and the stuff of greatness," Jack said. "Shall we go?"

Side by side, they walked out into the night.

The next day, Jack sat on the end of a pier, kicking his feet idly over the waters of the inner harbor, and thought about what to do next. Time was heavy on his hands. All around him, the wharves thronged with people, longshoremen and sailors and teamsters and touts and peddlers, all shouting and calling out to one another as the business of the port carried on in the normal manner.

Elana had not left word for him at the Cracked Tankard, at least not yet, so he could not retrieve the book from its hiding place and collect the balance of his fee. He had a night and a day to wait yet before he could deliver the Sarkonagael. The next Game event was not for two nights yet, so there was little opportunity to continue his attack on the Riddle of the Seven Faceless Lords or to determine who Lady Mantis and Lord Tiger were and what it was they were up to.

Morgath and Saerk hadn't put in an appearance for days; presumably they'd followed Anders out of town in an effort to steal or recover the ruby the Northman held.

Marcus and Ashwillow hadn't shown their faces since that one unfortunate encounter in the alleyway near Jack's apartments.

Iphegor the Black had not been observed to leave his tower since the untimely demise of his familiar after Jack's burglary.

Ontrodes had run him out first thing in the morning when Jack dropped by to find out if the sage had learned anything more about the Sarkonagael. Even though Jack had the book in his possession, he was still interested in finding out what exactly it was so that he could figure out why Elana wanted it. He'd tried to read it, of course, but the cursed thing was obscured in a mage script he couldn't unravel. Of course, he didn't show Ontrodes any of the book—that would invite trouble, especially considering how diligently the sage was working for Zandria. Jack had the feeling that Zandria and the Sarkonagael would not mix well.

He looked up at the blue sky, streaked with high, wispy clouds. "At least it finally stopped raining," he remarked to no one in particular. He polished a stolen apple on one sleeve and took a reflective bite. The Brothers Kuldath suspected him of stealing their rubies. The Knights of the Hawk suspected Elana of *something* and associated him with her. Doubtless Iphegor the Black very much wanted somebody's head on a plate, although it was unlikely that the wizard would believe for long that Marcus the knight-commander was the perpetrator of his familiar's cruel end.

Jack took another bite and picked up a small book and a quill, thoughtfully transcribing a few more Game clues into the journal. Every clue rang of authenticity; Jack had seen dozens of official clues now, so he knew exactly how they were worded. In fact, the journal he was creating featured half a dozen accurate hints, just to add a patina of truth to the utter fabrication of the rest of the clues. The trick of it was losing the notebook at the right moment of the next Game gathering, without making it look like it had been lost on purpose. With any luck, a few participants would knock themselves out of the Game with Jack's forgeries.

That task attended to, Jack blew on the page to dry the ink and then put the book away in his vest pocket. The Game was attended to; Elana was not prepared to meet with him yet; that left Zandria and *her* riddle as the next item of business on Jack's agenda.

"And that means I'll need to speak to Tharzon," he said.

He finished his apple and tossed the core into the water, then scrambled to his feet—only to find a hulking figure in a dark hooded cloak standing over him. "Not so fast, friend Jack. I'd like a word with you."

"Anders?" Jack peered under the hood. "Please announce your presence next time with a Northman's drinking song or perhaps a wild war-whoop. You frightened me out of my wits, creeping up on me like that."

"Someone's looking for you, then?"

"My talents are widely sought. Failing that, so is my head. Back from Tantras already?"

Anders nodded. "A pair of bandits waylaid me, but I *discouraged* them from pressing an attack. They did manage to lame my horse by stringing a rope across the road, so I had to walk the poor beast the rest of way there and back."

Jack glanced around the busy docks, but no one seemed to be paying any special attention to the two of them. "And the ruby? How did you fare?"

Anders offered a gap-toothed grin and held up a small purse. "Better than expected. I fenced it for eight hundred and fifty gold crowns."

"Excellent! So my share would be four hundred and twenty-five, then."

"I think your recollection is faulty, friend Jack. We agreed on a sixty-forty split in my favor. To spare you the trouble of figuring it, I have already done so; it's five hundred ten for me, and three hundred forty for you."

Jack scowled. "That's hardly fair."

"You agreed to it. I don't consider it fair that I was hounded across the city by a ten-foot-tall demon and now seem to be held responsible for a robbery we committed together while you walk about free and clear." Anders dropped the purse into Jack's hands. "Your share. Count it if you like."

"Later," Jack replied. "Regarding those bandits: by discourage, do you mean chased off or discouraged in a more permanent manner?"

"Chased off, I'm afraid, although one will walk with a limp for the rest of his days." Anders frowned and looked down at Jack. "You didn't hire someone to waylay me, did you, Jack?"

"No, of course not," the rogue said quickly, holding up his hands. "It's very bad business to betray one's partners, after all. Word gets out, and then no one wants to work with you." He could see that the Northman was not entirely convinced, which stung Jack to no small degree. Making a show of another glance around the wharves, he reached up to put his arm around Anders's shoulder and said in a low voice, "I consider you to be one of the most trustworthy cutthroats I know. And, since I know that you feel that I have been less than forthright in my dealings with you of late, I earnestly desire the opportunity to win back some of your trust. What would you say if I told you I had another prospect that could prove very, very promising?"

Anders regarded him suspiciously. "Such as?"

"The opportunity to loot one of the most famous of

Sarbreen's hidden vaults? A potential king's ransom, waiting just beneath our feet?"

"And the opposition?"

"Not opposition per se, but rather rivals seeking to beat us to the prize."

"Based upon my previous associations with you, I interpret those statements to mean that you've learned of a hitherto unnoticed pile of dwarven coppers for which we must strive against an army of angry demons conjured by ill-tempered Thayvians."

"Nothing quite so bad as that. And we have an advantage; the competition doesn't know that what we intend or what we know."

Chewing his mustache thoughtfully, the Northman watched the longshoremen and sailors thronging the wharves, hard at work. "What's the prize again?"

"The Guilder's Vault, a crypt in which the masters of ancient Sarbreen entombed Cedrizarun, the master distiller and a leader of the city." Anders appeared to waver so Jack decided to set the hook. "Come with me, and I'm sure Tharzon can answer your questions."

"The dwarf tunneler? Are you cutting him in, too?"

"The very same. And yes, I intend to take him on as an equal partner. Can you think of anyone more knowledgeable in the ways of Sarbreen's passages and vaults?"

The Northman shook his head. "No, Tharzon would probably know more than anyone. Very well, I admit that I'm interested."

"Follow me, then," Jack said and set off at once.

The two rogues hurried up Cove Street and took a left on Nightlamp, following the road to DeVillars Ride and turning right again. Two blocks brought them to Rhabie Promenade, and then they turned left again onto Manycoins Way and followed that road the length of the Temple District, through the Market District, and on into the neighborhood of Torchtown. Hidden in the back alley off of Vesper Way they found the Smoke Wyrm, a small taphouse in the solid stone cellars under a merchant's office. The place was favored by many of the dwarf craftsmen who lived and worked in Torchtown, and featured some of the best beer in the city.

In the middle of the day, the place was virtually empty; no self-respecting dwarf would consider drinking when there was work to be done. The only occupants were a couple of Sembians engaged in hard drinking despite the hour, and a sturdy dwarf barkeep—Tharzon.

"Jack Ravenwild," the dwarf rumbled. "I hold you responsible for a lack of sleep of late. That puzzle you gave me has me tied in knots. Anders Aricssen, good to see you again."

"I had hoped that you might have solved my riddle by now," Jack said. "Draw us two mugs of Old Smokey, friend Tharzon; we've much to discuss."

Tharzon eyed him balefully but complied, filling a pair of clay mugs from one of the numerous casks behind the bar. He set it on the worn wooden bar but didn't slide it toward Jack until the rogue rolled his eyes and set a silver talon on the table. Jack blew the foam off the draft and took a cautious sip; Old Smokey was good dwarf-work, and it would fuddle a man's wits in two mugs, if not one.

"Did you have any luck at all with it?" Jack asked.

"Some," Tharzon admitted. He nodded at Anders with a look at Jack, but Jack waved him on. With a shrug, the dwarf reached into his leather apron and pulled out a folded piece of paper, carefully unfurling it with his thick fingers. "I won't know whether I've solved it or not until I stand in the Guilder's Tomb. Here it is again:

> *"Other hands must take up my work*
> *Other eyes my works behold*

At the center of all the thirty-seventh
Girdled by the leaves of autumn
Mark carefully the summer staircase
*   and climb it clockwise thrice*
Order emerges from chaos; the answer made clear."

"A rather obtuse riddle," Anders remarked.

"Hmmph. Well, whoever translated this from Dwarven missed a couple of words. Instead of 'girdled,' it means 'encircled,' and instead of 'the leaves of autumn,' it could be read, 'these leaves of autumn.'" The dwarf shook his head. "And where it says 'mark,' you should probably think of it as 'measure.' Hasty work, poorly done."

"Interesting," Jack said. "I don't see that it changes the meaning much."

"No, but you never know what might be significant. Clearly this is a set of instructions for finding the entrance of the vault. Missing even one word might mean that you never find it."

"It seems to me, friend Tharzon, that understanding this puzzle depends on understanding three things: the thirty-seventh, these leaves of autumn, and the summer staircase. I suppose you could add climbing the staircase to that list." Jack took another sip and offered a foamy leer. "Fortunately, I have already divined the meaning of the thirty-seventh."

Tharzon leaned forward, his thick arms planted on the bar. He actually stood on a short runner behind the counter, raising him to Jack's height. "I hate guessing games, Jack. Just tell us."

"The thirty-seventh refers to a superior brandy, the Maidenfire Gold of the year 637 (Dale Reckoning) distilled by Cedrizarun. He was, of course, the master distiller of old Sarbreen. It is supposed to be the most noble spirit ever crafted east of the sea."

"That would be more than seven centuries old," Anders rumbled. "I am sure it was very fine in its day, but none can possibly survive any longer."

"Don't be so sure," Tharzon said. "A human lifetime burns brightly and gutters out in less than a hundred years, but my folk sometimes live to see their fourth century. We contemplate works requiring decades, even centuries, that humans would call impossible. I have seen dwarven spirits two or three centuries old; the Master Distiller might easily have crafted a spirit that might pass decades like a human-wrought brandy would pass years." His eyes grew dark and thoughtful as the dwarf contemplated the notion. "But where would you find such a thing? And how much would it cost? A single bottle might bring a thousand gold crowns—two thousand gold crowns—in the heart of a dwarven kingdom. I cannot imagine where else you would find it."

"I know someone who has a bottle," Jack said. "For the moment, let us assume that we can borrow it when we need it. Why would a seven hundred year old bottle of brandy be at the center of all? What can it mean to this riddle?"

"Where was the inscription found?" Tharzon asked.

"My acquaintance with the expensive taste in liquor took the whole design on this parchment as a rubbing from Cedrizarun's tomb. No, I don't know exactly where that lies yet; again, let's assume that we will be able to gain that knowledge when we need it."

"That is twice now you have assumed that a very difficult obstacle to your plan will be easily overcome," Anders pointed out. "I am not reassured."

"Friend Anders, the boldest plans and the loftiest designs demand a mind that is capable of spanning insuperable difficulties to apprehend the most fantastic rewards." Jack indulged himself in another draught of the

ale. "An impossibly rich prize is, by its nature, impossible to obtain, so therefore the prize that is *almost* impossibly rich is therefore *almost* impossibly difficult. And if something is *almost* impossible, well, that means that it is really possible but simply damned hard. Let us not turn away from a wondrous prize until we are certain that it is truly impossible to attain."

Tharzon laughed in a low voice. "No one doubts the excessive reach of your ambitions, Jack. It is the length of your grasp that is in question." The dwarf paused to draw himself a mug of Old Smokey. "This riddle is inscribed on Cedrizarun's tomb. The vault in which his funerary wealth is interred will be located somewhere near that spot, concealed by the most cunning secret entrance the master masons of old Sarbreen could devise. This riddle must tell you how to find and open the secret door."

"Are you certain that Cedrizarun did not intend a good jest at the expense of future tomb robbers?" Anders said. "How do you know that this has anything to do with a vault? For all we know, this is simply his favorite beer recipe, encoded for future brewmasters."

"I have spent almost fifty years learning all that I can about Sarbreen's old wealth and the disposal thereof," Tharzon said. "Trust me; the Guilder's Vault exists, despite the fact that it has never been found. Cedrizarun could not be certain that his descendants would retain the secret of his vault's entrance over the years, so he created the riddle as a clue in the event the knowledge was forgotten."

"Yes, but why leave any hints at all? Why leave an entrance to the vault, if it was simply designed to hold the wealth that Cedrizarun chose to take to the grave?" Anders wiped his mouth with the back of his hand. "Forgive me for saying so, Tharzon, but everyone knows that dwarves despise grave robbers. Why leave potential thieves any kind of a chance at all?"

Tharzon's eyes glittered—he'd made quite a handsome living by looting the crypts of his forefathers, even though he viewed it as restoring the glories of lost Sarbreen to their place in the light—but he held his temper. "Because Cedrizarun would want his sons, and their sons, and their sons after them to one day be buried at his side. His body doesn't lie under the stone or slab this inscription was found on; it lies inside the vault itself, with other places prepared for those who would one day join him there. That is why they would leave a door, Anders Aricssen."

"Back to the riddle," Jack said. "What of 'these leaves of autumn'? Does that make any sense?"

Tharzon shrugged. "No, not to me. I have been—"

"What about these?" Anders reached over and pulled the parchment toward him. "The dwarf-runes are all carved here, in the center of the stone, but there's a border around the inscription. Grape leaves, perhaps? Could the inscription refer to the border around the words?"

Tharzon frowned and pulled the parchment back, looking at it more carefully. "I think you are right. Look, in the leaves—see how strangely the vines and the veins are worked? There are runes hidden in the border!" He studied them furiously for several minutes, ignorant of the fact that the Sembians in the other corner demanded more ale. The dwarf didn't even object when Anders got up and threw out the two merchants, barring the door behind them. After a long time, the dwarf rubbed his eyes and looked up. "Damn it. They mean nothing. Pieces of letters and words, but nothing complete, all of it jumbled together."

"But it was deliberate?" Jack asked. "Not a coincidence of design?"

"The carver worked hard to put them in and conceal them," Tharzon admitted, "but they don't make sense! It's gibberish!"

Jack put his chin in his hand and thought hard, staring at the riddle. "What if," he said slowly, "these fractional runes align somehow when you encircle them around something? Say, a particular bottle of brandy?"

"Hard to imagine wrapping a stone marker around a bottle," Anders remarked.

"Yes, it is," Jack agreed. He picked up the rubbing parchment and looked at it. "But not so hard to imagine wrapping a piece of paper on which the design has copied around a bottle, is it?"

Tharzon stared at him. Then he seized an empty mug from behind the bar and set it on the counter. "Go on," he said. "Try it."

Jack took the parchment and wrapped it around the mug. He quickly discovered that the parchment simply covered itself up on multiple windings without revealing anything in the border marks. But if he angled the parchment, he created bands in which the border overlapped with the border of the layer underneath. And some of the marks *might* line up to make whole runes . . . if he knew just how big the bottle was supposed to be, and how sharply the border strip should incline on its circuit of the bottle.

"I think," he said, "that we need the bottle now."

Zandria's home was a strong lodge of stone and timber nestled in a quiet alley of Swordspoint. Once the building had been a woodcarver's shop, with a large workshop in the stone-walled lower floor and a set of small apartments for the craftsman's family in the wooden floors above. Finding Zandria had been harder than Jack had expected. Raven's Bluff was a city that teemed with adventurers, so asking after adventurers took some time. But persistence, silver, and a little luck brought him the address he sought.

And so on the next morning he found himself in front of the old woodcarver's house, now converted into a small fortress and stronghold for Zandria and the band of monster slayers, dungeon delvers, tyrant topplers, and peasant protectors who followed her.

"Illyth would give her eyeteeth to listen to the tales you'd tell," Jack said to the building. "Noble deeds, daring exploits, glorious battles, and grisly death. What more could a girl ask for?"

He laughed aloud and bounced up to the door, guarded by a whitewashed shield and scarlet falcon emblem hung over the lintel. It stood open to the old woodcarver's workshop; Jack knocked once on the doorframe and stepped inside. "Hello?" he called. "Is Zandria here?"

Two men worked inside, stoking a fire at the center of an improvised armorer's shop. Several chain mail shirts rested on thick wooden mannequins along the wall, four suits of full plate armor stood mounted on the opposite wall, and dozens of helms, greaves, vambraces, pauldrons, epaulets, and all the other pieces that went into a fine suit of field armor lay scattered about. Both fellows turned as Jack walked in—tall, powerfully built fellows dressed in smiths' aprons and marked here and there by various scars, tattoos, nicks, and scrapes. Freebooter swordsmen, Jack decided, now tending to their battered gear.

"Who wants to know?"

"I am a messenger in the service of Ontrodes the sage."

The two swordsmen exchanged glances. One shrugged

and wiped his hands on his apron. "Up the stairs. After you, of course."

Jack bowed and trotted up the stairs to the upper floor. He emerged in a large common room, dominated by a vast oak table with eight chairs. Trophies and banners decorated the walls—orc battle flags, old Sembian tapestries, Vaasan shields and swords. At one end of the table sat Zandria, surrounded by dozens of texts and manuscripts.

"Brunn, I told you I was not to be disturbed!" she snapped without looking up. Then she did look up, and her face grew livid as her eyes fell on Jack. "Incredible. Your nerve simply defies belief. Do you *want* me to burn you to a husk of smoldering ash? Do you have some unnatural desire to meet your death this very instant?"

"Against my better judgment, I have decided to give you the opportunity to contract my services as guide, advisor, and confidant," Jack said. He pulled up a chair at the opposite end of the table and poured himself a goblet of watered wine from a silver ewer service. "I will now entertain your solicitations for my assistance."

"Zandria, should I throw him out?" the swordsman—Brunn—asked. He moved into a menacing position directly behind Jack.

"No. Beat him within an inch of his life, and then throw him out."

Brunn's hand came down on Jack's shoulder, and the powerful fighter started to haul the rogue out of the chair. "Nothing personal," he grunted. Pinning Jack with his iron grip, he drew back his other hand to begin the pummeling.

"I've solved Cedrizarun's riddle," Jack said conversationally. He tried not to shrink from the impending blow. "And I know how to find the Guilder's Tomb."

Brunn furrowed his brow. He had a heavy jaw and a

flat, square face that might have looked dull-witted except for the keen alertness in his hard blue eyes. "Zandria, you've been trying to make heads or tails of Cedrizarun's riddle for weeks now. He says he can help. What's the harm of hearing him out?"

"You don't know him like I do," she snapped.

"So? Who is he, anyway?"

Zandria just crossed her arms. Brunn shrugged and turned to Jack. "Fine. So who are you, anyway?"

"I am Jack Ravenwild. I am an adventurer like yourself, although I am currently between companies. I have some learning, some skill at difficult places, and some magic." He carefully extricated himself from Brunn's grasp and fished out the copy of the tomb inscription from his belt. He held it up so that the swordsman could see it. "I'll tell you how to read this if you consent to my presence on your upcoming expedition and agree to cut me in for a fair share of the Guilder's loot."

"That's it," the mage growled. She stepped around the table and stalked up to Jack, murder in her eyes. "There is no arrangement, no employment, no consulting fees. We want nothing to do with you, do you understand me? Now get out of here before I flay the skin from your worthless carcass!"

Jack flinched from her vitriol. He stood in silence for a good minute, weighing her words. Then he nodded slowly. "Very well. I shall not trouble you with my presence again, my lady." He rolled up the parchment and stuck it through his belt. "If you'll excuse me, I have an appointment with the mage Skellar the Unjust, of the Company of the Dead Troll. Perhaps he'll be interested—"

"Stop right there," Zandria whispered in a deadly voice. "You will *not* show that parchment to anyone else."

"Then allow me to show it to you," Jack replied. "Bring me your bottle of Maidenfire Gold."

"That brandy is worth a thousand gold crowns," Zandria replied. "I am not going to let your larcenous hands get within ten feet of it."

"Then you might as well cut my throat right now!" Jack roared. " 'At the center of all the thirty-seventh!' Do you want to know what that means or not?"

The mage eyed him coldly. Thinking, then she spun on her heel and stormed out of the room, returning a moment later with the ancient bottle, almost black with age. She set it on the table in front of him without another word.

Jack took the parchment and spread it flat beside the bottle. "See this exquisite border work? Leaves, vines, a curiously undwarven design? Why do you suppose it is there?"

Behind him, the swordsman shrugged. "Cedrizarun was a distiller and vintner," he said. "Not all dwarves work in stone and steel."

Jack took the sheet of paper on which he'd copied the rubbing and turned back to the bottle. " 'At the center of all the thirty-seventh, encircled by these leaves of autumn.'" He looked carefully at the bottle; it was spun glass that had been shaped while warm, pressed and sculpted with a relief showing dimly a field or farmland. The same design was repeated four times around the bottle's circumference—the field under winter snow, spring plowing, summer with high waves of grain, and autumn reaping. The sun shone down over each scene. " 'Mark carefully the summer staircase."

Using the sun over the summer scene as his starting point, Jack wrapped the parchment clockwise around the bottle. The distance that the sun stood over the field he used as the rise of the winding.

The inscription fit exactly three times in circumference. And it inclined just enough that the bottom border overlapped itself, revealing a faint line of dwarf-runes concealed amid the leaf design. "Bring me some sealing wax," Jack said softly, holding the parchment in his hands. Zandria stirred and retrieved a block of red wax from her work desk, muttering a small cantrip to soften it. "Now adhere the sheet to itself at just this position. I will hold it steady." The mage did so, frowning in concentration as she worked around Jack's hands.

Gingerly, Jack released his grip and stepped back, leaving the bottle standing on the table in its parchment wrapping. He bent low to study the runes without touching or displacing them, Zandria's face just beside his.

"Another message," she breathed in wonder. *"Ten paces south. Speak 'kharaz-urzu.' Raise the sevenstone."*

Jack stood up straight and grinned in delight. "Shall we discuss terms?" he said.

CHAPTER SEVEN

They settled on two of eleven shares for Jack, which was better than he had expected. Zandria's adventuring company included five other full partners, each entitled to a full share. She claimed three shares as the leader of the band. The remaining share was set aside to split between several men-at-arms and specialists retained by the Company of the Red Falcon in order to shore up its numbers for the recovery of a major hoard from the depths of lost Sarbreen. Zandria was willing to assign Jack one share for solving the puzzle, but refused to consider more than that until he promised to share in the company's risks and labors by participating in the expedition.

Even then, Jack thought that the mage agreed too quickly. Upon leaving the company's headquarters, he went straightaway to Anders and Tharzon and began planning the operation by which Zandria's band would be relieved of the burden of managing their newfound wealth. And he also set the Northman to watching Zandria's band night and day, expecting that she would be tempted to use the knowledge he'd provided without actually observing every detail of their agreement. In Jack's experience, a quick assent in any negotiation of this sort meant that the other party had decided they could get what they wanted by more expedient means.

That attended to, he returned to his apartment to prepare for the day's more significant event—the exchange with Elana. He'd been thinking of her more and more frequently as this day approached, until he found himself almost shaking in nervous anticipation as sunset neared. He bathed and dressed with care, selecting clothes that marked him as a serious professional, a man confident in his own abilities, a man who got what he wanted by hard work and hard choices.

Elana was a trained swordswoman, a woman versed in discipline and confidence; she had no patience for fops or dandies, but a fellow thief, daring but not boastful, businesslike but not mercenary . . . who knew what might happen?

"After all," Jack told himself in the mirror as he shaved, "it would be a matter of common sense to make it as easy as possible for the lady to uphold her end of our arrangement."

Jack dressed in plain black with a padded doublet of glossy leather and well-brushed boots that matched handsomely. He disdained any flamboyance, covering his head with a simple cap and sheathing both rapier and poignard on his left hip in the Vilhonese style. Then he disarmed the numerous traps he'd set over the Sarkonagael's hiding place, wrapped the heavy tome in plain burlap, and stuffed the whole thing into a leather pouch secured to his shoulder.

He sallied forth an hour after sunset, turning up his face to the fine mist that hung in the air. More spring rain—a sign of turbulent weather to come. Yellow lanternlight gleamed on the wet cobblestones, and Burnt Gables was quiet save for the occasional carriage clip-clopping by in the damp night.

"How perfectly suited for clandestine meetings and secret doings," he said with a laugh. "An auspicious start to the evening's festivities!"

A ten-minute walk brought him to the Cracked Tankard. The place was unusually crowded, choked with crewmen from two Chessentan galleons that had tied up at the city's wharves earlier in the day. Jack threaded his way through the crowd, elbowing a space at the bar. No fewer than three barmaids plus the barkeep Kirben were manning the rail tonight; they rushed back and forth, serving draughts as quickly as they could draw them. Jack dropped a silver talon on the countertop as the tavern-keeper stomped past.

"Ho, Kirben! Perchance have you a message for me?"

"Ho, yourself," the barkeep snapped. Kirben swept the coin into a pocket of his apron and handed Jack a small envelope sealed in red wax. "Don't say I never did anything for you."

Jack broke the seal and scanned the note inside. *The Storm Gull, Aldiger's pier. Make sure you lose any tails. Don't leave this message here.* Skullduggery and dark doings, he thought. A dangerous prize and a lovely lady!

"I won't be back tonight," he told Kirben, stuffing the note into his pocket. Then he headed out into the night again, winding his way through the city toward the harbor neighborhood known as Silverscales.

He turned south on Blacktree Boulevard and followed it to the harbor, pausing at the intersection of Blacktree and Fishleap to look for any signs of pursuit. A man in a dark cloak about twenty yards behind Jack casually halted and began to inspect the goods displayed in a store window; Jack ducked out of sight into a dark alleyway and worked a minor illusion that altered his appearance, taking the form of a hulking half-ogre longshoreman with stooped shoulders and long, powerful arms that hung almost to his knees. Adapting a drunken sway to his walk, he stepped out of the alleyway and roughly shouldered the black-cloaked man aside.

"Outta my way," he rumbled ominously.

"I beg your pardon, sir," the man said. He turned and dashed down the alleyway, intent on reaching the other end to keep Jack in sight, not realizing, of course, that he'd just run right past his quarry.

Jack leered with a mouth full of peglike teeth and continued on his way. Magic was so useful and so easy, it was almost like cheating. He wondered why more people didn't take it up. Wizards and magicians claimed that it took years of tireless study and punishing apprenticeships to glean even the beginnings of the Art, but it had always come naturally to Jack. They studied pages full of exhaustive formulae, pored over ancient texts, scrabbled for hints and ciphers in the works of their predecessors. Jack just thought of things he'd like to be able to do, sharpened all his will and attention on *wanting* to be able to do them, and through trial and error found out how, through nonsense words and simple gestures and patterns or focuses he could concentrate on, just like a man playing at ninepins might stand on one foot and pull in an arm while trying to *will* the ball to strike the lead pin dead on.

"Faerûn's wizards have, no doubt, a long-standing agreement by which all initiated into the Art swear to make it look as difficult and obtuse as possible," he mused as he walked. "Therefore they ensure that anyone paying for their services believes that he is hiring a rare and talented professional indeed, the one man in a thousand who can make sense of magic. Why, if they let slip that *anyone* could do it, the whole lot of them would be ruined. Hah!"

He followed Fishleap through Bitterstone and around

the end of the city wall into Silverscales. Here a dozen ramshackle piers and wharves jutted out into the outer harbor, crowded with three or four times that number of galleys, caravels, carracks, and yawls. Stomping along the boardwalk Jack came to the last pier, the one opposite Aldiger's Cut, and scanned the ships moored there. At the end a small sloop rocked gently by the wharf. "The *Storm Gull*," he read from the lettering across the ship's stern. Jack threw one more glance over his shoulder and didn't spot anyone paying him undue attention, so he resumed his own appearance and trotted down the pier to the ship.

Two easterners in metal-studded jerkins lounged on the ship's deck, watching Jack without saying a word. They were strange-looking fellows, with bronzed faces and straight black hair, perhaps from the fantastic lands beyond even Thay or Rashemen. Jack boarded the ship and nodded politely.

"Take me to Elana," he said.

The first easterner straightened with a rattle of steel and pointed at a companionway leading down to the *Storm Gull*'s main cabin. "That way," he said through a thick accent. He returned to his watch, studying the wharves and streets intensely.

Jack clattered down the steep ladder and found himself in a short passageway lined by several doors. At the end of the passage, the door leading into the stern cabin—presumably, the master's quarters—stood slightly ajar. With a shrug, Jack pushed it open and went inside.

The decor showed a distinct preference for the remote East; paper lanterns hung from the beams overhead, a low desk or table surrounded by cushions sufficed for furnishings, and tall screens of carved and inlaid wood were secured to the walls. Elana knelt comfortably behind the desk, examining a small explosion of paper. Behind her, a tall mage in yellow robes and a high-collared vest or tabard of tooled red leather stood watching, his scalp shaven and his face marked by a long, drooping mustache. He, too, was an easterner. Elana looked up as Jack entered, carefully covered her work by sweeping it into a wooden valise, and gestured at the opposite place at the table.

"Jack Ravenwild. Please, sit down."

Jack dropped to the deck carelessly, sitting cross-legged before her. He glanced around the cabin, admiring the eastern furnishings. "You surprise me, dear Elana. I would not have suspected you of having a taste for the exotic. Shou Lung?"

She offered a slight smile. "No. Shou work tends to be more ornate, more complex than this. The screens, the lamps, and the table are from the island empire of Wa. I prefer its austerity and simplicity." She raised one hand to indicate the tall shaven-headed mage at her side. "This is Yu Wei, Adept of the Seventh Mystery, Sublime Dragon of the Black Pearl Order. He is my chief advisor in magical matters."

The tall adept inclined his head. Jack returned the gesture. "Yu Wei felt that I should not have left the retrieval of the Sarkonagael in your hands, once you'd told me that you knew where it was," Elana continued. "You persuaded me to allow you to try your hand at the task. How did you fare?"

Jack unlocked his satchel and removed the burlap-wrapped book. He set it on the table and removed the cloth cover, revealing the sinister black binding with its silver skulls.

"May I present the Sarkonagael, or the Secrets of the Shadewrights?"

Elana smiled coolly and reached out for the book. She opened it carefully, running her fingers over the ciphered text absently, and then handed it to Yu Wei.

"See if the spell is there," she told him. The tall mage bowed deeply and then left the cabin, stooping to pass through the low door. He did not speak a word. "Well done, Jack Ravenwild. My sources inform me that you bearded Iphegor in his lair and then defeated him in a confrontation in the street shortly thereafter."

"Your sources? It seems you are well-informed, my lady."

"I'm surprised that you chose to confront Iphegor. I would have thought that escaping anonymously was more important to you."

Jack shrugged. "I did make use of a disguise, so I doubt that Iphegor will easily discover my identity. In any event, he shouldn't give me much trouble for a long time. Unfortunately, his familiar was killed when he confronted me, and you know how much that discomfits a wizard."

Elana smiled. "Indeed. I hadn't thought you so ruthless."

"Not ruthless, dear Elana. Merely—businesslike. I do what must be done." Jack leaned forward and offered a charming smile. "Are you satisfied with the services I have rendered?"

She didn't reply immediately. Instead, she rose to her feet with one smooth motion and glided over to a small wooden chest by one wall. She opened it and removed a pouch that clinked enticingly. "Your payment, plus a substantial bonus."

Jack ignored the money and stood also, stepping closer to Elana. He pulled her into his arms and drank one long, perfect kiss from her lips—but her hand came up between them and gently but firmly pushed him away.

"No, not that," she said.

"I thought that we had an understanding—"

"Did we, Jack?" Elana turned away and paced over to the shuttered windows looking out over the stern. "I never specifically stated that I would grant you my favors upon completion of your mission, did I?"

The rogue gaped. "You led me to believe that was the case."

"What you believe, dear Jack, is your own business." Elana looked over her shoulder at him and brushed one dark lock from her face. "There is a substantial bonus included in the purse. I honored my word."

"Oh, just a moment!" Jack swept around the table to confront her. "You all but said that you would reward me with your most intimate embrace in lieu of any sum of money, and frankly, dear Elana, I considered it worth-while!" He waved his hand at the cabin, the ship around them. "If this is your sloop, and these your belongings, I don't doubt that you could easily afford the sum you offered to retain my services. Why then would you hint at more if you had no intention of living up to it and no need of deceit? Do you take pleasure in toying with men?"

"Since you have been in my employ, Jack, you have spent a great deal of time playing at the Game of Masks—using the advance I gave you—with Lady Illyth Fleetwood. You have skulked from place to place engaged in an effort to solve a riddle bedeviling the Red Wizard Zandria of the Company of the Red Falcon. Now answer honestly, Jack. Would you have applied yourself to the modest task I set before you if I hadn't allowed you to find some additional motivation for yourself? Or would you have wandered off into some other scheme or plot?" Elana's face grew as hard as a blade. "I remind you again that I showed you as much good faith as you showed me. If you don't like games such as that, Jack, perhaps you shouldn't play them."

Jack stared at her. "How do you know these things? Illyth, Zandria, the riddle? Have you been spying on me?"

"I have my sources," Elana said. "I warned you, Jack, the first night we met. When you accept my money, I consider you to be in my employ. That places certain responsibilities upon my shoulders and certain obligations on yours. I am utterly loyal with those who follow me and deal with them with no mental reservations. I require the same in return."

Jack took two steps back and sat in the window seat spanning the aft bulkhead of the room. "Who *are* you?" he said quietly.

Elana watched him, a cat playing with a wounded bird. "Are you certain you want to know, Jack? If I tell you, you no longer have the option of walking away. All I can tell you is that you will be well rewarded, you will be engaged in dangerous and frequently undesirable work, and that you will be one of a very small number of people who will tear down Raven's Bluff and rebuild it as something entirely different. People will get hurt, people will die, and you may not live to see if I am ultimately successful or not. This is your last chance to say no."

Jack looked down at his hands and rubbed them together. He could see what Elana was doing, of course. She was setting the hook. How could he possibly say no to all that? He'd grown up a guttersnipe, an orphan, entitled to nothing more than he could pilfer with his own hands. Elana offered him a chance to be a power, a lord over men, a shaper of events and dreamer of great dreams.

And, of course, she offered him the chance to *know*, the opportunity to find out what she was hiding under all the secrecy, and maybe—just maybe—a chance to win her favors after all. If he left now, he wouldn't see her again. He was certain of it, but if he stayed, if he showed her what he could really do, who knew?

He looked up and said, "I understand. I will not abandon

my existing enterprises altogether—after all, I have given my word to others, and I am inclined to keep it in a couple of instances, but I accept your conditions. Now, Elana, who are you?"

The swordswoman bared her teeth in a smile that would have intimidated a tiger. "I am more widely known as Myrkyssa Jelan," she said, "but for you, dear Jack, Elana will do. Sit down again, and I will explain to you how things must be."

"Myrkyssa Jelan," Jack repeated dully. "The Warlord, Terror of the Vast, shaker of mountains and destroyer of cities." He took two steps back. "On second thought, I believe I prefer to think of you as Elana. If you don't mind, I shall bid you a good night."

Jelan narrowed her eyes. "It's not as easy as that now, Jack." One hand slid down to rest on the hilt of the slender sword at her side.

The rogue tilted his head thoughtfully. "I beg to differ, dear lady," he said. He worked a spell of shadow-jumping that whisked him from Jelan's cabin in the blink of an eye, teleporting him to the lonely wharves a few hundred feet distant. It was perhaps the most difficult spell he knew how to work, but useful beyond compare when he needed to absent himself from tricky situations. He staggered then straightened again; the shadow-jump was strenuous.

Jack looked around, blinking to adjust his vision and regain his bearings. There was Jelan's ship, rocking softly by the pierside. No hue or cry sounded from its decks, but Jack hadn't expected any. Instead, he turned and hurried quickly back into the shadows of the alleyways and rambling streets.

At first Jack thought to bolt for his apartments and drop out of sight for a couple of days, in case Elana—Myrkyssa Jelan, he corrected himself—objected violently to his flight. But between the outcome of the mission he'd undertaken for her and the ugly turn in the Game of Masks, he discovered the need of a few stout ales. He briefly considered whether or not it was wise to choose the Tankard for his relaxation this evening, but he could detect a very tangible and nigh-irresistible pull gently tugging his feet into the familiar direction. He had a heavy purse full of coin, and the Cracked Tankard was just the place to make it a little lighter.

"Besides," he told himself, "Elana must realize that I am well aware of the fact that she has found me twice in the Cracked Tankard and cannot possibly regard it as a safe place to avoid her attention. Reasoning thus, she will not even trouble herself with looking for me here, so this is the perfect choice for my evening's entertainment. I'll exercise due caution, and no trouble will come of it."

He reached the corner of Red Wyrm and DeVillars, pausing to check for any followers. A coach trundled past in the warm night, wheels gleaming in the lamplight. Jack straightened his doublet and adjusted the fit of his cap. Then he strode boldly inside, instantly comforted in a small but familiar way by the press of bodies, the haze of smoke, the laughter and music and babble of a score of conversations all shouted over each other. With a small sigh of relief, Jack found his favored table and drew up a seat. Briesa worked the common room of the Tankard this evening; Jack offered her a wink and a leer that brought her over ahead of three other tables demanding service.

"Why, Jack! I've hardly seen you of late," the pretty barmaid laughed. "I was beginning to fear that you'd forgotten me!"

"How could I forget you, when my every waking

moment is filled with longing, and my nights are immortalized by the passion we share in my dreams?" Jack replied. He pulled her onto his lap and held her there for a moment. "Would you be a fine lass and bring me a flagon of that Sembian wine you keep above the bar?"

Briesa disentangled herself from his grasp. "And how would you be paying for that?"

Jack dropped a small handful of gold crowns on the table. "I am lately come into a small inheritance. From this moment forward, I shall settle all my tabs and make good on all my previous promises. Perchance have you seen Anders tonight?"

"He's making use of one of the upstairs rooms," Briesa replied. "Shall I tell him you're here?"

"I'll wait. It won't be long."

Jack sent her on her way with a good-natured slap on her fanny. Briesa gathered up the coins in her apron and danced away toward the bar, slipping through the press with the expertise of experience.

He had time to pour and drink two goblets of the Sembian red before Anders Aricssen came thumping down the narrow staircase, his fair features flushed with drink and his swordbelt slung over one shoulder. The Northman spied him at once and pushed through the crowd straight toward him.

"Jack! I've been looking all over for you. Where in the world have you been tonight?"

"Concluding business with a beautiful, yet disappointing, lady," Jack said glumly. Briesa returned with the wine and two goblets. Jack poured a cup for himself and one for Anders as she moved off to look after dozens of shouting patrons. "It's a strange night, friend Anders, filled with veiled peril and dark deeds."

The Northman slumped into the seat across from him and drained his goblet at one mighty go, red rivulets streaming through his beard. "That does not tell me much," he observed. "Say, that wasn't half bad. Your business must have concluded reasonably well, Jack; I can gauge the success of your ventures by the quality of your drink."

Jack nodded absently, still thinking about his encounter with Elana. She'd paid him well enough, he supposed, if not in the coin he'd hoped for. That was disappointing enough, but he found himself considering her words again. Something about obligations and responsibilities to those in her employ, and the commensurate degree of loyalty she expected in return . . . dangerous words indeed, especially to Jack's way of thinking. He'd made a career out of avoiding entanglements of that sort.

"Anders, did you perchance ever meet the Warlord Myrkyssa Jelan?" he asked suddenly.

His question was ill-timed, catching the Northman in the middle of a quaff of wine. Anders's eyes widened, and he choked comically, spewing a fine red spray of Sembian wine in Jack's general direction. Coughing and gagging, the Northman hunched low in his seat and seized Jack's arm with one hand.

"Curse it, Jack! Don't bring up that name anywhere near me!"

"No one's paying attention to us," Jack answered. "Besides, who cares what side you fought on in the Warlord's siege? I'm sure you fought well and valiantly, and deserve all the honor and respect accorded veterans of that fierce war."

"They lynched a fellow over in Pumpside just last month after they discovered he'd served under the Warlord's banner," Anders muttered. "He was a carpenter, with a wife and a family, a law-abiding citizen of Raven's Bluff ever since Jelan's army broke itself at the Battle of Fire River. Could you imagine what might befall me, given my lack of vocation? I'd be lucky to spend the rest of my days on the prison barges!"

"The sooner you answer my question, the sooner I'll stop pestering you about it," Jack observed. "Did you ever meet the Warlord during your time in her service? Do you have any idea of what she looks like?"

"I was only a footsoldier in a mercenary company, Jack. Captain Aeldar was called to the Warlord's council more than once, but he was the only one of our company who met with her." Anders chewed on his lip, thinking. "I saw her from a distance on several occasions, riding past with her commanders on whatever business she had at the moment. She wore armor of black, lacquered plate that gleamed like jet in the sunlight. Her helm covered her features." He laughed nervously. "She could be in this room, and I wouldn't know it."

"What do you know about her?"

Anders shrugged. "About as much as anyone in her service, I suppose. Captain Aeldar brought us to her army late in the campaign. We joined her banner only two months before Fire River, so we weren't with her from the beginning. According to the soldiers who'd served with her longer, she came out of the east three to four years ago at the head of a small band of mercenaries. They said that she recruited men in Narfell and Damara before shifting south to the Impilturan frontier and the Earthfast Mountains. She embarked on a campaign of conquest, hammering tribes of orcs and ogres and giants and other fell creatures into a restless horde under her command. It's said that she won their allegiance by defeating tribal champions in one-on-one combat and deposing chieftains at the point of her sword."

"It's also said that she is ten feet tall and breathes fire," Jack pointed out.

Anders nodded. "I don't necessarily rule it out. I'd

believe almost anything I heard about the Warlord. Somehow she united tribes that had spent generations killing each other and made them follow her banner. Two springs ago, as the snows melted in the high passes, she led her horde down the valley of the Fire River, marching straight on Raven's Bluff."

"Why Raven's Bluff? Hlammach, Lyrabar or Filur would have been closer. Tsurlagol or Tantras would have been easier targets."

"She didn't consult with me, Jack. All I know is that Aeldar marched us all over the Vast keeping up with Jelan's army."

"What else?" Jack asked. "Wasn't she supposed to be immune to magic? I seem to remember stories to that effect."

"I heard that many Ravenaar mages and priests spent a great deal of time and effort attempting to divine her location and her intentions but failed, and I heard stories from soldiers who'd seen her in battle. They reported that no magic seemed to harm her." Anders paused, then continued, "You should also keep in mind that I heard stories claiming that Jelan could fly, grow to a giant's stature, tear the hearts from fallen warriors and devour them raw, and uproot hundred-foot trees with the strength of a titan. Tyr knows who she really was and what she was capable of."

Jack tugged at his thin stripe of a goatee. He would give a lot to know the truth. Did she still plot the destruction of the city? Or had she decided to pursue her inscrutable goals in some less distasteful manner? For that matter, what were her goals? What did she need the Sarkonagael for? Why did she risk her life by hiding in the very city she had tried to conquer, surrounded by thousands of people who wished her dead?

"It makes no sense," he sighed, waving a hand in dismissal. "On to less difficult questions. Have you any news to report of Zandria and her intents?"

"She's preparing to descend into Sarbreen the day after tomorrow at first light," Anders replied. He drained another gulp of wine, evidently relieved by the change of topic. "Just as you said, friend Jack. She and her company mean to visit the Guilder's Tomb without troubling us for our assistance."

"Brilliant, capable, and predictable," Jack remarked. "That, of course, is the very reason I asked you and Tharzon to watch Zandria's company night and day. I knew that she would think twice about retaining my services for a share of the loot."

"So, what's the plan? Follow her and fall on her band when they lead us to the tomb?"

Jack raised his hand. "No, no, no. Follow her, allow her and her companions to loot the tomb, and *then* fall on them if need be. First of all, the Guilder's Tomb may be guarded by all manner of unwholesome guardians and devious traps, so we shall allow Zandria and her stalwarts to take the measure of their strength. Second, if the tomb's wards claim some of her companions, Zandria may be amenable to a renegotiation of our arrangement."

Anders grinned. "Ah, so you'll rob her at swordpoint after she's spent her strength in forcing the tomb and removing the loot. An excellent plan, Jack."

"Robbery is such a hard word. I prefer to think of it as encouraging her to generously reconsider our mutual association. After all, I am rather fond of Zandria, and I would hate to have her be sore with me."

"I am not concerned with how she feels about the situation," Anders said.

"Ah, but isn't it better to provide her with an opportunity to *purchase* our assistance in the event that Sarbreen's deadly traps and ancient defenses put her company in a bad way?" Jack sipped at his wine. "If the right circumstances develop, friend Anders, she might give us the lion's share of the loot and feel glad that she had the opportunity to do so. Now *that* is a plan."

The Northman furrowed his brow, thinking hard through his intoxication. Anders was one of the most lucid drunks Jack had ever known; no amount of ale or wine ever seemed to fog his wits. "And what if Zandria and her company recover the loot with little trouble? She'll have no need of us then."

"In that event," Jack said, "we'll consider more direct measures."

Despite his best efforts, Jack discovered once again that copious amounts of drink drown one's troubles in only the most transient and misleading manner. Hours of conniving, plotting, and planning with Anders and an imprudent amount of wine developed no certain plans for dealing with Zandria's expedition and did nothing at all to alleviate Jack's concerns about his meeting earlier in the evening or his enemies in the Game of Masks. But he did become quite drunk and had a roaring good time when he wasn't trying to think too hard.

The next morning eluded Jack entirely, as he was unable to dispel the miserable stupor smothering him after the night's festivities. He rose about two hours past noon and spent most of the next hour dressing slowly and painfully, one article at a time. Eventually he rallied enough to stagger out into the street and purchase bread, cheese, and a half-dozen boiled eggs for his breakfast, after which he felt much better.

"Illyth would undoubtedly say that I deserved my earlier misery," he mused while he ate, perched under a ramshackle porch in front of the grocer's shack. "She does not view overindulgence with the good-natured humor one looks for in that sort of situation." Then Jack sat bolt upright and smacked his hand to his forehead. "Illyth! The Yellow Lord's tournament is tonight!"

He looked up to the sky; the sun was only two hours short of setting, and the next Game event was only an hour off. In a panic, Jack dashed back to his apartment, dressed quickly in his best clothes, and then hired a coach to drive him out to Fleetwood Manor as fast as he could get there.

After a very anxious half hour for Jack, the carriage turned into the short, shady lane that led to Fleetwood Manor, passing another coach on its way out. He was only about a quarter hour late in picking up Illyth, which was better than he'd expected when he remembered their date. He was dressed rather casually for the evening, with tight black cannons and a pleated tunic of yellow and maroon. The coach stopped at the ivy-covered manor door; Jack hopped out before it had stopped rolling and took the short flight of steps two at a time.

"Lord Jaer Kell Wildhame for the Lady Illyth," he told the major domo.

The man didn't say a word in response. Jack turned on him in some annoyance—after all, he was running late— and found that the manservant was simply staring at him in amazement. The man's astonishment darkened visibly into suspicion.

"The Lady Illyth left with Lord Jaer Kell Wildhame just a moment ago," he said, motioning to a pair of house guards nearby. "Who, may I ask, are you?"

"I beg your pardon," replied Jack. "Did you say that Lady Illyth just left with me?"

The major domo nodded at the coach that had been departing just as Jack arrived. "There she goes. If you are not in that coach, sir, I do not know who is."

"Nor do I," said Jack. He dashed back to the coach he'd

rented and climbed up beside the driver. "Quickly, man! After that coach!"

The driver, a stout old man with flowing white mutton-chops, hesitated just a moment before snapping the reins and shouting. The two-horse team snorted and started off, wheeling the carriage around the drive and out toward the road. Jack could hear sounds of consternation and pursuit behind him, but he ignored them. They thundered down to the end of the lane and turned onto the road, heeling dangerously before finishing the turn.

"Faster!" cried Jack.

"We're running all out!" the driver replied. "What are we going to do when we catch them?"

"I'm going to jump," said Jack.

The driver looked aside at him. "You're daft," he said.

Jack just motioned him to keep after the coach ahead. They were closing fast; the other coach was rolling along at a quick trot, while Jack's was bouncing and clattering at a full gallop. Jack stood up on the coachman's seat, balancing easily atop the jolting carriage. The road wasn't wide enough to allow two coaches abreast, so he'd have to jump from behind. Fortunately, he knew a jumping spell that would work—as long as he didn't misjudge his leap and sprawl in the road in front of his own coach.

"Be ready to rein in when I jump," he told the driver. "I'm going to stop the other coach if I can."

The horses in Jack's team raced up behind the other coach, slowing only as the animals realized that the rolling obstacle in front of them was not going to get out of their way. At that moment, Jack worked the spell and leaped forward, sailing clear over his own team and alighting with a thump on the roof of Illyth's carriage. He dropped into the coachman's seat and shoved the other driver off the bench without ceremony. The man grunted in surprise and tumbled off into the ditch at the side of the road, rolling over and over. Jack seized the reins and hauled back, slowing the team. Then he vaulted to the ground and yanked open the carriage door.

Illyth screamed. Jack stood dumbfounded, staring into his own face. A short, wiry man dressed in black and gold ceased an assault on Illyth to leap out of the coach, knocking Jack flat. Jack scrambled to his feet as Illyth hurriedly covered herself with her torn dress. He turned just in time to get the other Jack's boot in the center of his chest, hammering him back against the carriage. Jack responded with a spell of magical energy that knocked down his opponent and drew the sword at his side. The other Jack mirrored his movement, drawing his own sword. They circled, looking for an opening.

Jack had a long moment to study his opponent. The other Jack was his identical twin, except there seemed to be a dark cast to his features, a hint of dusky gray that didn't show in the shadows but became clear when the other Jack happened to step into the long, slanting rays of sunlight from the setting sun. Jack shook his head in disbelief.

"Sir, you seem to have borrowed my features and my date. Who are you, and what offense have I offered you?"

The shadow Jack grinned an idiot's grin and leaped forward, stabbing murderously here and there with his blade. Jack yelped and dodged, parrying the attacks as best he could while he gave ground, circling behind the coach. The other fellow didn't have a great amount of skill, but he was blindingly fast and exceedingly agile, leaping and jumping with the energy of a madman as he slashed and stabbed.

"*Jack!* What in the world is going on here?" Illyth appeared behind the shadow Jack, still holding up her dress with one hand. "Who—?" The noblewoman halted in amazement, watching the duel between Jack and his twin.

"Illyth, get back!" Jack cried.

He met a high swing by ducking under it, then rolled to one side to avoid a follow-up thrust that would have gutted him had he been a hair slower. He responded with a couple of wicked jabs in the general vicinity of the shadow Jack's midsection, but his evil clone merely rolled aside. They exchanged another blinding pass of swordplay in which neither could penetrate the defenses of the other, and then sprang apart.

"Insolent mimic!" Jack snarled. "Who are you? Why do you steal my likeness?"

The shadow Jack merely grinned and worked a spell of invisibility, vanishing from sight.

"He can do that?" Jack asked in amazement. He worked the same spell and vanished likewise, stepping softly away from the last place he'd stood. Matching him in physical skill and agility was one thing; that made the shadow Jack a dangerous adversary, but one that Jack could defeat. But if the shadow-clone actually shared all of his abilities, all of his knowledge, all of his magical strength, Jack couldn't imagine how he could beat the fellow.

Illyth whirled, looking for some sign of either one. "Jaer Kell Wildhame, if you've left me standing in the middle of this dusty road with a torn dress and no escort for the Game tonight, I am going to be quite upset. I demand an explanation!"

The dusty road! Jack smiled and froze in place, looking carefully at the ground. If his opponent was still moving—there! Stealthy footfalls, right behind Illyth! Jack hurled himself forward and swung his sword in a waist-high arc. His invisibility spell failed as he broke the enchantment by striking out, but he was rewarded with the unexpected clang of steel and a soft resistance to his blow. The rapier wouldn't cause much of a wound wielded edge first, but droplets of dark blood spattered the earth, and a slim blade appeared in the dirt, skidding to a halt.

"Hah! I have disarmed you, villain!" Jack gloated. He snatched up the other weapon and swung wildly with both blades, groping for contact with his adversary.

Instead his adversary fled. Jack caught sight of a couple of quick footfalls in the dust, and then the brush and branches up on one side of the road rustled violently. Droplets of blood marked his assailant's trail—but the blood drops lasted only a moment before sizzling away in some strange dark vapor.

"Come back here!" Jack roared. "You have much to answer for, my friend!" He ran a couple of steps in the general direction of his foe's retreat, swinging aggressively, but there was no sign of the shadow Jack. "Curses!"

"Is he gone?" Illyth asked.

"I'm afraid so. He ran off, as if to mock the character of that noble hero whose likeness he so impudently stole," Jack said. He leaned against the carriage, suddenly tired beyond belief from the strenuous duel. "Do you have any idea of who that was?"

Illyth rounded on him with a look of such anger and amazement that Jack took a step back. "In the names of all the gods, why should *I* know who that was? He was your identical twin! Are you telling me that you have no idea why someone who looks exactly like you showed up at my doorstep, ushered me into the coach, and started pawing at me like a lovesick orc?"

Jack shook his head, although he couldn't shake a very odd sense of guilt over his double's actions, as if he were somehow responsible for what anyone who looked like him did. "Dear Illyth, I am many things, not all of them reputable, but I have never sought to force my attentions on anyone. And I would never do so to one of my dearest friends. I am at a complete loss to explain who that person was or what he was doing." He paused, and then added, "I am just glad that I was able to drive him off before he did you any harm."

The noblewoman looked down at her dress. She had to hold it with one hand to cover her bosom. "Who would want to impersonate you? And why would he want to abduct me? What can this possibly mean?"

"I suspect that this stone was aimed at me and not at you. I seem to be collecting enemies at a very unhealthy pace."

"Which of your enemies would take the trouble to impersonate you so perfectly?" Illyth asked. "Tell me a name, and I'll see to it that the authorities arrest him. I have some friends in high places, and I want that . . . that *person* locked up safely in a cell somewhere."

Who, indeed? Jack thought for a moment. The House Kuldath? Zandria? Morgath and Saerk didn't have the means or motive to strike at Illyth, and creating doppel-gangers to strike at those close to her rivals simply was not Zandria's style. The Knights of the Hawk? Marcus and Ashwillow would certainly have nothing to do with such a scheme. Iphegor? Now there was a possibility, although it seemed overly subtle for the necromancer, and Jack couldn't imagine that even a black-hearted scoundrel like Iphegor would willingly strike at Illyth to get at Jack.

No, what they needed was someone who was anxious to strike at both Jack and Illyth.

"Lord Tiger and Lady Mantis," Jack said. "I am sure they were behind this. Who else would have reason to strike at both of us together, or to strike at you alone? Somehow they must have determined our identities out-side the Game, and they mean to silence you and dis-credit me."

"Or to silence you by framing you for rape, murder, or worse," Illyth added. "It makes sense. Oh, Jack, what should we do? We have to find out who they are so that we can involve the authorities before they try again!"

Jack wasn't quite so certain that involving the authorities would be a wise move on his part, although he couldn't fault Illyth for thinking so. Best to move softly and avoid coming forward unless he absolutely had to.

"I know that you were looking forward to tonight's Game, Illyth, but do you think it would be wise to attend? If we fail to appear tonight, Tiger and Mantis might guess that their ploy has succeeded, and we might finally have them at a disadvantage. Perhaps they'll make a mistake."

Illyth looked down at her dress. "Solving the riddle of the Seven Faceless Lords doesn't seem as intriguing as it did an hour ago," she said. "I don't share your certainty that Tiger and Mantis are responsible, but I agree that attending the Game isn't a good idea at the moment. That person escaped, and who knows where he's going to strike next?"

"I intend to confront him at my earliest convenience and settle this issue," Jack replied. "The Green Lord's banquet is in four days, correct? By then I will have certainly apprehended the miscreant who borrowed my appearance, thus ending the threat." He offered Illyth his cloak and draped it over her shoulders, then helped her to his coach. "I'll stay with you awhile and keep watch, in case he returns, and we'll pass the time by comparing clues, as we'd planned."

"That's right," Illyth said, narrowing her eyes. "Jack, you were late by nearly an hour!"

"Punctuality is a virtue I never claimed to possess in abundance, dear Illyth," Jack said. He climbed into the coach behind her and signaled to the driver. "Back to Woodenhall, good man. We will be staying in this evening."

CHAPTER EIGHT

Jack passed the night comfortably stationed in the parlor of Woodenhall, ostensibly watching for any return of the doppelganger or shadow that had attacked Illyth earlier. But well before dawn he rose and slipped away, anxious to get back to the city in time to meet Anders and Tharzon. He left word with the staff that Illyth was to be guarded carefully and made his preparations for an expedition into Sarbreen's depths. He should have been trembling with anticipation, given the situation; if all went well, he might take possession of a prize so valuable that Elana's commission and the Game of Masks would pale in comparison. But Jack still couldn't help but feel that Zandria had excruciatingly poor timing. He had too many other things to think about, so, with a mind full of dark suspicions and an uneasy heart, he met Anders and Tharzon near the house rented out by the Company of the Red Falcon and followed Zandria into Sarbreen.

The Guilder's Tomb proved to be a surprisingly accessible place. From the sewers beneath Tentowers, an old vertical shaft led to a deep drain tunnel far beneath the city. Deeper tunnels and complexes intersected the shaft at various intervals, like floors of a building connected indirectly by a laundry chute or dumbwaiter. About sixty feet below the city sewers, a long, vaulted passage slanted across the vertical drop, leading to a broad chamber guarded by fierce-looking stone statues of grim dwarves. Zandria's company splashed through the sewers for a time, then rappelled down to the intersecting passage and marched only a hundred yards to reach the place. Jack, Anders, and Tharzon followed at a discreet distance.

Dwarves were hewers of rock and carvers of stone; Sarbreen, their ancient city, was bored through the rocky prominence of Raven's Bluff, in some cases hundreds of feet below the surface. The place was a maze in three dimensions, an endless labyrinth of shafts and passages, halls and chambers. In over a century and a half of human habitation on the hillside above, no one had ever mapped more than a tiny portion of Sarbreen's lost halls, but no part of Sarbreen was more than an hour's walk from the city above—if one knew the way.

If one didn't, the dwarven ruin might as well have been a wilderness the size of a kingdom. Most expeditions returned empty-handed after wandering aimlessly for hours or days through the same chambers. A few encountered old dwarven traps, hidden pits, and deadly blades that scythed out of dark alcoves, and some ran into dangerous and deadly monsters—undead things that hungered for the blood of the living, ferocious scavengers that fed from the city's effluvia drifting down from above, and horrifying aberrations that crept up into Sarbreen's halls from even more mysterious and remote depths far below the light. Jack had abandoned dungeoneering as a pastime after one such encounter. Hours of tedium punctuated by rare moments of utter terror hardly seemed like a heroic pursuit to him. Besides, the few expeditions that were successful brought their loot back to the surface, where rogues like Jack could easily help themselves to someone else's good fortune.

Following the brilliant magical lights of Zandria's company, Jack and his companions carefully tailed the band to the broad chamber at the end of the passageway. They carried no lights of their own; Tharzon's dwarven eyes were more than capable of piercing the darkness, and Jack worked a spell he knew that sharpened his own sight. Anders they led carefully along until they were close enough to see by the distant light of Zandria's expedition. The three rogues found a spot to wait about a hundred feet down the hall and settled in to watch.

"What do we do next?" whispered Tharzon.

Jack replied, "Let's see if Sarbreen's legendary perils do that work for us. Zandria is not a mage to be trifled with. She has at least two capable swordsmen with her—I met them when I visited their stronghold in the city. See, there they are." In the yellow light flooding the end of the hall, Zandria's companions spread out to search the chamber, while the Red Wizard consulted papers and notes before a gleaming slab of stone in the center of the far wall.

"Those other two in armor are probably priests," Tharzon added. He pointed to a short, stocky man and a young, athletic woman with a shaved head. "See the emblems of Tyr, there, and Tempus? Best to figure that they are both trained warriors, too, as well as potential spellcasters." The dwarf shifted slightly to change his view. "There's another fellow in dark clothes, probably a lockpick or burglar."

"That makes six to our three," Anders observed. "We should have brought a couple more stout lads to even the odds. Jankizen from Shadystreets would be useful."

"Jankizen can't add two and two twice and come up with the same result," Jack snorted. "Besides, more help means more shares." He peered down the hallway at the small pool of light.

Zandria and her allies were busy readying for a fight, checking weapons and arranging potions and scrolls so that they could be easily found in a hurry.

"They're getting ready to open the tomb. Wait here, lads. I'll creep a little closer to see what unfolds."

"Don't get caught," Tharzon muttered.

Jack winked at the dwarf and wove his spell of invisibility, vanishing from sight. He stepped out from behind the broken columns they'd chosen for cover and advanced toward Zandria's company, picking his steps carefully. Invisibility did not make him inaudible as well, and the crunch of a thoughtless footstep on rubble or a carelessly kicked stone would alert Zandria. Mages had spells to reveal things invisible, and Jack had no wish to put the Company of the Red Falcon on its guard.

At the moment, the adventurers stood in a loose half circle surrounding Zandria as she faced the wall opposite the entrance—except for the swordsman Brunn and the Tyrian priest, who deliberately watched the hallway outside for the approach of any enemy from that quarter. Jack nodded in appreciation; these were professionals, as he'd suspected. He stopped about ten feet short of the two sentries and studied the scene.

Now choked in rubble and ruin, the chamber had once been grand indeed. Two twenty-foot pillars had been carved into the likeness of grim dwarven sentries, guarding the entrance to the room. The chamber itself was a high rotunda, its walls lined with tall columns. A great carving in relief circled the entire chamber, a pastoral scene of grain fields and vineyards. In the center, directly opposite the entrance, stood a smooth glossy stone with a smaller, more intricate carving.

"Zandria's inscription," Jack whispered to himself. "Excellent!"

The red-haired mage stood with her back to him,

facing the wall. She carried a long staff of dark, rune-engraved wood and wore a short sword of strange black metal at her side. Holding the staff in the crook of her elbow, she studied a parchment scroll.

"Now, ten paces south from here," she said. "South is toward the entrance, correct?"

"Aye," said the priest of Tyr, speaking over his shoulder. "The hall outside runs straight north and south."

Zandria turned and began pacing straight toward Jack, her expression fixed in concentration. She counted ten paces and then halted, very near the entrance to the chamber. She referred to her notes again.

"Now, I speak the words *kharaz-urzu.*"

As soon as the dwarven words left her lips, a bright silver light softly grew in the chamber. High above, shining orbs hidden among stone carved to resemble the boughs of trees began to glow magically, overpowering the adventurers' own spells of light. The swordsmen shifted nervously, vigilant for any sign of impending attack, but instead of heralding the arrival of some ancient guardian, the light simply cast a glimmering field of slanting silver beams throughout the room as each ray bounced and rebounded from hidden, polished surfaces.

"What's happening?" called out the priestess of Tempus. She whirled from side to side, her battle-axe poised to strike. "Zandria?"

"Hold a moment. Nothing threatens us," the wizardess replied.

She turned slowly, studying the patterns formed by the argent beams. Six rays gleamed in the chamber from six silver apples hidden in the stony leaves at the apex of the room; each reflected four times from smooth, glossy spaces cunningly hidden in the carving that surrounded the room, creating a cage of light that spiraled down to meet at one common point in the center of the chamber—

a large seven-sided stone that stood perhaps an inch higher than the rest of the floor.

"The seven stone," Zandria breathed. "Brunn! Kale! Crowbars, quickly! Raise the stone in the center!"

The swordsman, Brunn, abandoned his post at the entrance to the rotunda and shrugged off his pack. The slender half-elf in gray joined him. Both men rummaged through their backpacks and came up with short iron crowbars. Then, silhouetted by the silver light, they worked the tools under one edge of the stone and slowly levered it up. The stone was about six or seven inches thick, and almost four feet in diameter.

"There's a staircase hidden under here!" called the half-elf.

"The Guilder's Tomb," Zandria whispered. She glanced around. "Thieron and Durevin, stay up here and guard our exit. Kale, you take the lead. Be wary of traps; Sarbreen's full of them. Brunn, you follow Kale, and I will follow you. Maressa, you bring up the rear. Any questions?"

"It's dangerous to split up," said the priest of Tyr. "What if you have need of Durevin and me when you get to the other end of the passageway below?"

"We'll call for you to join us if it looks like we might lose contact, Thieron," Zandria said. "All right, then, let's get to it."

The scout—Kale—nodded once and dropped quickly into the stairwell, alert and cautious. Brunn, the big swordsman, came after the thief, jingling in a mail shirt that hung to his knees. Zandria followed and then the priestess of Tempus. Jack debated returning to where his friends hid and then decided that the opportunity was simply too good. He glided forward between the Tyr priest and the other swordsman, who stood watching warily in all directions, and followed Maressa down into the staircase.

The stairwell opened out into a long, low hall, leading into darkness. They advanced a long way, passing entirely beneath the rotunda by Jack's reckoning, and then began to climb back up another flight of stairs.

"We're right behind that damned memorial stone," observed Kale from the front of the party. "All this time wasted solving the riddle, when we could have tunneled or blasted our way through with magic!"

"I am not certain that would have been the case, Kale," said Zandria. "The master stonewrights of Sarbreen had secret ways of strengthening stone, reinforcing against magical attack. It wouldn't surprise me if they had guarded the vaults behind the rotunda with these techniques."

"Door ahead," the thief said by way of reply. A great valve of shining silver stood at the top of the stairs at the end of the secret passage, only six feet in height but almost as wide. The likeness of a dignified elder dwarf was embossed in the center of the portal.

"Cedrizarun himself, I believe," Zandria said. "Search for a means to open it, Kale, but be careful. There may be a trap."

The lockpick nodded and moved closer to inspect the door. The rest of the group fell silent as they allowed Kale to do his work. "Ah," said the thief. "Avoid the handle, here. It triggers some kind of mechanism—a pit trap beneath this staircase, I believe. Instead, all we need to do is simply slide the door aside. It's on a very well concealed track."

"You mean it doesn't open? You just shove it aside like a decorative screen?" Brunn laughed. "Not very secure, is it?"

"That's not all. Some magical force prevents the door from moving. I suspect that we need a password of some kind, as we did above."

Zandria nodded. *"Kharaz-urzu!"* she stated. Nothing

happened. The others waited, shifting nervously, but no silver light appeared, and the door remained immovable. "Damn, I'd hoped it was the same word. Very well, then. Stand back, I'll work a spell of opening."

The other retreated back down the stairs a few steps as Zandria raised her staff and struck once on the silver barrier, muttering old magical words. The silver surface glimmered and then began to roll aside. As it opened, an arc of darkness appeared at one corner and then twisted up and around, replacing the silver wall—the door was wheel-shaped, rolling aside in its seamless stone groove. Zandria waited for the door to move aside and then thrust her staff into the space revealed, conjuring a brilliant burst of magical light to illuminate the space beyond.

Gold glittered and sparkled in the darkness. Jack blinked in amazement; the vault was full! Dwarven arms and weapons gleamed in the light, tall banners from a dozen battles lined the walls, and everywhere he looked great painted vessels and gilt coffers bulged with gold and jewels. A single share of this loot might be worth thousands upon thousands of gold crowns!

"Oh, my," said Kale. The lockpick took one tentative step toward the waiting riches and licked his lips. "Oh, my."

Zandria barred his way with her staff. "We will examine the treasure carefully and completely before we begin to remove it from the vault. Remember, the first thing we want is the Orb. Anything after that is merely a pleasant bonus, and for Azuth's sake, exercise caution! Who knows what traps the Sarbreen dwarves might have planted within the vault itself?"

The Orb? Jack thought to himself. What in Faerûn is Zandria looking for that all this wealth barely impresses her? He carefully trailed the adventurers into the vault, noting with some appreciation that Brunn and Maressa were engaged in wedging an iron spike under the rim of the door-wheel so that the heavy silver circle would not roll back into place and trap them all inside. The vault was arranged in a simple cross shape, with a small round room at the intersection of three short arms; the entrance was at the base of a somewhat longer arm. In the center of the round room stood a great stone sarcophagus.

Zandria and Kale split up, wandering through the vault without disturbing anything large, although Kale quietly pocketed a few interesting baubles when Zandria was not looking. Jack smiled and indulged his own larcenous impulses when neither the mage nor the lockpick was looking his way, filling his pockets as quickly as he could. He filched a fine-looking dagger of strange dark steel, a ring evidently carved from a single piece of onyx, and a dusty bottle that might or might not have sloshed with some small amount of Cedrizarun's legendary brandy.

"Ontrodes will bless me until his dying day." Jack smiled. Now for the real trick, he wondered: How do we separate this much wealth from the Company of the Red Falcon without a fight?

There was a vertical lift of over sixty feet on the way back to the surface, he recalled. Jack could post himself in the middle of the shaft, armed with a knife, then, when Zandria's companions hoisted up bags of loot, Jack could cut the line and drop the loot to the bottom of the shaft, where Anders and Tharzon waited to make off with the booty.

"That would fetch us only a fraction of the take," he muttered. "One or two bags at the most before they became suspicious."

Maybe he could substitute bags full of rocks for the gold, quietly switching the treasure one sack at a time as they hauled it past him, but he'd have to count on no one opening a sack at the top until all the sacks were up, and Jack couldn't imagine how he could encourage Zandria's friends to leave the sacks alone that long. Unless . . . unless there was someone up there when the sacks arrived, a passer-by who innocently engaged Zandria and her allies in conversation. Of course the Red Falcons wouldn't inspect their sacks if Tharzon and Anders happened by, engaged in a routine exploration of Sarbreen's upper levels. Zandria might order the two killed in order to protect their secrecy, but Jack doubted that she was made of such ruthless stuff. She'd probably chase them off after a few minutes. In the meantime, Jack would keep hauling up loot as if there were nothing wrong up above. He grinned widely. There was a plan worth putting into action!

"Come here!" Zandria stood by the sarcophagus, gazing at the stone carving on the lid. The top of the sarcophagus was worked into a likeness of Cedizarun, reposed on his back, a noble bottle clasped to his breast. "Brunn, Maressa—the sarcophagus holds a secret compartment!"

Jack looked over at the adventurers, now clustered around the dwarven tomb. Zandria carefully removed the stone bottle from the statue's grasp, a perfect piece of stonework that no doubt had taken years to carve. The stone grated coldly as the mage carefully pulled the stone bottle apart into two pieces. Inside, a brilliant white orb of pearly luminescence glimmered.

"The Orb of Khundrukar! Hidden in Cedrizarun's grasp, literally!"

"Is it magical?" asked Brunn.

"Very much so," Zandria replied. "although I am unsure of its properties." She took the Orb, wrapped it in a soft silk cloth, and tucked it into a pouch at her waist. "Help yourselves to the rest of the hoard, then. I have my prize."

Jack took that as his cue to slip out the door. It would take them some time to sort through all that treasure, enough time for he, Anders, and Tharzon to set up a careful pilferage of the treasure as the Red Falcons transported it back to the surface. Of course, he would have loved to get his hands on the Orb, but he'd settle for a king's ransom in gold and jewels. He was just setting up the operation in his mind when he heard shouts of alarm and the clash of arms from the other end of the passageway.

"Anders must have decided to rush the sentries," he realized. Quickly he dashed ahead to take the priest and the warrior from the rear, hoping to silence the fight before it spoiled his plans. Jack reached the staircase leading up into the outer rotunda and started to climb up, when suddenly Anders and Tharzon appeared at the head of the stair, leaping down in utter flight.

"Seal the door! Seal the door!" Tharzon bellowed.

An instant later, the priest Thieron followed the Northman and the dwarf. "Who in Tyr's seven hells are you?" he bellowed after them. "Where do you think you're going?"

"Out of the way, you idiot!" Anders yelled. He reached up and started to haul at the great stone slab that covered the hidden stairway.

The priest gaped in indecision, and then *something* outside made a kind of long, wheezing grunt and slithered close. Jack couldn't see it, not with Tharzon and Anders and the priest tangled up at the head of the stairway, but Thieron could.

"Tyr's hammer! A dragon of the deep! Durevin, flee!"

From outside Jack heard hissing and the soft scrape of scales on stone. Suddenly a great roar sounded, and a man screamed high and horribly. A sword dropped down the staircase, ringing as it clattered from step to step to land at Jack's feet. Half the length of the blade was gone, leaving a charred, corroded fragment that smoked and sizzled. He looked up again, just in time to see Anders, Tharzon, and Thieron the priest come down the stairs in a bouncing, swearing knot of limbs and weapons. He tried to scramble out of the way but was caught and knocked flat by Tharzon as the dwarf rolled down the steps. A hard-driven elbow knocked the wind out of him, and the collision spoiled his spell of invisibility. Jack saw stars.

When his vision cleared, he found himself looking up the now-empty staircase at a great crocodile-like snout and gleaming yellow fangs. The dragon was a small one, as these things go, probably not much bigger than four or five draft horses lined up nose to tail, but its head was as big as a sixty-gallon tun and its eyes gleamed with intelligence and malice.

"More rats in the hidey-hole," the creature hissed. "Don't worry. I'll be down in just a moment."

Jack scrambled backward on his hams about ten feet, staggered to his feet, and ran for his life. He risked one quick look over his shoulder and saw the monster gliding down the staircase. It was very snakelike in build, with no limbs to interfere with its passage and a pair of great black gleaming wings that folded back along its length. He picked up the pace and passed Tharzon and then the priest Thieron, joining Anders as he raced up the stair at the other end of the passageway that led up to the vault.

The three thieves and the Red Falcon piled into the treasure room in an explosion of armor and oaths. Brunn and Maressa drew weapons and leaped forward to defend their find against the invasion of strangers, but Anders and Tharzon ignored them, instantly turning to the wheellike door and kicking out the spike in order to roll it closed. The great valve boomed shut just as the slithering dragon-snake appeared at the bottom of the stairs.

"Come out, come out!" the creature laughed. "I think you have locked yourselves in, little mice. I shall be most cross if I have to come in after you!"

Jack, Anders, and Tharzon turned away from the door only to find the Red Falcons lined up against them. Zandria stepped forward, her face livid.

"What in the hell is going on here?" she demanded.

Jack started to answer, but Thieron spoke first. "Durevin and I were standing watch, when all of the sudden the dwarf and the big one came running up the outer passage, screaming 'Dragon! dragon!' At first I thought it some kind of ruse or ambush, but they ran right by us into the hidden staircase. When I looked up again, I saw what they were running from—a deep dragon, as fast as a racehorse and as big as a coach." The priest's voice faltered. "Durevin tried to check its advance. He had time for two, maybe three swings, and then the creature dissolved him with its breath. He's dead."

The door boomed with a great hollow sound. "That would be the creature just outside the door?" Zandria asked.

"Yes," said Thieron. "I am sorry, Zandria. We didn't have time to do anything but flee."

The mage absorbed the information with an expression of irritation, as if the priest had told her that a dress she liked had been ruined in the wash. "Understood. Everyone, get ready for a fight. The dragon's breath may be powerful enough to eat through the door." Then she turned to Jack and said in a cold voice, "Now what are you doing here? And who are these two?"

"Why, we were engaged in a routine exploration of the upper halls of Sarbreen," said Jack, "when we had the great misfortune of encountering the monster who now batters at our door. Deeming discretion the better part of valor, we chose to search for a more advantageous position to stand our ground. Unfortunately, we fled into the very dead end where your two companions stood guard. We advised them of the situation and took the liberty of using the passage you've found."

" 'Advised us of the situation'?" said Thieron. "You ran past screaming 'dragon'! Or those two did, anyway. I didn't see you until we came down the stair."

"Well, you were advised that there was a dragon in the vicinity, and that we had elected to execute a minor tactical withdrawal," Jack replied. He looked around at the great golden hoard that surrounded them, as if noticing it for the first time. "Dear me! Zandria, by any chance are we standing in the Guilder's Vault?"

"Why yes, Jack, so we are," the mage replied. "I don't doubt that you followed us here quite intentionally."

"Really? Why, I should hope that you were here on some other business altogether, dear Zandria. If you came to the vault without me, well, that would seem to imply that you had decided not to live up to our agreed-upon bargain of two-elevenths of the treasure." Jack allowed himself a smug smile. "Now who was going to steal from whom, I wonder?"

"Choose your words carefully," grated Brunn. He stepped forward. "There are five of us and only three of you, and we're better armed."

Anders met the swordsman's gaze levelly. "I guess we'll find out about that, now, won't we?"

"Silence!" Zandria's voice cracked like a whip. "We all share a much bigger problem. There is a dragon at the door, in case you've forgotten."

"Oh, don't mind me," hissed the dragon, its voice distant and muted through the door. "I am enjoying this tremendously. It's quite uncommon for my prospective meals to argue with each other in this fashion. I'd like to see how it turns out. Do continue."

"If there is anyone on the face of this world that I would rather not be caught in this predicament with," Zandria said, "I think it might be you, Jack Ravenwild. But I cannot change that now, so I suggest that we consider how we might cooperate to get out of this."

"Very well." Jack looked around. "First things first. There are eight of us now here. I suggest eight equal shares, should we survive, and Zandria, you and I as the leaders of our respective parties shall dice for the Orb of Kundugar."

"That's the Orb of Khundrukar, you idiot, and that is completely unacceptable," snapped Zandria.

"On what grounds do you reject my proposal?" Jack said with hurt in his voice. "It's actually quite fair. In fact—"

He was interrupted by a sudden blast outside, muted by the thick door and the dense stone. A faint whiff of something sulfurous tainted the air; the great silver door began to blacken and sizzle ominously.

Zandria snarled in anger, "Damn, I don't think that door will hold. Jack, you and your accomplices have two choices. You can stand and fight alongside us, or you can stand and die like sheep. There's no exit from this chamber, so you're out of places to run."

A small hole appeared in the door; a great black dragon snout rammed into it, buckling the portal and breaking free great, slagged slabs of the door. The dragon drew in its breath, preparing to fill the small room with its horrible corrosive vapors again.

"Wait!" called Jack. "Don't do that. This chamber is filled with treasure."

The dragon paused. It wriggled and shifted, so that it could peek through the holes widening in the melting door. "Why, so it is! And I might have ruined it all. Thank you for bringing that to my attention."

"Don't mention it," Jack muttered. "Umm, would you consider a modest bribe to leave us alone? Say, half the treasure in the room?"

Zandria and her companions muttered angrily, but they held their tongues. The dragon was silent for a few moments, evidently considering the offer. "If you strip and leave your weapons and gear in this chamber, I'll allow you to leave," it said. "All of the treasure, of course, would have to stay."

The humans and the dwarf exchanged glances. "I don't believe it for a moment," said Tharzon. "Dragons are notorious liars."

"Why, I would offer my sacred bond to any who threw themselves at my mercy!" the dragon replied. "I value my word very highly."

"We decline," said Zandria. She studied the chamber quickly; the door was at the bottom end of the southern arm. She gestured sharply and sent the surviving Falcons back to the west arm, then hissed at Jack. "You three to the east."

Jack, Anders, and Tharzon retreated to the east arm of the cross-shaped room. Jack wasn't a great tactician, but he appreciated the arrangement at once. The dragon wouldn't have anyone standing right in front of it when it forced the door. It would have to enter the room bodily and then turn to attack the Falcons on its left or the rogues on its right. One band or the other would have the opportunity to attack the creature from behind.

The dragon snarled in rage and threw itself against the ruined door. The ancient dwarf-made valve held for a moment and then failed utterly as the very stones it was anchored in were jarred from their place. Metal shrieked and groaned, stone cracked like thunderbolts, and then the creature was inside the room, a great dark serpent lunging forward with incredible speed and power. Its wings battered the walls, knocking treasure in every direction. It glanced once into the east alcove, its curious yellow eye gleaming, and then it hurled itself toward the west and the Red Falcons.

"Die, monster!" shrieked Zandria.

She worked a spell of lightning, blasting at the dragon with a brilliant blue bolt of energy. Thieron began chanting a priestly spell to summon strength and fortitude against the creature, while Brunn and Maressa leaped forward, blade and battle-axe flashing. The dragon drove them back with huge snaps of its fanged maw.

"Come on, Tharzon!" shouted Anders.

He leaped forward with his greatsword in hand, the dwarf only a step behind, war-axe high. The two struck at the gleaming dark flank of the dragon, barely marking the creature's scaly armor, and then the dragon twisted with a powerful motion and slammed its long, whiplike tail through the alcove, sending both Northman and dwarf flying as it pulverized them. Jack leaped over the lashing tail and conjured a ball of magical force, hurling it at the dragon's back. The detonation brought a roar of pain from the monster. It twitched its tail and upended Jack, too.

"This isn't going all too well," he mumbled as he picked himself up from the stone floor.

He looked up just in time to see both Anders and Tharzon knocked off their feet again by the dragon's tail, while across the room Zandria—now levitating in the air and blasting at the dragon with darts of brilliant magic—was suddenly swatted across the room by a wing the size of a small sail. She hit the stone wall hard and fell stunned to the ground on the east side of the chamber.

The dragon's lashing tail suddenly twisted away from the alcove, replaced by one dark wing. The half-elf Kale was dragged into view, caught in the coils of the deep

dragon's body like a small animal trapped by a constric-
tor snake. The thief screamed shrilly, feebly stabbing at
the dragon with a small dagger, and then something
cracked loudly enough to be heard over the dragon's bel-
lows and the shrill ringing swords. Blood started from
Kale's mouth, and he dropped his dagger, his head vanishing beneath the dragon's coils.

Jack looked around. The door was dicey, but he had
other ways to leave. He picked himself up from the floor
and then darted forward to set one hand on Tharzon and
the other on Anders.

"Come on, lads! Let's quit while we're ahead!"

"But the dragon—" Anders began.

"Is not our fight," Jack finished.

He summoned the energy for his travel spell, shaping
the chaotic spiral with care; this spell taxed him, and he'd
never tried to carry two companions at once. The dragon
whirled about, sensing that something was happening,
but before it could strike again, the room faded into mist
and darkness—

—and they were somewhere else, falling to the cold
stone floor in silver light. Jack landed heavily and lost his
breath. Anders and Tharzon fell to the ground right
beside him, their weapons ringing on the stone. His head
swam with dizziness, but Jack staggered to his feet. As he
thought, they were in the outer rotunda. The silver light
still caged the room, but against one wall a great smear
of smoking, bubbling stone showed where Durevin had
met his end in the dragon's vile corrosion.

Tharzon sat up slowly. "What happened? Where are
we?"

"I used a spell of transport," Jack answered. "The
range is short, no more than a hundred yards or so. I
thought we'd get around the dragon by returning to the
nearest safe place I could reach."

"You dragged us out of the fight and abandoned Zandria to that monster?" Anders asked. "The Guilder's Vault was ours! All we had to do was beat the dragon, and we would have walked out of there with a king's ransom!"

Jack pointed at the open stairway leading down to the long corridor. Sounds of battle echoed up from the opening. "The fight's still going on, Anders, not more than thirty or forty yards down that hallway. Please, feel free to rejoin the fray. I doubt that the dragon's going anywhere."

Anders stalked in a circle, frustrated. "But all that gold!"

"All that gold does not serve a dead man at all," Tharzon remarked. "Did you line your pockets at all while we were in there, Anders?"

The Northman nodded. "I scooped up a handful of trinkets before the dragon broke down the door."

"As did I, and as did Jack," Tharzon said. "Come on, friend Anders. You aren't leaving empty handed, and it was only a morning's work."

Jack caught the Northman's arm and pulled him toward the entrance to the rotunda. "We would be well-advised to absent ourselves from the scene. Zandria and her friends will defeat the dragon, in which case it may come this way again, or they will be defeated, in which case it may come this way again. Either way, I mean to be in the Cracked Tankard enjoying an ale by the time that comes to pass." He laughed and patted his pockets. "In fact, I will even buy the first round. Now let me tell you about the plan of genius I hatched to pilfer the treasure from the Red Falcons before that oversized snake ruined it all."

CHAPTER NINE

Jack, Anders, and Tharzon celebrated their escape from the Guilder's Vault with steins of beer and flagons of wine for most of the rest of the day. Between the three of them, they had pocketed a handsome amount of dwarfwork valuables. Jack did not see fit to mention the small brandy bottle nestled safely inside his jacket. He didn't know whether to sell it (Cedrizarun's work was doubtless worth many hundreds of gold crowns, possibly thousands), share it with his comrades, drink it himself, or give it to that old sot Ontrodes for a lark.

"That weighty decision must be delayed until I have given the issue due consideration," he told himself. "The tragedy of using this irreplaceable liquor poorly would haunt me for the rest of my days."

Now that he'd had some time to reflect on their narrow escape, he seemed to recall that a month or two back the Lady Mayor had issued a proclamation offering a generous reward, a very generous reward, to the plucky soul who had braved Sarbreen's awful dangers and hungry deep drag-ons in order to recover various artifacts from the depths, including the Orb of Khundrukar. Some-thing to the effect of a noble title and ten thousand gold crowns for recovering the dwarven device . . .

"Perhaps she might pay handsomely for a ring, a dagger, and a bottle of the most superior brandy residing in mortal hands today. Failing that, perhaps she might pay handsomely to learn that the Red Wizard Zandria had recovered the Orb or perished in the attempt," Jack mused.

Jack bid his partners a good night and left to find a bed. He even left his fair share of the night's tab on the table and sauntered off into the cool spring evening, humming a merry air as he strolled down the streets leading toward home. Perhaps he'd purchase a small manor out in the countryside, nothing ostentatious or crass of course, a few dozen acres and servants to maintain his modest yet comfortable lifestyle.

"Women such as Illyth or Zandria might prove eager to attach themselves to a person of my status and dignity," he mused. "Why, I might—"

Someone threw a cloak over his head from behind and wrapped it tight in the blink of an eye. A flurry of punches and jabs battered Jack through the heavy coat, and he was wrestled and dragged a few steps only to fall into a muddy, foul-smelling pool of water. He flailed about, trying to defend himself, but hard-driven fists hammered into his head, shoulders, and back, knocking the wind out of him and pounding him mercilessly. Jack gibbered in panic.

"Wait! Stop—unh! Who—agh! Stop!"

"Well, well, well. If it isn't—"

"Jack Ravenwild. Where's the ruby, Ravenwild?"

"You know, dear sir, we've been quartering the city looking for you. We've discovered that the ruby stolen from House Kuldath was sold in Tantras a few days ago. Perhaps now you may be inclined to—"

"Tell us where the money is, or we'll slit your throat."

Twisting in agony, Jack managed to wriggle out of his cloak. He rolled over on the cold cobblestone and found himself staring up at Morgath and Saerk. The two thieves stood over him, short truncheons in their hands.

"Your persistence astonishes me, gentlemen," he gasped. "I thought we understood that I had nothing to do with your employer's unfortunate loss."

"You were seen taking money from a big, blonde-haired Northman—" Morgath began.

"—who was observed selling a ruby the size of a pigeon's egg to a dealer in Tantras for the sum of thirteen hundred Ravenaar crowns," finished Saerk. "The Northman fenced it for you. Now how do you think we can satisfy our employer's demands for justice and the gem's return?"

"Clearly, we cannot return the gem, so we should discuss the issue of reparations," Morgath said. "Now, let's start with what's in this satchel."

Thirteen hundred crowns? Why, Anders cheated me of almost two hundred pieces of gold! Jack thought first of all. Then the rest of the thief's statement reached him regarding the disposition of Jack's satchel. Jack shook his head, trying to clear it of intoxication and pain, and looked up. Morgath was holding the pouch in which he'd stashed the pick of his pickings from the Guilder's Vault! Slowly he levered himself up off the street and carefully brushed off his clothes.

"That," he said slowly, "has nothing whatsoever to do with you."

"Oh? If it's valuable and it is yours, then it might very well have something to do with us—"

"We'll just keep it until you produce the ruby." Saerk laughed. The thin thief was really an unpleasant fellow, gaunt and bony, and his laugh sounded like the shrill whinny of a skeletal horse. He dropped the truncheon and pulled out a wicked knife. "I think we'll keep a couple of your fingers, too, by way of thanking you for the trouble at the Tankard last week."

Jack was not about to let these two filchers walk off with his hard-won loot. He drew himself up and looked at the two men, then glowered, then scowled. "I believe," he said clearly, "that I have had all that I care to stand." He muttered a spell, the spell of seeming, and slowly began to alter his appearance. "You see, gentlemen, I am not as I appear. Until now, it has suited my purposes to disguise my true form, but you, you have given me cause to forget my restraint and resort to more direct measures." He grew taller, heavier, more gaunt. His skin darkened to an infernal coal black as his ears assumed wicked points and long, sharp tusks thrust their way out from his lower jaw.

The two thieves took a half-step back, fumbling for their weapons. "Stop that," squeaked Morgath. "You can't fool us with a simple trick like that!"

Jack grew taller still, now towering over both men. Wisps of steam escaped from his mouth when he talked, as his voice deepened into a low, menacing rumble. "I am a visitor from a far land," he continued. "I had hoped to pass peacefully among your kind, perhaps observe human customs, learn human ways, but I refuse to be assaulted with impunity, and I refuse to be hectored and badgered and threatened, and I refuse to have the two of you pawing through my personal effects. Despite my best efforts to avoid this, you have forced my hand, and so now I must *rend the two of you limb from limb and feast on your steaming organs before your dying eyes!*"

He finished by throwing back his head and bellowing in sheer ogrish rage, rolling his eyes and raising his huge taloned hands over his head as if to conjure down upon the two terrified thieves the very instrument of their doom with no further delay.

Morgath and Saerk stood petrified for one awful instant, gazing up like sheep standing under the butcher's knife, and then they broke and ran, abandoning the satchel and their truncheons in their haste to depart the vicinity. Jack roared after them as they fled pell-mell down the alleyway and bolted out in the street. Morgath turned left and Saerk turned right, a prudent tactic had they been in the correct position to execute the maneuver, which they weren't. As it so happened, they collided, the short one upending the taller, and the taller knocking down the shorter. Jack took two steps and roared again, at which point the two thieves yammered in terror, picked themselves up, and ran off screaming into the night.

Jack used the spell to assume the appearance of a uniformed city watchman and picked up his belongings. He could hear the screams of the two thieves, now fading into the cool distance. Sooner or later, the authorities would come running to investigate reports of a berserk ogre mage rampaging through the Anvil, and it wouldn't be wise to wait for that to happen. He changed his appearance back to normal and departed the scene, congratulating himself on his own cleverness. The night was cool and fresh, the air was sweet with rain, and even if he ached in the ribs and shoulders and arms from the drubbing the two thieves had given him, in the end he'd run them off.

He was only a block from his apartment when someone *else* threw a cloak over his head and pummeled him mercilessly to the cobblestones. Flailing wildly to tear the cloak from his face, Jack's arms were pinned, and then his assailant threw him face first into a hard brick wall, hammering a big fist into his kidneys two, then three times. Jack cried out and fell, only to be savagely kicked several times before he heard a voice through the red haze of pain.

"That's enough, Marcus. We're supposed to arrest him, which implies bringing him in alive."

A heavy boot kicked him once more in the stomach, doubling him up like a broken doll. Then the cloak was pulled away. A large pair of leather-booted feet stared him in the eye, and a little farther back a somewhat smaller pair of leather-booted feet of a more feminine slenderness waited their turn.

"This defies all probability," Jack coughed. "Two beatings in one night, commenced in the exact same fashion. I shall henceforward trust no man wearing a cloak."

"Hello, Jack," purred Ashwillow. The Hawk Knight knelt so that she was able to meet his eyes. "You've been quite a busy burglar of late, haven't you? Dueling wizards in the streets, socializing with the privileged classes, crawling around in Sarbreen doing who knows what . . . honestly, I don't see how you find the time."

"I know of several black-hearted scoundrels who bear me a striking resemblance," Jack wheezed. His guts ached as if red-hot skewers had been stuck through him. "I would love to help you, dear lady, but I am afraid I cannot be held answerable to their misdeeds."

"What did you steal for Elana?" demanded Marcus. "Where did you meet her? Time's running short, and I am not going to play games with you." To emphasize his point he dragged Jack to his feet and threw him against the wall with great disregard for both rogue and building.

Jack tried to straighten up but couldn't; his stomach hurt too much. He panted for a long moment, trying to master the pain. Someday, he promised himself, I am going to find out where Marcus lives, and then when he is on his way home from a late night at a tavern, I am going to jump out of the shadows and beat him with a board.

He considered whether or not he should tell them the truth about Elana. After all, he hardly owed her any loyalty. Three things stopped him: first, telling the truth was foreign to his nature; second, admitting that he'd unwittingly aided the Warlord Myrkyssa Jelan didn't seem like it would make the Hawk Knights leave him alone; third, and most significantly, Iphegor the Black appeared in a sulfurous belch of smoke and screamed at Marcus, *"There you are! Oh, now shall I have my vengeance upon you, wretched thief and craven mouse murderer!"*

"I beg your pardon?" Marcus said, blank bafflement in his face.

"Remarkable," Jack managed.

Obviously, Iphegor had used some spell to transport him to the vicinity of the man who'd pillaged his tower and wrought the end of his familiar, because here he stood. But Iphegor did not know, *could* not know, that Jack was Jack and not Marcus, since the thief had used the seeming spell to take on the Hawk Knight's appearance during the unpleasant affair in the necromancer's tower.

Jack looked at Marcus and Ashwillow and straightened a little bit. "Oh, are *you* in for it now."

Iphegor, already in the process of casting some dire spell, hesitated half a heartbeat as he glanced sideways at Jack. The two knights goggled in amazement, still trying to grasp the implications of the sorcerer's spectacular appearance. Then Iphegor dismissed the small, well-pummeled popinjay before him as insignificant to his mission, stepped back, and raised his voice, conjuring a horrible doom down upon the unfortunate Hawk Knights. Marcus sprang toward the necromancer to halt his spell, while Ashwillow dove for cover.

Jack worked a simple spell and jumped straight up with all his might, carried aloft by dancing emerald energy. He gained the rooftop of Eldritch, Lightfoot, Findrol, & Company with one bound just as Iphegor's spell detonated under him, filling the narrow alleyway with black, searing flames that washed out into the street and erupted into the sky overhead. Jack risked one glance below, just enough to see a very singed-looking Marcus seize hold of Iphegor's throat while the wizard raised a very deadly looking wand to smite him again. Sorcerous black flames engulfed both the trading house and the building across the alleyway, burning weirdly without light but igniting the buildings nonetheless.

Ashwillow rose up from behind a high stone curb, only partially singed. She aimed a wicked crossbow in Jack's general direction, but before she could let fly with the bolt, Jack conjured a solid sheet of billowing vaporous fog in the alleyway, obscuring all vision. The knight's quarrel flew off over his shoulder.

"The roof! He's on the roof!" Ashwillow cried.

"Bugger the spy! *Help me!*" Marcus replied, striving to keep Iphegor's deadly wand from his face.

Jack turned and ran for his life. Behind him, spells thundered and steel rang in the fog and confusion as Iphegor and the Knights blundered and fought in the mists.

"You will not escape me so easily, thief!" shrieked Iphegor once, distantly, and then Jack abandoned the scene altogether.

Since it was clear that his apartments were under the surveillance of various parties that wished him ill, Jack elected to avoid going home. "The hour is late, drink has fogged my wits, and I desperately require sleep," Jack mused, perched on a rooftop several blocks away. A roaring fire filled with golden sparks marked the place where Jack and Iphegor had recently parted ways, and he saw no reason to return to the scene. "My various bolt-holes and haunts throughout the city may be watched tonight, so I need to find a place of comparative safety and seclusion."

He thought hard for a moment, considering and discarding various plans, until he struck upon one that seemed workable. "Ontrodes has plenty of room in his tower. I am sure that a gold crown will purchase a night's stay and cheerful hospitality in an atmosphere of rustic scholarship and charming antiquity." At once Jack alighted from the rooftops and set off toward Shadystreets, splashing through the rain-soaked streets and whistling merrily to ward off cutpurses and murderers lurking in the dark alleyways of the poorer neighborhoods.

He reached Ontrodes's street and picked up his pace, anxious to be inside. Few streetlights burned in this part of the city, and the evening here had a restless, watchful feel to it, as if unseen eyes studied his every move in breathless patience. Jack hurried about halfway down the street and then stopped in confusion.

"Evidently, I am more intoxicated than I thought," he muttered. "Ontrodes's tower is *not* on this street, which begs the question, which street am I on?"

He halted and looked about to get his bearings. On his right hand stood the Dyddow Barrelworks, exactly where it was supposed to be at the end of Riverview Road, and he'd just passed the Red Ravens firefighters' hall on his left not fifty yards back. This was the right spot, but Ontrodes's tower was not here. Narrowing his eyes suspiciously, Jack turned in a slow circle, studying his surroundings carefully on the off chance that some incredibly ambitious trickster had *moved* the sage's tower in order to have a hard-earned laugh at his expense. A dilapidated house joined to a shapeless mound of rubble caught his eye.

"Wrack and ruin!" Jack cried. "Ontrodes's tower has finally collapsed entirely!" And indeed, the precarious angle at which the sage's small round tower had leaned for years evidently proved too much for mere stone and mortar to bear. The small house still stood, although it leaned drastically in the other direction now that it had been freed of the tower's pull. The stone archway joining house to tower remained more or less intact and was now covered loosely by a ragged piece of canvas that hung damply in the rain. Books and fragments of books lay crushed beneath the rubble or strewn here and there across the muddy streets.

Jack shook himself out of his amazement and bounded up to the cottage door. He cast one more glance at the stones piled up beside him, and then hammered on the door to the sage's dilapidated demesnes.

"Ontrodes, Ontrodes! Open up! I have urgent business with you!"

There was no immediate response, so Jack decided simply to hammer continuously on the door until he provoked one. Certainly the sage's neighbors began to express their dissatisfaction after a few minutes of Jack's attention, screeching obscenities out of open windows and threatening him with horrible violence if he didn't cease and desist.

After two or three minutes of incessant hammering, the door was suddenly thrown open from within. Ontrodes, dressed in a wine-stained robe, stood there, rubbing his eyes blearily as he stared at Jack. "What harm have I ever done to you, you impudent whelp? Have you not done enough? What is it to be now?"

Jack paused and rubbed the heel of his hand, somewhat sore from pounding on the sage's lintel. Ontrodes stared at him with undisguised contempt, even anger, but that of course was to be expected when waking the old codger in the middle of the night.

"Wise Ontrodes, what has become of your domicile? What catastrophe befell your noble residence?"

The sage's face darkened into a drunken, bitter anger

so vehement that Jack took a step back. "You ask me what became of my tower? *You* ask *me?* By Gond's wondrous brass *balls,* Jack, do you think that I find anything *amusing* about this? I am a peaceable man, a man of wit and learning, but I swear by Cyric's black heart that if I ever catch sight of you again, I will pull off your head and *defecate down your throat!*"

With that the sage slammed his door so thunderously loudly that two more stones jutting out from the maimed wall of his home clattered down onto the rubble, and the door-latch flew from its place to land in the mud at Jack's feet.

"That," thought Jack, "was not the expected result of this conversation."

He walked in a small circle, thinking hard. Ontrodes was clearly incensed—no, enraged—at him, but he still needed shelter and he did earnestly desire to understand exactly *what* he had done, other than waking the man in the middle of the night, that could possibly have earned him such vitriol. He wrapped his arms around his torso and stamped, growing chilled in the damp night air. The old dwarven bottle was round and warm in his coat pocket.

Gingerly, Jack stepped up and rapped his knuckle on the door. "Ontrodes!" he called softly. "I do not know how I have caused you such anger, but I would dearly like the opportunity to make amends. I have brought you a distillation concocted by old Cedrizarun himself, seized just yesterday from the jaws of a dragon in the Guilder's Vault! Please, allow me to make a gift of it to you!"

The sage snuffled and grunted in his cottage, but remained silent for a long time. Jack began to fear that he might not reply at all, but finally the door creaked open again.

"I do not believe you," the sage said through an inch-wide gap, "and there is no liquor on the face of the world that could possibly atone for the wrong you have done, but, just for the sake of curiosity—show me."

Jack withdrew the dark bottle from his coat and held it up for the sage to see. "I found it in Cedrizarun's tomb," he said quietly. "Look at the bottle. It matches precisely the bottle Zandria showed you, does it not?"

"You probably stole it from her, poured out the contents in ignorance, and filled it with swill," Ontrodes said, "but the bottle itself may be valuable. Give it to me!"

"First, wise Ontrodes, noble Ontrodes, I wish to know: Why are you angry with me?"

The sage's face reddened, but with the prize suspended before his eyes, he managed to retain a deadly calm. He waved one hand at the wreckage of his tower. "Is it not obvious?"

"You believe that I caused the collapse of your tower?" Jack snorted in amazement. "Ontrodes, the tower was decrepit. It might have fallen for any number of reasons. I certainly had nothing to do with it."

"Oh? I thought that the magical blasts you used to destroy the beams holding up the second floor hastened my tower's demise considerably!" Ontrodes snapped. "How can you stand there pretending innocence, when not six hours past you were dancing around my crumbling home, singing those inane, insulting limericks and hurling blast after fiery blast into my very home! Why, if I hadn't thrown myself out the window of the study, I would have been killed!"

"I have no memory—" Jack began, and then he halted. Of course he didn't have any memory of wrecking the sage's tower, because he did not do it. But was it not possible, perhaps even likely, that his shadow had been here instead? "Ontrodes, believe this or not, but it is the truth: Two days past I discovered that I have a sinister and malicious copy at large in the city, a spiteful fellow who wears my likeness and apparently delights in tormenting my friends and acquaintances. My doppelganger wrought the ruin of your tower."

The sage merely blinked at him. "You expect me to believe that? What an incredibly convenient explanation!"

"I had thought I might call on you and ask for shelter for the night," Jack continued, stroking his beard, "but now I see that I have need of your professional services too. Here, I freely offer you this rare and exceedingly valuable dwarven brandy by way of apologizing for my counterfeit's uncouth actions." He handed the sage the bottle from the Guilder's Vault and then stepped inside, easily avoiding the old man's groggy attempt to impede him at the door. He would have gone straightaway to the sage's study, but that of course no longer existed, so he turned instead into Ontrodes's kitchen and drew up a chair by the hearth. "Now what are the means by which some villain might copy one's appearance or create an evil duplicate of a person?"

The sage stood by the doorway, bottle in hand, still grappling with the fact that Jack had eluded him and was now ensconced in his kitchen. "Come back tomorrow with one hundred pieces of gold, and I'll consider your question. Until then, Jack, I want nothing to do with you."

"Sample the brandy, then. It is Cedrizarun's work. A chance to savor it should be worth a thousand gold crowns, let alone a hundred."

"I expect that you have simply poured more Sembian horse piss into this noble vessel, hoping to deceive me in that manner," Ontrodes rumbled, but he complied.

He took a pair of sturdy tongs from a hook on the wall and carefully broke the seal of the bottle, removing the cork with surprising deftness and care. Then he held the bottle to his nose and inhaled.

Ontrodes's bloodshot eyes flew open wide, and his

mouth fell open. He stared down at the bottle in frank amazement and then inhaled again.

"I do not know if this is Cedrizarun's work or not," he whispered, "but it is surely an old, mature, exquisite and potent dwarven brandy. There can be no doubt of that! Jack, I might almost find it in my heart to forgive you the destruction of my home." He hurried to find a suitable glass.

Jack smiled. "As I said before, what are the means by which a person might copy someone's appearance or create a duplicate of the target for nefarious ends?"

Ontrodes poured a dram of the golden liquid into a fine tall glass on the sideboard. Jack used a minor cantrip to do the same for himself, bringing his glass dancing through the air to his hand. The sage glared at him, but Jack had been careful to help himself to the merest portion.

"I am not an expert in these matters," the sage said. "My learning lies—"

"I know, I know, Ontrodes. Liqueurs, cordials, wines, and brandies. I seek your advice in this matter fully cognizant of your limitations."

"Fine, then. I can think of five principal methods on first examination: spells of illusion, spells of transformation, magical items permitting the same, the natural abilities of certain monsters such as doppelgangers or demons, and simulacra or clones. There may of course be other means."

"Could we narrow the field by limiting the means to those that would copy abilities other than sheer physical characteristics? For example, personal knowledge or magical ability?"

"That is easily done. Illusions and transmutations do not generally confer any special knowledge or magical ability upon the person changed, nor do magical devices duplicating their effects." Caught by the question, Ontrodes thought for a long moment. "I have heard of doppelgangers that could copy such things, but only by slaying the target and devouring his brain."

"We can rule out that one, thank the gods," Jack said.

"Then I imagine that you are left with two likely explanations: a simulacrum of some kind or one of the more mundane means employed by a mage who has carefully researched the target."

The second made sense—any competent mage could work the magic that Jack had seen his shadowy twin employ, and any competent cutthroat could have observed his comings and goings to learn of his association with Illyth, but the first confused him.

"The latter seems more likely, but I do not rule out the former. What is a simulacrum?"

"A magical construct or creature built from snow, or mud, or something similar and then infused with a kind of pseudo-life. It is perfectly accurate to casual observation, but its abilities are only a pale mirror of the person it is built to resemble. A clone, on the other hand, is a real, living person magically grown from some tiny part of its model. Both of these things are, of course, exceedingly rare and powerful magics, Jack." The sage narrowed his eyes suspiciously. "You're not thinking of trying to copy somebody, are you?"

"Ontrodes, have you heard nothing I have said? It seems that somebody has copied *me*," Jack said glumly. "Two days past I encountered a rather gray-faced fellow who looked like me, fought as I fight, and even seemed to know some of the magics I know. I cut him once, but he didn't bleed normally. His blood was dark and seemed to vanish after a moment on the ground."

"That is very odd," murmured the sage. "Gray faced, you say? Did he have a different appearance when he stood in shadow and when he stood in sunlight?"

"It would be hard to—wait, no, I think he did. Yes, definitely he did. It struck me as very peculiar."

"Doubly odd," Ontrodes said. With trembling hands he raised the glass to his lips and tried one tentative sip, swilling the liquor in his mouth, an expression of purest bliss etched on his coarse features. "Exquisite, exquisite! Remarkable! Be careful with your taste, my boy, this is potent stuff!"

Jack tried his. The taste was extraordinary, a glimpse of pure fire captured in a stream of gold. The fumes seemed to burn delightfully all the way through his skull, yet the taste was sweet and strong, indescribably so. He grinned in delight, then turned back to the issue at hand.

"What was doubly odd about that?"

"What? Oh, the shadow. You see, that is a characteristic usually observed in a shade."

"A shade?" Jack leaned forward, interested. "Now, what in Faerûn is a shade?"

"Not from Faerûn at all, dear boy, but the plane of shadow. Another rare and difficult process, in which a person exchanges his own life-force for the stuff of shadow."

"So a mage hostile to me has made himself a shade, studied my habits and appearance, and worked a simple illusion to borrow my appearance?" Jack shook his head. "That seems far-fetched."

"The other possibility is that a mage has found a way to create simulacra using shadow stuff as the working material, so to speak. I suppose it could be done."

"Who would go to that much trouble to discomfit me?" Jack wondered aloud.

Tiger and Mantis were still his first guess, but who else might be responsible? Iphegor the Black certainly had the motive, but he had already demonstrated an interest in a much more direct sort of retribution. Morgath and Saerk almost certainly lacked the magical skills to do such a thing. Marcus and Ashwillow would never move against a noble of the city in order to get at a common thief, and besides, they probably lacked the magical skill as well. Zandria had the skill, but it was not clear why she would strike at Illyth. Of course, there was Elana, who knew people who had the skill, and who might be sufficiently ruthless to order Illyth's abduction.

It didn't make sense. As far as he knew, no mage he'd ever heard of might be a shade. That left the other possibility, that some wizard hostile to him had learned how to make shadow-simulacra.

The Sarkonagael: Secrets of the Shadewrights.

He'd delivered it to Elana, allowed her to reveal her true identity, and then refused her. She might not be a wizard herself, but Yu Wei was in her employ, along with others perhaps. Could Elana have ordered Jack's elimination by means of a spell from the book he'd stolen for her?

"Damn," he muttered. "I'm going to have to track her down, and I'll have to find out if she is really behind this or not."

"Track who down, Jack?" asked Ontrodes.

"Noble Ontrodes, I hesitate to say more lest I endanger you as well," Jack replied. "You are better off ignorant of my affairs."

"That's hardly fair. Knowledge is my livelihood, and you certainly owe me an explanation. When can I learn more?" the sage demanded.

Jack stood suddenly and drained the rest of his brandy. His head reeled pleasantly, despite the fact he'd had only a swallow. "Strong stuff, indeed," Jack said. "With luck, I may be able to explain more in a day or three. But first, I have a shadow to catch." He let himself out into the night and stood outside Ontrodes's ruined tower, thinking about where to spend the night.

Rooming with Ontrodes was clearly out. The sage had

formerly commanded room to spare in his tower, but that was clearly no longer an option. Jack was hesitant to return to his apartment. Fortunately, he'd made plans for an emergency of this nature. Despite the late hour, he retraced his steps westwards on Riverview to Sindle, cut north one block to Thavverdasz, and followed the road to the point across from the Ladyrock. There he hired a boatman waiting on late fares to ferry him over to the island-neighborhood for the exorbitant price of two silver talons. After a short scull of perhaps two hundred yards, he climbed out of the ferry onto the wharves of the Ladyrock in the middle of the river mouth.

Several months ago Jack had discovered that one of the smugglers living on the island was dead, and that no one else was likely to know that he was dead, and that no one in particular was likely even to miss the departed. He left a cottage of three rooms, sited very near a small paper mill that created a perpetual miasma of stench in this portion of the islet. The cottage itself was not in particularly good condition, with walls that didn't run true and a roof covered in wooden shakes that curled up at the edges like dried old leaves, admitting an unfortunate amount of weather and vermin into the place, but it was otherwise a good place for Jack Ravenwild to drop out of sight for a time. He made up the bed, trying not to pay attention to the heavy scent of mildew from the straw-stuffed mattress, and built a small fire in the hearth to warm the place and dry it out a bit. Then he stretched out on the damp, cold pallet and drifted off to blissful sleep.

The next day, the beginning of Tarsakh, was windy and bright, although the cool, damp air of spring still left an unpleasant chill in the shade. Jack stocked his new residence with nonperishable hardtack, dried sausage, cheeses, and jerky, just in case he might have to stay out of sight for a few days. Then he dressed as an adventuring swordsman in a shirt of fine mail and spent most of the afternoon making inquiries across the city regarding the whereabouts of a short, wiry fellow dressed in black with an impudent manner and a marked predilection toward chaos, mayhem, and murder. He spoke to innkeepers by the score, tavernmasters restaurateurs, fences and (carefully) city watchmen, harlots, strumpets and fishwives. He soon discovered that while a person answering to that general description had been seen in half a dozen places throughout the city, no one knew the dastard's whereabouts. So Jack's investigations were checked for the day. As the sun vanished behind the late afternoon fog banks rolling in from the Inner Sea, he returned to the Ladyrock in order to prepare for the Green Lord's banquet.

"I will surely apprehend that villainous duplicate, that duplicitous villain, at my earliest convenience tomorrow," he muttered angrily, dressing for the Game. "I simply have more important business to attend at the moment than dealing with the likes of him. The charming Lady Illyth awaits, and I cannot disappoint her."

He caught the public ferry departing the isle a half hour before sunset and hired a carriage on the Bitterstone wharves to take him out to Woodenhall. The six-mile trip was becoming quite familiar by now, and Jack had long since tired of watching the scenery. Still, he bounced out of the coach with a lively step and donned his most charming grin when they arrived at the manor to pick up Illyth for the evening.

"My dear Illyth!" he cried. "I presume no uncouth blackguards have troubled you today?"

Illyth climbed up into the coach, taking Jack's hand, and settled in the plush seat. She was dressed in a beautiful dress of green brocade, trimmed with white lace at collar and cuff.

"Your ill-mannered twin hasn't shown himself in three days," she said. Then she reached behind her back and drew out a slender wand of dark wood, tipped with burnished brass. "But, just in case, Father bought me a wand charged with a dozen lightning spells. I hope the rascal shows himself again!"

"I didn't know you had any talent for wizardry, my dear." The coach rolled off across the cobblestones and into the humid night.

"Very little, I'm afraid, but I know enough to discharge this wand. There are a couple of elm trees in the woods behind our house that are somewhat the worse for my practicing." Illyth returned the device to whatever hidden pocket she'd removed it from and then turned her dark, serious gaze on the rogue. "So, what have you been up to for the last three days, Jack? Have you learned anything more about the shadow, or the doings of Tiger and Mantis?"

Jack shrugged, choosing his words with care. "A fruitless investigation into the nature of my enemy," he said, which was not entirely untrue. "I didn't learn much." He cobbled together a largely fictional account of the last several days, emphasizing the frustrating and hopeless search for his shadow-copy. It was not his best work, but Illyth skeptically accepted it, until the coach clattered up to the Raven's Glory. "Excellent!" said Jack. "And look, we are here."

The Green Lord's banquet was to take place in the pretentious restaurant, ballroom, and tavern known as the Raven's Glory. Three stories high, the establishment had been rented out in its entirety to the Game of Masks for the evening, no doubt enriching the fat coffers of the equally fat Veldarno Khalabari even more than hundreds of patrons engaged in a wild evening of expensive dinners, free-flowing wine, and festive dancing would have done. Jack and Illyth were helped down from the coach at the front door of the banquet hall by two manservants in pristine livery and walked inside to robe for the Game.

Masked as Lord Fox and Lady Crane, they moved on into the great room. The floor was crowded with several dozen Game-goers in their magical masks, a splendid sight. The proprietor Khalabari, short and sweaty, dashed from place to place like a lump of butter on a hot skillet, hardly tending to one task before another caught his attention and whisked him away in a flutter of unctuous courtesy.

Jack and Illyth climbed up to the balcony overlooking the dance floor, keeping their eyes open for Tiger and Mantis. The conspirators had not yet made their appearance, which unnerved Jack greatly. If the two plotters simply didn't show, he would have no way to find out whether they were surprised to see Illyth and him together at the revel. Beyond that, he lacked any more sophisticated plan.

"I am afraid that I am considering this whole affair to the point of distraction," he said aloud.

"Murder? Kidnapping? Impersonators and shadow wizards?" Illyth shook her head. "Jack, I do not see how you can possibly give the matter too much attention. What shall we do when Mantis and Tiger show up?"

Jack thought on that for a moment. "They've been careful to cover their identities so far. What if we simply unmask them and discover who they are?"

"We would be disqualified at once," Illyth pointed out.

"Perhaps we could lure one or both somewhere out of sight, where we could quickly identify our antagonist without revealing our own identities?"

"All we might do is start a scuffle, in which we are as likely to be unmasked as they. And if Tiger and Mantis report that we have unmasked them, we might be disqualified anyway."

"Why, then it should be their word against ours, and that rarely carries the day in any dispute," Jack replied.

"You mean we would blatantly deny having anything to do with them?" Illyth seemed honestly repelled by the idea.

"Correct, my dear. Besides, I may have a trick or two to ensure that no scuffle ensues." Jack scanned the crowd again but did not spy the familiar masks. "I see no sign of them yet. Do you perchance have your Game journal with you?"

"Yes, but playing the Game—"

"—is exactly what we came here to do, dear Illyth." Jack took her by the elbow and steered her toward the buffet table. "So, what do we still need to learn?"

Illyth showed him the book, holding it close so that no one nearby could easily see its contents. She'd recorded each clue they had actually seen in one section, and then the clues they'd traded through hearsay a little farther on. In the last part, she'd carefully drawn a large table across two pages, showing by each title the kingdoms and names. With a charcoal pencil she'd filled in the information they knew, and the information they suspected. "We need a number of clues yet," she said. "I fear we've fallen too far behind by missing the Yellow Lord's tournament."

"Shall we attempt to garner more clues, then?" Jack asked.

Illyth reluctantly nodded, looking about for any sign of Tiger or Mantis. "I suppose so. We—oh, wait. What's this?"

With a sudden fanfare on the ballroom floor below, a pair of coronets sounded. Randall Morran, the chief game judge, cleared a small circle in the center of the dance floor. "Ladies and gentlemen! A contestant chooses to attempt the solution of the Riddle of the Seven Faceless Lords!"

"Oh, dear," said Illyth. "We're too late!"

"Not necessarily. Be ready to write down the answer given; if it is wrong, we may learn a clue through elimination," observed Jack.

On the floor below, a stout lady with a goldfishlike mask stepped forward, escorted by a tall gentleman with the noble features of a lion. "Attend, please, the Lady Carp and Lord Lion!" the Master Crafter called.

Lady Carp turned and curtsied to the waiting assemblage. She withdrew from her sleeve a slip of paper, examined it for a moment, and then began to read: "Here is my solution," she said. "The Red Lord is Buriz, his kingdom Pentar. The Orange Lord is Fatim, his kingdom Quarra. The Yellow Lord is Dubhil of Trile. The Green Lord is Alcantar of Unen. The Blue Lord is Erizum of Dues. The Purple Lord is Geciras of Septun. And the Black Lord is Carad of Hexan. Is it solved?"

Randall Morran made a great show of consulting a small parchment sealed in a ribbon-wrapped envelope, standing clear of any observers. He allowed the wait to become deliciously long, and then shook his head. "Alas, Lady Carp, your solution is incorrect in four particulars. A noble effort, but not enough to win."

The Green Lord strode up beside the Master Crafter and stood before Lady Carp, silent and tall. He pointed at Carp and Lion solemnly, and then drew his finger across his throat ceremonially.

Morran bowed and said, "For your failure, the Green Lord condemns you to death. You may unmask and remain to enjoy the festivities if you wish, or you may depart and retain your anonymity."

Lady Carp sighed. "Oh, it's a silly game anyway." She

drew off her mask. Jack didn't recognize her, or her escort, an older gentleman with a white goatee. "Better luck to the next!" she called to the crowd, and then she and her date departed to the polite applause of the crowd.

"Did you record her solution?" Jack asked Illyth.

"Yes, but we don't know which part was wrong. Which four parts, in fact."

"True, but look here—her solution for the Orange Lord matches our own, which we have confirmed completely with real clues. Therefore, the four errors in her solution must lie elsewhere." Jack grinned. "I think that we can use her solution in its entirety as the basis for our own, simply asking ourselves for each item: was Lady Carp right or wrong? Then we examine our own evidence item by item to see if we can confirm or refute her solution. We will be left with a small number of yes-or-no guesses with which we can attempt the solution."

"Clearly, Lady Carp guessed on at least four points, probably more, and got them wrong," Illyth said.

"Yes, but I promise you that someone else will attempt that very strategy later in this session," Jack said. "I doubt that we have the luxury of solving the puzzle in its entirety. Someone will narrow the solution down to a few guesses and hope they get lucky in the interest of solving it first."

Illyth frowned. "I prefer a more deliberate solution."

"Faint heart never won fair lady or the Game of Masks," Jack said. He studied the crowd below one more time and straightened. "Or caught a conspirator. Look, there's Tiger now."

"What do we do now?"

"Stay with me, and follow my lead," he told her.

Jack glided across the room and down the wide stairway, moving casually to intersect Lord Tiger. Illyth hesitated, mustering the courage to follow, then hurried after him. Jack caught the tall lord just as the fellow reached the foot of the stair and deliberately stepped in front of him, halting his progress.

"Hold a moment, my lord. I would like to have a word with you."

Tiger studied him, his feral eyes gleaming in his predatory mask. "To what end?" he snarled.

"You know as well as I," Jack ventured. The lord hesitated, perhaps trying to gauge the depth of Jack's confidence. The rogue decided to set the hook. "It pertains to your conversation with Lady Mantis."

Now the conspirator guarded his response. "What do you think you heard?"

Jack glanced at the surrounding revelers. "Shall we discuss it here, or should we adjourn to one of the private chambers upstairs?"

Behind the mask, Lord Tiger seemed to glower. "Very well, then," he spat.

Without waiting, he pushed past Jack and hurried up the staircase, past the dining hall on the second floor to the quiet, dark reaches of the uppermost floor. Here, Veldarno Khalabari had created a dozen small rooms for private dining and other entertainments secluded from the revelry below. Few Game participants were on this floor at the moment, although as the evening grew old a number would doubtless avail themselves of the facilities rather than endure a long, cold carriage ride home. Tiger went to the first open room and stepped inside, turning warily to keep an eye on Jack and Illyth.

"Speak your piece and be quick about it," the lord snapped.

"Your hostility is unbecoming, sir," said Jack. He advanced into the room, Illyth a step behind him. Lord Tiger folded his arms across his broad chest and glared at him. "In particular, I found my shadow-double to be a particularly obnoxious assailant. I believe you owe the lady an apology for the liberties it attempted to take with her person."

Tiger looked from Jack to Illyth, his anger fading into a sullen glower. "What in Cyric's screaming hells are you talking about?"

Jack waved his hand. "You lie poorly, sir. We survived your assassin's attack. Now explain to us why you sent him, or we shall have no choice but to remand the entire matter into the hands of the proper authorities." Behind his back, he tapped Illyth's waist; the noblewoman picked up on her cue at once and moved a step, separating herself from Jack and dividing Tiger's attention.

"I do not have to answer to your delusions," Tiger snapped. "You threaten to expose me? Fine. I call your bluff. You are nothing to me, but if you continue to pester me, you will be eliminated from the Game and more. Do you understand me?"

Illyth took another step and then said something that shocked even Jack. "Lord Tiger, you should answer to my companion. Otherwise I shall have to arrange for the Watch to receive evidence implicating you in a conspiracy to commit murder under the cover of the Game. You remain free only on my sufferance."

Tiger wheeled on her. "Evidence? What evidence?"

"If we told you, you might be tempted to rash actions and desperate measures," Jack replied, stepping in to cover Illyth. "Rest assured that it is completely incriminating."

"If that is the case, why are you speaking to me?" Tiger said after a moment's pause. "A bluff, then. You know nothing, just as I thought." He drew himself up and strode to the door, shouldering Jack out of the way and turning his back on Illyth.

In that moment, Illyth reached out and snatched his

mask from his head. The Tiger illusion vanished; the man whirled in rage, reaching for the sword at his side. He was young and dark complected, with a scalp shaved down almost to stubble and fierce bright eyes.

"Damn you! Give me that!"

Jack seized the light slip of cloth from Illyth's hands and hurled it over Tiger's shoulder. It cleared the railing and fluttered down to the dance floor below. "Careful, Lord Tiger! You seem to have lost your mask."

The man started after the mask and watched it fall. He turned a venomous glare at Jack. "If you think that trick will spare you—" he began.

"Of course it will!" Reaching for Illyth's hand, Jack worked the transport spell and blinked them both across the hall to a dark stairwell across the ballroom. He turned and looked back; Lord Tiger was casting about for them furiously, a glint of steel in his hand. Jack grinned and kissed Illyth on the cheek. "Well done, dear Illyth! Perchance did you recognize him?"

The noblewoman still seemed amazed by the turn of events. "I think so," she said slowly. "A merchant's lieutenant named Toseiyn Dulkrauth, of the Storm Dragon House, I think. You realize that we have made an enemy of him now?"

"Yes," laughed Jack, "but now we know who our enemies are!" He tried to ignore the way Illyth's silence seemed to speak louder than his own bravado.

CHAPTER TEN

Of course, unmasking Toseiyn Dulkrauth didn't really prove anything about the shadow Jack. Even if he was satisfied that Mantis and Tiger were not responsible for the appearance of the shadow, Jack had only eliminated one possibility. Jack gave up and returned his attention to Illyth, the Game, and the discomfited Toseiyn Dulkrauth, watching warily to make sure that Lord Tiger did not find an opportunity to slip up behind him and put a dagger in his back when no one was looking.

As the Green Lord's banquet came to a close, Jack returned Illyth to her manor and warned the servants there to be on guard for someone answering to his own exact description. "And you be careful as well," he told Illyth. "I am not the sort of person checked by a single failure, and it may be that my evil twin is similarly persistent. He may try to carry you off again."

"Don't worry about me," said Illyth. "The house guards are aware of the imposter now. They won't let someone who looks like you get anywhere near me." She laughed. "It wouldn't surprise me if my father had ordered the guards to shoot you on sight or something like that. I'd better check into it."

"Please do," Jack agreed. He climbed back into his coach and signaled the driver. The man flicked the reins with a small sound of encouragement, and the coach rattled away from the manor house. Jack settled in for the long ride, thinking furiously about Dulkrauth's hidden agenda and secret goals. "Some Game," he remarked, considering the situation. "Murder, conspiracy, kidnappings, and all the brightest of Raven's Bluff socialites and sycophants to weigh as suspects."

"Did you say something, sir?" the coachman called from above.

"Do you know where the Cracked Tankard lies?"

"I do, sir, although I advise against it. A person of your station would find the place squalid and coarse, filled with lowborn ruffians plotting robbery, murder, and worse."

"The very place!" Jack smiled, even though the driver could not see him. "Take me there at once!"

The hour was now growing late, and the Tankard was filled with local merchants, laborers, and clerks who preferred to take advantage of the tavern's comforts over those of their own homes. Several huge roasts sizzled invitingly over the fire, and Jack comfortably settled himself in his usual place. Briesa had the night off, but Jack flirted with another of the barmaids and won himself an unusually large helping of beef. He had barely started on his dinner when a large boot came down in the middle of his chest and rocked him back on his chair, pinning him against the wall.

"Hello, Jack," said Zandria. She held a dangerous-looking wand in his face. "I've been looking all over for you."

Now I remember, Jack said to himself. The Cracked Tankard is the place I come to when I want people to find me, interrupt my dinner, and threaten me with violence. "I need to find a new tavern to frequent," he muttered. He looked up at Zandria. The mage looked moderately charred, with black holes eaten in her leather jacket and an extremely close haircut, as if she'd angrily hacked off hair too singed to save. "Dear Zandria, is this uncomfortable approach absolutely necessary?"

"Where are the ring and the dagger, Jack?" the mage replied. "I found the Tomb's riches; I fought a deep dragon to keep them; I lost comrades and friends in doing so. I have no patience whatsoever for your petty larceny. You stole prizes that I worked very hard to acquire, and I want them back."

"You chased off the dragon? Excellent! When and where shall we meet to count out my two-elevenths share of the loot?"

"Your impudence was tiresome the first time you crossed my path, you sniveling little worm," Zandria snapped. "How *dare* you bring up such a matter, when you abandoned the field and left my company to stand alone against that monster?"

Jack shoved Zandria's boot from his chest and stood up as quickly as the blink of an eye, jamming one finger at her. "How dare you bring up the circumstances under which I departed the fight, when you went out of your way to make sure I would not show up in the first place! We had a deal, Zandria, and you broke it before I did!"

"You insinuated yourself into my company! I didn't ask you to eavesdrop on my conversation with Ontrodes, I didn't ask you to illicitly copy my notes, and I most specifically *did not ask for your help!*"

"But you accepted my aid when I had something useful for you, by which I refer to the solution to the Guilder's riddle. You would not have found the tomb at all if it hadn't been for my interference, and you sought to reward me by cutting me out of my agreed-on share. So who's the thief here, dear Zandria?"

The mage's eyes burned dangerously. "Choose your words carefully, Jack Ravenwild. You are an instant away from annihilation."

Jack deliberately turned away from her to straighten his chair and took his seat again. He drank one sip from his mug and wiped his hand across his mouth. "Very well. Sit down, dear Zandria, and we'll examine the situation rationally. Both parties have claims and both have damages, so let us try to find a compromise that suits the situation."

"I have no interest in negotiating with you. Give me what is mine, and count yourself lucky that you walk away in the shape you were born to."

"I have always responded poorly to threats. In this case, I will make an exception. We have the Guilder's hoard; I want my two-elevenths. And, aside from the hoard, we have the Orb of Khundrukar—presumably in your possession—which I also was promised a two-elevenths stake in."

"I made no such promise!"

"Examine our contract, Zandria. The wording runs something to the effect of 'all items and treasures discovered in the Guilder's Tomb and any other regions jointly explored.' The Orb is certainly included in that." Jack fished around in his coat pocket and found a small pipe. He rarely indulged in pipeweed, but this seemed like an appropriate occasion. He tamped leaf into the pipe and lit it with a minor magic. "I would be willing to forfeit my two shares if you will forfeit your claim to the Orb."

"Impossible," Zandria said. "The Orb is not subject to discussion."

"If we remanded this matter to the local courts, I am certain they would uphold my claims on two-elevenths of the treasure, and they would assign me two-elevenths ownership of the Orb." Jack puffed on the pipe a moment.

"However, I have no particular wish to engage in an ugly legal battle with such a dear comrade as you. I would prefer a more informal and mutually satisfactory arrangement."

The mage glared at him for a long moment, thinking hard. Then she shoved her wand back into a holster at her hip and drew up the chair opposite Jack's. "I'll see to it you receive your two shares of the hoard. You give me the magical items you stole. You are bound by that contract, too, and I have a nine-elevenths ownership of the ring and the dagger. Does that meet your requirements?"

Magical items? Clearly, Zandria believed that the ring and the dagger were enchanted, which meant that they were more than mere baubles to be pawned at the first opportunity. In fact, magic rings had a reputation for potentially concealing extraordinary powers. Jack had thought that the gems and coins he'd stuffed into his pockets were the prize for his efforts in Sarbreen, a few hundred crowns of loot quickly converted into cash. But if he had a magic ring and an enchanted dagger in his possession, he might have scored far better than he'd thought.

Of course, there was no point in acknowledging this to Zandria. Jack carefully controlled his reaction and frowned studiously. "I accept two shares for the two items for the sake of argument, as long as we add the value of the ring and dagger to the hoard before calculating my cut, but the Lady Mayor's advertised reward for your Orb is ten thousand gold crowns and a noble title. What value shall we place on that?"

"We cannot split a noble title," Zandria said slowly, as if explaining weighty matters to a child.

Jack smoked and nodded thoughtfully. "I propose this: we place eleven marbles into a bag, two black, nine white. We shake up the bag and hand it to an impartial stranger, asking him to draw one marble from the bag without looking. If he draws a black marble, I win the entire reward due the finder of the Orb. If he draws a white marble, you win."

"I will not settle this question by gambling! Who knows how you might fix such a game?"

"We seem to be stuck," Jack remarked. "Clearly, you want the title. I will settle for cash. I'll give you ring and dagger for two-elevenths of the hoard (including the value of ring and dagger!) You give me the ten thousand crowns for the Orb's reward and keep the title."

The mage winced, but nodded. "Done. Now give me the ring."

"Not so fast," said Jack.

It was a shame to give up a chance at the noble title, but frankly, he preferred cash in hand, and he had too much on his mind to do a proper job of holding the Red Wizard over the barrel. Beside, he had no idea what Zandria might do if he made it too hard for her to deal honestly with him. He looked at Zandria and studied her for a moment, making a great show of thinking things through carefully and slowly.

"While I have no real idea of the value of those two items, your intense interest in them would seem to indicate that they are quite valuable indeed. Therefore, I will hold the ring and the dagger as security against my cut of the treasure and ten thousand gold crowns. I will redeem them when you make good on my agreed-upon share of the loot."

"Security?" asked Zandria incredulously. "Your impudence is beyond compare! I should incinerate you where you sit, and take both ring and dagger from your smoldering corpse!"

"You might do that, of course, but you would be disappointed. You see, dear Zandria, I do not have either ring or dagger on my person at the moment." That, of course, was a bald-faced lie; the ring nestled in Jack's vest pocket, while the dagger was tucked into his left boot. "Why don't we plan on meeting here again in, say, two days? That will give you time to turn in the Orb and collect the reward. Do you agree?"

The mage rolled her eyes, but nodded. "Fine. I agree."

"Excellent! Then let us share a drink to commemorate the agreement."

Jack signaled the waitress, but Zandria waved her hand in disgust. "I have no interest in toasting your health, Jack Ravenwild. I will assemble the money you require. Be warned: if you fail to produce the ring and the dagger, I will not entertain any further negotiations. I shall simply kill you on the spot regardless of repercussions or arrangements. I admit that may cause me some small trouble, which is why I did not end your life tonight, but you will be a smoking corpse, Jack, dead as every slaying-spell at my command can make you. Do not try my patience again."

The Red Wizard stood and turned on her heel, marching out of the room with her fury blazing like a brand in the night. Longshoremen and teamsters twice her size caught one glance of the expression on her face and fell over themselves trying to get out of her path. Jack raised his goblet to her back and smiled.

"Your health!" he called. "I shall see you in two days!"

Jack lingered another hour at the Tankard, enjoying the sense of security engendered by passing time in a room crowded with familiar faces while he planned his next move. Zandria had given him much to think about; he fished the ring out of his pocket and examined it again. It was a single piece of smooth gray stone flecked with red, quite handsome in its own way, although not particularly valuable at first glance. He whispered a few words and worked a minor magic to detect whether or not it was enchanted, and blinked in surprise—the stone ring radiated magical power to any who could sense such things!

"Perhaps you might be worth keeping after all," Jack said. He slid the ring back into his pocket.

The next Game event was three days off. Before then, Jack decided he had three things he needed to do. First, he needed to find his shadow double and take whatever steps were necessary to stop the fiend and discover its origins. Second, he needed to plan a safe and equitable exchange (or a shameless confidence game) to obtain the thousands of gold crowns that were rightfully his. And last, but certainly not least, he needed to stay out of the sight of the various parties who meant him ill, including but not limited to Iphegor the Black, Marcus and Ashwillow, Morgath and Saerk, Tiger and Mantis, and possibly the Warlord Myrkyssa Jelan.

"It is probably a bad sign when one's enemies significantly outnumber one's friends," Jack said sadly.

He drained the last of his wine and stood up to leave. Jack was so distracted by the plots at hand that he almost walked right out of the Tankard's front entrance with no regard for who or what might be watching. He paused in the rickety swinging door by the taproom's mossy walls and ducked back inside at once, cursing his carelessness.

"Having just discovered considerable wealth on my own person, it would be unwise to stumble into my enemies' hands again," he told himself.

Instead, he made himself invisible and used the spell of shadow-jumping to whisk himself to an empty rooftop he knew of three blocks away. The tactic seemed to work;

he was not followed or accosted on his way to the Lady-rock. By the time he reached the hovel by the paper mill, midnight was hours past.

Jack passed the rest of the evening in a restless, vermin-pestered slumber. He eventually dozed off until well after noon on the following day, when he was awakened by a gang of neighborhood children engaged in a game of throwing stones through the rotting shakes of his cottage roof.

Jack groggily chased off the ragamuffins, ate a cold breakfast of old bread and hard cheese, and considered his schemes and designs. "My appointment with Zandria is not until tomorrow evening, leaving me a day, a night, and a day to occupy myself," he observed to an attentive cockroach who shared his quarters. "I should keep an eye on Zandria to make sure that she doesn't forget the terms of our bargain again. I should take steps to ascertain the current whereabouts of my accursed shadow. And I should also seek to unravel whatever plot Toseiyn Dulkrauth, the esteemed Lord Tiger, is up to. What to do first?"

None of the vermin infesting the premises offered any suggestions. In fact, they were so unhelpful that Jack resolved to spend the rest of the afternoon improving his conditions by effecting what minor repairs he could to the cottage and using various noxious magics to render his domicile unappetizing to rats, mice, insects, and their ilk. This involved the theft of quite a large amount of timber, straw, tools, and plaster from various businesses nearby, which Jack accomplished without any real challenge. With that attended to, he pilfered several days of food-stuffs and other supplies to see him through the week.

Finally, when he had rendered the cottage as tolerable as he could make it, Jack decided that it was worth a few hours of his time to learn more about the ring and the blade he'd stolen from the Guilder's Vault. He took both objects out and set them on the battered wooden table before the hearth. Then he slowly and methodically worked out a spell of identification, an enchantment that could analyze and decipher the spells folded into the very being of the ring and the dagger.

The dagger, he learned, was a highly enchanted weapon wrought with spells of secrecy and silence, the perfect blade for dark deeds and backstabbings in shadowed alleyways. It seemed well suited for his hand, a blade made for a rogue such as he. It also possessed the very curious property of retaining its enchantment in places where other magics failed.

"Potentially useful," Jack admitted, "but I cannot guess why I would willingly go into such an environment." He shrugged and returned the dark blade to his boot.

The ring, on the other hand, was a device whose maker cared little for subtlety. It was a manifestation of the power of stone and earth, fused with potent magics allowing one to command elementals or even the earth itself to do one's bidding. Passages might be opened where none existed before, walls raised or torn down at will. The user might even call upon the ring's power to imbue himself with the strength and toughness of stone itself.

"Very useful," Jack grinned. "Defense, offense, transport, and general utility all incorporated in one superbly wrought dwarven ring. I can see why Zandria lusts after you, my little prize."

Since he was loath to part with either device, Jack decided that he would have to strike a different bargain with Zandria. He'd keep the ring and the dagger as his two-elevenths of the hoard proper, leaving him with the ten thousand gold crowns associated with the reward for the return of the Orb. The gold was certainly sufficient to his means for the moment, and with the magic of the

Guilder's artifacts, he could easily steal more anytime he liked.

"The only trouble lies in persuading Zandria to accept a renegotiated deal," he said aloud. "She probably cares little for the gold itself, and is far more interested in acquiring the magic in my possession; Red Wizards are like that. It might be useful to make sure that Anders and Tharzon are nearby, in case she is unusually resistant to the notion."

Without further delay, Jack departed the Ladyrock and set off in search of Anders and Tharzon. Both Northman and dwarf hadn't seen much reward for their labors in Sarbreen, so an opportunity to enjoy a cut should be welcomed by both. He decided to call on Anders first, taking the ferry over to Bitterstone and then heading north into the Temple District. The streets were crowded with workers heading home after a long day's labor, women scurrying out to purchase something for the stew pot, and gaily dressed rakes and ladies beginning the night's revelry a little early. Jack liked crowds; they provided him with a comfortable anonymity and plenty of opportunities.

He followed Blacktree Boulevard all the way through Holyhouses and Gowntown to the Market District. Anders rented a small room in the shadow of Purtil's Tower, a ramshackle structure of stone and rusted iron that comprised the city's oldest water tower. Jack turned east on Broken Bit Lane and then north again into the narrow alleyway winding almost beneath the dilapidated columns of the water tower. He crossed a small, sodden courtyard strewn with garbage and climbed up the wooden staircase that zigzagged across the back of Anders's building. The Northman lived in a very modest room on the uppermost floor.

He had just set his foot on the topmost stair when the deluge struck. From the water tower's flank fifty feet above, a great torrent abruptly broke loose. Metal groaned and stone creaked ominously as tons and tons of water poured out of the torn side of the tower and fell atop the boarding house where Anders lived. Jack was washed back down the stairway, striking step after step until he caught himself halfway down and found his feet again.

"Catastrophe! Calamity!" he cried in astonishment. "What now?"

As if in response to his question, the roof of Anders's building gave way beneath the weight of water falling from the tower overhead. Jack recalled that it was not much of a roof in any event, a frail structure of wooden shakes that admitted freezing drafts in wintertime and clouds of noxious insects in warm weather. The cascade of water continued from the breached tower, filling the upper floor faster than it drained away to the floors below.

The entire building groaned horribly. Inside, beams cracked beneath the watery assault, and the boarding house started to *lean* noticeably to Jack's right. The rogue hurried down the stairs and dashed out into the open courtyard to get clear of the failing structure. Rivulets of water ran past his feet.

"Anders!" cried Jack. "If you can hear me, run for your life!"

At that moment the Northman's door on the uppermost floor burst open, revealing the tall warrior. Anders Aricssen was soaked to the skin, and a torrent of water followed him out of the doorway. He was burdened with a double armful of whatever possessions he'd managed to gather up. Without ceremony Anders hurled his valuables from the porch. Then he caught sight of Jack in the courtyard below.

"You fiend!" he shouted. "You backstabbing, underhanded wretch! You whelp of a she-goat and a goblin! If I—"

The Northman was interrupted by watery disaster. The boarding house sagged over entirely on its side in a rumble of falling timber and a gush of water from every window. The wooden stairs collapsed like matchsticks, leaving Anders comically suspended in midair for one brief instant before joining the general ruin of his home. A wave of water half a hand high washed over Jack's feet where he stood, rooted to the spot in amazement. The torrent pouring out of Purtil's Tower slowed to a stream, then a drizzle, and finally a drip.

Jack looked up, craning his head to study the side of the water tower. Dozens of neighbors and passersby stood gawking at the scene, just as he was, but atop the tower he caught sight of a familiar black-clad figure—his shadow!

"It seems my twin has a great liking for mischief," Jack muttered.

The dark figure leered down at the ruined building, white teeth flashing in a fierce grin, and then vanished from sight. Jack sighed and doffed his cap, wringing water from it. Jack approached the sodden wreckage of Anders's house carefully, looking for any sign of the Northman.

Anders was pinned under a tangle of heavy wooden beams that should have killed him outright, but some fluke of chance had left him mostly unharmed from the building's collapse. Battered, bruised, and dazed, the Northman stared up into the sky, speechless.

"Good Anders, are you all right?" Jack said, picking up a board and heaving it aside. "Can you speak?"

"When I can stand," Anders said from beneath the rubble, "I mean to rend you limb from limb."

Jack paused in his efforts to extricate his friend, and surreptitiously rearranged the wreckage to hinder Anders if he suddenly tried to get up. "What offense have I given you?" Jack said slowly, although a terrible suspicion was forming in his heart.

"What offense have you given me? *What offense?* You have ruined my house and inundated my belongings! You came within a whisker of killing me! *What offense have you given me?*" Anders howled in rage and struggled to find his feet again, shrugging off hundred-pound timbers like matchsticks. "I am going to tear off your arms and beat you to death with them, O very prince of dung beetles!"

Jack backed away cautiously. "Anders, I should take this opportunity to advise you that I have been illicitly copied. For the last three days, a dark and sinister copy of me has been prowling the city, causing all kinds of mischief. I am afraid that the scoundrel has wrought the destruction of your house. I had nothing to do with it."

"You don't recall taunting me not ten minutes ago? Calling me an unwashed barbarian and promising me a bath? Twisting my nipple and pulling my beard?" With each exclamation the Northman heaved another board out of the way, drawing closer to freedom. "I take great pride in my personal hygiene, Jack. I swim every day. I am hardly unwashed, and *I did not need a bath!*" Anders staggered to his feet, bruised and bleeding, eyes burning like coals.

"Anders," said Jack, "how am I dressed?"

The Northman kicked a broken step out of his way and closed on Jack. In fact, Jack was dressed handsomely in red and yellow, with a plumed cap and a blue velvet waistcoat. Anders halted, squinting at the rogue.

"Ten minutes ago you wore gray and black. When did you change?"

"As I said, I am plagued by a duplicitous doppelganger who delights in harrying my friends. Two days past he pulled down Ontrodes's tower. Today he visited you. Believe me, the minor inconvenience you have suffered in the loss of your home and the destruction of your personal property is nothing compared to the lasting damage the villain has inflicted on my good name and honorable reputation."

"If this is some kind of trick—" Anders growled.

"Anders, would I stand here before you and tell you a story of such an outlandish nature if it were not strictly true?"

The Northman glowered. "I suppose you are going to tell me that you had nothing to do with the fire started in the Smoke Wyrm yesterday by someone answering to your exact description? Or the shameful fashion in which noble Tharzon's beard was dipped in flammable wax first, so that he ran down the street with his head on fire until he managed to smother the flames by plunging his face into a filthy mud puddle in the middle of Manycoins Way?"

"Tyr's eyes! My deceitful shadow did that?" Jack swallowed nervously. Tharzon would simply kill him on sight; there was no way he could ever stumble across the dwarf again, explanation or no explanation. "The dastard!"

"Not only that, but you—your shadow, I guess—hired seven street mimes to ape poor Tharzon's flight and extinguishment directly afterward, thus shaming the poor fellow seven times over in front of hundreds of passersby on the busiest street in the Market District." Anders raised an admonishing finger. "That was ill done."

"Street mimes?" Jack fought hard, very hard, to keep a straight face, despite a twitching of his lips and a snigger in his voice. He could see them blundering down the street, beating at their heads, only to fling themselves into the nearest pile of ordure— "I tell you, friend Anders, not in a thousand years could I have imagined such a base deed. I am responsible for neither Tharzon's scorching nor your drenching!"

"I believe you—for the moment, but if I should ever learn otherwise . . ." Anders held Jack's gaze for a long moment, naked anger riveting the rogue to the spot. Then he harrumphed and kicked the wreckage aside. "You'd best find out who is imitating you and bring this to an end, or you won't have a single friend in this entire city!"

Jack glanced skyward, scanning the rooftops. There was no sign of his dark twin, although that did not mean that the villain was not lurking there invisibly.

"I shall henceforward devote my entire existence to the discovery and punishment of this fiend," he promised.

Leaving Anders to the unenviable process of drying what little was left of his material possessions, Jack spent the rest of the evening and all of the following day searching all of his favorite haunts and places, asking people he knew when they'd seen him last.

The barkeep at the Cracked Tankard gave him a strange look and said simply, "Last night. Why do you ask?"

At the Wizard's Guild, the doorman squinted and muttered but admitted he hadn't seen Jack in a week or more. He checked various food stands, alehouses, and taprooms all over the waterfront, to little avail, and he avoided the Smoke Wyrm, because he already knew his shadow had done its work there.

"It would seem," he told himself after hours of wandering the city, "that my shadow twin frequents different establishments than those I favor." Finally he turned his steps toward the Cracked Tankard again, expecting any kind of mischief from the various parties that he'd learned were looking for *him*. The Knights of the Hawk had apparently been asking after him all over the city, along with a mage who might or might not have been

Iphegor, and a pair of thieves who might or might not have been Morgath and Saerk.

"Zandria!" Jack stopped and put his hand to his head. "We are to meet this evening and discuss the division of the loot! I'd forgotten!" And he had no preparations at all for allies to back him up in the event the Red Wizard chose to deal dishonorably. He stepped off the street and onto the covered boardwalk running along Waelstar Way, perching atop a barrel of pickled herring outside a provisioner's shop while he thought. Anders wanted little to do with him, Tharzon he dared not approach, and any other blackguard he could think of was simply much too untrustworthy. Ontrodes was a drunkard, and Illyth a noblewoman—and neither would be much use in dissuading Zandria from treachery if the sorceress were so inclined.

"Elana would be a good accomplice," Jack muttered, "as she is extremely competent and claims to be immune to magic, a handy thing when one is confronting a wizard. It's a shame that she is the Warlord, and her minions are trying to kill me. Otherwise she'd be perfect."

Reluctantly he decided that there was nothing to do but trust in Zandria's honorable nature, so he hopped down from the barrel and continued on his way. She had agreed, after all, to pay him two-elevenths of the treasure plus ten thousand gold crowns of the reward—all told, a sum that must be close to thirty thousand gold pieces. "I could never transport such wealth," Jack thought. "I shall have to arrange for a detail of guards from some reputable counting-house to take custody of the coinage and convert it into more convenient sums later. If I do so, Zandria will see that I mean business and will not easily be cheated. And I can always try to ransom the ring and the knife back from her by offering cash for the articles of interest."

Quickly Jack hurried to the offices of House Albrath and

there contracted for the services of six sturdy armsmen and a secure coach to await his negotiations with Zandria that evening. The cost was exorbitant—more than two hundred gold crowns—but Embro Albrath himself assured Jack that discretion was his watchword. For the deposit and a mere five percent of the value of the transaction, the mustachioed Albrath would see to it that Lord Jaer Kell Wildhame's wealth reached a secure location and that Jack was provided with the means to access his gains or convert them into other currencies at his leisure.

By the time Jack concluded his arrangements with the merchant, the sun was setting over the Inner Sea and the shadows ran long in the city streets. The day's warmth faded rapidly before the onslaught of a cold, damp offshore wind, bringing evening fogs to the city streets and a chilly, cloying mist to those workmen and wayfarers who had not found their suppers yet. Jack wrapped his cloak closer to his body and shivered his way across town again, riding inside his rented coach in the company of the garrulous Embro Albrath while his hired soldiers tramped alongside. He and his procession arrived at the Cracked Tankard an hour after sunset, creating quite a commotion.

"You and your men may wait outside," Jack told the merchant imperiously. "My business should be concluded swiftly."

Embro Albrath—a stout man dressed in red, wearing a sea of golden chains around his neck and a gold ring on each finger—shook his head. "I shall accompany you, my lord," the merchant said. "I have no wish to pass an hour or two in this clammy cold while a friendly fire warms yon taproom."

Jack began to protest but stopped himself. Albrath's presence lent an illusion of credibility to the transaction. He might do well with the moneylender at his side.

"Very well, but I must ask you not to interrupt, no matter what transpires. My affairs are complicated and my partners unreliable."

"I am the very soul of discretion," the merchant promised.

Jack nodded in appreciation and let himself out of the coach. He glanced once more at the six soldiers standing by vigilantly, then ducked inside. Embro Albrath trailed him by a step. The merchant hesitated half a heartbeat when he noted the location in which Jack intended to do his business, but he smiled broadly beneath his mustache as if he approved of the informal setting and said nothing.

The common room of the Cracked Tankard was filled, which was not at all unusual given the time of day. Jack studied the room carefully and saw no sign of Zandria, nor any agents or thugs who might have been in her employ. He caught the barkeep's eye and flashed a couple of silver talents, learning that Zandria awaited in a private dining room in the back of the alehouse.

"Excellent," said Jack. "Let us proceed!"

He bounded up the narrow staircase leading to the private rooms on the upper floor, confident and energetic. Zandria would deal honorably with him; Red Wizards might be prideful and dangerous, but if word got out that a Red Wizard's word was no good, why, the entire organization would suffer immeasurably! In fact, it would be far wiser for the leaders among the Thayan magocracy to sternly advise their lesser brethren to scrupulously honor the letter and spirit of any agreement struck, so that all people everywhere would know that a Red Wizard's word was his bond.

"Zandria is arrogant, condescending, and overbearing," Jack remarked, "but her integrity must be beyond reproach!"

"I beg your pardon?" said Embro Albrath, huffing slightly as he hurried to keep up with Jack's nimble ascent.

"Oh, nothing," Jack replied. "Look, here we are." He stopped at the indicated door, paused to adjust his fine coat and tug at his cuffs, then boldly entered the room.

Zandria sat at one end of a long table set with a modest meal, the swordsman Brunn standing behind her. The warrior's left arm was in a sling, but his face showed nothing but deadly competence and readiness for action. Six heavy wooden coffers lined up against one wall caught Jack's eye immediately; he knew a coin chest when he saw one. The Red Wizard and her champion faced a small, dark figure in a blue waistcoat very similar to Jack's—no, exactly similar to Jack's—and as Jack entered, all three glanced in his direction. The wizard looked sharply at her dinner companion, back to Jack, and to her companion a third time.

"Now *this* I was not expecting," she muttered darkly.

The shadow Jack grinned widely and pointed at Jack, standing in the open door. "And there, Zandria, stands the villainous doppelganger who even now fondles your stone ring and your black dagger in his larcenous pockets. The temerity! The impudence! I beg you, rid me of this accursed copy for the betterment of all mankind!"

Jack stood stock-still in astonishment, gaping at the scene. Behind him Embro Albrath halted in confusion, as Jack now occupied the entirety of the doorway and moved neither forward nor aside to permit the merchant to follow. The gold-chained moneylender craned his head and leaned to the left to peer over Jack's shoulders.

"What is it? Is there something wrong?"

Jack—the real Jack—found his voice, at least in part. He squeaked, "You can speak!"

"I recommend that you place him under a spell of dominion or holding at once," the shadow Jack continued to Zandria. "He is a crafty and cowardly fellow and will flee instantly if you do not restrain him!"

"My lady Zandria," Jack said quickly, "You have been deceived by that miserable wretch who sits at your table. He is a simulacrum of me, possessed of a spirit so malicious and spiteful that every moment you spend in his presence invites unforeseen disaster!"

"I would, of course, say the very same thing if I were a murderous doppelganger attempting to reverse your rightful suspicions back upon the noble personage I had so insidiously copied," the shadow Jack purred. "It is the oldest trick in the book when dealing with an identical copy of oneself."

During this entire exchange Zandria's expression had darkened from amazement to smoldering anger. Her eyes blazed furiously, and her cheeks burned red. "I don't know which one of you speaks the truth, and I don't care," she said, slowly standing and reaching for the wand at her belt, "but one or the other of you had better produce my ring and my dagger this very instant, or there will be hell to pay."

"Alas, fair lady, I cannot. My imposter stole them from me, just as he stole my shape," the shadow said. "Kill the felon and examine his belongings; you'll find the items you desire, concluding our business, and I'll take the gold and refrain from troubling you in the future."

"That's *my* gold!" Jack cried indignantly. "Zandria, I must insist that you remove this viper from the premises at once! Our business cannot proceed until he is no more!"

"Better kill them both, Zandria," Brunn advised in his rumbling voice. "It's the only way to be sure, and you keep ring, dagger, and gold all."

The wizardess pointed her wand at the shadow Jack, then at Jack, and then finally at a point more or less in between from which she might menace either one. She glared at each. They were dressed in the exact same manner, both faces were split by the same insincere mouth and framed with the same stripe of thin beard. In the dim lamplight of the dining room, the shadow Jack was fully substantial and vital, grinning with excitement, alert and alive and animated so convincingly that Jack's own mother would have been hard pressed to tell the difference between the two.

"I think you have the right idea," Zandria said to Brunn. She raised the wand and pointed it at Jack.

"Wait!" cried Jack. "I can prove that I am the authentic Jack, and the other one a work of foulest sorcery!"

"The obvious ploy," the shadow Jack replied. "Do not fall for his desperate manner, dear lady. He seeks to play upon your tender feminine mercies."

"At this point, I don't care which of you is real and which is not," Zandria remarked. "Somebody has my ring. I mean to have it, and whichever of you produces it will be paid appropriately. After that, the two of you can throttle each other to death as far as I'm concerned."

"Do you have the ring the lady refers to?" asked a very nervous Embro Albrath from Jack's left shoulder. "If so, I advise compliance. Continued uncertainty can only result in poor decisions and hasty acts."

Jack scowled deeply. He wanted to work out an arrangement that would allow him to keep the ring; he saw all kinds of possibilities in the device. But as long as his nemesis stood before him, he would never be able to negotiate any kind of deal with Zandria. On the other hand, the six chests along the far wall presumably contained close to thirty thousand gold crowns . . . and that made the prospect of losing his prizes from Sarbreen much less odious. Better the gold at hand, he reasoned, than death at Zandria's hands.

"I came equipped to execute our arrangement in good faith," Jack said loudly. He reached into his pocket and produced the stone ring, then pulled the dagger from his boot, advancing to set them on the table. "Here are the items I recovered from the Guilder's Vault. If you please, I will inspect the coinage now."

"As I told you! He had them all along!" the shadow crowed to Zandria. "The ring and the knife are yours, dear lady. In keeping with our bargain, I will take the gold and go."

"I brought the ring and dagger," Jack retorted. "Your business, dear Zandria, is with me. Ignore this treacherous cur. He offers you nothing but lies!"

Zandria frowned, but sheathed her wand and stepped forward to scoop the two items from the tabletop. She looked at Jack and said, "You've delivered on your end of the bargain; I'll deliver on mine. Take the gold and go." Then she turned to the shadow Jack and said, "Whether you're the authentic Jack Ravenwild or an imitation, your twin produced what I wanted, so I am honoring the deal I made. If you dislike it, take it up with him."

The ingratiating smile fell from the shadow Jack's face, and his eyes grew dark and hard. Without another word he vanished, disappearing in the blink of an eye.

Brunn swore and stepped out into the center of the room, hand on sword hilt. "Blast! What now?"

"Be careful," Jack advised. "My clone knows everything I know. He may be gone, or he may have turned invisible." He moved swiftly to put his back against a wall and scanned the chamber for any hint of a stealthy unseen presence.

"No matter," Zandria scoffed. "My business here is done. Removing the gold is your concern." She dropped the ring and the dagger into the pouch at her belt and secured the cover. "Come, Brunn. We are finished here."

At the wizardess's hip, her dark and dangerous wand gently slipped up and disappeared. Jack saw it just as the magical weapon vanished into someone's invisible grasp. "Zandria!" he gasped in alarm. "Your wand!"

The Red Wizard snatched at the holster on her hip and cursed in Thayan. She whirled, a spell on her lips, but at that moment the shadow Jack appeared with her weapon in his hand and an expression of infernal glee on his face. He pointed her wand right at Zandria and activated the device. Blue flame engulfed Zandria and washed past her to blast a great swath of destruction across the table, the floor, the ceiling, and the far wall. A blast of heat seared the room, and the fiery roar drowned out Jack's very thoughts. The rogue only avoided Zandria's fate by throwing himself to the floor; Embro Albrath survived simply because he backpedaled so swiftly that he fell down on his broad bottom in the doorway.

"Help!" the moneylender called. "Magic! Murder! Betrayal!"

Zandria screamed and staggered back, engulfed in flame. The swordsman Brunn drew his blade so swiftly that Jack didn't even see him do it and struck out at the shadow Jack, but the nimble devil darted back three steps and turned the fiery wand on Zandria's companion, blasting him as well. The room itself was fairly well alight with the second blast, curtains and exposed beams dancing with sheets of flame.

Jack picked himself up and launched a deadly magical attack of his own, a pair of streaking force globes that hammered into the shadow and detonated with brutal force. The shadow flew back into the wall and hit hard, slumping awkwardly to the ground. Zandria's wand clattered from his fingers to the floor. Smoke and fire filled the room, and amid the roaring of the blaze Jack could hear cries of consternation and panic from nearby rooms in the Tankard.

This villain is destroying my favorite tavern! he

thought, then he darted forward, drawing his rapier to finish off his foe.

The shadow scrambled to his feet and returned Jack's spell, blasting Jack off his feet with two hammer blows of magic that caught the rogue at hip and torso. For a moment Jack saw nothing but stars, twisting in agony on the burning floor. Blood ran between his fingers and his entire left leg felt numb. Across the room, the shadow also tried to recover and stand. He levered himself up by the table.

Near Jack, Zandria rose to all fours, hunched in pain. She should have been burned to a crisp, but the blue flames died out swiftly, leaving her scorched but not seriously injured—a spell of protection, Jack guessed. The sorceress straightened up, kneeling, and directed a brilliant bolt of lightning at the other Jack.

"No one steals my wand!" she howled. The thunderclap left Jack's ears ringing and blew a hole the size of a large man through the dining room wall and into the room beyond.

Unfortunately, it missed the shadow Jack, although the stroke of lightning contributed mightily to the impending demise of the Cracked Tankard. The shadow dodged with a quick roll that brought him close to the wizardess, at which point he kicked her in the jaw as hard as he could. Zandria spun in a half circle and dropped to the floor. The contents of her pouch scattered across the uneven planking, odds and ends of spellcasting, coins and gems, and—most significantly—the stone ring, which rolled almost to Jack's hand.

Jack snatched the ring and shoved it onto his finger, invoking its powers. The impervious toughness of stone hardened his skin; the cold, remorseless strength of rock flooded his limbs. He stood and recovered his rapier, advancing on his nemesis.

"Come on, you miserable copycat! Do you dare to face me with steel in your hand?"

The shadow Jack grinned and drew its own sword. "It's what I was made for," he hissed.

He lunged at Jack through the smoke and the flame, the dark steel of his rapier moving faster than a striking serpent. Jack parried the blow with unexpected strength and blocked a surprise attack of the shadow's poignard simply by batting it aside with his hardened hand. Then he returned a murderous thrust right at the center of the shadow's torso.

The shadow Jack attempted to parry, but Jack's rapier punched through the simulacrum's defenses, driven by the strength flooding into him from the ring. In utter astonishment the shadow looked down at Jack's blade, buried in its black heart. "Not . . . fair," the simulacrum gasped. Then the creature discorporated in one swift instant, melting into cold shadows that seemed to sink through crevices and divisions in the wooden floor as if returning to whatever cold hell had birthed it.

"Take that, you fiend," Jack snarled.

He stepped back, watching dark shadowstuff run from the blade of his rapier, then glanced around the room to gauge the damage. Zandria sprawled unconscious on the floor. Brunn had been fairly well incinerated by the full blast of the fire wand. There was no helping him. Of Embro Albrath, there was no sign at all; the stout merchant had fled the scene early and precipitously. And, of course, the room was now a blazing inferno, with roaring flames shooting up the walls and a blast-furnace heat beating on Jack from all sides. If they saved the tavern, it would be a miracle.

"Time to go," Jack decided.

He still wore the ring; that was a good place for it. The dagger was nearby, so he returned the dark dwarven blade to his boot. Then he picked up the unconscious Zandria and draped her over one shoulder (easier than he would have thought, with the magical strength of the ring to fortify his small stature). Flames blocked his exit from the room, so he simply used the shadow-transport spell to step from the fire-engulfed tavern to the cool, dark street outside.

After the roaring heat and searing flames, the streets were oddly dark and silent. Jack set down the Red Wizard, who groaned and stirred. The Cracked Tankard's roof was a mass of yellow flame, lighting up the entire block. From all directions citizens hurried toward the scene, hoping to extinguish or contain the blaze before half the city burned down. And with them came tramping squads of city watchmen, doubtless filled with questions and anxious for resolutions. Jack quickly examined himself— singed, battered, injured but not permanently. Zandria seemed to be in about the same condition, or perhaps a little bit worse for the wear.

"You'll forgive me, my dear Zandria, but I believe I will leave now," Jack said. "Since my share of the gold is now engulfed in an inferno, I'll just keep the ring instead. Farewell!"

If the Red Wizard protested, Jack did not notice. He had already darted away down the nearest dark alleyway.

CHAPTER ELEVEN

Jack made his way back to the hovel on the Lady-rock, slept, and then spent most of the following morning analyzing the events of the last few days and trying to make sense of them. He owed the summoner of the shadow Jack some measure of retribution, but he didn't even know against whom he should direct his vengeance. In any event, both Iphegor and Jelan had good reason to attempt his assassination or embarrassment, so striking at the responsible party (given the unlikely eventuality that he could determine whether the wizard or the warlord was at the root of the insult) would seem to be nothing more than perpetuating a costly and inconvenient vendetta. "And that," he told himself, "is not good business, nor is pouting like an angry child. I have great works ahead, and mighty labors to attain noble ends."

Toward sundown the weather grew clear and cold, a sharp wind picking up off the sea, and he returned to his cottage to prepare for the next Game session, the Blue Lord's theatre. He picked up Illyth at the accustomed time, noting with satisfaction the number of armed guards and scowling wizard soldiers who thronged the Fleetwood estate.

"A fierce defense," he observed professionally.

"What was that, Jack?" said Illyth as she climbed into the coach.

"Your father seems to have taken matters most seriously," Jack replied. He waited for the noblewoman to seat herself, and then climbed up beside her and rapped on the door panel to signal the driver. "I forgot to tell you, but you should know that I have dealt with my imposter. He will trouble you no more."

Illyth looked at him and sighed in relief. "I'm glad to hear it. Do you have any idea of who sent him after me, or why?"

"No, I do not," Jack admitted. He nodded back at the estate. "You should probably retain your armsmen for a little longer, just in case. I have no evidence that would give me to believe that there was only one shadow simulacrum instead of two, or three, or a score."

"Oghma's word! Let's hope not—one was trouble enough!" Illyth shivered; the night was growing very clear and cold, as if winter had saved one last evening for the city despite the advance of spring. They rode on for a time quietly, watching the countryside roll by. "Listen, Jack," Illyth said, breaking the silence. "If you would prefer to abandon the Game, I will not hold it against you. It's clear to me that you have other things on your mind, and you are endangering yourself by participating."

Jack shifted in his seat to meet Illyth's gaze. "I refuse to be intimidated by Tiger and Mantis. Do not lose heart yet! We are close to puzzling out their plot, I can feel it."

"There must be something more that we can do."

"Play the Game," Jack said with a shrug. "We are close to a solution. Finishing the Game quickly may bring other plots to a head, too. Tell me, do you have Lady Carp's solution recorded?"

"I do, and I spent an hour yesterday examining it. We

can confirm eight of the fourteen variables in the solution, and we suspect answers to four more variables." Illyth took out her notebook and worked a small cantrip to illuminate the interior of the coach with soft blue light. "See here? We saw a clue that stated that the Blue Lord does not dwell in Dues, but Carp's solution failed there. That is one of the four items she missed."

"I see. And the others?"

"We have clues eliminating only three or fewer possibilities, or hearsay that leaves several answers open."

"And how would you answer the riddle at this very moment?" Jack asked.

"We can confirm the identities of the Red, Orange, Yellow, and Black lords. We suspect the identity of the Purple and Blue lords, and we don't know about the Green lord—"

"Just a moment," Jack said. "If you suspect the identity of Purple and Blue and you know the others, you must suspect Green's identity as well simply through the elimination of possibilities. If you're right about Purple and Blue, then Green must follow."

"But I don't *know* that I'm right about them," Illyth countered. "As for the kingdoms: we can confirm Red, Orange, Yellow, and Blue. We suspect Green and Black. And we're not certain of Purple."

"Good. Great!" Jack reached over and rifled back to Lady Carp's answers. "Red, Orange, and Yellow we know for a fact, and we see that Lady Carp's answers match ours. Therefore, the four errors she made must lie in these eight answers: the identities and kingdoms of the Green, Blue, Purple, and Black lords. We *know* the identity of the Black lord—which Lady Carp got wrong, by your notes—and the kingdom of the Blue Lord—another failure on her part.

"So, as far as our answer is concerned, Lady Carp

made only two mistakes that we cannot account for, and those mistakes must lie in the identities of the Green, Blue, and Purple lords, and the kingdoms of the Green, Purple, and Black lords."

Illyth frowned in concentration, examining her notes with brow furrowed. "I see. You may be right, Jack. We could be very close. Lady Carp stated that Alcantar was the Green king, Erizum the Blue king, and Geciras the Purple king. But we know that Alcantar is Black, and we don't know who Carad is supposed to be . . . in fact, we have contradictory clues about Carad."

"Contradictory?" Jack looked at her notebook again. "Oh, you can scratch out that one. I made that up."

Illyth did a double take. "You did *what?*"

"'Carad is not the Green Lord.' I made up that clue, when I was trading clues by hearsay with somebody. Lord Ram, I believe."

"Hmmph. I received that clue from Lady Nightingale, who is Ram's date for the Game. What a mess you've made of this whole thing, Jack!"

The rogue smiled. "A good thing you discovered it, then. Look, we're almost here." The coach rolled up a short, steep street, halting in front of one of the city's theatres, rented out for the night by the Game organizers. He hopped out and helped Illyth down; they joined the throng of Game-goers waiting to enter.

Lords and ladies chatted gaily, bundled up in furs and heavy cloaks against the chilly weather. Jack and Illyth passed through the atrium, donned their masks, and joined the revelers milling around in the main lobby of the theater. The entire chamber was decorated in shades of blue. Azure arrases covered the walls, the ceiling overhead was painted to resemble clear sky, and the footmen and attendants were dressed in dark navy blue waistcoats.

"I see no sign of Tiger or Mantis," Illyth observed.

"Maybe they've given up their plotting. It would be a pleasant change simply to play the Game for once."

"I suggest that we should do what we can to examine our last remaining possibilities," Jack said. "Look for players you haven't spoken to before now, and see if their clues help to settle things."

Illyth nodded. The crowd began to shuffle toward the entrance to the theatre proper, filing out of the lobby and into the darkened auditorium. The chamber was small and intimate, filled with ornate boxes and stands that lined the walls. An usher greeted them and showed them to a small box low on the left-hand side. In a few minutes, the entire chamber was filled with masked Game players, continuing their conversations from outside, circling from box to box and leaning over the balustrades to gossip with each other. In the first box, high on the right wall, the Blue King sat enthroned, attended by guards in lacquered ceremonial armor.

"The play will interfere with the Game," Jack observed. "It seems as though the entertainment is not well thought out."

"Oh, no one really watches anyway," Illyth said. "When you go to the theater, it's all about talking to anyone seated nearby and speculating about who's been seated with whom and why."

"I thought you were a fan of the theater!"

"I am, but most people aren't." The curtain rose, and a couple of actors in ridiculous costumes marched out onto the stage and began a comic scene of some kind. Scattered Game-goers watched and laughed, applauding the clever lines, but most turned to their neighbors and continued their conversations as if nothing else was taking place.

Jack and Illyth cast about for some additional clues but failed to find anything definitive. In the meantime, the play—a short skit of only twenty minutes or so—came to an end, and the actors departed the stage. The Master Crafter Randall Morran took their place and raised his arms for attention.

"Ladies and gentlemen! Another contestant dares the Riddle of the Seven Faceless Lords!"

Illyth groaned. "Oh, no!"

Jack shook his head. "Wait and see," he said. "It might be nothing more than a series of guesses. We aren't finished yet."

This time, Lord Hawk and Lady Hare took the stage. Hawk, a rather short and unassuming fellow whose grand title seemed at odds with his appearance, cleared his throat and pulled out a small journal.

"Our solution: the Red Lord is Buriz of Pentar; the Orange Lord is Fatim of Septun; the Yellow Lord is Dubhil of Trile; the Green Lord is Carad of Quarra; the Blue Lord is Erizum of Unen; the Purple Lord is Geciras of Dues; and the Black Lord is Alcantar of Hexan." He finished with a confident smirk, evidently pleased with himself.

"Alas, my lord Hawk, your solution is erroneous in three respects," Morran said. He turned to face up to the box where the Blue Lord sat. "My lord king? Your judgment in this matter?"

The Blue Lord extended one arm and turned his thumb down.

Randall Morran laughed and turned to Lord Hawk and Lady Hare. "Off with your heads, then! You may unmask and remain for the rest of the evening's festivities, or you may leave now and protect your anonymity."

Hawk shrugged. "I'll stay," he said. "I want to see if anyone gets it right." He doffed his mask to a polite applause and helped Lady Hare down from the stage.

"You see? We are not done," Jack said. "Optimism is a virtue, my lady—Illyth?"

Illyth ignored him, rifling through her journal and hurriedly making notes. "Lady Carp said that Alcantar was the Green Lord," she muttered to herself, "but we know that he's the Black Lord. So that means that Carad, Geciras, and Erizum are in some combination the Green, Blue, and Purple Lords, since we have confirmed the identities of four others. Lord Hawk said that the Orange Lord ruled Septun, but we know that he rules Quarra. That means that Green, Purple, and Black must rule Hexan, Septun, and Dues . . ."

"Are you onto something?"

"Quiet! Lady Carp made four errors . . . we know that Alcantar is the Black Lord, which is one of her errors—*but we also know that Alcantar can't be the Green Lord as she said, so there is a second error!* And we know the Blue Lord rules Unen, where Lady Carp said Dues. There are three mistakes. And thus when she said the Green Lord rules Unen, she made her fourth mistake." Illyth looked up from her journal. "Jack, I know all four errors in Lady Carp's solution."

Jack leaned over to study her journal. "Then you should mark in everything *except* those four errors in her solution as tried and confirmed, and add it to the list of variables we have already confirmed. Now how does it look?"

"That confirms every lord except the Green Lord—who must be Carad since no other is left!" Illyth's voice rose in excitement. "And every kingdom except the Green Lord's, which must be Dues! Jack, I solved it!"

"Quick, summon a Game attendant! No sense waiting now!"

Jack helped her up and ushered her to the corridor outside the box. Together, they hurried down to the theatre floor, winding down the steep stairway at the side of the building. They rounded the last flight in a breathless rush and ran right into Tiger and Mantis. The two were speaking with a couple of theatre ushers just inside the curtains separating the lower corridor from the theatre floor.

Jack and Illyth halted in surprise, as did the other couple. They stood a long moment on the carpeted staircase, staring at each other in fox, crane, tiger, and mantis masks, frozen for two, then three heartbeats. Applause rippled from the theater beyond, then laughter and catcalls, the play must have resumed, Jack thought. Lord Tiger—Toseiyn Dulkrauth—took one menacing step toward them, drawing a long knife from his belt.

"You two, go," he said to the ushers. The men nodded and ducked outside. "I've been waiting for this," he hissed through his mask. "Mantis, watch Fox! He is a mage!"

"We have urgent business elsewhere, sir," Jack said, backing up a couple of steps. "If you'll forgive us?" He quickly worked the spell of shadow-jumping—

—only to be blocked at once by Mantis, who raised her hand and countered his spell with a snarl. "You won't vanish into thin air this time!" the lady snapped. Then she followed by conjuring a ball of roiling black acid and hurling it at Jack's head. The rogue ducked and hauled down Illyth, slipping on the stairs as the murderous spell hurled over his head and scorched a foot-wide hole in the wall behind him. Tiger lunged forward and missed his stomach by inches, burying the wide-bladed knife in the step below Jack with a wooden *thunk!*

Illyth screamed, "Jack, watch out!"

The rogue rolled away from a second thrust and found a perfect opportunity to plant one boot in the center of Dulkrauth's chest, shoving him back hard. The merchant captain flailed his arms for balance and staggered back three steps into Mantis, almost knocking her down too. Jack took that as his cue to scramble to his feet and leap up the staircase back toward their box. He caught Illyth by the hand as he went.

Behind them, Mantis dodged away from Tiger and turned to track Jack and Illyth up the stair. She snarled something else and hurled a lance of dark energy at the two of them, destroying the wooden banister in a shower of splinters and gouging a great dark furrow in the wall beyond.

"Come back here!" she shrieked.

"Not likely," muttered Jack.

He burst back into their former box and hauled Illyth close. Tiger and Mantis pounded up the stairs, only a few steps behind them.

"Jack, we're trapped!" said Illyth. "They have us cornered!"

"Not yet," Jack said.

Without even stopping to think about it, he caught hold of Illyth and vaulted over the balcony edge, working the spell of jumping even as he did so. Below them Game-players screamed or gasped at their sudden appearance, but instead of plummeting into the stage twenty feet below, Jack alighted easily and set down Illyth. All around them the players in the current skit gaped in astonishment, utterly unprepared for a member of the audience to leap into the middle of the play.

"Do continue," he told the actors, and then half-dragged and half-carried Illyth back down into the orchestra pit.

In the balcony box, Tiger and Mantis stood fuming for a long moment, evidently considering whether or not they dared to continue their assault in the full view of everyone present, but discretion won out. Masks contorted in sheer fury, the two conspirators ducked back out of sight before any attention fell on the vacant box. Jack imagined that Mantis hissed some dire promise of doom at him before vanishing, but he couldn't be certain; the lady retreated even as the theater burst into an uproar of noise.

"You're spoiling the show!"

"What is the meaning of this?"

"Are you mad?"

"Down in front!"

Jack and Illyth looked around at the musicians and the actors, still waiting for them to clear the area. The Master Crafter hurried up, wringing his hands. "My lord, my lady, are you well? Why did you make such a prodigious leap? Are you hurt?"

"Lady Crane has solved the Riddle," Jack said instantly. "She wishes to announce her solution at once!" He heard Illyth gasp beside him, perhaps mortified by the sudden attention of the entire audience, but he squeezed her hand and winked at her.

The Master Crafter bowed. "Very well, then. I am sure the entertainers will not mind if we briefly interrupt their skit. After all, great events are afoot!" He stepped up onto the stage proper and bowed to the assembled players. "Lords and ladies! The Lady Crane attempts the riddle!"

"Jack, I'm not—" Illyth began to whisper.

"You'll do fine. Now, give them the answer."

Illyth swallowed and faced the crowd. She cast one more nervous glance at Jack, and then started. "My answer follows. The Red Lord is Buriz of Pentar. The Orange Lord is Fatim of Quarra. The Yellow Lord is Dubhil of Trile. The Green Lord is—" she checked her journal surreptitiously— "Carad of Dues. The Blue Lord is Erizum of Unen. The Purple Lord is Geciras of Septun. And the Black Lord is Alcantar of Hexan."

Morran made a great show of consulting his sealed scroll. "My lady," he said quietly, "you have won! The Riddle is solved!"

The chamber stood silent, then erupted in applause.

"Three cheers for the Lady Crane!" called out one voice from the back of the theater. "Huzzah! Huzzah!" Illyth curtsied and tried to conceal her own surprise behind a calm demeanor, but she couldn't help rubbing her hands unconsciously and beaming from ear to ear behind her mask, creating a very curious expression for a crane.

Randall Morran raised his hands for quiet. "My lords and ladies! Although the riddle is solved and the Lady Crane has claimed the grand prize of the event, the Game continues! The Seven Faceless Lords have discarded their signature robes and masks, and now stand among you in masked anonymity. Now, gentle persons, you must put your fellows to the question and determine who among you is not what they seem. I will even offer a hint to get you started: each lord attended only the gathering he sponsored and this evening's theatre, and knows nothing of the events or occurrences at the revels of the other Faceless Lords."

"I see that you were prepared for the possibility of an early solution," Jack murmured to the Master Crafter.

"We have already made arrangements for three more Games," the fellow replied jovially. "It would be a terrible waste to end the Game in its entirety tonight."

"I wager you have another development in mind should your Faceless Lords be unmasked too quickly," Jack observed. The Master Crafter merely smiled and inclined his head. "Your resourcefulness is to be commended. Now regarding the prize—"

"Excuse me," said Illyth. "I think you'll have to reconsider the next step of the Game."

"I beg your pardon, my lady?" Morran asked.

"The Seven Faceless Lords are standing right over there, in their full robes and masks." Illyth said pointing.

At the other end of the theatre, the robed actors slowly filed in, solemnly proceeding toward the stage.

The Game players looked at each other and whispered or muttered, checking with their neighbors to make sure they had heard the Master Crafter correctly. The marching figures silently surrounded the audience.

"What is this?" Morran muttered under his breath, so quietly that only Jack and Illyth were close enough to hear. "This is not in the script!"

In years of thievery, swindling, pursuit, and evasion, Jack had developed a distinct knack for sensing trouble when he chose to apply himself. The mysterious robed figures stood over the audience, positioned more or less in front of each exit from the room.

"An ambush," he realized. He reached out and caught Illyth's wrist, starting to pull her back from the stage.

As one, each of the robed figures withdrew a slender wand from its sleeve and pointed it toward the crowd. Game players surged up out of their seats, suddenly aware of the danger, while attendants stood frozen in shock and panic.

"Come on!" Jack yelled at Illyth, hauling her into the nearby conductor's box and ducking for cover.

At that moment each figure unleashed great bolts of brilliant lightning through the masked crowd, splitting the air with painful *cracks!* and then booming thunderclaps a second later. Brilliant blue shadows flickered and pulsed across the walls, leaving bright spots in Jack's eyes even though he was not looking directly at the bolts.

"Tymora's teats!" he cried. "What now?"

Outside people screamed in pain and fear. In the space of a heartbeat, the theatre became a scene of absolute bedlam. Ruthlessly, the robed figures shifted their aim and discharged their lightning wands again, burning great swaths through the seething press of nobles and merchants and Game-attendants who charged, fled, or cowered as their personal courage demanded. Suddenly the massive bulk of Randall Morran skidded into the conductor box, knocking both Jack and Illyth to the wooden floor.

"My apologies, Sir, Madam," the Master Crafter huffed. He was singed in a couple of places, but mostly unharmed. "Your selection of shelter seemed sound and well advised."

"Morran, what's going on here?" Illyth demanded. "Is this some kind of drastic plot twist?"

"No, fair lady. It seems that someone has taken this occasion to assault the noble and privileged among our Game players. We had nothing to do with those villains casting lightning bolts." The bard's speech was punctuated by another pair of deafening thunderclaps. Jack noticed that Illyth's hair stood on end from the near miss.

"I have no quarrel with the Faceless Lords," Jack said. "Illyth, might I suggest a withdrawal from the scene?"

She cringed, but nodded. "Which way?" she asked.

"Behind the stage. There should be an actor's exit unobserved by our assailants."

Jack scrambled up out of the box and turned to help up Illyth, crouched double to keep low. He glanced out over the theatre floor; several of the Faceless Lords were now embroiled in a furious scuffle with burned Game players, while others kept the crowds at a distance and continued their murderous work. Dozens of players seemed to have been killed or injured; the screams of the wounded and the wails of their companions filled the auditorium with a hellish cacophony of noise, still punctuated by the frequent *crack!* of more lightning.

"Dear Oghma," Illyth murmured, shocked by the carnage. "What could possibly bring this about? Who would want to do this, and why?"

"I deem that a matter worthy of investigation but not at the moment," Jack replied.

He led her across the stage, darting for the wings. The Green Lord spied them and leveled a bolt of white death in their direction, but his aim was spoiled by a sudden assault from two angry young noblemen armed with small swords. The robed figure collapsed under multiple stabbings as Jack and Illyth dived headlong behind the curtains, followed a moment later by the Master Crafter.

The actors in the skit Jack had interrupted seemed to have had the same idea. Unfortunately, they had discovered that their exit had not been overlooked. Standing in the doorway, two theatre ushers—the very same two that Tiger and Mantis had spoken with before Jack and Illyth encountered them—stood in the doorway with bared blades. Lord Tiger himself stood behind them, snarling in anger and vehemence. Several dead or unconscious comedians lay crumpled on the floor before the door.

"Fox and Crane," the lord hissed. "Time to settle our differences at last!"

Jack understood everything in one moment of perfect clarity. For his own reasons, Toseiyn Dulkrauth and his mysterious accomplice had decided to strike at the city's most indolent nobles and pretentious merchants by arranging a slaughter in the Game of Masks. Dulkrauth had replaced the theatre's ushers with his own hired blades to seal the exits. Then he'd dressed assassins with a knack for magic in the robes of the Faceless Lords, equipping each with a deadly wand of lightning.

"I would like to take this opportunity to apologize most sincerely for any inconvenience I have caused you, sir," he stammered. "The lady and I were just leaving. Please, don't let us interfere with your busy schedule."

He started to edge back, hoping that no lightning-armed wizards in hooded robes were watching the stage. Illyth, on the other hand, stood her ground and set her chin defiantly in the air. "Why, Master Dulkrauth? What do you possibly hope to gain from all this?"

"Gain? New faces in the city's councils, dear lady, terror and fear and consternation, chaos and uncertainty, the opportunity to profit by the deaths of rivals. You, I fear, are merely in the wrong place at the wrong time." The merchant captain nodded at his blades. "Kill the girl and the bard. Leave the fox-faced one for me."

Jack dragged Illyth back out onto the stage, rushing through the curtain. The Master Crafter darted in the other direction, toward the stage wings. The floor of the theatre was a charred wasteland, with a score of Game-goers dead in their seats and small fires smoldering everywhere from the touch of the lightning. People ran and screamed, two or three knots of men struggled with tall robed Faceless Lords, and behind him he could hear Dulkrauth and his mercenaries lunging after them in pursuit.

"Jack!" Illyth cried in alarm.

The rogue looked to her side; there the Blue Lord burned down a Game attendant and looked up, spying the two fugitives on the stage.

Without a second thought Jack leaped up and down, waving his hands in the air. "Hey, you! I'll wager you can't miss at this range!"

The murderer slowly raised his wand to point directly at the pair of them; Jack seized Illyth and threw her to the ground just as Dulkrauth and his armsmen burst out of the curtains right where they had stood. Then the Blue Lord loosed his bolt. White light crashed all around them like the fall of a brilliant hammer. Then the thunderbolt seemed to pick up Jack and fling him back down to the stage again.

Ears ringing, he looked over his shoulder. Dulkrauth and his two swordsmen had been fairly felled by the Blue

Lord's attack. Before the sorcerer could correct his aim, Jack scrambled to his feet and helped up Illyth.

"Backstage again!" he cried.

"Where are we going?" the girl cried in the confusion. "Jack, you almost got us killed!"

"I am improvising, Illyth," he responded.

He bolted for the stage exit, only to run headlong into yet another complication. A tall, stern-faced mage carrying a staff the size of a small tree stepped silently into the backstage area from the dressing rooms, an aura of power crackling audibly around him. He halted and gazed on Jack and Illyth with cold dispassion, speaking not a word.

"Master Alcides!" gasped Illyth. "You don't know how glad we are to see you! There is an ambush in the theatre—sorcerers are striking down all the Game players!"

"Master who?" asked Jack. Then the name rang true. Alcides von Tighe, the archmage of the Wizard's Guild, probably the most powerful wizard for a hundred miles around. Just the fellow to deal with a hornet's nest like this, he thought. "Oh, of course. I recommend warding against lightning if you have any spells of that sort," Jack volunteered. "You'll find seven villainous fellows in the chamber just outside. Deal with them as you see fit; in the meantime, I am afraid I must escort the lady to safety."

Alcides conjured a small, winged monstrosity with needle-sharp fangs and evil yellow eyes. The devil hovered in the air before him, flapping its leathery wings while its tail, armed with a venom-dripping barb, lashed back and forth angrily.

"Slay them both," the mage commanded with an imperious wave in the direction of Jack and Illyth.

"Master Alcides, wait!" Illyth cried out. "I am Illyth Fleetwood—"

The venomous devil beat its wings once, twice, and then it darted straight for her, stabbing with its barb just as a knife fighter might slash and thrust with a poisoned blade. Illyth jumped back, tangled her feet in the curtain ropes, and fell heavily on her backside. Jack grabbed a small three-legged stool from the set and threw it at the little monster, driving it back from Illyth. The creature recovered instantly and came after him. Jack drew the dagger at his belt and slashed wildly at the thing, trying to avoid its sting.

"I fail to see how Master Alcides's arrival has improved the situation," he said to Illyth, as the tall stern mage strode past the stage.

A sudden bright flare of lightning from just beyond the curtain threw a brilliant white glare all across the backstage. The mage looked back at them to see how its minion fared and then stepped out onto the stage. In the light, Alcides's face was gray, almost insubstantial. Shadowlike.

"It's another one, Illyth!" Jack said. "A shadow simulacrum!"

He defended against a sudden furious attack on the part of the imp, who missed with its venomous barb but managed to lock its small, sharp jaws on Jack's left arm and started to worry at him like an infernal terrier. Jack gave out a strangled cry of disgust and pain and fell back into the curtain, but he managed to seize the monster's stinger with his right hand and wrestled it away from his face.

The archmage—or to be exact, his copy—stepped boldly onto the stage and was instantly targeted by several crashing bolts of lightning. They struck some kind of invisible shield or barrier surrounding him and died out as if they were nothing more than pretty lights. The shadow-Alcides grinned feverishly and filled the theatre floor with a great blast of fire that shriveled the Red and Black Lords to ashes and started the whole place burning merrily. Game-players still fought desperately to escape the killing place, hemmed in by Tiger's armsmen at the exits. What can this possibly signify? Jack wondered for one fleeting instant. Then the imp started scratching at his face and throat with its claws while it still ripped and tore at his arm with its teeth and stabbed at him with its stinger. Jack howled in pain.

Something big hit the devil from behind, then again, and again. The creature crashed into the stage floor next to Jack, bludgeoned there by a short board wielded by Illyth.

"Hah! Take that!" the noblewoman cried. She jammed the end of the plank hard at the imp's head, but the creature released its grip on Jack's arm and twisted out of the way.

The timber slammed into the stage only a few inches from Jack's face, but he ignored it and reached out to seize the devil by the throat. Reversing its sting, he jammed the barb into the little monster's belly and squeezed, pumping its own poison into it. The thing wailed in agony, a high scream like a tea kettle hissing on a hot stove. Then it disappeared in a puff of stinking sulfurous smoke. Jack coughed and gagged, but Illyth reached down and hauled him up.

"Come on," she said. "If your shadow was close to a match for you, we don't want to be anywhere near Alcides's shadow. He's an archmage. Oghma knows what he might do next."

Jack risked one more look at the battle in the theatre. Hovering in midair, protected by a spell shield, Alcides directed radiant blasts of magic at whatever target struck his fancy—Game players, Faceless Lords, armsmen, or now at the city watchmen who appeared on the scene, trying to fight their way into the auditorium.

"I agree," he said. He clamped his right hand around

the bloody bite wound on his left forearm, and led Illyth toward the stage exit again.

This time, no one blocked their escape. They clattered down the short flight of rickety wooden steps leading into the alleyway behind the theatre and headed out toward the street. Smoke poured out of every window; people screamed inside, and a handful of Game-players and attendants scrambled out of windows facing the alley and jumped or fell to the dubious safety of the narrow lane outside.

"There must be dozens of people dead," Illyth said. "Oh, Jack, I just can't believe that Dulkrauth's plot was so murderous. What kind of person would do something like that?"

"Be thankful we have survived more or less uninjured," Jack replied.

They reached the end of the alleyway. In the street, dozens of city watchmen and firefighters rushed about, trying to make sense out of the chaos. Mages from the Ministry of Art watched the building, preparing to use their magical powers to aid in the effort to quell the riot and extinguish the fire.

"There he is!"

Jack glanced up in surprise, Lady Mantis stood beside Ashwillow, the Hawk Knight, and several city watchmen. The conspirator pointed at him. "I saw him speaking with the mercenaries before the attack. That's the man!" The watchmen nodded and advanced on Jack.

"Is there any way this situation could get worse?" Jack muttered to himself. He raised his hands and adopted an expression of earnest contrition. "Ashwillow, listen to me. Lady Mantis seeks to shift the blame for this fiasco. She and her accomplice, Lord Tiger, arranged this whole thing. Now she hopes to convince you that I am in some way responsible."

The Hawk Knight narrowed her eyes. "You can explain it all to the magistrate, Jack Ravenwild. In the meantime, I am placing you under arrest on charges of murder, conspiracy, arson, assault, unlicensed magic, and high treason. Gentlemen?" The last remark was aimed at the watchmen who now closed in on Jack.

"I understand, dear Ashwillow," Jack said with a shallow bow. "I hope you'll forgive me if I attend to my defense against these charges?"

He started to work the spell of shadow-transport—only to have his feet kicked out from under him before he'd even muttered a single syllable. Someone standing behind him knelt and caught him in a hammerlock, beating his forehead into the cobblestones hard twice, then three times, until his ears rang and all he could see were stars.

"I knew you were going to do that," snarled a familiar voice. Marcus bound his hands tightly behind his back, and then gagged him as well with little gentleness. "There, that should keep you from working any spells. You're not going to get away quite so easily this time."

Jack was hauled to his feet and held up by his arms, although his vision swam and blood ran down his face. He caught one glance of Illyth's horrified face, and then he was wheeled about and frog-marched down the street in the center of a knot of watchful guardsmen.

CHAPTER TWELVE

As might be expected of someone in Jack's line of work, he was no stranger to the city's gaols. Fortunately, he had endured no long incarcerations, nor had he ever been convicted of any serious crimes. More than once, he'd simply waited until no one was looking to charm a guard and talk himself out of prison or absented himself from the judicial process with a well-timed spell of invisibility or disappearance. In fact, Jack had acquired a dangerous level of confidence in his ability to avoid legal complications.

This time, the city officials were not treating him as a common burglar, rumored fence, or suspected swindler. They were treating him as a murderer, traitor, and spy, whose known magical powers merited the utmost caution. He was fitted with a set of enchanted fetters that utterly blocked any attempt on his part to wield magic, then he was interred in the strongest, most secure, and incidentally most dismal cell in the city, in the prison-fortress of Ill-Water.

Ill-Water was not actually located in the city proper; it was built on an artificial island of massive stone slabs a few hundred yards out beyond the harbor entrance, surrounded by the cold waters of the Inner Sea. Raven's Bluff reserved

Ill-Water for prisoners whose crimes, abilities, or stations were so far beyond those of the common criminal that no possibility of escape could be allowed. For cutthroats, brawlers, smugglers, and highwaymen, the city's prison hulks offered weeks, months, or years of backbreaking labor. For crimes of a less violent nature, the Nevin Street Compter sufficed, but for those who had aligned themselves against the powers of Raven's Bluff, Ill-Water was the fortress of last resort.

Jack saw no other prisoners, no exercise yards, no mess halls, nothing of the outside. He was ferried to the island prison in the lightless hold of an armored prison barge, led through a cyclopean maze of winding stone passages and massive iron doors, and then finally deposited in an oubliette four feet square and about fifteen feet deep, reached only through an iron trapdoor bolted and locked from outside. A grill of thick iron bars about a foot square in the center of the trapdoor provided the entrance for food, water, and a thin glimmer of yellow light. A similar grill in the center of the cell's cold stone floor served as the means by which his wastes exited.

And there he remained for some interminable time in the darkness, relieved only by the pale gleam of torchlight from some distant spot in the hallway above, and in the silence, sundered only by the unending dull thundering of the surf breaking against the prison's massive foundations. Neither condition showed the slightest fluctuation or variance; before he'd slept even once, Jack had lost track of whether an hour, a half-day, or even several days had passed. He tried talking to himself, singing, thinking up dirty jokes, challenging himself with mental puzzles, marching in place, and straining at the iron fetters that bound him, but ultimately the tedium overcame him, rising up like a dark and sinister flood, drowning him in despair and futility so that he simply slouched on the floor and gazed upward longingly at the light.

Jack had always imagined that any incarceration might be an arduous and exacting kind of adventure, an opportunity to survive a difficult experience and then escape from it in a particularly daring and skillful manner, the kind of experience that would only add to his fame and renown. What he had not expected was to be buried in a cold stone shaft and simply forgotten about. He hadn't expected to be alone, with nothing but the mocking half-light and the maddening reverberation of the distant surf to keep him company.

After he'd slept twice, he was awakened by a guard's passage. Jack leaped to his feet in excitement, amazed at how so common an occurrence as a human being walking by overhead could seem like the most entertaining break in the tedium. The small grill in the center of the trapdoor opened; a basket containing a flagon of water and some tough black bread was lowered on a length of twine.

"Remove the bread and the flagon," directed the voice from above. "You can keep the container until your next meal. You'll put the flagon in the basket, and it will be refilled. Do you understand?"

"Yes," said Jack. "Listen, I would like to speak to—"

"One more word, and you'll miss your next meal. Two more, and you won't eat for three days. You are not to speak at all, unless asked to. Do you understand?"

"Yes," said Jack.

He fidgeted and grimaced, desperate to say *something,* anything to keep the person above nearby, but he did not doubt for a moment that the jailer would do exactly what he said he would and skip him for the next few rounds.

"Good."

A shadow moved across the light above; the basket

was abruptly drawn up again. Jack resigned himself to chewing on the tough bread and washing it down with the icy water, and considered whether or not he should begin a count of feedings by way of marking the time.

He slept again, awoke and spent a long time staring at the walls, and then the basket was lowered to him again. He received another chunk of coarse bread and a refill for his water flagon. The cycle repeated several more times. Jack wondered if strangling himself with his fetters might be preferable to eternal incarceration, and to divert his mind from such a grisly prospect, he began to hatch for his own fancy the most outrageous escape plots he could imagine.

"I could scale the cell walls chimney style, seeing as they have carelessly been left so close together," he mused. The shackles were unfortunately fixed to a heavy bolt in the cell floor, preventing him from climbing anywhere near the trapdoor above.

"I see that my jailers thought of that already," Jack muttered after trying the scheme. "Then perhaps I shall work at dislodging the grate below. I am a small fellow and may be able to fit through the opening and discover where the cell's wastes are discharged. Given that this place is built upon an artificial island, they are almost certainly emptied into the sea. It is a foul path indeed, but I am desperate and cannot be fastidious in these matters."

The bars were as thick as spear shaft and evidently anchored deeply in the stone walls. With the strength of an ogre he could not have pulled them loose.

"Very well, then. I did not care for that scheme, anyway. Instead, I shall remove these enchanted shackles, thus making available magical abilities that must surely suffice to free me from this dismal place."

The shackles were enchanted quite well. Hours of

experimentation convinced him that he'd have to break most of the bones in his hands to free himself of the irons on his wrists. Broken hands, of course, would drastically inhibit his ability to work magic, and there was no way that his feet could be crushed or pulped enough to slip out of his ankle irons.

"Even if I could free myself that way, I would have two broken hands and two broken legs," Jack mused. "Beginning my escape in such a condition would not be advisable."

Before Jack had determined which of the unattractive options promised the best chance for escape within the next decade, he was interrupted by the approach of booted feet, a number of them, in the corridor above. The procession stopped above his cell; a moment later, the trapdoor was pulled open. Lanterns bright enough to make Jack shield his eyes shone down on him.

"Jack Ravenwild," stated one of the guards above. "You have been summoned to appear before the Lord High Magistrate to answer to charges of treason, murder, arson, conspiracy, assault, and various other crimes and misdemeanors."

The guards lowered a narrow ladder into the cell. Two climbed down and freed his fetters from the bolt in the wall, then escorted him back up to the hall. There he was chained securely, blindfolded and hooded, and finally manhandled through the prison's labyrinthine passageways and out into the open sea air. He could hear a boat scraping against the stone quay, rocking up and down in the soft swell.

"The prisoner is ready for transport," said one guard aloud.

"Put him in the boat," another replied. "Chain him securely. The Lady Mayor herself wanted this one tried and condemned speedily."

"Are we going to see him again?" asked the first guard.

"That's up to the Magistrate," said the boatman. "I suspect that you'll hold him for a day or two, and then he'll be put to death." Someone prodded Jack with a cudgel and shoved him down into the damp bilge of an open boat. His chains rattled and clanked as they were secured to the boat in some unseen manner.

"It seems," Jack muttered to himself, "that attending my own trial is the only opportunity I will have to leave this place."

Jack was transferred from the boat to a small, shuttered wagon that trundled through the streets. The normal bustle and commerce of the city was missing altogether. Jack guessed that the hour was very late, but he'd thought that he had felt weak sunshine through the heavy hood during his short voyage across the harbor in the prison scow. If the sun was up, then the quiet of the city was very peculiar. He shrugged and set the issue aside; he had far more important things to worry about.

The wagon halted, and Jack was dragged out and hauled up a steep flight of stone stairs. Heavy doors creaked open ahead of him, only to boom shut when he and his captors passed. The quality of the sounds changed—footfalls echoed, the mail of his escorts jingled shrilly. They were inside a large building, which he guessed must be Ravendark Castle, seat of the city hall and location of the city's High Court. In all the years he'd lived in the city of Raven's Bluff, Jack had never once set foot in the place. Suspicious guardsmen and nosy bureaucrats made it a bad place to visit, if one's chosen vocation was not entirely sanctioned by the civic authorities.

He was ushered into another chamber, and his chains

were fastened to a post or rail nearby. A soft murmur of voices sounded anxiously in the middle distance, the muted buzz of a hushed crowd or gathering.

"If the prisoner is secured, remove his hood," commanded a strong voice nearby.

"The shackles prevent the working of magic, my lord," responded someone very close to him. "He is helpless."

"Good. Unhood him, but maintain a careful watch. He is known to be quite elusive."

Jack was roughly handled for a moment as unseen hands worked at the bindings of his hood, and then the heavy leather mask was pulled away from his face. He stood in a prisoner's pulpit, his hands chained together, with the chain anchored to two heavy stone columns. Shafts of dim sunlight slanted across a small, high chamber of stone. Blinking to accustom himself to the light, he twisted around to look behind him. He was in a courtroom, the gallery filled with several dozen people, and in front of him behind a tall stand stood a very stern-looking man with a dour face and large, powerful hands clasping a rod of office. The judge looked over at a mailed guardsman standing by the prisoner's rail and nodded.

"Jack Ravenwild, you stand accused of high treason, murder, arson, assault, burglary, swindling, the malicious use of magic for sinister designs, and conspiracy to overthrow the rightful rulers of the city of Raven's Bluff," intoned the bailiff. "You stand before Lord High Magistrate Tordon Sureblade. What say you to these charges?"

"I believe there has been a terrible misunderstanding—" Jack began.

The bailiff cut him off. "You may plead guilty, not guilty, or no contest to the charges," the officer said.

"Not guilty then. I am innocent of every charge brought against me, and I warmly greet this opportunity to answer each one in due course." Jack cleared his throat and added, "If it please the court, may I be set free of these bonds? I confess that they distract me terribly from the grave matters at hand, and I fear that simply appearing in irons may unconsciously sway the court to view me in an unfavorable and undeservedly criminal light."

"Note the accused's plea as not guilty," said the Lord High Magistrate from his lofty vantage, "and leave him in his shackles." In another corner of the chamber, a court clerk hastily scribbled into a large leather-bound book, evidently recording the proceedings. Then the Magistrate turned his attention to Jack. "Understand, sir, that I am vested with the full and solitary power to hear your case, adjudicate your guilt or innocence, and pronounce sentence. As the High Magistrate for this city, I am the only appellate authority and the final arbiter of all matters of justice and order. You stand before me instead of a lesser magistrate because the charges laid against you are extraordinary in nature and capital in punishment. Do you understand?"

Jack managed a feeble nod. What little confidence he might have felt at regaining his sight and powers of speech was rapidly dwindling. He suspected he would have a hard time baffling Tordon Sureblade with a convoluted fabrication or warming his heart with charm and earnestness. In fact, he suspected that he would do very well to treat the Lord High Magistrate with the same caution he might give to an angry dragon.

"I do, my lord."

"Very well. Officers of the Watch, you may present the evidence against this man."

One by one, the city authorities paraded through the court the Brothers Kuldath, Iphegor the Black, Marcus and Ashwillow, Zandria and those who survived in her band, several shopkeepers and ferrymen from the Ladyrock, the

Master Crafter Randall Morran, a woman by the name of Lady Milyth Leorduin (Jack identified her as Lady Mantis by her voice and virulence), Briesa and other waiting-staff from the Cracked Tankard, and even Ontrodes the sage.

"That is the man we saw in our house!" cried the Kuldaths, pointing their bony fingers at Jack and quavering with mercantile rage. "He stole our ruby!"

"I deny any such doings," Jack replied in turn. "At the hour stated by the Kuldaths, I was engaged in charitable work among the poor. It's not much, but I do what I can."

Iphegor the Black came next. "There stands he who burglarized my tower and murdered my familiar," snarled the wizard. "If you do not execute him, my lord, I beg you to remand him into my custody. I would be only too happy to take care of the matter for you!"

"I heard of the incident of which Master Iphegor speaks," Jack said with a frown of true concern. "While I grieve for his loss, I believe that the man seen to exit his tower answered to a description not unlike that of Sir Marcus of the Knights of the Hawk, or so I heard, anyway. Might I ask if any investigation has been made into his involvement in this sordid affair?"

Meritheus, the agent of the Wizard's Guild, followed. "He represented himself as 'the Dread Delgath' and joined the Guild under a false name," reported the stout mage. "As he is an accused felon, we revoke his membership immediately and disavow any association with his actions."

"I have no idea what he is talking about," Jack replied. "I am not now, nor have I ever been, a member of the Wizard's Guild. Given the spectacular destruction visited upon the city's theatre quite recently by the archmage of that villainous collection of necromancers and ill-doers, I should hope never to become a member in the future!"

Marcus and Ashwillow took the stand after that, each in turn. "Our sources observed the accused's meetings with a swordswoman calling herself Elana on several occasions," stated the Hawk Knights, each telling the same tale. "As we privately stated to the Lord High Magistrate earlier, we have conclusive proof that Elana is an agent of the Warlord Myrkyssa Jelan, which means that the accused is very likely to be engaged in Jelan's plots against the city. He also resisted arrest and questioning on two occasions."

"Elana did, in fact, contact me about a very mysterious matter of employment," Jack admitted ruefully. "I turned her down at once, of course, and immediately commenced a thorough investigation of all her affairs. In fact, I had amassed a fair body of evidence indicating that she might have something to do with the Warlord and was engaged in preparing to turn over my findings to the proper authorities when the Hawk Knights evidently mistook my activities for collusion in her sinister schemes. Well, I am glad I had a chance to clear that up!"

The Knights of the Hawk were followed by Zandria the Red. "He interfered with my legitimate efforts to salvage treasure from Sarbreen's depths and was directly responsible for bringing my company into contact with a deep dragon, which led to the deaths of two of my partners," Zandria said. "He also pilfered my notebooks, stole treasure I was engaged in legally recovering, and spied on my preparations in order to prepare an ambush for me below the city."

"The Lady Zandria unfortunately suffered a serious blow to the head during the very expedition she refers to," said Jack. "She has entertained paranoid delusions ever since. In truth, I am her chartered partner in these operations and sought only to fulfill the terms of our contract. Regardless of what you do with me, please arrange medical assistance for her, before her delusions result in a true catastrophe."

"Six days ago, a cartload of fresh thatch disappeared from my workshed early in the afternoon," said one roofer Jack didn't recognize. "At the end of the day, I noticed that an abandoned house on the east end of the Ladyrock sported a brand new roof."

The thatcher's story was amplified by that of two carpenters and a bricklayer, who reported missing tools and materials they later discovered in and around the same house, while the tavernkeep of the Red Sail identified Jack as the very same man who'd suddenly taken up residence in the abandoned cottage.

"I visited the Red Sail, yes," Jack admitted, "but I do not maintain a residence upon the Ladyrock. And I certainly cannot be held accountable if its mysterious owner finally decided to fix the place up. Why do I stand accused of repairing his roof?"

Randall Morran, the Master Crafter of the city's bardic guild, climbed to the stand with a serious and weighty expression on his face. "The accused took part in the Game of Masks under the guise of Lord Fox," reported the Master Crafter. "I was present in the robing room on several occasions when he was given his mask for the game or removing it at the end of the evening. He was suspected of cheating by several other players, although I cannot honestly say that I witnessed it."

"Of course I participated in the Game," Jack said cordially. "I was given to understand that, within the Game, players were expected to make full use of all the resources at their disposal to solve the riddle. I would never condone any such behavior had the Game not required that sort of thing to begin with. That was part of the fun!"

Lady Mantis spoke next, although she wore no mask in the courtroom. "I happened to overhear a conversation between Lord Fox and Lord Tiger, whom we now know was Toseiyn Dulkrauth," Milyth Leorduin reported. "They were planning some kind of attack or ambush within the Game, something about arming the Faceless Lords with magical wands and striking during the Blue Lord's Revel. I regret to say that I deemed their conversation to be nothing more than a game within the Game. If only I'd known that they plotted a real murder!" She wiped real tears from her eyes and sobbed delicately. "I cannot imagine what kind of fiend would plan such a thing as the attack at the theater the other night!"

"Ah-ha!" said Jack. "The Lady Mantis seeks to reverse her guilt upon me! She reports the very evidence I would have given against her. I require her immediate arrest upon the charges you have mistakenly assigned to me!"

"The fiend burned down my skewer stand and made off with the receipts of a full day's business," complained a vendor in sausages from the Anvil, "and he fondled my wife as well!"

Jack squinted at the fellow and shifted nervously. He didn't remember doing anything like that. "Perhaps the gentleman has confused me with somebody else," he offered timidly.

"I found him spying upon my girls in their dressing rooms, lurking about invisibly while they bathed after a performance," stated the proprietor of a festhall and dance revue. "When I cornered him, he worked an enchantment upon me that led me to distribute all the money in my coffers and crawl to the Temple of Loviatar on my hands and knees, groveling for forgiveness!"

"I am certain I had nothing to do with that!" Jack cried. "Besides, if I was invisible, how in the world does he know it was me?"

"Because you threw off your spell in order to ride upon my back, lashing me with a cat-o-nine-tails and composing shameful limericks the whole way!" the man stated. "What did I ever do to you, you villain?"

An awful suspicion began to dawn in Jack's heart. He hadn't burned down the sausage-vendor's shack or harried the whoremaster all the way to the temple of the bitch goddess, but it was not inconceivable that his shadow-self might have done these things during the days it was free to make use of his appearance and abilities. He looked over to the gallery where witnesses waited, observing the trial. Dozens of sullen, angry stares weighed upon him like leaden chains.

"Are they all here to testify against me?" he asked the bailiff in a stage whisper.

The officer shrugged. "Only a dozen or so. The rest are here to beg the Lord High Magistrate for your death, on account of the injuries you wreaked on their loved ones, property, and acquaintances."

"Oh," Jack replied. He turned to face the Magistrate as the last witness filed down from the stand. "My lord, is it truly necessary to hear anymore evidence of this sort? It is clear to me that the city has built a flimsy case out of hearsay and circumstantial evidence. I beg you, let us end this farce before we exhaust one more moment of your undoubtedly important time. I am feeling quite magnanimous and shall generously forgive my slanderers for any misstatements or untruths they spoke, in the interest of speeding along these proceedings."

"It is ironic that you should speak of truth," Tordon Sureblade said grimly. He held up one hand—a glint of gold encircled one thick finger. "I wear upon my left hand a ring of truth, which prevents me from speaking any falsehood. It also makes clear to me the falsehoods of others. You, sir, have twisted and wormed your way through the entire hearing, mixing lies and falsehoods with glimmers of a false earnestness. Never in my years of serving this city on the bench of high justice have I encountered such a morally dissolute and utterly despicable person as yourself!"

"I didn't lie about the Lady Milyth's testimony! Or about the sausage vendor's wife, or the whoremaster's tale!"

"Rare exceptions over the course of the last three hours," the magistrate said. He threw a stern look at the gallery, where Lady Milyth Leorduin sat in a noble's box with a small retinue. The noblewoman's face was set in a look of utter serenity, as if she deemed the proceedings completely beneath her notice. "And I will look into these anomalous testimonies. But the fact remains that you are guilty of burglary on at least two accounts, conspiracy, and most seriously of all, high treason by way of your association with the Warlord's agent in the city. Can you present any evidence or testimony to contradict these findings?"

Jack nodded vigorously. "Yes, I can, Lord High Magistrate. I require several days of liberty—escorted by city officers, of course!—to build the case for my defense. I can contest each and every one of these very serious charges."

The magistrate held up his hand, on which gleamed the ring of truth. "I didn't think so," he said in a tired voice. "Bailiff, remove the prisoner. He is to be incarcerated in the fortress of Ill-Water for a period of one tenday, during which time I intend to open an investigation into the affair of the Game of Masks and Lady Milyth's role therein, as well as the other charges of which the defendant was truly ignorant. Then he is to be hanged by the neck until dead unless the circumstances of the investigation warrant a stay of execution."

The courtroom buzzed with excitement over the verdict, including one or two strong remarks suggesting that it would be much better to put Jack to death on the spot and then investigate the other allegations. Jack looked up at the various witnesses who had spoken against him;

the Kuldaths glowed with triumph, the Master Crafter Randall Morran seemed disappointed, the commoners ranged from whoops of glee to smug nods of satisfaction. The bailiff and the guards escorted Jack out of the room and back to a holding cell in another part of the castle, hooding him again.

He found himself sitting on a hard wooden bench in a small wagon, doubtless locked and barred and enchanted against any possible escape, with a pair of guards sharing the cramped space.

"So it's back to Ill-Water?" Jack asked through the hood.

"Silence," one guard grated.

Jack shrugged as best he could given his bonds. The wagon trundled off over the cobblestones, rattling and swaying. He listened closely for any signs of business or activity in the city; the roads from Ravendark Castle to the boat landings wound through the busiest parts of Raven's Bluff, and he strained for the sounds of conversation and commerce from the streets beyond the wagon's walls. He heard nothing but the creaking of the wheels.

After a surprisingly short ride, the wagon halted. The door squeaked open, and the two guards climbed out, the wagon shifting with their weight. Someone else climbed in and sat beside him; a soft feminine hand grasped his.

"Oh, Jack," said Illyth in a small voice. "I just heard the verdict."

"Illyth? What are you doing here?"

"I arranged a short visit before you're to be returned to prison. I've been trying to see you all week, Jack, but they won't let anyone go out to Ill-Water." She laughed softly, a sound that almost ended in a sob. "I bribed the guards to allow me to see you before you reached the landing. Jack . . . is there anything I can do? There must be some way to reverse the magistrate's judgment!"

"I do not know," he answered. "The only thing I can think of is to call in whatever favors you can to delay the execution for as long as possible. The magistrate said he would order an investigation into Milyth Leorduin's involvement in the Game (she's Lady Mantis, apparently) so you might work with the investigators to clear me of that charge, at least."

"Done," said Illyth. "What of the other charges, Jack?"

He remained silent for a long moment. "I don't think there is much you can do, Illyth. Most of them are true. I'm pretty much what they say I am."

"Oh, Jack," she whispered. "You helped Myrkyssa Jelan?"

"I didn't know that I was helping her at the time," he said. "I thought it was simply another job. I'm a burglar, a thief, a scoundrel, but I am not a traitor, not wittingly, at least. And I've never killed anybody other than Iphegor's mouse, and that was an accident!"

Illyth was silent for a long time. He could hear her sobbing quietly. The door at the back of the wagon opened again, and the guards reentered.

"Sorry, m'lady, but we cannot delay any longer. We're expected at the landing, and questions will be asked if we're late."

"A moment more," Illyth said. She returned her attention to Jack. "Jack, there must be something we can do!" she said urgently. "You don't deserve to be put to death for what you've done!"

He leaned back against the wagon's wooden interior, his shackles clinking together. Given the fact that he would probably not get a chance to escape, what could be done? He thought hard and fast.

"The only thing I can think of is this: approach Marcus and Ashwillow, and let them know that I'd be willing to cooperate with them in locating Jelan and her agents. I've

seen several of them, so I might be able to find them or
testify against them, if need be. I might have some value
as a means of unmasking the Warlord's plot."

"It's time to go, my lady," the guard repeated.

Jack felt the wagon shift again as Illyth retreated. "I
know," she said to the guard. She paused. "Jack, I'll do
what I can. Everything has been so strange lately. The
Game plot, and now these shadow people are showing up
all over the city . . . I know that the authorities want to
find out what's going on. Maybe you can help them."

She suddenly leaned forward and kissed his hand,
then clambered out of the wagon. She murmured something to the guards, and Jack detected the unmistakable
jingle of coinage changing hands. Then the guards closed
the door again, and the driver flicked his reins at the
horse drawing the prison wagon. They clattered off
through the silent streets.

As far as Jack could tell, the Ravenaar guards
returned him to the exact same pitlike cell that he had
occupied before. If it was not the same cell, it was identical to the first in every detail that mattered. Freed of the
stifling hood, he enjoyed the sense of relative freedom
and the ability to stand, sit, or lie down as he pleased.
But the enchanted fetters on his wrists and ankles still
denied him the ability to access any of his magic, and the
dull booming of the surf through the fortress's seawalls
reminded him that he was interred quite securely in a
place he would likely never leave alive.

He quickly became bored with pacing the narrow floor
and occupied himself for a time by considering whether
he might have influenced the Lord High Magistrate's
decision through a more cogent and eloquent defense.

The magistrate's ring of truth was quite tricky; there ought to be a law requiring him to disclose the fact that he used such a device before defendants said a word to him, Jack reflected. The careful absence of fabrication in his defense would have been quite challenging. On the next occasion, he would work hard to suggest or imply falsehoods he wished to impart to the authorities through half-truths and omission. For example, he might have damaged the value of Zandria's testimony by stating the terms of the agreement they had reached regarding the reward for recovering the Orb and simply asking the magistrate whether she would gain his cut of the treasure if he should happen to be convicted. No lies spoken, but a damning suggestion that Zandria stood to gain thousands of gold crowns by helping to ensure that he was not available to collect his share of the contract.

In fact, if he had *known* that the Magistrate could discern lies, he might have simply told the truth about why he undertook the recovery of the Sarkonagael for Elana. He certainly didn't know that she was an agent of Myrkyssa Jelan (actually, Myrkyssa Jelan herself!) at the time, and the magistrate must have accepted that as a mitigating circumstance against the crime of treason. The charges of murder and conspiracy were brought into question by Lady Milyth's false testimony, so all that would be left were charges of theft and burglary. "And those," reflected Jack, "are not capital crimes. I should therefore be incarcerated in the Nevin Street Compter for some inconvenient period of time until I arranged my escape, not awaiting death in ten days in the most secure facility available to the city authorities. What a dismal prospect!"

Jack reexamined his fetters again, hoping that there might be a way to remove them. If he could regain his magical abilities, he could remove himself from the situation in the blink of an eye. Within an hour he'd be aboard a ship bound anywhere else on the Inner Sea, Impiltur or Procampur or Westgate or Marsember or anywhere but Raven's Bluff. Unfortunately, the manacles still defied his skill.

"A fiendish device, unnecessarily cruel and entirely uncalled for," he mumbled. The infernal reverberation of the ceaseless surf held no answers for him, so he closed his eyes and dozed off for a time.

He was awakened by the approach of someone in the hallway above. Anticipating his crust of bread and flagon of water, he groped around in the darkness for his flask and stood up with a rattle of chains. But the light seemed dimmer than that carried by the guard on his rounds, and the motion above somewhat more furtive. Quietly the bolt securing the trapdoor was drawn back, and the cover to his cell opened stealthily.

A woman's voice whispered, "Jack Ravenwild?"

"Yes! Yes! I am he!" Jack replied.

"Good." She stood up and moved away. Jack suddenly feared that, having gone to some trouble to locate him, his mysterious guest now intended to leave him exactly where she had found him, but then she whispered, "Bring a light," to another person or persons above.

A moment later, she returned holding a small lantern to look in on Jack. He squinted up at her, shielding his dark-adapted eyes against the light. The Lady Mayor Amber Lynn Thoden crouched at the top of the cell.

"Hello, Jack," she said. "We have some things to talk about."

CHAPTER THIRTEEN

The *Storm Gull* glided silently past the quiet wharves of the city, lanterns lighting the way at bow and stern. The hour was late; the docks, so crowded and busy during the day, were virtually abandoned. Not a single person could be seen in the halos of streetlights glowing through the soft rain. Jack wrapped a borrowed cloak closer to his body and considered whether it might not be better to leap into the water and swim for it. Icy eel-infested waters seemed a better proposition than continuing on his current course.

He looked around, furtively studying his captors. The Lady Mayor—no, Myrkyssa Jelan—stood at the helm of her sloop, guiding the boat confidently up the Fire River. Jelan had abandoned her pose of Lady Thoden as soon as she'd escorted Jack from the depths of Ill-Water and boarded her dark cutter. Beside her, the Shou mage Yu Wei stood stock still, engaged in some inner meditation that left his face even more expressionless and serene than usual. A half-dozen very capable-looking people rounded out the crew—Hathmar Blademark, a drow swordsman; a cold woman called Amarana, who wore the emblem of the night goddess Shar; and a short, powerful Tuigan in leather and iron, who introduced himself to Jack.

"I am called Tenghar," he had said. "I will kill you if the Warlord wishes it done."

Several others worked the boat's sails and sounded the waters as the sloop glided upstream.

"Kel Kelek! Take the helm!" Jelan waited while one of the other men, a tall and rangy Nar with a frightening pattern of facial tattoos, clambered back to take the ship's wheel. She tapped Yu Wei on the shoulder and then addressed Jack. "Master Ravenwild, if you would be so kind as to join me in my cabin?"

"I would be delighted, my dear," the rogue replied with false joviality.

No point in allowing her to see how nervous he was with this development. When Jelan had abducted him from prison in the guise of the Lady Mayor, he'd been anxious to leave regardless of the circumstances. Certainly, anything was better than death row. Now he suspected that the Warlord would make the cost of her generosity known to him.

"At least she is unlikely to simply silence me in some permanent means," he muttered. "That she could have done without removing me from my cell."

He followed the warrior and her sorcerous advisor down the narrow companionway and into the sloop's rear cabin. The Shou (no, Wa, Jack reminded himself) decor was unchanged, a delicate and spare arrangement of white screens and paper lanterns with a wide dark table of gleaming wood set at knee height so that one could sit on the floor and eat or work comfortably.

Illyth Fleetwood sat dejectedly on the floor. The girl looked up sharply as Jelan, Yu Wei, and Jack entered the room. "Oh, Jack!" she cried. "They've got you too!"

"You might say that," Jelan said with a small laugh. "Do not worry, Illyth. No harm will come to either Jack or yourself as long as Jack improves his behavior."

She was still dressed in the handsome dress and fillet of the Lady Mayor, but as she talked she undressed to reveal dark leather armor and steel beneath her robes. Jack recalled his brief flirtation with the Lady Mayor on the first night of the Game, amazed that he hadn't spotted the resemblance then, but the disguise was so skillfully done, including mannerisms and posture and voice, that it seemed that Elana—Jelan—the Lady Mayor were really three different women altogether.

"Extraordinary," Jack breathed. "The Hawk Knights comb the city for any sign of you, yet you stand in the very center of the city and direct their search."

"Who could expect it?" Jelan said. "But tonight the deception ends."

She unbuckled her sword belt, leaned the weapon against one wall, then knelt behind the table. Jelan indicated the opposite place with a tilt of her head. Jack sat down a little awkwardly, while Yu Wei took up station somewhere behind him, standing silently by the door. Illyth moved over to sit beside Jack.

"You are probably considering your escape already," Jelan began without preamble. "No matter. I only require your services for the next few hours, and if you do what I need you to do, I'll gladly let you go."

"I fail to understand why I am so important to you, my lady."

"For one thing, you agreed to hear her out, after you were warned that you should not do so unless you were prepared to accept what must follow," Yu Wei said. "We are not forgiving of broken promises."

"You retrieved me from Ill-Water to make me abide by my word?" Jack asked in amazement. "I didn't tell anyone that I had learned your identity. It was in my own best interests to keep your confidence."

Jelan smiled in a predatory manner. "I am not so

forgetful of my obligations as you are, Jack." She began to let down the braids in her hair, shaking the rain from her dark tresses. She kept her gaze on Jack's eyes, refusing to allow him to look away. "Where I come from, that would be reason enough to justify the trouble I went to this evening, but, as it so happens, I do have a specific purpose in mind for you."

"You desire something else stolen, my lady?" Jack asked.

"Jack, have you ever studied to be a wizard?"

Jack leaned back, his brow furrowed. Illyth shifted uncomfortably beside him, but held her tongue. He could not see where this was going.

"No, not really. Anyone can work magic, simply through an act of will and a little practice. All those who purport to study wizardry have been pulling the wool over everyone's eyes. None of that mummery is required!"

Jelan looked up past Jack to Yu Wei. Jack craned his head to glance at the Warlord's wizard; the mage simply stood impassive, but his eyes were deep and thoughtful. He tugged at his white wisp of a beard and spoke.

"Consider this possibility, Ravenwild: for the great majority of people who seek to use magic, all that 'mummery' as you call it *is* required. But for certain special individuals—you, for instance—magic is something else entirely. Is that not every bit as likely as your assumption that there is a universal conspiracy subscribed to by every wizard on the face of the world?"

"Perhaps," Jack admitted, "but that would imply that I am something special or unique, and any theory that begins with such an assumption is usually a poor one."

"A wiser statement than I would have expected from you," the Shou said. He smiled in satisfaction.

"Jack, have you ever heard any tales of wildfire?" Jelan asked.

"My lady, I confess that I am at a complete loss as to the goal of this interrogation," Jack began. Jelan raised her hand, forestalling his argument, and simply waited for him to answer her question. He sighed and shrugged. "Well, of course I have. Some people say that once in a while a Ravenaar born and bred may exhibit the unusual reaction of lashing out with magic when threatened. It's always a person who has never wielded magic in his life, and it's said that the wildfire-wielder cannot control or summon his powers at will. It is an involuntary reaction to danger, noted no more than once or twice a year in the entire city."

Jack suddenly smiled and wagged his finger. "Ah, now I understand! You and your wizard here believe that my powers constitute a manifestation of wildfire! Well, I am sorry to say that you must be mistaken. I have full and voluntary control over my magic."

"Perhaps you are able to control your ability to an unprecedented degree," Yu Wei said. "Where do you think wildfire comes from, boy?"

Jack glared at him. "Who knows? Maybe it is something that only one person in a thousand anywhere can do."

"The phenomena has been observed only in Raven's Bluff, Jack," said Jelan. "Why here? Why is it that a small number of people living in this city are simply blessed with inexplicable magic? Something about Raven's Bluff instills magic in a small number of its citizens, apparently at random. And, in your case, the magic is quite versatile and strong."

"What does it all signify?" Illyth interrupted. "Where does this magic come from?"

"It comes from a device that I call the wild mythal," said Jelan. "Raven's Bluff is built on top of Sarbreen. Sarbreen was built on top of an older and deeper city, a drow stronghold thousands of years old. Here, in the deeps beneath us, the mightiest wizards of the drow once gathered to forge a mythal of their own, a font of power akin to those made by the most powerful elven wizards of centuries long past."

"A mythal?" Jack asked. He shook his head. "I don't understand."

"The mythals were the most powerful magics ever devised by the elven courts of old," Illyth said, nodding. "At Myth Drannor, Evermeet, Calmaercor, and other places too, mythals were forged of elven high magic to serve the elven race. They guarded the elven realms against all harm and made possible works of wonder now forgotten."

"The dark elves did not overlook the potential of the mythal magic," Jelan added. "In their long war against the surface elves, the drow came to desire a similar device of their own, one with the power to bend or break the surface mythals. And so they toiled for many long years, forging their own mythal stone somewhere in the ancient city under Sarbreen, but their mythal failed. It gathered an enormous amount of magic, but it could not be tamed to their will. They abandoned the whole city, and the warped magic of their failed device has slowly seeped into the very earth and air and water of this place for centuries now. Raven's Bluff, by pure chance, was built upon a fountainhead of magic that is probably unique in all the world."

Jack looked at her with understanding. "That is why you raised your horde, my lady? To control the fountainhead of wildfire?"

Jelan nodded. "I had other reasons, too, but yes, that is the primary one. I intend for the wild mythal to be the keystone of my kingdom, a source of power that would make my conquest unassailable. There are dozens of cities in the Vast that might be easier to take or more easily pacified. Raven's Bluff, however, is unique in this regard, and the fools don't even know what they have."

"What of the Sarkonagael? Why did I steal it for you, if the wild mythal is your real target?"

"It contains spells that I needed Yu Wei to possess—"

"The shadow simulacra!" Jack interrupted. "You are the source of the shadow copies! Do you have any idea of the kind of trouble those constructs are causing in the city?"

The Warlord nodded. "A good idea, yes. You see, Jack, Raven's Bluff is also unusual in that it is home to a disproportionate number of powerful individuals: swordsmen of epic stature, knights of unsurpassed faithfulness and strength, mages and priests and other magic wielders of dire power. The city is a city of heroes, and while Hawk Knights and Wizard's Guilds and dozens of interfering bands of adventurers stand about keeping an eye open for trouble, I find it difficult to achieve my goals. Two years ago, my armies would have overrun the Ravenaar defenses with no trouble if it had not been for the heroes who flocked to the city's defense. This time, I have decided to strike at the heroes first. When the city's most powerful defenders are dead or discredited due to the actions of their simulacra, Raven's Bluff will fall with hardly a blow."

"I am perhaps more sentimental than I thought I was," Jack admitted, "since I find that I do not care for the idea of laying waste the city I grew up in."

"I do not intend to lay waste to the city, Jack. My quarrel lies against only a small fraction of the city's inhabitants, the handful of powerful nobles, guilders and so-called heroes who rule this place. When they are gone, I shall stay my hand. I have no interest in devastating the people I intend to rule wisely and well."

"Your horde of two years past indicates otherwise,"

Illyth remarked boldly. "Orcs, goblins, giants, and ogres, all eager to sack the city and carry off its population in their entirety. Your quarrel at that point would seem to include all within the city's walls."

The Warlord lost her composure for a moment. Her face, until this moment set in a faintly amused and indulgent smile, hardened into something sharper than a blade.

"Did you ever wonder," she said with acid, "why, two years past, the battle for Raven's Bluff turned when it did? *I achieved my purpose without razing the city.* When it suited me to do so, I allowed my army to be defeated. In fact, I contributed significantly to the security of my future conquest by bringing before its walls a generation of orc and ogre warriors, only to have them cut down in sight of their goal. It will be ten years at least before the tribes can muster another army like that one, and by then I intend to have made Raven's Bluff completely unassailable.

"Clearly, I succeeded in some goals and failed in others when I brought the horde against Raven's Bluff. That was a tool that was wieldy for the job at the time. Now I find that other, subtler tools are better suited to my purpose. And that is all you need to know."

"I still do not understand how I fit into your plans," Jack said.

"In three ways. First, I have taken you into my service. That in itself is sufficient. Second, I believe that through you I may take control of the wild mythal. Third, your talents are particularly well suited for some tasks I have ahead of me."

There was a knock at the door. The Nar swordsman— Kel Kelek—appeared in the doorway. "My lady, the landing is near."

"Excellent. I'll be up in a moment," Jelan said. She

stood and buckled on her swordbelt again. "Jack, I am no fool. I have little reason to trust you, even though I believe it would be in your best interest to serve me willingly. I would have asked Yu Wei here simply to work a geas upon you, but he informs me that the results may be unpredictable given your talents, so I have resorted to a more simple security—Illyth. I have no wish to harm her without cause, but I will if I have to. Do not give me cause."

Jack frowned and carefully controlled his response. "I understand. I will cooperate, but you must promise that Illyth will not be harmed."

Illyth recoiled. "Jack, don't do it! Who knows what harm could come of her plots?"

"The Warlord honors her word to the letter," Jack admitted. "She will do exactly as she says. I don't have a choice."

"A wise decision." Jelan pulled leather gloves over her hands and strode past Jack, pushing her way past the Nar swordsman and climbing up the companionway. Then she turned on the stair, ducking a little to meet Jack's eyes. "Yu Wei recovered your weapons and magical devices from the prison's lockbox," she said. "Ready yourself for an expedition into Sarbreen."

The Warlord's party, Jack and Illyth included, entered the subterranean ruins of Sarbreen through a tunnel mouth excavated in the floor of an abandoned warehouse. The ancient dwarven city had few streets or thoroughfares. It was an endless series of chambers and halls and foundations, a lightless and directionless labyrinth that defied Jack's attempts to perceive the underlying symmetry. Smooth polished granite blocks covered the walls, almost untouched by the passage of seven hundred years since the city's destruction. Rainwater, run-off, and less pleasant waste dripped through the old dwarven hold from the human city above, turning some of the larger corridors into sewers.

"I've never been in this part of Sarbreen before," Jack said in a low voice to Jelan. "Where are we?"

"The Armory," the Warlord replied as they hurried through the darkness. "Many of Sarbreen's dwarves died in this place, defending the priceless weapons stored here from the pillaging horde of orcs and goblins. They died in vain."

At the end of the hall they passed through a great gate of wrought iron, sundered long ago by some terrible magic that peeled back the iron plate like soft putty. Dozens of moldering skeletons lay scattered nearby, along with a few scraps of rusted armor and the shards of broken weapons. Hathmar, the drow swordsman, led them onward through a number of small, winding passages that wandered between stone living chambers, rooms graced with shattered statues and tattered banners. "Living quarters of the weaponsmiths," the mercenary captain explained, "also looted long ago."

"Be careful, but hurry," warned Jelan. "We were followed from the Ladyrock, and I wouldn't be surprised if the Hawk Knights are on our trail. Keep your voices low, and be ready to douse our lights if we spot any light behind."

They came to several broad halls that had collapsed into rubble, with great rockfalls spilling out onto the floor from the walls and the ceiling. At one time the rooms must have been noble and majestic, each sixty or seventy yards in length and perhaps half that in breadth, but now they were cluttered with mounds of debris. In single file Jelan and her companions picked their way between the rockfalls, slipping and clattering over the wreckage.

"Revel halls," said Hathmar Blademark. "Take care, the Dragon Hall is close by."

At the far end of the collapsed halls they found a broad alcove or antechamber filled by a great dark well. A set of stone stairs wound down into the pit, circling around and around.

"Dim your light," said Jelan. "We do not want to advertise our presence to anything that might wait below."

Yu Wei complied, masking the glowing golden ball his magic had conjured. Then they groped down through the darkness, each with his or her hand on the shoulder of the person in front, the drow leading the way with his superior dark vision.

After several hundred steps they reached the bottom of the well and filed out into a high, sharply arched hall. The Tuigan and the Nar ran out ahead, weapons ready, but no dark-lurking monster waited; the vast chamber was empty.

"The Hall of the Dragon," Illyth whispered to Jack. "I never thought to see this place with my own eyes! It was the public meeting place of Sarbreen's guilders and masters, the seat of the city's government."

"I didn't realize you were so well versed in Sarbreen lore, dear Illyth," Jack replied.

"Fully half of the adventurers whose careers I studied explored Sarbreen at one time or another, and a number of them died in these depths. I suppose it just stuck with me."

Jack nodded, concealing his nervousness at the notion of people just like them meeting terrible dooms in these darkened dwarven halls, and turned his attention to the chamber itself. Dark galleries ran along the walls, providing room for hundreds of dwarves to watch the proceedings on the floor of the hall. Now nothing but a soft wind sighed through the high balconies. At the far end of the hall, a great stone dragon was carved in bas-relief forty feet tall. Its noble features grimaced in a terrible battle challenge.

"The Stone Dragon of Sarbreen!" Illyth breathed. "Jack, this is the stuff of legend! No one has seen this place in a hundred years and returned to tell the tale."

"That is not entirely true, my lady sage," Jelan said, sauntering closer. Yu Wei, Amarana, Hathmar, and the others stood guard warily, watching the numerous dark tunnel mouths that opened into the great chamber. "I myself have been here three times in the last six months in attempts to reach the Wild Mythal, but this barrier—" she gestured at the massive relief on the chamber's far wall— "has frustrated me every time. It is my hope that Jack can help me here."

Jack glanced up at the formidable structure. "I have no great skill at digging, but if you wish, I will take pick-axe in hand and do what I can."

"If only it were so easy," the Warlord said. "Beyond that wall lies a rift or passageway descending into the true underdark beneath the very deepest dwarven works. Yu Wei's divinations clearly show the way to the Wild Mythal, but to reach it we must pass through the doorway concealed in this wall. And that barrier has frustrated all the efforts of mighty wizards and priests both. It will not yield to me."

"But you, Jack Ravenwild, are a Ravenaar born and bred, infused with the chaotic energies of the device this barrier protects," Yu Wei intoned. "We believe you can open this passage."

Jack sighed and followed Jelan's gaze. He was inclined to allow the Warlord to stand frustrated before this wall until the end of time, but that was why Jelan had brought Illyth along. Clearly, this was not the time to challenge her.

"What do I have to do?"

"Come here," said Yu Wei.

The Shou wizard stood at the feet of the great image. The dragon was head-down, as if it had been frozen in the act of descending the wall. Serpentine coils and vast batlike wings shadowed the upper portions of the bas-relief, lost in the darkness high overhead, while the creature's fierce claws gripped a great orb ten feet across at the bottom, just beneath its open mouth and noble countenance.

"This sphere in the dragon's claws marks the doorway, but no opening spell at my command can part it, and more destructive spells are defeated outright."

"The wall is blank stone. What do you propose?"

The Shou scowled. "If you know an opening spell, attempt it. Perhaps the stone will accept your magic where it refused mine."

Jack shrugged and did as Yu Wei suggested. He stepped close and murmured the words to his passage spell, reaching out to caress the cold stone of the sphere-shaped surface. For a long moment he felt nothing. Then, abruptly, a streamer of emerald energy caressed him, dancing up from some wellspring far below his feet and winding left and right to stay in contact with him, no matter where he went. He gasped in shock and opened his eyes to look on the spiraling magic with his human vision. He saw nothing at first, although he could still feel it nearby. Then he realized that Yu Wei stared silently at something in front of them.

In the center of the stone sphere, beneath Jack's hand, a blot of darkness edged in green-glowing magic had appeared. Emerald energy whirled and darted around the aperture, which rapidly widened to fill the blank stone between the dragon's claws.

"Jack, you opened it!" said Illyth. She hugged her arms

around her shoulders, excited despite the circumstances.

"Indeed," said Yu Wei. The wizened sorcerer turned to the Warlord. "My lady, we should make haste. The aperture may not remain open for long."

Jack simply gaped. He hadn't even finished the spell . . . or so he thought. Could he have cast a spell without even realizing it, simply by concentrating on the feel of magic from the floor beneath his feet? What else might happen if he tried to channel the power he could sense?

"Excellent!" said Myrkyssa Jelan.

She checked her arms and armor, then joined them by the doorway. The others in her party—drow swordsman, Shar priestess, Tuigan warrior, and the others—followed quickly. Jelan looked at Hathmar and inclined her head; without hesitation the drow ducked into the dark opening, scouting the path ahead. "Now we shall see what the dwarves chose to conceal."

"So where does it go?" Jack asked.

"Down to the deeps," Yu Wei answered. "My divinations show a—"

"Silence!" hissed Jelan. She pointed at the stairwell behind them. A flicker of yellow light danced on the walls. She doused her own light. "Everybody, through the door! Someone is following us!"

Jelan glanced at the dark doorway, then took Jack by the elbow and guided him toward a deep niche in the wall guarded by a mighty stone statue of an armored dwarf.

"Go ahead!" she told her mercenaries. "I want to see who follows, but we'll withdraw as soon as we know. Jack, you will stay silent or Illyth suffers."

Yu Wei and the others ducked through the archway in the shadows beneath the dragon claws, carrying Illyth away with them. At the rear of the hall, yellow light grew brighter, closer, in the circling stairwell descending from the halls above. A sudden clatter echoed from the antechamber, and the glimmer of light flickered and flared wildly. Jack leaned forward, watching carefully now. Footsteps clattered on the stairs above, followed by the ringing of steel and distant cries of distress. A voice cried out in pain, another shrieked words of magic, and then something *inhuman* roared in challenge, a deep-throated growl that echoed throughout the entire room.

Jelan snorted softly beside him. "Be ready to move when I command," she said. "Someone is about to bring their battle into our presence, and I deem it wise to abandon the vicinity before we are caught up in an argument that isn't ours."

The archway in the opposite wall filled with yellow light and motion as several figures clattered down the last of the spiraling stairs in the antechamber and retreated out into the floor of the great hall. Marcus and Ashwillow, at the head of a handful of city soldiers, turned to face whatever it was that pursued them.

Out of the dark shaft in the adjoining chamber, six gray shapes suddenly dropped, with great leathery wings snapping out to break their plunge. They were about the size and shape of a man, but so heavy and powerful that the flagstones at the bottom of the shaft cracked under the impact of their descent. With roars of battle rage, the creatures surged out of the bottom of the well and assaulted the Hawk Knights and their soldiers.

Blades flashed and steel rang as the knight slashed out at his attackers. One recoiled, cradling a mangled arm and hissing in pain, but two others pummeled Marcus to the ground with blows powerful enough to powder stone. Ashwillow barked out a magical word and sent a jet of scorching blue flame into the middle of the pack. The creatures—some kind of gargoyles, Jack guessed—were driven back for a moment. Two soldiers seized Marcus by the arms and dragged him up, retreating from their assailants.

"That's enough," Jelan snarled. "Come on. We'll leave these fools to their fate."

Jack cringed. Marcus and Ashwillow certainly wished him no good and it might solve some problems later if they met their doom in Sarbreen today. Still he begrudged no one a chance to escape a grisly death at the claws of a flight of gargoyles.

Jack took one more look at the fight across the great room. The creatures had already recovered from Ashwillow's fiery attack, ignoring the patches of black, cracked hide that smoked across their broad backs and massive wings. With cries of rage, they took to the air, streaking across the vast space of the dwarven greathall like catapult stones in flight. The rogue ducked into the open passage and found a long tunnel lined with cool, smooth stone that gleamed in the reflected light. Yu Wei, Illyth, and the others waited thirty yards down the tunnel.

A moment later, Jelan darted into the passage behind Jack. "Move quickly," she called ahead. "We are pursued."

Three of the powerful gargoyles appeared in the darkness behind them, screeching with rage. They hurled themselves forward, crowding the small passageway and scrabbling past each other to reach Jelan first. The Warlord cast one cool glance over her shoulder and picked up her pace, keeping safely ahead of the flight. Jack decided to do the same. The passageway behind the sphere ran for almost a hundred yards, as straight as an arrow, before opening up on a tall, narrow cavern cleft by a great crevasse. The Warlord's party was trapped on a wide ledge, unable to flee any farther. Wind howled up from below, a roaring blast of air that rumbled and echoed in the cavern like the thunder of a nearby waterfall.

Illyth plucked at Jack's sleeve and pointed. "Look!" A round stone platform floated in midair in the center of the crevasse, level with the floor on which they stood. A wooden dock or landing extended out over the abyss to meet the edge of the stone platform.

Jack moved over to peer over the edge. As far as he could see, the crevasse plummeted down into the dark. He raised an arm to shield his eyes and blinked in astonishment.

"What is this place?" he shouted.

"The road to our goal," Jelan replied. She turned and drew her blade, preparing to defend the mouth of the passageway against the pursuing monsters. Tenghar and Hathmar joined her, forming a hedge of steel to seal the tunnel's exit. The gargoyles were almost upon them. "Yu Wei! Bar their passage!"

The Shou sorcerer inclined his head and raised his hands, muttering words and weaving his fingers. Golden flames suddenly exploded from the stone floor to fill the tunnel behind them, creating a sheet of leaping death that sealed the tunnel mouth completely. Jack could feel a small warmth on his face and hands, no stronger than sunlight on a clear day, but the heat must have been far more intense on the opposite side of the fire barrier; the gargoyles bayed in misery and retreated, shielding their faces with their great dark wings.

"The wall will hold them for a quarter hour!" Yu Wei cried. "After that, the monsters will be free to pass!"

"Well done," the Warlord said. "That will do for now. Turn your attention to the platform and determine how it operates. We will keep watch."

They waited a few minutes, buffeted by the winds, the scorching heat of the wizard's shield defending them from the gargoyles in the tunnel. Yu Wei muttered and mumbled, inspecting the floating platform.

At length he stepped back and said, "I believe I understand the device, Warlord, but it may be prudent to test it first in order to make sure that I have mastered the enchantment."

"I trust you implicitly, and we do not have much time," Jelan replied. She brushed by the sorcerer and jumped across to the stone platform as if she had absolute confidence in the precarious engine. It bobbed a little under her weight but remained stable. "Come on, then, everybody aboard. Jack, you stay close by me," she said. "I want you where I can keep an eye on you."

"I am completely trustworthy," Jack protested.

He followed Jelan and tried not to think about just how much of a drop might wait under his feet. He gave his hand to Illyth and helped her onto the platform, then moved aside to make room for the rest of Jelan's picked warriors.

"Nevertheless," Jelan said. "Trouble follows you like gulls following a fisherman's dory." She turned to face the rest of the party. "Keep your eyes open, friends. I am very concerned about what might or might not come up behind us in the dark."

Yu Wei stepped aboard last and carefully touched the heel of his staff to the old dwarven stone, speaking a word that Jack did not recognize. After a moment, the platform began to sink, dropping quickly and smoothly down the crevasse as the walls seemed to climb away from them.

The wind screamed like something flayed alive as they dropped into the darkness.

"Dungeon delving," mused Jack, "is an occupation for those unfortunate souls who have demonstrated that they are too stupid, ill-tempered, or incompetently noble to hold down any honest job."

He gazed out into the great vast darkness around him and shivered. For several minutes the stone platform had descended through empty air, as the crevasse had widened drastically hundreds (or perhaps thousands) of feet below its upper entrance. The walls were now well out of sight, and still they dropped. At least the platform hadn't yet taken them into any life-threatening peril, but that, of course, was no guarantee that it wouldn't at any moment. A cold, damp stream of air raked the open platform, hinting of vast subterranean spaces stretching away around them. The platform was a bubble of golden light, sinking into darkness like a coin dropped into a bottomless well.

"Surely recovering treasures long forgotten is better than outright theft and burglary?" Illyth replied.

"It's dangerous, but it's honest."

Jack stood close by her, holding her closely to keep her warm. Jelan had not provided Illyth with garb particularly suited for marching around in the frigid depths, and the noblewoman shivered constantly.

Jack shrugged and threw his cloak over her shoulders. "I'll trade risk for guilt any time," he said with a laugh.

Illyth's disapproving look stung him, and he fell silent. They gazed into the limitless dark, wondering when the descent would come to an end.

"Hathmar, what do you know of the depths beneath Sarbreen?" Jelan asked the drow swordsman. The Warlord did not take her eyes away from the wall of darkness around them, watching vigilantly for any sign of trouble. "Are there any monsters common to this region we should watch for? Hazardous conditions that might cause injury or death?"

"I have never walked these ways, Warlord," the drow said. "In Sarbreen's day, the region beneath the city was vigorously patrolled by the dwarven city above. If drow had lived here when Sarbreen was great, there would have been war. My people lived in the deep Underdark near this region, but they must have been long gone by the time of Sarbreen's founding. Certainly the Sarbreenaar never had any truck with them."

"Silence," hissed Yu Wei. "We've reached the bottom."

Around them long spires of rock now appeared at the edge of their bubble of light, gleaming wetly in the darkness and growing thicker and wider as they descended toward the giant stalagmites' unseen bases. Jack had the curious fear that the platform would settle on one of the rocky points and upend itself, but the makers of the ancient mechanism were not so careless; the platform came to rest on a square of polished granite with a soft grating sound. Jack hopped to the floor of the chamber and helped Illyth down; the others dismounted carefully, searching for any signs of danger.

"The gargoyles did not pursue us," Jelan said, looking up into the darkness. The Warlord frowned in concern. "They have wings. Why didn't they chase us down here?"

"Perhaps they have not yet broken through Yu Wei's wall," Amarana, the Shar priestess, said.

"Or perhaps they have no wish to be where we are now," Jack muttered. "It could be that they feared to follow you into the chasm."

"A cheerful thought," said Jelan. She shook herself and looked around the stone forest surrounding them. Great needles of stone rose into the darkness, as tall as the turrets of a castle. "Which way now?"

"According to my divinations, we should seek a lake of darkness," Yu Wei said. "We will find the wild mythal there." He consulted a small, dark orb held in his left hand and studied it for a moment. Then he pointed off into the darkness. "That way."

"Hathmar, you lead," said Jelan. "Amarana, would you join him? Your dark lady favors you with sight in places such as this. Yu Wei, Kel Kelek, follow them. Jack, you and I will stay close to Illyth. Tenghar, you and the rest cover the rear. And make sure you keep your eyes open."

With the drow and the Shar priestess in the lead and half a dozen swordsmen guarding their backs, they set off between the huge stalagmites, winding across an uneven floor of natural rock that surrounded the dwarven platform at the foot of the long descent. Jack offered Illyth an arm to steady herself and picked his way carefully across the damp stone. He could *feel* something now, even without closing his eyes or concentrating on it, a subtle tide that seemed to tug on his soul. It almost felt as if he were caught in an undertow, the race of water receding away from the shore to gather for a tremendous wave still unseen. And the power of the magic streaming past him resonated, recharged him, so that he felt full of power and skill and confidence. With every step he could sense his magical strength replenishing itself, a sensation he never experienced on the surface.

"I think we're getting close," he told Illyth. "I can feel something ahead of us, a very strong magic indeed. I don't think I've ever held this much power."

"The lake," called Blademark from the front, softly.

A moment later they all reached the shore. The water was oily and blacker than night, a great dark expanse whose farther shores might have been a hundred yards away or a hundred miles. Here, at least, the shore seemed to indicate a sizable body of water. Small waves lapped at the gravel strand, and a band of damp stones above the waterline hinted at a small tidal range. Left and right the shore was bare, marked only by boulder falls and rare pinnaclelike stalagmites rising up into the darkness.

"Are we supposed to swim from this point forward?" Jack asked.

"If necessary, I can arrange it," Yu Wei retorted. "We will do what must be done."

"Quiet," said Jelan. "Look." She pointed toward the center of the black lake. Out over the water, hundreds of yards beyond the limit of their vision, a green aurora danced. Emerald energy twisted in an ever-changing spiral, weird and ethereal. Jack felt each undulation as a tremor in his bones. "The wild mythal. That must be where it lies." She smiled and started forward—

—only to be abruptly lassoed by a slimy, brown tendril from the darkness to their right. Two more shot out, tangling her arms and wrapping several times around the Warlord's torso.

"Look out!" she cried. "Ropers!"

In the murk and shadows of a large fallen boulder, three dark, pulsing *things* shifted and gaped. Each looked like a stalagmite that had suddenly sprouted six long, thin tentacles. Jack caught a quick glimpse of bright teeth in their huge maws, and then more tentacles shot out, looping around Yu Wei, Amarana, and Jelan again.

Tenghar shouted a battle cry and leaped forward to hew at the tendrils binding the Warlord, only to be caught in turn by four more tendrils. He had the curious misfortune of being lassoed by two of the creatures at the same time, and between them the monsters were far stronger than him. The Tuigan was hauled off his feet and dragged toward the waiting fangs.

"Get off me!" he shrieked, flailing ineffectually with his tulwar.

His cries rose to a fevered pitch as he was dragged within reach of the ropers' maws. Something crunched in the darkness, and Tenghar abruptly stopped screaming.

"Merciful Oghma!" Illyth choked. "Those monsters—"

"I know," said Jack.

He looked around quickly. Jelan's warriors rushed forward to hack at the monsters. Yu Wei burned away one tendril, but two more seized him. Amarana fought to invoke her dark powers, but whipping tendrils spoiled her magic. The Warlord fought silently to keep from being dragged closer. She suddenly dropped flat and braced her feet against a ridge of rock, wedging herself in place. Calmly she released her sword and drew a dagger to begin sawing at the tendrils binding her.

"Kel Kelek! Hathmar! Aid Yu Wei and Amarana! The rest of you, slay those things!"

Jack saw his opportunity. Every one of the Warlord's followers was engaged by the ropers. He took Illyth's hand and quickly worked the spell of shadow-jumping, moving several hundred yards into the darkness and broken rock of the cavern floor. One moment they stood in a circle of yellow light, caught in the middle of a furious battle against monstrous predators; the next, he and Illyth stood alone in the darkness, listening to the sounds of a far-off battle.

Illyth recoiled in panic and cried out. Jack quickly caught her hand again.

"Shhhh," he said quietly. "We're safe. I took the opportunity of the ropers' attack to abandon the Warlord's expedition."

The girl panted in the darkness nearby. Her breathing slowed after a dozen heartbeats, and her hand stopped shaking. "I understand," she whispered back. "Jack, they'll come for us as soon as they finish with those—things."

"They might," he admitted, "but we will be hard to find. And it may be that Jelan has no further use for us and does not wish to spend the time tracking us down."

Illyth fell silent for a moment. Her hand gripped his tightly. "Jack," she said, "Could you please make some light? I don't like this."

"It's not wise, Illyth. Even a glimmer might be seen from a long way, and remaining inconspicuous is our best defense at the moment."

"I know, but . . . what if something like those ropers, or worse, is waiting out here in the darkness?"

Jack shivered despite himself. "Very unlikely," he lied. He looked around, and noted a faint glow of green in the distance. "Look, over there. I suspect that the mythal lies in that direction, and the lakeshore as well. We will head in that direction and then backtrack toward the stone platform from there. I'll have you out of here in an hour or two, and you'll have an adventure of your very own to write about in your journals."

"Are we going to abandon the wild mythal to the Warlord?"

"Illyth, what else are we supposed to do? She's leading a dozen extremely skillful and ruthless mercenaries, including a very powerful mage and a couple of top rank swordsmen. And Jelan herself is quite competent, too. There's only the two of us. Our best move is to get out of the way and hope that she doesn't find what she's looking for down here."

"Still, I feel that we ought to be doing something," Illyth protested.

"We'll notify the proper authorities the moment we get out of Sarbreen," Jack promised. "Now take my hand, and try to be quiet. We should keep moving."

Jack and Illyth spent the better part of an hour picking their way carefully through the darkness, listening for any signs of pursuit by the Warlord's party—or the telltale sounds of some abominable monstrosity native to the Underdark preparing to make them its next meal.

Although he knew it might be dangerous, Jack relented and created just a tiny glimmer of light, no brighter than candle flame, and used his magic to send it dancing ahead of them, illuminating dimly their path. Fortunately, they encountered nothing more dangerous than strange-looking lichens and odd, spikelike fungi sprouting from beneath heavy round boulders, and even then Jack gave the subterranean growths a wide berth.

The sounds of battle from the Warlord's encounter with the ropers had long since died away, but not before a pair of thunderclaps and a blast of searing white flame had blasted through the darkness hundreds of feet away. Jack decided that the wizardry probably meant that Jelan's party had eventually bested their attackers, since ropers weren't known to use lightning bolts to finish off their prey. The question was, what had the Warlord decided next? Had she ordered a search for Jack and Illyth, or had she continued on toward her goal?

"Jack, look. I think that stalagmite looks familiar." Illyth broke his train of thought, tugging on his sleeve and pointing. A towering peak the size of a castle turret rose above them, vanishing into the darkness. "The stone platform came to rest nearby."

"Illyth, we've passed a dozen just like in the last hour," Jack said. "How do you know?"

"I have a good sense of direction," the noblewoman replied. "I think we're near the platform."

Jack was inclined to argue the point, since he had been unsuccessfully trying to find that very spot for most of the last hour by navigating across the dark, featureless cavern floor, but he decided to indulge her. "All right, but let's be careful. Jelan may be lying in wait for us here, since she knows that this is our route back to the surface. I'll render us invisible as a precaution; keep hold of my cloak, or we'll never find each other again!"

Illyth agreed with a nod, and Jack worked the spells. The magic came swiftly and easily to him, another sign that the wild mythal was nearby. In the darkness, it was hard to tell if anything had changed or not, but Illyth clung tightly to the hem of his cloak.

"This way," she said.

Jack allowed Illyth to take the lead and followed her around the huge rock spire. At first he thought she'd missed her guess, but the square level came into view as they rounded a shoulder of the rock.

The platform was missing.

"Oh, dear," said Illyth. She shivered and pulled closer. "How are we supposed to get back up to the top again?"

"It might be a blessing in disguise, when you consider that the chamber above might be filled with angry gargoyles," Jack mused. "Of course, I have no idea how we can get back home otherwise." He looked up into the darkness overhead, trying to guess how far they'd descended on the levitating platform. A small globe of yellow light hovered far above, sinking toward them as Jack watched. He nudged Illyth and pointed before remembering that he was invisible and his arm could not be seen. "Look up. The platform's coming back down, and someone with light is riding it."

"The Hawk Knights?"

"It could be. I doubt that the Warlord has had time to return here, ascend, and start to descend again. Let's find a good place of concealment and await their arrival. If nothing else, we need to use the platform when the current riders are done with it."

Jack drew her back a little ways behind the rock, and they settled down to wait. The platform descended quickly, dropping hundreds of feet in no more than two or three minutes. It slowed and stopped soundlessly atop the square plaza in precisely the same manner as before.

Five figures stood atop the stone, encased in a dome of blinding light: Zandria, the Red Wizard; Marcus and Ashwillow, Knights of the Hawk; and the thieves Anders and Tharzon, knights of the post. Jack blinked in surprise.

"This is an unexpected alignment, to say the least," he muttered.

"I recognize the two Knights of the Hawk," Illyth whispered. "They're the ones who arrested you at the Blue Lord's theatre. And I saw the Red Wizard at your trial, but who are the other two, and what are they all doing here? Are they friend or foe?"

Jack realized that he honestly could not answer the question. Not only did he not know, he didn't even have a good guess. Marcus and Ashwillow would arrest him on sight. Zandria's reaction might be anything. And with Anders and Tharzon, it all depended on how much they resented his shadow-twin's humiliating assaults. But . . . even if all five wanted him dead on the spot, they had no quarrel with Illyth and might be counted upon to get the noblewoman out of the Underdark and back where she belonged.

"We will present ourselves and hope for the best," he told Illyth.

Before she could ask another question, Jack stepped out from behind the rock and dropped his spell of invisibility. "Good day, gentle persons," he called. "I must confess I am glad to see you all!"

All five whirled to face him, weapons ready. It was clear that they'd seen no little fighting recently, and their reactions were almost comical. Jack was careful not to smile. He gestured toward Illyth and then approached the light. Anders seemed relieved to see him, but Tharzon scowled darkly. The dwarf was clean-shaven, the first time Jack had ever seen him thus. Marcus and Ashwillow advanced on him, weapons drawn; Jack decided to blunt their attack before it began.

"If you are looking for the Warlord Myrkyssa Jelan, she is not here. We had a falling out, and she proceeded without us. But I can show you where she went, and I am afraid she is up to no small mischief."

Marcus wasted no time. "Where is she?" he demanded.

Jack pointed toward the dim green haze, far off in the darkness. "A short march from here you'll find a subterranean sea, and the Warlord somewhere out on or under its dark waters." He looked over the two knights again, noting the furrows gouged in their steel cuirasses and the various bruises and cuts covering their features. "Last I saw, you led a detachment of Ravenaar soldiers. Where are your men?"

"Dead or dying," Marcus growled. "Your mistress led us into an infernal ambush. You've much to answer for, street rat." He advanced again, blade weaving.

"Hold, Marcus," called Zandria. "Many people wish Jack dead, but that does not mean you are free to kill him." The wizardess stepped forward, intervening. "We have more important things to do."

"Indeed," Jack said. He turned to Anders and Tharzon. "Good friends, what brings you here, and in this company?"

Tharzon growled something unintelligible. Anders shrugged. "I'd thought I might break into Ill-Water and extricate you from your predicament, mostly because I believe you still owe me quite a large sum of money. And Tharzon agreed to help, so that he could kill you with his own hands instead of allowing the city to deprive him of his rightful vengeance. While it's true that Tharzon and I still hadn't resolved the question of what to do with you when we got you out, we both agreed that the first step was to remove you from Ill-Water. We rowed out in a black-painted dory and were about to commence our rescue when the *Storm Gull* appeared, and the Lady Mayor ordered your release. So we followed, hoping that we'd find it easier to free you from a small party surrounding the Lady Mayor. Then she led us straight into the darkest depths of Sarbreen."

"You truly intended to free me? After the misery my shadow wrought on both of you?" Jack found his heart swelling with pride. "What wretched thieves! Any cutthroat worth his salt would have let me swing!"

"Your untimely death would have left too many mysteries unresolved," Anders finished.

"If it turns out you weren't responsible for the *incident* on Manycoins Way," Tharzon added in a low rumble, "Anders convinced me that it might be possible that you can tell me who *was* responsible. I live to settle that account, Jack."

Jack turned to Zandria. "So I can explain to my satisfaction the presence of Marcus, Ashwillow, Anders, and Tharzon," he said amicably, "but I don't understand how you come to be here, dear Zandria."

"Three reasons," she said brusquely, "the ring, the dagger, and the death of Brunn at the hands of your simulacrum. Tempting as it is to blame you for the last, I know better. Whoever made that shadow of you bears responsibility for its actions. Like your fellow cutthroats, I intended to remove you from Ill-Water so that I could recover my property and discover the identity of your enemy. I followed the Lady Mayor as well, until I encountered these two ruffians and accosted them. We compared notes and resolved to join forces for the moment. Later, in the chamber of the stone dragon, we encountered the Hawk Knights here and struck a deal with them as well." She crossed her arms, eyes blazing.

"And, you rescued me from the burning tavern when you might easily have left me to die. Consider the debt repaid."

Illyth spoke up from her place by Jack's side, revealing herself. "So, what do we do now?"

Five hostile stares turned on her. "We have what we came for," Anders remarked. "We've found Jack. The sooner out of this place, the better."

"Unlikely, barbarian!" Marcus snapped. "I am taking Ravenwild into custody. He is staying right where I can see him, and I am not going back to the surface until I've caught the Warlord as well."

"I believe that we all have more important business here than bringing me to trial," Jack said. "You said it yourself, Marcus—the Warlord is down here, too, and she is much more noteworthy a felon than I."

Marcus scowled. "What of it? The accusations against you demand our attention." He advanced on Jack, sword ready. "Ash, watch the ruffians. We'll sort this out when we have him in custody."

"No one is taking anyone into custody!" Zandria raised her hand and created a flash of light to seize attention. "While we stand here arguing, the Warlord comes closer to reaching her goal."

"Stand down, Sir Marcus," Illyth said. "The Red Wizard speaks the truth. Regardless of Jack's guilt or innocence, the Warlord's plans proceed. You should concern yourself with matters of justice after we have addressed matters of the city's survival."

The two Hawk Knights exchanged dark looks but did not refute Illyth's point. "Agreed," said Ashwillow, speaking for both. "Stopping the Warlord's designs takes precedence, but I cannot make any promises about what happens when we return to the city."

Jack bowed. "Then may I suggest that we resume our

quest? If you'll follow Illyth and me, we'll show you which way the Warlord went."

Moving swiftly, they set off across the cavern floor, nervously scanning the darkness around them. They walked a couple of hundred yards and came to the cold lakeshore, where three dead lightning-blasted ropers marked the scene of Jelan's battle against the monsters.

The green spiral of energy out over the water was even stronger, more distinct, than before, a twisting emerald strand weaving slowly back and forth. Jack could hardly take his eyes from it; the others were awestruck as well.

"I think the wild mythal lies beneath that," Illyth said quietly. "That's where Jelan and her henchmen went."

"So how do we reach it?" said Tharzon. "That must be five hundred yards, at least, and this water will be icy cold."

"Swim or sail," Anders replied. "Flying would work too, I suppose. Given those options, perhaps we should look around for anything that might serve as a raft."

"You omitted an option," Zandria said.

The mage stepped into the water and waded out until it was knee deep, reaching down to stir her staff in the blackness. She muttered a few words and gestured, working a spell. Instantly the water in a large circle around her changed in texture, color, filling with streams of bubbles.

"We can walk. I have cast a spell to render the water in this circle breathable. If you stay close to me and remain within its bounds, you will be able to breathe with no trouble at all."

Tharzon balked. "I'll pass, thanks. My father didn't raise me to walk on the bottoms of lakes."

"It is perfectly safe," Zandria said.

"Then I will not concern myself on your behalf," Tharzon replied. "You can go ahead without me, but I am not walking into that lake."

Marcus sighed and sheathed his sword. He waded into the water beside Zandria and motioned to Ashwillow and Anders.

"Come on," he said. "If we stand here trying to argue a dwarf into doing something he doesn't want to do, we'll be here all day. The Warlord is still ahead of us."

The Hawk Knight and the Northman shrugged and waded in as well. Jack joined them a moment later, Illyth following behind them. Tharzon remained on the shore. Jack turned back and waved at him.

"Better to stick together," he said. "Who knows what might be lurking out there in the cavern?"

"Who knows what might be lurking in that lake?" Tharzon grumbled, but the dwarf winced and walked into the cold waters, axe held high over his head.

Jack nodded and turned toward the lake. Zandria waded deeper, the circle of changed water following her. The water was bitterly cold, and he still felt as if he stood waist deep in any normal lake, but he had confidence in Zandria's magic. He followed her, and when the water rose to his neck, he ducked under and tried a very cautious breath. The changed water felt strange and cold in his mouth and throat, dense and humid, but it was indeed breathable.

"Not pleasant, but tolerable," he said aloud, and he was surprised to hear his voice echoing in his ears as if he'd spoken more or less normally.

With one last look at the cold stone-strewn shore, Jack turned back into the lake and allowed the waters to close over his head entirely.

They marched across the bottom of the lake floor for a strange, indeterminate time, chilled and wet despite the airy water that encased them. The lake was virtually life-less, the ground beneath their feet smooth and weedless gravel only marked by an occasional haze of algae or detritus. The buoyancy of their bodies imparted a very long, bouncing stride to each of them, carrying them through comically awkward steps. It seemed to Jack that they moved through some kind of dark and sinister dream world.

It soon became obvious that maintaining a straight course to the center of the subterranean lake would be next to impossible. Marcus halted in indecision, unable to tell whether he marched straight toward the gyre of energy that was visible from the lakeshore or not. Jack could feel the tug of the mythal so strongly that he doubted he could walk in any other direction, even if he wanted to. He moved up and took the lead, guiding the others across the rocky bottom toward the unseen font of magic ahead. Jack trudged on for a time, and then he saw a dim glow ahead through the darkness, a bubble of green light on the lake floor ahead.

"Douse our light, Zandria," he called through the strange medium. "There is something up ahead."

The mage complied without a word, leaving them in blackness so complete that Jack had to repress his body's natural rebellion at being in the cold, lightless wet. But with their light's absence, the light ahead grew stronger. Jack led the others toward the other light, and as they drew closer it became clear that an emerald column glimmered from the lake bottom up to the unseen surface overhead, surrounded by a wall of water that streamed sluggishly around it. In fact, Jack could feel the tug of the current crossing their small circle. He advanced closer, halting only when they were a few feet from the perpendicular wall ahead. The circling current was so strong that Jack and his companions had to use their hands to steady themselves on the rocks of the bottom in order to keep from being pulled out of Zandria's circle.

On the other side of the glassy wall, Jack could dimly see a stone platform on the floor of the lake, surmounted by a massive stone pillar thirty or forty feet in height and at least ten feet thick at the base. The surface was far out of sight above, easily a hundred feet at this point, but the weak maelstrom circling the stone on the lake floor left a channel of air all the way to the surface, a gleaming emerald shaft that glistened with reflected light.

"The mythal," Jack said. The water carried away his words.

Zandria tapped his shoulder and pointed to one side. There, ten figures surrounded the wild mythal, distorted and dim behind the swirling water wall. Jack could not distinguish anything other than the largest details in any of them—relative height, whether they wore light or dark clothing, where they stood in relation to each other.

"The Warlord and her men," Zandria cried. "What now?"

"Can we breach the wall of the maelstrom?" Marcus called.

"The spell of airy water will not prevent it, but it depends on what magic holds the water at bay," Zandria said. "The only way to know for certain would be to try."

"We must be virtually invisible to them," Anders said. "They would see nothing but a wall of black water from their side. We can take them unawares."

"You mean to attack?" Jack asked.

"That is why we came down here," Zandria said, "to foil the Warlord's plans and to bring her to justice. Can you think of any other way to accomplish those ends?"

Jack took the question seriously and thought hard. They were seven against ten, and one of them was not a

296 • The City of Ravens

combatant—Illyth would have no place on a battlefield. But they would possess the advantage of surprise, which counted for a lot, and ultimately, Zandria was right. They'd come here to stop the Warlord. Myrkyssa Jelan would undoubtedly resist. That meant that he had to prepare for a fight.

"No," he admitted. "We will have to hit them hard and fast while we have surprise. Yu Wei is a very dangerous wizard—he is an old Shou who wears yellow robes. Make sure we hit him first!"

Marcus drew his sword, a bizarre motion in the water. He lowered his visor. "On the count of three, we will all try the barrier together. All of us through, or none of us. One . . . two . . . three!"

With the others, Jack scrambled forward and threw himself at the bright wall ahead, unsure of what to expect. It yielded before him, distending inward, and then he burst into open air in a spray of water and mist. He stumbled and went to all fours, then scrambled to his feet and ran forward to get clear of the maelstrom's walls. Beside him, Illyth stumbled, while Marcus plowed through the barrier like a bright knife slicing through a sheet of wax paper.

Jelan and her followers whirled to confront the threat, goggling with astonishment. In the open air Jack could hear the wild mythal throbbing and crackling, an aura of emerald motes dancing around the device in an endless coruscation. The floor beneath his feet was cool tile, inlaid in an exotic spiraling design that circled the colossal stone in the center. He ignored it and worked his force globe spell, hurling two potent spheres at the Shar priestess, as she offered the most convenient target.

"Beware, Jelan!" he called. "I have returned!"

To his amazement, the spheres flew from his fingertips

and tripled in size, fed by the streaming emerald energy dancing around the mythal. Amarana managed to dodge one, which blasted a mercenary swordsman with the impact of a giant's hammer, but the other blew her legs out from under her. The mail-clad priestess screeched and hit the tiled floor hard, her legs badly broken by the force of Jack's spell. The mythal, he realized. Its magic powers are my own!

Then one of Jelan's followers stabbed at him with an evil gout of black flame that twisted to follow Jack despite his efforts to evade the sorcerous fire. The searing heat and crackling energy contorted his limbs and crumpled Jack to the ground, but now the battle was joined all around him. Zandria hurled a bolt of brilliant lightning straight at Yu Wei. The Shou sorcerer screamed as the white energy illuminated him like a living pillar and then channeled through his incandescent body to strike at the mercenaries who were unfortunate enough to stand near by, linking them all in a bright and deadly pinion of energy. Marcus dashed at Jelan, who had some-how eluded the fire and the lightning, but from the knight's left, a mercenary captain raced forward, forcing Marcus to break off his attack and meet his instead. They circled in a flurry of hard-struck blows, swords ringing in the damp air.

The lightning chain flickered to nothing. Jack blinked the afterimages from his eyes, trying to get his bearings, and looked up just in time to see Yu Wei crumple to the ground, a burnt husk. Three of Jelan's swordsmen fell with him. Heartened, Jack struggled to his feet and rejoined the fray. To the left, Marcus and the captain continued their duel. On the right, Anders fought for his life against the blindingly fast drow swordsman Hathmar Blademark. Zandria traded spells with the Nar warlock Kel Kelek, parrying his spells with counterspells of her own. The tattooed warrior screamed with frustration and abandoned his attempts to breach her defenses, rushing the red-haired mage with his long sword. He crashed into her and knocked her to the stone floor, struggling to bring his sword to bear.

Jelan! Jack realized. Where is she? He searched the battlefield for the Warlord and spotted her pacing deliberately toward the wild mythal, moving strangely.

"Illyth, help Zandria!" he cried, and then he ran straight for the mythal stone.

He made it within ten feet before something kicked his feet out from under him. An invisible force repelled him from the stone, spinning him to the floor. Jack looked up just as Tharzon rebounded from the same transparent barrier he had struck.

"Moradin's beard! What is this?" the dwarf groaned.

Jack turned, expecting an attack from Jelan—but the Warlord simply ignored him with nothing more than a quick glance of appraisal. Jack rolled over and stood up, trying to determine why she hadn't run him through as he lay helpless on the floor. Then his eyes fell on the spiral pattern that surrounded the base of the drow mythal.

A faint, emerald glimmer surrounded the mythal at a range of twenty feet or so, rising in delicate sheets like a mirror maze made of green diamond dust suspended in the air. Jack stood just inside the outer barrier. Tharzon scrambled to his feet only an arm's length on the other side. The dwarf tried to step through, but the magical field repelled him again.

"Damnation! I can't move through!" Tharzon cursed in anger.

"It seems that I can," Jack replied. "You help the others. I'll see what I can do about Jelan." He turned back to the Warlord.

Jelan carefully approached the stone itself, glancing over her shoulder to keep an eye on the battle. She spotted him and smiled in a warlike fashion.

"Stand back," she commanded. "I bear you no particular malice, Jack, but I will not tolerate interference!"

Jack frowned. Jelan was a very skilled swordswoman, and he was hesitant to resort to force. But no one else in his party would be able to come to his aid for some time yet; the skirmish still raged outside the emerald field.

"If you'll tell me what you are doing, I might decide that I have no reason to obstruct you!" he called, hoping to distract her.

"Ending a curse," she replied, "and mastering this stone."

The former didn't seem too bad, but Jack didn't like the implications of the latter. He steeled himself for a fight and stepped toward her.

"Not if I can help it, dear Elana," Jack said. He summoned up a green spiral of energy, vibrant and powerful, and lashed out at her.

The bolt crackled across her torso and did not affect her in the least. Jelan smiled sweetly.

"Magic cannot touch me, Jack. You'll have to do better than that!" Then she danced away around the stone, circling away from him. The shimmering energy seemed denser, more substantial, the closer he moved to the stone pillar. Clearly, it wasn't a matter of walking up and manipulating the device; one had to carefully negotiate the fields of chaotic energy wreathing the wild mythal.

"What happens when she reaches the stone?" Jack muttered to himself.

He had a suspicion that he did not want to find out. He resumed his pursuit, slipping toward the stone as fast as he could while trying to keep Jelan in sight.

Outside, the impetus of his companions' attack had

stalled. Anders and Marcus were matched by swordsmen every bit as skillful as they were, if not more so. Zandria and Illyth struggled against Kel Kelek. Ashwillow worked spell and blade against three of Jelan's picked swordsmen, determined fighters who sought to corner her and cut her down. She halted two of them with a spell that rooted them to the spot, holding them in place through the force of her will, but the third swordsman reached her and slashed her across the torso. Ashwillow cried out and fell, curled around her wound, as the swordsman looked around for his next opponent.

Tharzon crashed into the man who'd struck down Ashwillow and knocked him to the floor. With one hand he slapped the swordsman's helmet from his head, and with the other he split the fellow's skull with his axe. The dwarf picked himself up, just as Hathmar wounded Anders and drove the barbarian to one knee with a series of blinding slashes.

"Hold on, Anders! I am coming!" Tharzon called.

Jack returned his attention to Jelan and moved closer, completing a circuit of the mythal stone three and a half laps behind Jelan. He turned the corner and suddenly found that she had halted, facing a smooth flat patch that marked one side of the stone. She'd reached the center, and he was only ten or twelve feet behind her. Jack circled carefully, warily, nearer. He was almost in sword reach, and it wouldn't help anything if he allowed her to gut him just as he caught her. I need to distract her, he decided.

"Jelan! Your lieutenants and swordsmen are defeated! You have no hope of victory. I call on you to surrender!"

Jelan glanced over her shoulder at him, measured the distance from the mythal face to the spot he currently occupied, and smiled. "Your friends have the upper hand," she admitted, "but my soldiers are still fighting. I see no need to give in yet." She turned back to the mythal.

Jack scowled. He plucked the poignard from his belt and threw it at her, but the repelling force that protected the mythal from his approach also defeated missiles. The dagger clattered to the ground only a foot from where it had left his hand. Jelan did not even take notice. Instead, she faced the stone and seemed to raise her hands in supplication, closing her eyes and stretching as if she could embrace the colossal pillar if she tried hard enough.

"Whatever it is you're attempting to do, you are out of time," Jack promised darkly.

He spared the battle outside another look. With Tharzon's aid Anders fought his way to his feet again, blood streaming from several wounds. The powerful Northman beat aside the drow captain's attack and rammed forward breast-to-breast with the mercenary, shoving Hathmar back toward the wall of water surrounding the stone. Feathers of white water streaked away from the drow as he breached the barrier, and then Anders hammered him all the way through, losing his balance as the maelstrom swept away Hathmar. He drifted back into the black depths of the lake, caught in the current and swept back from air and life. Helplessly, the drow vanished into the dark depths.

Anders spotted Jack and Jelan and dashed straight at them, only to encounter the same barrier that restricted Jack. He rebounded and went down hard.

"I have an argument with you, Warlord!" he cried.

"So?" Jelan laughed. "You, too, are not in time." She completed whatever ritual or preparation she had performed, and then slashed open the palm of her left hand with a dagger. Then she pressed her bloody hand to the cold, dark stone.

With a detonation that tossed Jack, Blacktree, and everyone else nearby to the ground, the wild mythal exploded with emerald energy. Whips of green power flailed against the water, the stone, the darkness above with the fury of wildcats, sizzling and snapping. The maelstrom's eye blasted apart in a spray of cold water and reformed fifty yards wider than it had been, hammered backward by the power pouring from the mythal stone. And in the center of it all, Jelan arched and screamed with ecstasy and delight as the energy poured into her body, filling her, dancing across her skin like fire.

"I have done it!" she cried.

Done what? Jack wondered as he picked himself up and staggered to his feet. The magic streamed into Jelan as if she were a bottomless well, drinking and drinking without reaching satiation. Dully he noticed that the tile paths were now marked by walls of emerald force, the invisible barrier now visible and unbreakable, completely encapsulating him with the Warlord and the wild mythal. Magic now ran from his body to the stone, draining from his soul as blood might drain from slashed wrists. Moment by moment he felt it slipping away from him.

"Elana," he coughed. "What have you done?"

"For ten generations my family has suffered," she cried triumphantly. "Once we were mighty sorcerers, born to wield magic, the most powerful of all Kara-Tur. Then our magic was stripped from us by a divine curse! Now, at last, I have undone that wrong! We will be sorcerers again, one with the Weave, strong in the Art! *It is in my blood!"*

"You wrecked Raven's Bluff for this?" Jack asked in amazement.

Magic buffeted him, ruffled his hair and clothing, howled around him like a demon, but he could not sense it. He only felt its effects, and the ache in his heart, the sense of something missing, was unbearable.

"This is my restitution," she shouted. Energy wreathed her dark hair like a crown of emeralds. "My penance! And my triumph! I have freed my bloodline of the antimagic curse, and I have claimed the first city of my empire. I am bound no longer!"

"What of the mythal?" Jack cried. "You are destroying it!"

"I am *taming* it," Jelan replied. "Within its domain, I am the arbiter of all magic, I *am* magic. My kingdom will be unassailable!"

"Who gave you the *right?*" Jack demanded. "We have no need of an overlord. We do not desire a tyrant to decide who may use magic and who may not. You broke your curse—good! You have righted an ancient wrong, but you have no legitimacy here, no claim to rule Raven's Bluff!"

Jelan met his eyes evenly. "I do not ask for the right, Jack Ravenwild. I take it! I once offered you a chance to serve me. This is your last opportunity to reconsider your answer. Will you swear allegiance to me, serve me as one of the rulers of this city? Or would you rather remain a street rat for the rest of your days?"

Jack studied her face. He could see death waiting in her eyes if he answered wrong. He glanced behind him, where Illyth, Anders, Tharzon, and Zandria waited and watched, hemmed out by the green fields of magic. All of Jelan's lieutenants and swordsmen were down, as were the Hawk Knights. *I didn't even see the end of the battle,* Jack thought to himself. *What happened?*

"Well?" Jelan demanded.

Jack's allies were silent. Perhaps they'd already tried to make themselves heard through the wall of power surrounding the stone and failed; they simply watched him now, their expressions unreadable. Hope, despair, anger, compassion—it didn't matter what they wanted. It was up to him. He turned back to Jelan and smiled.

"I decline," he said.

Jelan raised her hand and struck him with a bolt of icy green lightning. Jack howled in pain and collapsed in a seizure of pain, arms and legs flailing against the stone. He bit his tongue hard. Blood filled his mouth. After an eternity of pain, the seizure relaxed, and he moaned aloud. Awkwardly, he turned himself over and levered himself to his hands and knees.

"Your spells lack subtlety," he gasped, pushing to his feet. He picked up his rapier and advanced on her.

The Warlord stepped away from the stone and drew her own sword. "Blades, then," she said.

Without hesitation she darted forward and slashed high at his head, a graceful and deadly arc that would have decapitated him with ease if he hadn't thrown himself to the ground to duck beneath it. Jack managed to get the point of his rapier up fast enough to back her off a step when she moved to finish him on the ground. Then he scrambled sideways until he gained his feet again.

The Warlord laughed and came at him again, offering him no chance to rest. She slashed and whirled like a dancer with a baton, impossibly swift and skillful. Jack deflected her blade from his heart by a lucky parry, blocked another by retreating behind a corner of the mythal stone, and then took a long, shallow cut along his ribs as he barely twisted away from a thrust that would have impaled him at the navel. He gasped in pain and backed away again. Already his limbs trembled with fatigue. I can't beat her, he realized. In a minute, maybe two, I'll slip or miss a parry and she'll run me through, and that will be it.

"You are not much of a swordsman, Jack," Jelan said.

"You might have been a good one, with some training. You've got good reflexes and an excellent eye, but you're not there yet."

"I'll work on that right after you kill me," he snapped.

Angrily, he called upon the power of the stone ring and felt new strength flood into his limbs, toughness imbue his flesh. Fueled by the ring's power, he counterattacked with everything he had, thrusting and riposting and lunging. Jelan simply laughed again and danced back, using graceful turns of her blade to deflect his stone-strength attacks. Jack overextended, dropping to one knee to reach her, and she slapped the rapier out of his hand with a wicked cut that would have laid open his right forearm if not for the ring's defensive enchantment. Jack cried out, stung, and staggered back.

"You've made a lot of poor choices recently," Jelan said. The smile faded from her face, replaced by something cold and deadly. "Time to face the consequences, Jack." She stalked closer, the tip of her sword unwavering.

Jack reached for his belt to draw his poignard, futile as it was. But he'd already thrown the weapon at her; the scabbard was empty. The dwarven knife! he remembered. As quick as thought, he stooped to his boot and threw the knife with a wicked underhanded motion using all his marvelous skill and the strength of the enchanted ring.

Jelan almost dodged the throw, twisting her torso with speed a cat would have envied and raising her sword point to deflect the dark knife. She wasn't quite fast enough. The dark blade took her on the left side of the torso, just under her breast, and pierced her fine armor as if it didn't exist. Myrkyssa Jelan grunted in pain and surprise, shuddering, and reached up to grip the knife handle.

"A treacherous blow," she gasped. "Hard struck . . . but not enough, not now."

Blood running through her fingers turned to green fire as mythal magic played over her wound. Jelan's mastery of the mythal permitted her to draw on the stone's magic to seal her injury and preserve her life.

"Mask's eyes," muttered Jack. "She's unbeatable." He had to do something unexpected, something extraordinary.

Impelled by desperation, Jack took advantage of Jelan's distraction and raised his left hand. The stone ring glowed with power as he willed it to life, this time calling on the impossible, seeking to shape the mythal itself. The mythal stone shrieked energy as the ring's magic fought to change it. Jelan must have felt the change through her connection with the device. She whirled and stared at the stone, trying to gauge its effects on her sorcery.

Jack threw himself forward and pushed her *into* the mythal stone. At the last moment Jelan sensed her danger and started to turn; cold steel kissed Jack's ribs as she struck out at him. But his momentum was enough to carry him into her, and she staggered back into the wild mythal itself. He sprawled to the ground at the foot of the stone, as the Warlord vanished into the rune-carved rock like a drowning woman sinking beneath black water.

Jack released the ring's power and allowed the stone to heal itself around her.

In an instant, the space Jelan occupied refilled with rock. He caught one last glimpse of Jelan as the stone walled shut, and then she was gone in a green flash of energy. Thunder shook the entire column, and the aurora scoured him like the blast of a furnace. The rings of energy barring access to the stone fell like curtains of water as Jack slumped to his knees, hand jammed against the cold dull ache under his rib cage. Then the maelstrom itself began to waver and collapse, the mythal's magic no longer sufficient to sustain it.

"Jack!" cried Illyth from a great distance. He turned to look behind him; the noblewoman and the others sprinted toward him, even as water began to cascade from above and darkness swirled up from below. He thought that Zandria was trying to work a spell—and then the dark waters swallowed him entirely.

EPILOGUE

White gauze danced over his head.

He was lying in a soft bed, surrounded by a thin curtain of translucent white that shifted and sighed in a warm wind. He ached all over, but his pain seemed very distant.

"Am I dying?" he wondered aloud.

"Do you wish to die?"

A dark-haired woman in blue sat beside him, her face impossibly beautiful. Wisdom gleamed in her eyes, and compassion, and strength, and a hundred things more that he couldn't begin to describe. She was completely serious in her question, and somehow he knew that dying would not necessarily be a bad choice now.

Since she asked in seriousness, he tried to answer her the same way. "Only if I have to," he said. "I am not certain that I am done living yet."

"Good," the lady in blue said. "I have something that I would like you to do for me, and it will be easier if you choose to live."

He looked at her again and tried to focus clearly on who he was, who she might be, but it was difficult. It seemed impossible that a lady such as she could have anything she needed anyone to do for her.

"What is it, my lady?"

"The wild mythal still exists, unbound, untamed," she said. "I could rend the Weave to silence it, but if I did so, I fear that no magic would ever work there again, perhaps not anywhere within a hundred miles of the spot where it stands. The safest thing to do is to disperse its power among a great number of people, as I have always done. In the hands of one person, a weapon may be dangerous. Break it into a thousand pieces and give it to a thousand people to carry, and it is much less threatening. I wish you to accept a greater portion of the load."

He simply stared at her. "Why?"

"The wild mythal also needs a will to tame it, a spirit to guide its sentience. The Warlord's will not suffice; you exiled her to a very distant plane when you expelled her from the stone. If you relinquish your bond, the mythal will select another, and its preference is likely to be dangerous. It has tasted of Jelan's ambitions and hungers for more. With my help, you will check the mythal's dangers."

"Am I to use it to help people?"

"Use it as you see fit," the lady replied. "It might be best if the wild mythal served no purpose, malign or benign, but it is a mortal magic and thus a mortal decision. I wish to make sure that the Weave remains whole. Fetter the stone for me, and that will be enough. Will you do this for me?"

He thought for a moment, understanding that this also was a serious question. Then he nodded. "I will."

The lady smiled and said no more. She faded away, leaving him adrift in a white maze.

Some time later, he awoke. To his surprise, the whiteness was still there. He rested in a white bed, in a white room with white curtains. And Illyth sat beside him, also dressed in white. She was reading a book, but she looked up at Jack when she felt his eyes on her.

"You're awake," she said in surprise.

"Did you see the lady?" Jack asked.

"Lady? You must have seen me watching over you," Illyth said. She smiled. "You've been unconscious for more than a week. We thought we would lose you."

Jack started to sit up, but the lightness in his head dissuaded him. He lay back down in the pillows. "A week? What happened?"

"What do you remember?"

"We were at the mythal stone. I used the ring of stone to shove Jelan *into* the mythal and then closed it on her. Then the water—"

"Zandria teleported us away just in time. A moment more, and I fear we all would have been drowned. As it was, you barely survived. Jelan almost killed you, Jack."

"What of the city, the shadows, all the rest?" he asked.

Illyth smiled and set down her book. She came close and laid a hand on his forehead. "Jelan had arranged for a coup to begin as soon as she mastered the mythal. She had hired companies of mercenaries throughout the city—there was fighting in the street all day, and her troops were backed by some of the merchant houses loyal to the Lady Mayor and noble houses seeking to settle old feuds during the chaos. The mayor's office is vacant, as you might imagine; the deputy mayor is filling in for the moment. There have been no shadow attacks since we were in Sarbreen. Zandria says that any shadows left might have dissipated when Yu Wei died, so things are getting back to normal, I guess."

"Do they still mean to execute me?" Jack asked.

"For your valor in defeating the Warlord and your help in unmasking her duplicity, the High Magistrate has granted you a full pardon," Illyth said. "Of course, that is dependent on the consensus of the Council of

Lords, but it seems likely to be confirmed when the noble council—or what's left of it—meets again."

"I'd better start looking into this," Jack said. He started to lever himself up and abruptly found himself flat on his back. Illyth had pushed him back down with one hand. He winced. "Maybe later."

"Maybe later," Illyth smiled.

FROM THE DARKEST REACHES OF FAERÛN'S PAST COMES A NEW ENEMY.

Return of the Archwizards
AN EXCITING NEW FORGOTTEN REALMS EPIC

BOOK I: *The Summoning*
TROY DENNING
A new evil returns to Faerûn after millennia spent in a shadowy hell.
March 2001

BOOK II: *The Siege*
TROY DENNING
The world-spanning schemes of Shade begin to take shape,
along with a new empire in the heart of the Great Desert.
December 2001

FORGOTTEN REALMS is a registered trademark owned by Wizards of the Coast, Inc.
©2001 Wizards of the Coast, Inc.

FORGOTTEN REALMS®

COLLECT THE ADVENTURES OF
DRIZZT DO'URDEN AS WRITTEN BY

BEST-SELLING AUTHOR

R.A. SALVATORE

FOR THE FIRST TIME
IN ONE VOLUME!

Legacy of the Drow
Collector's Edition

Now together in an attractive
hardcover edition, follow Drizzt's
battles against the drow through
the four-volume collection of

THE LEGACY, STARLESS NIGHT,
SIEGE OF DARKNESS,
and
PASSAGE TO DAWN.

_____

The Icewind Dale Trilogy
Collector's Edition

Read the tales that introduced
the world to Drizzt Do'Urden
in this collector's edition
containing *The Crystal Shard,
Streams of Silver,* and
The Halfling's Gem.

NOW AVAILABLE
IN PAPERBACK!

The Dark Elf Trilogy
Collector's Edition

Learn the story of Drizzt's
tortured beginnings in the
evil city of Menzobarranzan
in the best-selling novels *Homeland,
Exile,* and *Sojourn.*

FORGOTTEN REALMS is a registered trademark of Wizards of the Coast, Inc.
©2001 Wizards of the Coast, Inc.